The Courageous

Tim F. Miller

DEDICATION

To my wonderful parents, Tom and Mary Ann, who gave me the best childhood full of unconditional love and guidance. To my brothers, Mark and Jonathan, who made life a great adventure!

ACKNOWLEDGMENTS

Without a doubt, this book was a labor of love and insight. Spawn from a nightmare so vivid that I could remember intimate details. For some reason, I decided to write them down. Next thing you know, a novel was born. I am not a writer, per say, but a storyteller. I hope this book is both thought-provoking and entertaining. I am truly grateful to all those who read the early drafts of this book and sent helpful suggestions: Kirstin Miller, Mark Miller, Jonathan Miller, Ashley Twichell, Rick Neal, Mark Stewart, Jan Daniel, Brandon Whitaker, Matt Foley, Rick Sanderson, Stephen Bain, Lynn Delage and Barbara Sims. Thanks to Vizual Designs and graphic designers Michael and Kellan Davis for the book cover. The primary force and spirit present in my life has and always will be Jesus Christ—in whom all things are possible.

"The courage of life is often a less dramatic spectacle than the courage of a final moment; but it is no less a magnificent mixture of triumph and tragedy."

— John F. Kennedy

Tim F. Miller

Prologue
11 years earlier

Darkness finally fell across the night sky as millions of kids prepared for their annual pilgrimage to near and distant neighborhoods in search of the best ways to trick adults out of their treats. Next to Christmas, the Miller boys most enjoyed Halloween night. They could dress in an assortment of bizarre or familiar characters and be someone else for the night. The fantasy of stepping out of one's own skin and assuming another's appealed to young and old alike. One's mundane existence was temporarily suspended for a night of fantastic role playing. Kids cast themselves as superheroes, villains, ghosts, zombies and other make-believe characters that exercised their vivid imaginations. Halloween night provided the universal forum for children to be children and be rewarded with the greatest treasure— candy. However, children aren't always the only participants in this hallowed night of fantasy. Many adults reach back to their youth to re-live or revive the exuberance of imagination. Often lost to routine and the monotonous world of adulthood responsibilities, these "grown-ups" seek the opportunity to strike back at Father Time to reactivate moribund imaginations. Often the Miller boys saw adults dressed in costume to greet them at the door. Some were harmlessly clad in superhero spandex with a mask. Others simply wore outrageous wigs and make-up to stun the young trick or treaters. A few donned more elaborate costumes as corpses sitting up in a lawn chair on the front porch that suddenly came to life when the children rang the doorbell. These adults reveled in the shock and awe sprung back on the young, unsuspecting trick or treaters. A few of these adult pranksters went too far.

The Miller boys were at the perfect age for celebrating Halloween nearing the end of the twentieth century. The oldest, Joseph, was twelve and generally set the theme for the year's costumes. Whatever he decided, his younger brothers, Jack ten years old and Luke nine, simply followed. This year, according to Joseph, was the year of the dead. He determined the boys would wear old, torn clothes of the undead complete with pasty white make-up and fake blood oozing down their faces. This decision had been made by Joseph's neighborhood buddies who had little tolerance for the "baby" superhero costumes of the younger kids. Joseph's crew was determined to make this year's Halloween the scariest and most fun by preying and pranking all others.

The week leading up to Halloween was eagerly anticipated as the Miller's made their annual trek to Kmart for the costume selection. Their mother, Melinda, was disgusted by the very idea of Halloween and its association with celebrating the dead; wearing ghoulish costumes and haunting the streets seeking candy. Raised in a strict, Southern Baptist home in Hazard, Kentucky, Melinda and her older sister, Florence, were never allowed to participate on "Satan's Hallowed Day". Her parents ran a tight disciplined ship at home with a strict adherence to obedience. Her father, Ben, was a retired naval officer who believed children should rarely be seen or heard until they reached a certain age— that age was yet to be determined. Once Melinda left home for college, she opened her eyes a bit to a world outside of her father's realm. She met her husband, Matthew— studying to become a Southern Baptist minister, who further opened her eyes and mind to the odd and unusual world of boys with the third and final birth of their son, Luke. Through her boys she learned a great deal about patience, tolerance and noise. Raising three hyperactive, competitive boys meant there was never a dull moment in the Miller house though sometimes the "excitement" could be too much. Her serene childhood in the quiet mountains of Appalachia were marked by loneliness having shared a bedroom with her mentally handicapped older sister. The sixteen-year age difference, along with her sister's resentful disposition, made a close relationship near impossible. Her father's authoritarian rule for quiet and order in the house was equally complemented by her mother's, Edith, role as the traditional house wife with a domestic servant to clean the house. Edith raised her girls to love God, cherish the church, labor for the good of the family and community while respecting the hierarchy of authority in the house— which she placed a distant second. Melinda's childhood was quaint and deficient in the knowledge of boys and their abundance of chaotic energy. When Luke was born, her mother winced and said, "There'll never be peace and quiet in that house."

Though she didn't quite agree with the concept of Halloween, Melinda loved her boys with the fierce passion and fervor of a devout saint. If her boys wanted to participate in Halloween, then they would participate in Halloween. Matthew assured her that it was a harmless, secular ritual meant to entertain and spark the imagination of the young. Childhood was now cherished and nourished by fawning parents' eager to distance themselves from their own difficult upbringing. Although Melinda and Matthew were never shy about applying the rod to prevent spoiling the child, they would allow their children to exercise some independence on special occasions such as Halloween.

Joseph enjoyed this sense of independence and authority because he knew his brothers would acquiesce to his demands. Jack, two years younger, never really challenged Joseph's authority. There were the occasional skirmishes and screaming matches, but Jack could never overcome the size, strength and age difference. So, he followed Joseph's lead. Luke, on the other hand, the youngest, often voiced his opinion and demanded equality in the brotherhood— though he never won a fight or argument, he never stopped trying. He thought Joseph's zombie idea was too scary. Superheroes were far more appealing than walking corpses oozing blood and eyeballs and appealed to his mother's better judgement. Joseph instantly protested.

"Mom, superhero costumes are for babies! Me and my friends want to dress up cool like zombies and stuff!" Joseph whined.

"Superheroes are not babies!" Luke screamed back.

"Stop both of you! Don't make me take you out to the car." Melinda scolded quietly without moving her lips.

"Please Mom!"

"No, Joseph. Those masks scare your brother. Besides, I'm not sure its good for a Christian boy to go around the neighborhood with an eyeball hanging out and an axe embedded in your head."

"Come on Mom. The mask is awesome and besides its my mask not Luke's. He's a baby. I'm not going to be with him anyway."

"Oh yes you will. You will take both your brothers with you or you won't go at all."

"Oh, come on Mom. That's not fair. I want to hang out with my friends not these gross little babies. I do that every day."

"Hey…who are you calling a baby?", Luke cried and punched Joseph in the arm. Joseph immediately punched him back much harder in the arm and grabbed his mouth to keep him from screaming. Joseph's quick reaction was too easily accomplished to have been done just once.

"Look freckle-lips, nobody's talking to you. You're not going to ruin Halloween for me with your stupid scaredy-cat ways." Joseph whispered in Luke's ear.

"You don't scare me." Luke murmured through Joseph's hand.

"Oh, hush both of you. Joseph I've told you what's acceptable now take it or leave it. Its either these masks over here." Melinda stated firmly pointing at the less scary ghosts and skeletons. "Or you stay home. Which is it?"

"But Mom those masks are lame. They're not even scary. Just stupid looking."

"Nah-uh…I think they're scary in a cool way." Luke countered.

"Shut up! Nobody's talking to you!"

"Oh yeah, make me!"

Just as Joseph pulled his fist back to land it on his brother's chest, Melinda grabbed him firmly by the neck, digging her nails into the skin and marched him out of the store. Looking back at Luke using her low mother's intonation, she demanded he follow her immediately. As she was leaving the store, she instructed Jack to grab the three least offensive ghost costumes along the center aisle. Jack did as he was instructed. As the middle child, he felt compelled to obey authority figures like his parents, teachers and really all adults. He wanted to please everyone and hated confrontations. He felt bad for his brothers because he knew what they faced. Looking out the store window at the parking lot, Jack thought, *Oh man, they're in for it now. Mom's probably putting the death grip on their wrists and screaming in her low voice 'Christian boys obey their mothers'— they listen to her and instantly stop this constant bickering.' Now she's probably got them in the back of the van telling them to drop their pants cause she's going to spank them. Joseph's probably arguing that he's too big for spankings... but mom doesn't care. She's going to spank him first and harder. Luke is probably faking tears now to keep from getting spanked. Being the baby, he gets away with everything. Man...poor Joseph. This is all Luke's fault for being a scaredy-cat.*

While Melinda was out in the parking lot administering the righteous hand of God on her ill-mannered boys, Jack spied the perfect compromise. On the back aisle, behind the shelves of the harmless ghosts and skeleton costumes, Jack found the superhero section. He and Luke loved the Transformers' toys and cartoons. Optimus Prime was considered the best and had caused more than a few fights over who got to be him. Luke always lost those fights to the stronger, older Jack. He settled for Bumblebee, the beloved younger Autobot known for stealth and agility. Over time, Luke began to appreciate the younger Autobot because he could easily identify with the character seen as small, cute and deceptively courageous.

Jack quickly snatched up the two costumes, along with the gross zombie outfit and anxiously waited for his mother at the front of the store. *Boy, mom's goin to love this idea. It solves all the problems of Halloween. Joseph can still be that stupid, ugly zombie and me and Luke will be the cool Transformers. It won't be so bad being Transformers with Luke. He's alright sometimes and especially on Halloween. He won't act like a baby cause he'll lose the candy contest.*

The candy contest was just the latest competitive tradition started by Joseph. Like most competitions instigated by the oldest son, he usually won. Invariably the contests involved physical strength or cunning that gave Joseph the edge and usually had a high payoff such as money, candy, comic books or baseball cards. In this particular contest, conducted exclusively on Halloween, the rules were simple: those with the most candy won. There were a few caveats: chocolate candy counted as five points, gum two points and all other candy one point. The winner got to pick out two pieces of their favorite candy from the losers' loot. Again, Joseph created the contest, the rules, and supervised the count and its enforcement at the end of trick or treating. Joseph also determined when Halloween night ended. One year, Jack's bag appeared to be bigger than Joseph's, so he snuck out of the house to plunder more candy.

Jack watched his mother return to the store in a bad mood. Her pace was quick and determined and her usual cheerful expression was now a scowl with furrowed brows. He knew to tread carefully when she was in this state.

"Is everything okay Mom?" Jack weakly inquired.

"Yes…your brothers…well gimme those costumes. Certainly nothing to fight about. What's wrong with you kids? Why can't you agree on anything?" Melinda snapped in a forced whisper. Jack shrugged his shoulders looking up innocently at his mother.

"Oh well…why am I barking at you? You weren't fighting or causing me any problems."

"No, Mom."

"Well, if I hear one word from them about these costumes, they're sitting at home. No trick or treating."

Jack knew how to win over his mother by simply looking up at her with his big blue eyes, saying nothing.

"Oh, look at you. Such a sweet face. Well, which one are you going to be?", not looking at the costumes, "The ghost or the skeleton?"

"Neither one." Jack proudly announced pushing the costumes into her hands.

"What's this? This isn't…"

"Yeah, its better. See Joseph can still be an ugly zombie and Luke and me will be Transformers. You know how much we love them. And they're not against God or the church or nothing."

"Well?" Melinda paused quickly surmising the compromise.

"Mom, Luke will love this, and it won't scare him, and I'll go trick or treating with him." Jack confidently stated thinking he had sealed the deal.

"Well, Joseph's going with you boys. I don't care how big he thinks he is. He's going." Melinda affirmed. "Yes Jack, these costumes will do. It's a good choice and will please your father."

Being preacher's kids, the boys learned, carried an additional weight as they were watched and judged differently by some in the community. They were a direct reflection of their father; a revered minister and leader in the town. Hence, he had final say on these matters. Matthew Miller was no autocratic authoritarian. He tended to view many of these trivial childhood issues with a little common sense and a healthy dose of Biblical passages to guide his boys. When the family came home, he gave his sons the thumbs up. Melinda blew a sigh of relief; as yet another crisis had been averted.

❧ ❧ ❧ ❧ ❧ ❧ ❧

Alvin Wilkins was a respected member of the Nicholasville community. As a mailman, he often spent hours talking and "cutting up" with residents of his mail route. Some complained about how late they got their mail, but never to Alvin. His lively round face accented with sparse flecks of red hair along the sides and animated personality instantly soothed all anger. A slap on the back or a hardy handshake usually greeted each resident with delivery of the mail. It didn't take much effort to get Alvin to tell a joke or funny story. However, not all were amused by his yarns. Many were weary of his oft told stories and jokes but didn't have the heart to stop him. Some feigned illness or fatigue to avoid being trapped in an extended conversation. Others simply hid behind the door waiting for him to leave the street before retrieving their mail lest they be caught in his sights and held prisoner to a corny joke. He loved to gossip, but swore he never did. Serving his church as both a deacon and Sunday School teacher, Alvin tried to stay above any seedy rumor or unseemly tale, but some days he just couldn't help himself. Besides, the route residents and church members always gave him a pass because he was so affable.

Tonight, was Halloween, and Alvin was as excited as every kid in America. Though he was fifty-five years old, he dressed for Halloween to scare the children and make them earn their treats. His wife, Delores, indulged his odd enthusiasm for a child's event mostly because she couldn't have children of her own. She felt guilty about her inability to bring the joy and excitement of a child into their empty home. So, she tolerated Alvin's eccentricities because she loved him and felt sorry for him. *He should have children. He would make a great father. He's so kind and playful with kids. Oh, how I wish I weren't barren— its my fault he doesn't have any children. The least I can do is tolerate his childish antics.*

"Man, oh man, do I have the perfect set-up for tonight!" Alvin called out to Delores as he strolled through the front door from work.

"How was your day, honey?"

"Oh, the usual. Everyone wanting me to tell them a funny story or repeat some gossip. You know my rule about that— if its not fit in the Lord's House, it aint fit to be repeated."

"I'm sure." Delores replied with a knowing smirk on her face. She had heard through the community grapevine how many were more annoyed than amused by her husband's routine.

"Anyway, I have a special treat tonight. I'm bringing Sparkles out." Alvin announced.

"What? No…that's creepy. That old dummy clown should be thrown out and burned or something."

"What are you talking about?" Alvin snapped. "Sparkles is amazing. Kids love him. I always have him out on a lawn chair when we do yard sales and such…and the kids always come up and want to play with him."

"That's in the middle of the day with plenty of sunlight and their parents around. It'll be dark and scary tonight. In fact, I heard a storm will probably be rolling in. The sight of the that old ugly clown sitting in a chair will be terrifying."

"Exactly! Look, these kids today are sophisticated. Nothing really scares them anymore with all those graphic video games, movies and what not. But this will!"

"No Alvin. No. That's too much."

"Delores…don't you dare try to ruin this night for me." Alvin's face darkened lowering his voice, "Don't you dare. I've sacrificed so much for you. Don't think I'm going to allow you to ruin this. Don't even think about it." He knew exactly how to play his wife— which buttons to push.

Delores stared at him in disbelief. *I can't believe he's playing this card. Every time we get in an argument, he guilts me for not having children. I'm so sorry that I can't. He knows that, but still he brings it up and uses it like a knife to cut me up. To weaken me so he can get his way. It's not fair. He knows how much I, too, love children but…Oh God, why wouldn't you let me have kids.* Delores turned away and walked back into the kitchen to finish dinner. Alvin ran upstairs to get dressed and pull Sparkles out of the attic.

❧ ❧ ❧ ❧ ❧ ❧ ❧

"Mom, this is crazy making us go out now. Its not even dark! All the little kids and babies are out now." Joseph moaned in a futile attempt to persuade his mother.

"Joseph, I'm not arguing this anymore. You will go out now with your brothers or you won't go at all." Melinda snapped back. She never liked or understood this strange event. As a child, her parents forbade it. It was un-Christian and most likely an attempt by the devil to steal Christian children, her parents reasoned. But having discussed it thoroughly with her husband, Reverend Matthew Miller, she allowed her children to participate even though she would not. She turned the lights out on the front porch to signal trick or treaters that the Miller's would not be part of the devil's folly. She also refused to walk with the kids, as this too, would be seen as acceptance and participation.

"Ah right mom. Dang it. But they better keep up because me and Paul, Dewayne and Perry and some of the guys will be moving fast and we don't need little buttheads slowing us down."

"I'm not a butthead, you booger licker!" Luke retorted.

"Shut up, you little butthole!" Joseph parried quickly slapping Luke's Bumblebee mask sideways.

"Joseph Thomas Miller, you stop this now! Watch your language and stop hitting your brother or no one goes out tonight. Do you hear me boys?" Melinda was always alarmed by the foul language and awful way her boys treated each other. She never used such language, and if she had, her father would have worn her out with a hickory stick. She tried her best to raise her sons in a loving, Christian home that would not tolerate such filthy

15

talk and rambunctious behavior. Like her father, she believed in using the rod to keep from spoiling the child. The "golden ruler" and yardstick were often used and broken over the boy's backsides to remind them to behave and treat each other as they would have others treat them. After each spanking, the boys cried and promised to behave but invariably within a few hours they would be at it again.

"Yes, Mom. I guess Jack and Luke can ride their bikes to keep up." Joseph stated with resignation.

"Oh no we can't!" Jack inserted. "The last time we did that we nearly lost them."

"Ha, ha! You idiots almost lost your bikes cause you're too stupid to keep up with them."

"No… because you and your butthole friends grabbed 'em while me and Luke were at a house getting candy and then you hid them!"

"You're crazy."

"Then how come you were able to find them two days later when dad said he would let me and Luke use your bike?"

"Hey…I don't know anything about that. I just got lucky. I'm just better at finding things that you idiots lose."

"Because you took them and hid them!"

"You can't prove that butthead!" Joseph shouted pushing Jack against the wall.

"Stop it. Stop it now…geesh you boys fight over everything." Melinda flatly asserted. "Do whatever you want Joseph, but you have to keep an eye on your brothers. You're the oldest and the responsibility falls squarely on your shoulders. Do you understand me? You must keep watch over your brothers!"

Joseph slowly nodded looking away from his mother and directly at his brothers. *Man, why do I always have to watch out for them? They're stupid and ugly and its not fair that just because I'm the oldest I have to do this. Where is it written that the oldest ALWAYS has to be responsible for his brothers? It's not fair. Who's responsible for watching out for me? Huh? Man, sometimes being the oldest sucks bad. I mean, I like the attention and some of the cool things that come with being older like staying up later at night and staying outside longer with my friends but having to ALWAYS watch over my brothers…sucks!*

"Ah right mom. Come on guys, let's go. Come on Optimus Prime and Bumblebee." Joseph taunted using his baby voice that he knew annoyed his brothers.

"Don't worry Joseph, me and Luke will keep up. Won't we Luke?"

Bumblebee nodded up and down

"Well you better because we're meeting the guys off Third Street and heading into town?"

"Why are we going there? There's no good candy houses in town. Most of those houses don't even have their lights on?" Jack questioned.

"Shut up…I'll tell you outside." Joseph whispered.

"Okay…bye mom! We're leaving now with Joseph and meeting his friends at Third Street!"

"Okay, you boys have fun…and no fighting!" Melinda wishfully added.

The boys bolted out the front door and headed across the street to cut through the Hall's yard. This was a quick short-cut to school and town, but a bit tricky. The Hall's had a huge black mutt named Booger that barked and chased the boys all over the neighborhood. Maneuvering around him was never easy. Joseph, as always, devised a simple plan— he threw a large chew toy bone into the front bushes where Booger hung out. After a few minutes listening to sounds of biting and slobbering, the boys stealthily moved past the Hall's driveway into the backyard and out the other side to South Fifth Street that connected to Brown Street. The boys had traversed nearly every street in Nicholasville over the years exploring new ways to get to their school, church and downtown stores for baseball cards and candy. Keeping up with Joseph was never easy, and tonight it was especially difficult because he didn't want to be with his brothers.

"Hey Joseph, slow down!" Luke demanded

"No, you speed up!"

"Joseph stop a second! You said you were going to tell us why we are going to Third Street instead of Weil Lane."

"Alright." Joseph said turning back and waiting for his brothers to catch up. "Look, me and Paul and some of the guys heard there is a really cool haunted house in town."

"Where?" Jack inquired

"The old Walker Hotel. You know, across the street from our church."

"But that building is empty. There's no one there."

"That's what you think. Paul said he heard there were people setting up a cool haunted house".

"Cool!" Jack inserted

"I don't know. Sounds kinda scary." Luke warned

"Ah no it'll be alright Luke. Me and Joseph will be there the whole time. Don't worry."

"Look…I don't care what you guys do but I'm going. Now, come on. I can see the guys waiting."

❧ ❧ ❧ ❧ ❧ ❧ ❧

Alvin Wilkins finished applying the eye liner and adjusted the big fluffy orange wig in front of the bathroom mirror. Humming to himself, while looking over at Sparkles to make sure they were identical clowns— Alvin demanded perfection. He knew kids had a keen eye for fakes and wanted to make sure that there wasn't a hair's difference between the two. As a child, Alvin loved the circus and adored the clowns. He thought they were incredibly funny and entertaining. He won Sparkles five years ago at the county fair by ringing the bell five times on the High Striker. Delores begged him to sell it, or give it away, saying it was too creepy, and upsetting to guests who visited. They reached a compromise whereby he could keep it, and display it, but only on special occasions such as Christmas, New Year's Eve, the Fourth of July and Halloween. The rest of the year Sparkles lived in the attic.

Carefully pulling the life-size clown up over his shoulder, Alvin marched down the stairs and into the garage. On a pair of saw horses sat a crudely built pine coffin draped with a purple velvet cloth. At the head of the coffin lay an oversize pillow with a purple silk sham. Alvin meticulously placed Sparkles inside the wooden box while crossing its arms at the waist and closing its eyes shut. Next, he adjusted the overhead track lights in the garage to focus exclusively on the coffin. When he shut off the garage light, an eerie image emerged from the darkness— an image Alvin hoped would be talked about all over town for years to come. Exiting, he turned off all the lights, and closed the garage door with the remote then hustled into the kitchen to fill his bowl with candy. Passing by his wife's glare in his perfectly tailored clown suit complete with oversized shoes, he padded out to the front yard to take his post on a comfortable lawn chair with the candy resting in his lap.

His Halloween plan was quite simple. During the early daylight hours, when the younger trick or treaters were out, he handed out the candy as Sparkles. Here, his jovial nature shone as he teased, and joked with the little ones and their parents. Occasionally, he pretended to be asleep, waited for a child to reach for the candy, and then seized their arms and yell "Gotcha!". That was always good for a few screams and nervous laughs. However, as it got later in the evening, and much darker, Alvin opened the garage door to display the frightening image of Sparkles holding a cardboard sign that read "Dead Clown".

The illuminated coffin was enough to keep most away, but many of the older kids dared each other to peak in because the candy bowl was resting on Sparkles chest. Alvin sat in his lawn chair reveling in his caper and instructing kids to get the candy from Sparkles because his bowl was empty. *Wow, this is good clean fun! This is my best idea yet for Halloween. The kids are screaming, laughing and taunting each other. I'm sure word is quickly spreading all over Briar Patch and the rest of the neighborhoods about my house being the best and scariest! Boy, I can't wait to hear the neighbors and route residents congratulate me on such an awesome spectacle I created tonight. I'm sure to be the talk of the town* Alvin mused. *I'm sure the screams are alarming to Delores. She's such a killjoy. She has no idea how to entertain and delight children. Children are a joy to be cherished and amused. That's what I'm doing. Of course, she doesn't understand. She's incapable of having them and has always discouraged my attempts to have them over to the house. What does she know?*

❧ ❧ ❧ ❧ ❧ ❧ ❧

Jack and Luke were not happy when they finally caught up with Joseph standing next to five older kids.

They were all dressed in regular clothes that were cut up and torn with florescent white cream slathered about their face, neck and arms. An assortment of items were sticking out of their faces with streaks of blood all over their bodies. This ghastly zombie crew shocked Jack and Luke as they cautiously approached.

"What the hell are those idiots doing here?" shouted the zombie with a worm attached to his nose and an axe firmly splitting open his skull.

"Well...I kinda have to watch them?" Joseph said lowering his head trying not to look at his ridiculous Transformers.

"What...you gotta babysit these little shits?" offered the zombie with a dangling eyeball and mohawk.

"Hey, watch who you're calling little shits!" Joseph sharply turned staring at the dangle-eyed zombie.

"Oh yeah...who's goin stop me?" retorted the mohawked zombie, aka Perry Williams.

Joseph and Perry were natural rivals in the neighborhood, Weil Lane and Linden Lane. They were the same age, with a similar height and build, and a ferocious competitive streak to be the best in sports. Most days they were friends, but when they entered the sports arena, they were fierce rivals. The neighborhood sports revolved around the seasons. In the fall, it was football; in the winter, basketball; spring and summer was baseball. Each contest usually devolved into a heated argument, and occasionally, a fist fight. Joseph held his own against all the kids, even the older ones. He didn't necessarily win them, but he wasn't afraid to fight— that was key to winning the respect of the neighborhood.

These two always seemed to be on opposing teams, setting the environment for a hypercompetitive game, and potential fight. They argued often, but had yet resorted to blows to, once and for all, decide who was the strongest, toughest kid on Weil Lane/ Linden Lane. It was a fight most wanted to see, especially Jack and Luke who hated Perry's condescension towards them.

"I will!" Joseph said pushing up on Perry.

"Why are you defending these little shits? You hate them as much as everyone else?"

19

"No, I don't. Shut your mouth! Don't ever talk crap like that about my brothers." Joseph shouted feeling his blood pressure rising and preparing for an all-out fight. The anger, and defense of his brothers, caught him by surprise, but it had been building all day. He hated the responsibility of having to watch out for them as it often kept him from going off on his own with his friends. But at the same time, he didn't hate being with his brothers. They could be annoying, but they were fun to taunt, tease and occasionally play with. His mother's constant harping on being his brother's keeper had seeped into his unconscious mind and abruptly surfaced.

"Damn…back off Joseph…seriously, it's not a big deal." Perry offered meekly, not feeling the same level of anger as Joseph. To save face, he added, "Sure bring the little girls."

"Come on guys we're running late. You guys can fight later." Paul Milkens, Joseph's best friend, asserted.

The gang pushed onward at a fast pace. The Transformers fell further and further behind but caught a glimpse of them turning right off Third Street down a dirt path they had never seen before. Rushing to the entrance of the unmarked road, the younger Millers watched in trepidation as the gang disappeared down a worn path completely covered with overhanging trees. It was as if they had been swallowed up into the darkness. Looking at each other and then back at the hidden trail, Jack took off his mask.

"Luke, do you want to go in there?"

"Yeah…if you do…"

"Umm…it looks pretty scary."

"Yeah, its real scary"

"Well…umm…I don't think I should take you down there. Mom wouldn't like that, and I don't want to get in trouble."

"Yeah…anyway there's no good candy houses around here and I didn't want to go to that stupid haunted house. Can we go back and hit Weil Lane and all those streets?"

"Yes! Great idea, Luke. Come on, let's hurry. We can still hit a lot of good houses."

❧ ❧ ❧ ❧ ❧ ❧ ❧

The crisp autumn night air cracked with screams of terror and joy as children and their parents trotted all over the Nicholasville demanding candy for their adorable costumes. Some drove trucks with the kids riding in the back, while others were pulled in wagons or pushed in strollers. But most of the kids ran around unattended from door to door seeking the best candy. Alvin Wilkins was thrilled with how the night had gone. He was both funny and entertaining to the children and their onlooking parents. Alternating between playing with the children and pretending to be asleep and surprising them, Alvin grew restless. The gags were getting old. He needed something new and more terrifying. Though he had already opened the garage door to reveal the "Dead Clown" with candy, too few kids were approaching or even trying to go in. He devised a new plan. He switched places with Sparkles. Placing a sign on the dummy clown sitting in his lawn chair, Alvin quickly scrambled into the garage and into the coffin. He placed the candy bowl on his chest with the garage door remote in his hand. The sign on the dummy clown written in dripping red ink read "Candy in Garage…If You Dare".

❧ ❧ ❧ ❧ ❧ ❧ ❧

Optimus Prime and his sidekick, Bumblebee, ran across Hickory Hill, Nottaway Drive, Barberry Lane and Greenbriar hitting the houses at a quick clip. Between stops they heard many kids talking about the creepy clown house on Pinewood Drive. They said it was scary, but the candy was great because it was full size chocolate bars, not the "fun size" traditionally given on Halloween.

"Oh wow! That sounds awesome, Luke. Let's go. Full size chocolate bars have to count as way more points in the candy contest."

"I don't know…sounds kinda scary."

"Come on, Luke. This is no time to be a baby! Besides, its getting late and many people are starting to turn off their lights."

"Jack…you know I don't really like clowns."

"Why? What's wrong with clowns? They're happy and always falling down and stuff. There's nothing to be scared about."

"I don't know…why don't we just go home? We got plenty of good candy."

"Hey Jack, did you hear about Pinewood Drive?" blurted a small squat Spiderman.

"Yeah"

"They say its got this crazy clown scaring kids but giving lots of candy!"

"Yeah…are you guys going over there?" Jack said looking at an assortment of Marvel and DC characters.

"Nah…I was down there a few minutes ago but noticed how late it was getting and decided to go home." Hulk meekly offered noticing that no one really believed him.

"Ah you were just scared!" Jack quickly countered. He knew the "Hulk" was none other than Conrad Black, a kid that had bullied him since first grade.

"Who are calling scared? I just can't stay out too late and that street is too far outta the way."

"Sure it is."

"Listen bumble-gums, I don't have to explain anything to you. You're the scared one! Every time I push you to fight, you back off!" Conrad added with a shove that knocked Jack's pumpkin decorated bag onto the ground. Jack stared at him with his fists balled up but didn't move.

"That's what I thought! Still a little wussy! Come on guys, let's leave the little Transformers before Jack starts crying and we get in trouble." Conrad turned triumphantly mounting his bike.

Luke stared at his brother. *I can't believe he didn't punch that jerk. Why didn't he do anything? Man, he hits me all the time for nothing. He's just picking up his candy and not doing nothing!*

"Jack, why didn't you hit that idiot? He shoved you and everything?"

"I don't want to talk about it."

"But Jack…he called you bubble-gums. You hate that! You punch me and Joseph all the time for calling you that."

"That's cause…I don't want to talk about it. Look, I'm going to that stupid clown house to prove to those jerks, I'm not afraid. Are you coming?"

"Ah…I don't know…"

"Come on Luke. We have to prove to those jerks we're not afraid of stuff and what better chance than this? Come on, Luke…please."

"Well, alright."

Cutting through several yards later at night proved more difficult than the brothers anticipated. Many of the neighborhoods had begun turning off their lights and retrieving their costumed children. Climbing one fence on Greenbriar, the boys discovered two Doberman Pinchers with long chains. The dogs chased them toward the front gate and nearly bit Luke's arm before the chain restrained both, straightening them up, as they snarled and barked viciously at the boys. Jack leaned over the fence to help his terrified brother scramble over the gate.

"God…I hate dogs! They're so stupid and loud. Man, they tried to kill us in there. And where are the owners?"

"I know. But we're okay let's just walk down Pinewood and find that clown house."

"You still want to go after that crap? We were almost killed…what's wrong with you Jack?"

"I told you. We have something to prove!"

"You have something to prove. Not me."

"You too! If you don't come with me, they'll say 'why didn't your baby brother go?' You know they will. We BOTH have to do this."

"Alright…hey I think I see it. Look down the road a few houses down on the right. Do you see something sitting in that chair?"

"Yeah…come on. Let's get our big candy bars and go home."

As the boys approached, they turned around and noticed there wasn't anyone else on the street. Not a single costumed ghoul, ghost, princess, superhero or walking dead figure. It was eerily empty and darker as the clown house was the only lit house on the street and its light came from the garage.

"Well come on, Luke. They said the candy is just sitting on the clown in the chair." Jack asserted trying to instill confidence in his little brother.

When they came upon the seated dummy clown, there was no candy or bowl— just a sign that read "Candy in Garage...If You Dare". The Transformers looked at each other and then stepped back and gazed at the poorly lit garage entrance.

"Luke...it's alright. There's nothing to be afraid of. Just go in and grab some candy."

"You go in. This was your idea!"

"Come on Luke. This your chance to prove you're not a baby. Just go in real quick grab the candy and I'll tell everyone how brave and courageous you were. No one will ever call you baby or scaredy-cat or nothing because of what you did here tonight."

"Why don't you do it?"

"Cause...cause you're the one Joseph and his friends were making fun of. You're always the one they're calling baby and stuff. This is your chance to prove them wrong and I'll tell everyone!"

Luke's body stiffened. He hated being called baby. He hated being the youngest one always being blamed, left behind and picked on. He hated that he was seen as the weakest Miller in all the sports, and games in the neighborhood. He hated that Joseph was the "strong one", Jack was the "smart one", and *I'm the baby. The little wuss that everyone hates. I've got to go in there and prove I'm not afraid. I'm not a little wussy baby. Jack won't go cause he's the one that's really scared. I know. But I'll prove to him and everyone else that I'm not scared!*

"Okay, Jack. I'll do it. But you have to promise to tell everyone that I was the one that did it!"

"Of course!"

"And promise you'll not run off. Promise you'll wait for me."

"I'm just going to be standing over here in front of the garage by the road."

Luke turned toward the garage with a renewed sense of purpose. He was going to end this nonsense of him being a scaredy-baby, and instead be a hero in the Miller house, as well as the neighborhood. He poked his head into the entrance staring at the soft glow of the overhead track lighting focused on a wooden box. He could barely make out what appeared to be a shiny metallic bowl. *That must be the candy bowl. Okay I'll just walk over there, grab the candy and run.* Looking back, he noticed that Jack had moved. He was still there, just standing behind a short row of bushes. *Man, I can't believe he's moved back. He's the one that's scared, not me. Alright, time to get the candy.* Slowly creeping up to the coffin, Luke peered in and noticed there was no candy in the bowl. *Oh man…where's the stupid candy. Oh, there it is a big candy bar by his head. I'll just grab it. Reaching in for the treasured treat, Oh…oh God…that clown is so…creepy…* Luke stood still for several seconds terrified at the dead clown and then suddenly its eyes opened. Luke mouthed a scream, but no noise came out. Staring at the clown's red eyes, he felt a powerful hand clamp down on his reaching wrist and pull him toward the coffin. He heard the garage door start its downward rotation.

Jack watched in disbelief. Too stunned to move, he tried to call out for his brother, but the sound was lost in the wind. It was getting colder and darker with the sound of several dogs barking at once. Shaking his head, trying to make sense of what just happened, Jack instinctively moved toward the garage door. He didn't know what he was going to do but he had to do something. Inching out of his protective row of bushes, he spied several quick movements darting in and out of his periphery. *Oh God…what was that?* Squinting his eyes, trying to peer through a clump of boxes piled against the side of the house, Jack heard a loud bang and saw more quick movements. He turned on his heels and ran. Never once looking back.

৯ ৯ ৯ ৯ ৯ ৯ ৯

The Miller house was usually active, especially when the boys returned from some outdoor adventure or sporting event. They were highly competitive children with an unending bounty of energy. Melinda quickly adapted to the new, more interesting lifestyle of raising rambunctious boys. Gone was the sedentary lifestyle of her dull existence with her parents. Now, she lived a life full of excitement, adventure, and chaos. Her children showed her this different world— a world of boys that climbed furniture, spoke harshly to each other, ran in and out of the house, and almost always fought over anything and everything.

She had grown so accustomed to the frenzied Miller house that on those rare occasions when the boys were quiet, she would stir them up. Usually pitting one of the brothers against the other by asking, "Now which of boys can't hit the baseball very far?" or "I know Luke can't do it. He's too small." That stirred the boys into action through an argument or a fight. Melinda didn't necessarily want the fight, but she didn't discourage it either. She loved that they were active in Church, sports, and kind to everyone else. She prayed that one day they would get along and treat each other with love and respect, though that day seemed to be in the distant future. Folding laundry while watching TV in the living room with her husband, Matthew, she heard the front door slam shut.

"Boys…are you home?"

"It's just me Mom.'"

"Where are the other two, Joseph?"

"I don't know. Didn't they come home?"

"Of course not. That's why I asked you." Melinda snapped jumping out of her chair to confront her oldest in the kitchen getting a snack.

"Why are your brothers not with you? Joseph…I asked you a question. Look at me." Melinda demanded with a firm grip on his chin.

"They were slowing me down and my friends wanted to go to this really cool haunted house. And I knew they would be too scared to go. And I didn't think it was fair that I shouldn't go just because they wouldn't go."

Joseph could tell this salient point to his argument wasn't getting him anywhere. "Anyway… I left them at Third Street. I figured they would go back to Weil Lane, and stuff, since they have the best candy."

"Didn't you get any candy?"

"I got a little but we're not doing the candy contest this year."

"Oh really? Since when?"

"Umm…"

"Joseph Thomas Miller! You're changing the rules this year just because you're not going to win. That's not right. I know I told you boys I wouldn't interfere in your little contests and games. I wanted you guys to learn to resolve your own problems, but this…this is just wrong. Besides, where are your brothers?"

"Uhh…well…" Joseph's attempted stall to develop a story was interrupted with the slamming of the front door. Jack ran upstairs to his room. Melinda stared at Joseph. "Don't worry Mom. I got this. I'll just see what Jack's up to. I'm sure he's playing a game on Luke. I'll take care of it."

"Alright, go get your story straight and fix this little mess. Remember, you're the oldest and responsible for your brothers. I'm trusting you."

Joseph nodded his head having heard this line and verse far too often from his mother. Whether he thought it was fair or not, he was still held accountable for their actions. He quickly bounded up the stairs, darting to his left towards their room, but abruptly running in to a locked door.

"Hey retard, open the door!"

"Is Mom or Dad with you" Jack whispered with his face leaning against the door.

"No. Now open up."

Jack turned the dial and opened the door. He could see that Joseph was in a foul mood. Tensing up and expecting a punch at any time, he moved aside as his big brother pushed him back and shut the door.

"Where's Luke and where did you guys go?"

"Umm…well we went to Weil Lane and ran up and down all those streets behind it. We must have hit about fifty houses. Man, we cleaned up. Look my bag's loaded and so is Luke's."

"Yeah, well, where is he?"

Jack shoulders slumped as walked over to his bed and plopped down away from Joseph. After a few seconds of silence, Jack murmured, "Its all my fault…its all my fault…"

"What's all your fault?" Joseph demanded running to the other side of the bed to confront his middle brother.

"I left him at the clown house."

"The clown house? What clown house?"

"There was this creepy clown house on some street off Shun Road…Pinewood, I think, anyway some of the kids in the neighborhood said this house gave big candy bars, but everyone was too scared to go there. So, me and Luke went there to prove we weren't scared and…"

"And you dared Luke to do it because you were too scared to do it!"

"That's bullcrap! I wasn't scared…its just that Luke wanted to prove he wasn't."

"Whatever…so what happened. Why isn't he here?"

"Well, the candy was in the garage sitting on some box with a purple blanket or something. Luke reached in and then…" Jack's voice broke and then they heard the front door close shut.

"Well, there's my precious little Bumblebee!" Melinda wailed hugging Luke tightly. "Where in Heaven's name have you been?"

Luke stood with a blank stare as his mother pulled his mask off. She hadn't seen that look before and it sent chills down her spine. "Luke, are you alright?"

Hearing the commotion near the door, Matthew walked in.

"Luke, what's the matter?" he inquired growing more concerned by Luke's demeanor and absent expression. "Hey…Luke, are you okay?" Matthew continued grabbing his youngest son by the shoulders and lowering himself to eye level.

Luke slowly nodded returning the gaze back, and then wrapped his arms around his father's neck. The tight hug seemed to come from genuine fear.

"Son…what happened…you're shaking."

Again, no response.

"Jack! Come down here now." Matthew called to the upstairs bedroom.

"No, dad. Don't call Jack down. He didn't do nothing." Luke quickly responded.

"Well, I'm sure he didn't. I just wanted to get to the bottom of what happened. Wasn't he with you?"

"Yes…but…look dad I just got real scared that's all. There were some mean dogs that chased us and I guess we got separated. It's not Jack's fault."

"What mean dogs? Where? They should've have been chained up or behind fences."

"They were…but me and Jack climbed over some fences to cut through some yards."

"I've told you boys a thousand time not to do that. That's trespassing and anything that happens to you guys, legally, I'm responsible. If you get attacked by a dog or something like that, I can't help you."

"I know" Luke answered meekly with head bowed patiently waiting for the lecture to end.

Staring down at his son with anger rapidly rising, Matthew checked himself and slowly gathered his thoughts. "Well I hope this little scare will prevent you from doing anything like this again."

"Yes, sir. Can I go to my room now? I really just wanna go to bed?"

"You don't want to count your candy or stay up watching Halloween specials on TV?" Melinda asked in bewilderment.

"No."

"Alright…go on up and get ready for bed. We'll be up later." Matthew said looking back at his wife.

Melinda watched Luke listlessly climb the stairs leaving his candy bag by the front door. Turning back to Matthew, "Honey, I don't like this. I've never seen him this way before. He's been scared before, but this is…something different."

"I know, but he doesn't seem to want to talk about it. Maybe we'll get something out of him in the morning."

⚜ ⚜ ⚜ ⚜ ⚜ ⚜ ⚜

"Jack…Dad called you. You better go downstairs." Joseph insisted.

"I can't…he's gonna kill me?"

"Why? What did you do to Luke?"

"Nothing. Honestly, I didn't do anything?"

"Then why is Dad gonna kill you?"

Jack couldn't look at his older brother because of the shame he felt for running out on the youngest Miller. He, too, was Luke's older brother and next in charge. Joseph had always lectured him on that account— when he wasn't around it was Jack's responsibility to watch out for Luke. Jack had failed, and he knew it.

"What happened when Luke reached in for the candy?"

"I don't know…" Jack mumbled as tears began welling up. "I ran away"

"You did what? You ran away…why? You can't just leave Luke like that."

"You left us!" Jack shot back.

"No, I didn't. I kept you from going to that haunted house cause I knew you guys didn't want to go. I saved you from the embarrassment and teasing from my friends who would have called you names for not going in

27

to the haunted house. Jack, I ran down the secret short cut on purpose, knowing you guys would never follow because it was too dark and scary. I didn't leave you…I gave you guys the chance to go trick or treating without being bullied by the guys…I left you guys together. You were supposed to stay together. You know you're supposed to watch out for Luke when I'm not around. What's wrong with you?"

Jack had no response and no interest in defending himself. Normally, he never backed down from an argument with his brothers, especially Joseph, whom he was constantly trying to impress. But tonight, he knew he was wrong and there was no defense. He slumped onto his twin bed in the middle of the room between his brother's bed and tried not to re-live the night's transgressions.

Luke entered the room and quietly changed into his Spiderman pajamas. Looking down, he padded past his brother's beds trying to avoid any contact or interaction. He climbed into bed wadding his pillow into his chest and arching his butt up in the air while gently rocking back and forth banging his head against the headboard. The boys understood that Luke had always done this when he was scared or upset.

Joseph turned the light off. He wanted this night to end as quickly as possible knowing that what ever happened to Luke could easily be blamed on him. *Dad sounded really mad when he called up for Jack…but he didn't call again or even come up. Man, I know he's going to jump all over me for leaving those two idiots behind. Oh…I hate when dad makes me wait it out for his punishments. I wish he would just spank me and get it over with. I'm sure Luke told on me…man, I'm so busted.*

Jack knew he had to confront Luke about what had happened. The sooner the better because he hated these types of things hanging over his head. *Best to talk about it now…get everything straight. Whatever Luke said downstairs must have covered us cause dad's not up here screaming at us and spanking us. What did he tell mom and dad? I can't talk to Luke with Joseph around…what's it matter? Joseph's going to find out anyway. The least I can do is say I'm sorry.*

"Luke…Luke" Jack whispered facing Luke's bed hoping Joseph couldn't hear him.

Luke continued rocking back and forth.

"Luke…I'm sorry. I'm really, really sorry. I didn't mean to leave you. I just got…scared. I don't know why. I tried to call out for you and even went toward the garage door but there was some crazy noises around outside by the house…and I thought it might be those dogs or something. I'm really sorry."

Luke's rocking stopped. There was a long pause. Jack could hear Luke shifting his body around as he turned away from Jack facing the back wall.

"I promise you, Luke, I will never, ever leave you again. What happened tonight was my fault, not yours. You were the brave one, not me. I was a stupid coward and ran. But you…you were courageous. I'm sorry Luke. I'll never ever leave you again."

The room was still and quiet as Jack waited for some kind of response from his betrayed little brother. Staring at the back of his head, Jack watched for any movement or sound to let him know what was on Luke's mind. After a few minutes, listening intently, Jack detected muffled sobs. He could now see that Luke's body was trembling. He wanted to go over and try to comfort him, but he didn't know how Luke would react. *If I go over to him, he might scream at me and get mom and dad all upset and then I'm really in trouble… What? What is he saying? Sounds like Luke is mumbling something.*

"Luke…what did you say?"

Speaking in a low voice and choking back tears, Luke had trouble checking his emotions. Slightly raising his voice Luke cried, "I'm never goin to be afraid again. Never." Tears streamed down his faced as he started rocking again, back and forth.

Chapter 1

"The realm of dreams is a place where the subconscious mind is free and uninhibited to play out a fantasy that the conscious mind is afraid to face in reality."
—Author

Jack sat up immediately in his bed drenched in a cold sweat staring across the room. He couldn't quite tell where he was or what had happened as his mind was racing back and forth between two worlds: the present real world and the dream fantasy. He felt his heart pounding rapidly with his senses on full alert. Having traveled through the unconscious world of dreams and nightmares, Jack Miller, a senior at UK, was shaken to his core by what it may have revealed about him.

Before, he saw himself as a strong, confident, fairly intelligent guy who enjoyed campus life and all the extracurricular activities offered. Like many rising seniors, he wasn't certain what awaited him after school, possibly grad school or even law school. He was having too much fun to entertain the foreseeable future. Much of his confidence came after his first year in college when he began to seriously build his body with his roommates, Rick and Tater. The immaturity of his superficial mind created a self-image of strength and courage. However, that false narrative took a huge hit as he awoke covered in a cold sweat of self-doubt and delusion. He turned to his right to see a dark figure emerging toward him. Instinctively he backed away until he recognized the face of his old friend, Rick.

"Hey man...you okay?" Rick asked as Jack continued to stare at him without an answer.

"Dude, seriously...you okay? You just let out the most God-awful scream I'd ever heard in my life"

Again no response, just a blank stare.

"That must have been one helluva nightmare, Jack. But its okay...you're okay now. Whatever you just imagined or dreamed is over...its okay." Rick tried to console. "Damn, you're wet as shit. What the hell did you do in that dream that's got you so damn wet?"

Rick's calm, reassuring, familiar voice helped bring Jack back to the present. His body eased and relaxed a bit as he started to believe that he was truly back from the nightmarish realm that had quickly become fatal. *Oh dear God... thank you, thank you for delivering me from that Hell. Oh my...* Jack prayed taking deep, slower breaths. He wiped the sweat from his forehead looking down at his nearly naked body. He quickly ran his hand over his body checking for injuries. *My arms and chest seem fine and my legs...legs...my ankle...Oh dear God, thank you, thank you. The ankle's fine! Oh man that was the scariest dream...nightmare, I've ever had* he concluded.

"Dude... what the hell were you dreaming?" Rick anxiously inquired.

"Man...I don't know...I mean, damn...It was so real. So intense. Hell, I even woke up from the dream while in the dream."

"Dude, that's crazy! Sounds like some sorta drug-induced sleep or something."

"Yeah, but I don't do drugs...so I have no idea what caused this. I remember it so clear especially feeling hurt about Tater... Tater...where the hell is Tater?" Jack implored anxiously scanning back across the room towards his other roommate's bed.

Squinting their eyes in the hazy glow of the early morning, the two roomies could just make out a messy lump of blankets. Jack jumped out his bed and ran over to Tater's corner. He frantically pulled away the blankets, pillows and sheets to no avail.

"Jack, calm down dude. I'm sure he's alright. You know as well as I, he doesn't always come home. Hell, he probably found some ugly chick last night and stayed at her place." Rick offered with a laugh.

"Rick...this is what happened in my dream and Tater was dead!" Jack barked back.

"Oh, I'm sure he's not dead. You can't kill that crazy fucker. Hell, he's on too many steroids. Now, he might have..."

"Shut up Rick, this aint funny. Tater... Tater!" Jack cried out looking toward the kitchen and then back to the bathroom.

"Hey, look his shoes are over by the front door" Rick calmly asserted.

Jack scrambled out of the bathroom and into the den on the other side of the French doors of the bedroom. In the dark room, he could see a dark figure splayed out on the floor. Flicking on the light switch, Jack's eyes gleamed with joy at the familiar sight of Tater lying face down on the hardwood floor with his jeans down around his ankles and his t-shirt twisted half way off his head and swaddled under his face. He pounced on his beefy roommate and started shaking him in elation.

"Tater, Tater...you're alive. You're alive!"

Slowly lifting his head to come to his senses, Tater eased himself off the floor into a sitting position. Rubbing the sleep out of his red eyes, Tater felt a huge set of arms embrace him blabbering something about being alive.

"Damn Miller, what the fuck?" Tater mumbled.

"You big, ugly ape... you're alive. You're alive!"

"Of course, I'm alive. Damn, I just had a few extra drinks. Now get the fuck off me and stop hugging me and shit, fag!" Tater added shoving his ecstatic roommate away.

Jack smiled but obeyed knowing how cranky Tater was in the morning, especially after a full night of drinking before the start of school. Jack was still beaming in the excitement and realization that the long dark nightmare was now, truly over. He was alive and well, as was his party-happy roommate, Tater.

"Now, Jack…what's all this shit about me being dead. Of course, I'm alive. I was just passed out. That's all. Hell, you've seen that before. What made you think I was dead and why the hell are we up so damn early?"

"Oh man…it's a long, long story. Let's just say I had a horrible dream and bad things happened…especially to you, big boy."

"Me? What the hell happened to me?"

"Hey big boy, what the hell are you doing lying on the floor with a perfectly good bed just a few feet away and why the hell are your pants down around your ankles?" Rick added playfully.

The question was abruptly interrupted by a pounding on the door. They could hear a girl's voice demanding they open the door immediately.

"Who the hell's that?" Rick asked staring at Tater.

"Don't ask me…I didn't meet anyone last night. At least I don't remember meeting anyone… hell I have no idea…" Tater replied rubbing his head.

Jack stood up and opened the door. He couldn't believe he was looking at Heather Marie Mills. There she was, fresh from his dream standing in front of him glaring back.

He had known her since their middle school days as sixth graders in Mrs. Hall's homeroom. But it wasn't until high school, that he nursed a huge crush on her as the captain of the cheerleading team— who only dated upper classmen. Jack lacked the confidence to ask her out mostly because he felt insecure about his appearance. He had a handsome face but a lanky build. Compared to the guys Heather dated, he was painfully inadequate. On the basketball court and baseball field, Jack played with a fearlessness and certainty. In those athletic arenas, he knew what he was doing and experienced a great deal of success.

It wasn't until his senior year that he nervously asked her to the Valentine's Day dance— knowing there were no longer upperclassmen above him. They dated for a while, but she never seemed interested in him. It was just something to do to finish out her high school years. She dumped him before Prom and went with his best friend, Rick. Jack was devastated but understood— Rick was better looking and came from a wealthy family. In this field, he couldn't compete. However, he couldn't stay mad at Rick. He reasoned that, like in sports, he had just lost to the better man.

College helped Jack focus for the first time on his studies and his physique. With all the freedom of time living on campus, he played during the day, and partied at night where he met lots of females who only knew the confident, well-built Jack Miller at UK.

"Heather?"

"Yes, its Heather. Are you okay, Jack? I heard this awful scream from across the street and thought it could be you. That maybe you were hurt or in danger?"

"Oh, no…I'm fine…I …"

"He had a nightmare, Heather! That's why he's all naked and sweaty!" Rick inserted.

That last part hit Jack hard. He had forgotten he had just got out of bed and was in his night time attire: boxers. *Oh crap!* Jack thought as he quickly vanished behind the door.

"Oh, come on Jack. It's nothing." Heather reassured. "They're no different than your short shorts. Besides, since when did you become so modest?"

"Its true Jack. When did you develop this modesty?" Rick teased.

"I guess you're right" Jack retorted, "Anyway, Heather…I'm fine. What the hell are you doing fully dressed at this time of the morning?"

"Well, I was getting ready for our morning exercises across the street. You know, Beta Gamma Beta, when you startled everyone with that crazy loud scream. Are you sure you're okay? Did something happen?"

"Yeah, I'm fine…look Heather… there is something I would like to talk to you about if you've got time?"

"Sure, I've got a Pysch. class in an hour over at Whitehall. Care to walk me over?"

"Oh my God, really? You got a Psych class? So do I? Is it Psych. 121 at 8 o'clock?"

"Yeah." Heather smiled.

"Awesome. I'll meet you out in front of the Beta house in a few."

"Sounds good. You might want to put on some pants though… or not" Heather teased as she walked away.

Jack closed the doors and was instantly heckled by his roommates. Anytime one of them had a girl over, it was standard operating procedure to harass the roommate until they left. Jack simply laughed it off and jumped into the shower. *Damn its good to see her. She looked real nice. I haven't thought about her in a while. I wonder why she was so prominent in my dream last night? Oh well, life goes on! Beautiful, beautiful life goes on.*

Sprinting across the street in cargo shorts and a hooded UK pullover with his backpack slung over one shoulder, Jack spotted Heather talking to several girls in the parking lot behind the sorority house.

"There you are. I see you've added a bit to your morning wardrobe." Heather teased.

"Yeah, about that. I'm real sorry. I totally forgot how I was dressed" Jack regretted remembering how prudish Heather was in high school.

"Oh, it's alright Jack. Don't worry about it. Trust me, the worst part of my morning was going into that Chinese apartment next door. Those guys in there are disgusting!"

"Really? Why were you in there? What happened?"

"I don't want to talk about it. Let's just say those guys are gross and leave it at that. I was at their place by accident. I thought it was your place. It said, 'Three Amigos' next to the buzzer and they buzzed me in.'"

"Oh, shit that's funny. Damn, Tater must have switched the name plates again. He does that from time to time. He thinks its funny and yeah, those dudes are a little different. I think they are TA's working on their masters. They don't know a whole lot of English. You probably confused them" Jacked laughed.

"Oh well, they're sick. Anyway, what was that nightmare about that spooked you so bad?"

"Oh wow…where to begin? Look I don't want to bore you with infinite details to a dream that seemed too real but let's just say I witnessed two murders and thought I woke from that dream to find that I was still dreaming with the murderers chasing me all over campus."

"Wow that is weird. Kinda scary. You still look shaken from it. Did you know the murder victims?"

"Yeah…kinda. One was Tater and the other was some mystery girl I've never seen before in my life. I don't know…its really fresh in my mind and I really don't want to talk about, you know?"

"Oh okay." Heather nodded as they crossed Avenue of Champions and walked by Stoll Field. There was an awkward silence and then Heather asked, "So Jack, who you dating these days?"

"Oh, no one. You know, just sorta looking around. You know the shy guy from high school still" Jack added sheepishly.

"That's not what I hear"

"What do you hear?"

"I hear a lot and its not about some 'shy' guy. Jack Miller has become some whore dog bedding girls left and right." Heather teased.

"Oh…not true. They haven't been left and right. Usually right in front of me. Besides, what do you care? You rejected me in high school, remember?"

Heather stopped walking and looked up at Jack seriously. He could sense a lecture was coming but was confused about what it could possibly be about. *Damn Heather you broke my heart in high school and now you want to lecture me about dating others. Where's that coming from?* Jack inwardly inquired. She lowered her head trying to put the words together just right.

"Jack, I know I hurt you years ago in high school, but I've changed…you've changed. In high school, I was a bit superficial. I admit it. Who wasn't? Look, that's not an excuse. I dated seniors because they were more mature and by the time of our senior year, I guess I liked Rick more. He was the captain of the football and baseball team and just gorgeous. He was also really sweet and nice."

"Yeah…I get that. I was just some awkward skinny dude that fell for the best-looking cheerleader. You picked Rick. Its okay…really, I'm over that."

"No, no…let me finish. Since I've started college, I've seen you a few times. You've changed a lot and not just physically. You seem way more confident and sure of yourself."

Jack nodded looking away not quite sure where this was leading.

"I don't know Jack. I just feel I was wrong to overlook you in high school. I'm a different person at a different place in life and well, I guess I want a new start with you. We've known each other since sixth grade and were practically raised together in your father's church…which, by the way, you should attend more often."

"Oh, I know. My mom sends me text messages all the time. Well, anyhow…yeah that would be nice…to start over. Why not? Hey, its getting late. Better start heading up the hill to class."

Heather agreed as they started walking again with a renewed purpose. Heather had cracked back into Jack's world. It had been stewing on her mind for some time and she was happy that it was now out in the open. Jack was still perplexed about the conversation as well as how it connected to his thoughts of her in his dream. *I haven't seen Heather in three years and suddenly she's in my dream last night and now walking with me to class. She looks great and all, but this is just a bit weird. What does this all mean? Oh, stop overanalyzing a simple coincidence and enjoy her company. She's hot! Its true...anyway looks like a packed house up at the Classroom Building* Jack smiled as he instinctively climbed the stairs two at a time.

Jack waited for Heather at the top of the stairs on the massive patio landing overlooking the south end of the campus. He opened the tall heavy door for her as they circled around looking for room 121. *Damn…121…that number's weird for some reason. Can't quite put my finger on it. Oh well, here it is* Jack grinned as he again played the gentleman and opened the door for Heather.

The huge auditorium was filled with chatter and nervous anticipation of the new class and year. As always, Jack walked down a few steps on the center aisle and checked with Heather to see if this was a good place to sit. She nodded eagerly as they plopped down in the hard seats with a right-handed removable desk top. He pulled out his notebook and scratched out the name of the class at the top of his paper. Looking up, he noticed a message on the board in big bold print: **COURAGE VS. COWARDICE**.

"Oh my God…are you kidding me? What the…" Jack mumbled to himself and looked around the class.

"What's the matter Jack?" Heather inquired scribbling the white board message at the top of her paper.

"Oh…nothing. Just kind of a weird topic for our first class?"

"Oh, not really. Dr. Daniels is a highly reputably professor known for her edgy style of pushing students to the limit. She really delves into the psyche for answers" an overly impressed student inserted from behind nosing in on another conversation.

"That's …great…thanks. I hope you enjoy the class." Jack stated wryly as Heather laughed and elbowed him playfully.

There was a surreal feeling about the classroom. Everything from the way Dr. Daniels entered the room and sat up on the long desk in the front, to how eagerly the students responded to her probing questions. Jack couldn't help but feel he had experienced all of this before. It bothered and nagged at him. Suddenly his eyes caught the sight of a long-haired beauty walking down the far side aisle late. She stepped down several rows to a familiar face, smiled and threw her book bag down next to a hooded figure. She beamed and chit-chatted with the guy whose face and head were covered by his hoodie. *That smile…oh my God…she's gorgeous…and strangely familiar. Well, she's obviously into that dude. So, might as well stop looking over there* Jack assessed as he looked back at the professor down front. He still couldn't shake the eerie feeling that he had seen all of this before. Even some of the questions and answers Jack mouthed precisely as Heather stared at him in amazement.

"How did you know what that kid was gonna say?"

"I'm telling you Heather. There's some weird stuff going on and I … what the hell? Look Heather. Its my boy, Tater, arriving late as usual."

They watched in mild amusement Tater standing at the top of the auditorium with his back pack on his left shoulder scanning the room.

"What's he doing?" Heather asked.

"He's scoping the room for hotties." Jack whispered while chuckling, "Once he locks onto a hot girl sitting alone or where there's an open seat, he'll pounce. See… look, he's spotted someone now. There he goes, swooping in for the Tater-kill on some poor, unsuspecting girl…" Jack stopped in mid-sentence as he watched Tater walked down the far side wall and land right behind the beautiful long-haired girl and her hooded friend. *Oh shit…now what? No, no Tater, not her, dude. She's out of your league and besides she's obviously with the hooded boy! Okay…yeah, I see you Tater. You can stop waving and take that "shit eating" grin off your face.*

"Looks like he found someone" Heather smiled.

"Yeah." Jack nodded his head in disapproval.

"What's the matter, Jack? She looks fine…in fact she's breath-taking. Do you know her?"

"No…I don't think"

"What does that mean? You either know her or you don't."

"I don't." Jack stated flatly.

All during the class Jack's mind was running wild with an eerie sense of foreboding. He felt his heart race as he looked over several times at the girl and her hooded friend. He wanted desperately to see who was behind the hood. The girl was flirting openly with him and seemed to write on his hand which he playfully rubbed off. By this time, Tater had moved on to different game once he realized the long-haired beauty wasn't even aware of his presence or really anyone else besides hoodie. *God, she looks so much like the girl in my dream...Carly...no...Can...Candace. Candace! Oh my God, it's her! That's where I've seen her. Its Candace. My God, it looks just like her from my dream. She's even playing and flirting with the hoodie dude like I remember.* Jack's last thought was interrupted by the sound of students packing up their bags and leaving.

"Come on Jack, class is over." Heather instructed. "What's the matter? You looked as if you've seen a ghost?"

"Oh...no...its just a weird thought I had about what Dr. Daniels said about courage and cowardice."

"Whatever...you weren't listening. You didn't take one note." Heather laughed, "I can see, I'm going to have to pull you through this class."

"Yeah...probably. What's your next class?"

"I've got an upper level business class on the other side of campus. What about you?"

"I've got nothing again until one o'clock."

"Good...you can walk me over." Heather smiled climbing the auditorium stairs leading Jack out to the spacious Classroom building patio. *Wow, Jack's very sweet and seemed genuinely interested in me before class started and then...I don't know, he sorta weirded out. Like he knew what everyone was going to say and then he got real quiet when the tall beautiful girl walked in. Well, he's a guy...that's sorta what they do I guess. Still he seems freaked out and...now where did he go?* Heather panicked looking around in the mass of students moving in and about the building.

Jack had to know what was going on with this beautiful girl and why everything seemed so familiar. He watched the pair leave the auditorium but lost them in the crowd out on the patio deck. He stood over by the railing, peering down at the crowd of students walking down the big hill to the student book store. The tree-lined path had a long hand rail running down the center acting as a traffic median. *Come on Jack, get a hold of yourself. You've lost sight of the two and that's a good thing. You don't need to know what they're doing or really anything else. Its just a coincidence that she looks like the girl in your nightmare. She's obviously not, so...Oh shit. There she is! Walking down the path draped all over the hoodie dude... God...she's really something. I love how playful and full of life she seems* he pondered leaning against the patio railing.

Jack stared at the two who had stopped at the bottom of the hill near the "free speech" area of campus by the student bookstore. They were laughing and teasing each other. The hooded man turned toward the Classroom Building but kept his head down. Jack watched intently trying to see his identity. "Candace" broke from the hooded man's hold and ran to another familiar figure. It was a well-dressed light-skinned black man who smiled and hugged her as she pointed back at the hooded guy. Suddenly she darted back at him and pulled his hoodie off. Jack froze in astonishment. His eyes bulged in disbelief.

"Oh no…Oh no…Dear God…no, no, no! It's Luke! My God, it's my brother Luke! I've got to stop him!" Jack muttered.

"What did you say Jack?" Heather asked catching up to him by the patio railing.

"Oh my God Heather…you're not going to believe who the guy in the hoodie is?

"Who?"

"It's Luke. My brother, Luke!"

"So? He's with a cute girl. Good for him."

"No, Heather, you don't understand. That's the girl from my nightmare and she… Oh my God…was that a dream or a premonition?"

Chapter 2

"Don't be afraid of your fears. They're not there to scare you. They're there to let you know that something is worth it."

— C. Joy Bell

Luke rubbed his eyes trying to remove a sleepy film that clouded his vision. Squinting, he could just make out his bearings in a vaguely familiar setting. Staring through the foggy room illuminated by a single ray of light streaming through the corner of a window blind to his left, he could make out a beautiful woman astride the hood of a muscle car leering back at him. A smile eased across his lips. He knew exactly where he was, but wasn't sure why he was there. Scanning the room, his eyes focused on an ash tray sitting on top of a dresser near the door with a burned-out joint. There was no doubt where he was— Simon LaRue's apartment— but why? Looking down at his feet, he noticed his shoes were still on and was fully dressed.

Luke shook his head in astonishment at how often this scenario had occurred. Rubbing his temples, he tried to remember what had happened last night that landed him in Simon's place. *Damn…Simon…I saw him yesterday in Lexington. He wanted to talk to me about something…he told me to meet him at Three Goggles— I hate that fucking yuppie, frat/sorority place— too trendy. But I met him there around 10 o'clock…I think…damn, can't remember much of what we talked about, but I do remember meeting a smoking hot red-head. My God, she was nice…and could dance…man, she could dance. God, my head is killing. Must have had too many rum and Coke's…but that never hit me like this…*

Gently sliding his feet off the bed, Luke trampled over to the bathroom to relieve last night's endeavors. Washing his hands and splashing water on his face, one memory suddenly hit him like a wrecking ball— an eight-a.m. class at Whitehall Classroom building. *Damn, what was I thinking? Scheduling an eighter— rookie mistake and I'm a junior. Should've known better. But this is UK, not L.C.C.— my little JUCO stop to get my associates. I swear if Jack makes fun of that school one more time— Last Chance College. Not funny!*

Luke poked his head out of the bathroom and across the hall through an open door to Simon's room. He spotted Simon's alarm clock that read 7:32. He pulled a triple X gray hooded sweatshirt over his head that belonged to Simon because it appeared to be clean— though it was clearly too big. Looking back into the bathroom mirror, Luke ran his fingers through his sandy brown, wavy hair. He splashed more water on his handsome face with fair skin and a dash of freckles sprinkled about the cheeks and nose.

He always underplayed his physical appearance believing others were better looking or in better shape. He wasn't unhappy about his looks, just not confident that others saw him as attractive. Standing at six feet three inches tall and weighing approximately two hundred pounds, Luke had an imposing figure with an easy disposition— most of the time. When provoked, he could quickly rage in any direction and at anyone but was slow to cool down. Being the youngest of three active boys fighting for attention was never easy as Joseph, the oldest, was more accomplished and Jack, the middle brother, was overconfident.

Wiping his hands on a towel laying by the bathtub, Luke poked his head into Simon's room to make sure his long-time friend was okay. He eased the door open as a widening light spread across the room displaying an obese figure face down on his bed with limbs sprawled in every direction. Simon LaRue was Luke's best friend though he shouldn't have been.

They met in Mrs. Mathis' first grade class. Simon was the portly kid sitting behind Luke and harassing him with his super fat pencil that whacked him on the neck. Simon's parents insisted on purchasing the larger pencils because his chubby fingers had trouble gripping regular pencils. Initially this caused trouble as other kids teased him for his corpulent problem. But Simon turned the pencil liability into a weapon. At recess, he challenged and defeated everyone in pencil pop— a game whereby an attacker struck his opponent's pencil to break it. Veteran players learned to remove the eraser, bite down on the metallic band to sharpen it like a blade. Simon's prodigious scribbler bore a few battle scars about the middle section— mere chinks in the champion's armor. He had broken at least fifty pencils, including ten of Luke's.

One day, Luke's pencil had been snapped to a nub but he insisted on continuing the fight even though its reduced size exposed his knuckles to Simon's violent blows. Luke's cut-up knuckles weren't enough to concede the fight. Simon was in awe of his smaller classmate's grit and determination to fight on even when winning was no longer possible. This courageous act changed Simon's opinion and forged a bond of admiration. The smaller, scrappy Miller boy proved he was a worthy peer who could be counted on in a scrap— a frequent occurrence for Simon who had a knack for getting into physical confrontations.

Because he was bigger than most kids his age, Simon easily bullied his way around problems that often left him with few friends. He charmed Luke with his ignorant manners and careless attitude— a welcome change from his moralistic oldest brother. Joseph constantly questioned and criticized Luke's actions as being stupid or un-Christian. Around him, Luke felt conflicted and self-conscious, but not with Simon. Their friendship lasted through high school and into Luke's college years. Simon attended L.C.C. but became bored and gave it up to make money in construction as a menial laborer— pay was decent for a twenty-something with only a high school diploma and zero ambition.

Scanning Simon's bedroom for his bookbag was an act of futility as clothes, shoes, papers and magazines were strewn about the floor. Luke's aching head recalled that his bookbag never left his old beat-up Honda Civic. He quietly closed the door and entered the kitchen in search of something edible to answer his bellowing stomach. Pulling open the fridge door, Luke winced and quickly shut it. *Simon really needs to buy some basic food staples…beer and cheese aint exactly healthy. I need to get going. Finding a place to park on campus sucks balls! I'll most likely have a long hike to the Classroom building. Damn, why did I schedule an eighter!*

The advantage of Luke's compact, slightly dented car on campus was its ability to sneak into any available space on a street without any fear of it being robbed or broken into. Luke inched along Woodland Avenue searching for any nook or cranny. The treasured spot was located as Luke skillfully maneuvered the parallel park and quickly broke into a sprint as he had less than five minutes to get to class.

With his bookbag slung across his left shoulder, he jogged down Avenue of Champions past Stoll Field while slowing his pace up the hill to Whitehall. He entered the crowded classroom building twisting and turning his way to the front where he pulled out his schedule to see where his Psych. Class was meeting. *Ah…room 121. First floor and right in front of me.* Opening the tall double doors, Luke mused over its immense size. *Wow…so much bigger than anything at LCC. Stadium seating and its nearly full. Thank God, class hasn't started yet.*

He scanned the back rows for his usual seating preference but found most everyone else loved those seats as well. His eye caught glimpse of a small opening down front but away from the center of the classroom. Pulling his hoodie back over his head, Luke strolled across the top aisle and descended the wide steps to four empty seats. He nimbly slid past a few chatty "sorority types" and eased down into a seat leaving gaps on either side. He never felt comfortable sitting next to a stranger and hated the inevitable awkward chat that ensued.

Relieved that he was essentially alone, Luke pulled out his notebook and pen and instinctively looked up at three large white paneled boards with a black marker phrase **COURAGE VS. COWARDICE**. *Okay…this could be interesting. A topic with real world application. What makes someone act or fight and another run and hide? I can't wait to hear what Dr. Daniels says about all this. Oh shit, look what's coming down my aisle!*

"Hey Luke…I see you saved me a seat." The tall red-headed beauty smiled as she dropped her book bag and leaned up next to him. Luke was the envy of every red-blooded, able-bodied male that traced her graceful steps to his aisle.

"Hey…" Luke nodded.

"Seriously, Luke? 'Hey' is all you're gonna say?"

Luke stared at her for a moment as his mind raced back to last night and

Three Goggles night club. Her dark, tawny skin and emerald green eyes ensnared him. He could feel that he was different around her— more calm and relaxed. Very similar to another person he dared not think about.

"You don't even remember my name, do you?" she taunted.

"Of course…Molva?"

"Ha, ha! Very funny, Seinfeld"

"Seriously, I know… its Candace."

"Well I guess I did make an impression on you last night."

"Yeah, you're about the only thing I remember about last night. My head is splitting. I don't usually get that from rum and Coke."

"That's not all you drank last night."

"What? I drank something else? I hate trying new things."

"I know…I didn't think I was going to get you to try my drink, but you took one sip, and bam…next thing I know, you've ordered two more."

"Two more what?"

"Long Island Teas."

"Long Island Teas? Sounds like a sissy drink. What's in it?"

"Wow…you pretty much said the same thing last night…it has just about every liquor in it with some sweet additives."

"Damn, I vaguely remember any of that. I do kinda remember it tasted sweet but…"

"Yeah, you made a rookie mistake— drank too many, too fast." Candace added with a laugh. "But it loosened you up. You even got out on the dance floor."

"No way. There's no way I was on the dance floor."

"Oh yes you were, and you were fantastic."

"Ok, you're totally screwing with me 'cause I can't dance. You must have been with another Miller."

"Oh really? Who?"

"Never mind him…I'm sure he's already got a couple lined up." Luke mumbled.

"Sounds interesting" Candace beamed as she leaned closer. "Well you were fabulous on the floor and very light on my feet."

"Ha, ha…very funny. I'm sure I looked like an idiot."

"No, you didn't. You had fun. Dancing is supposed to be fun and carefree. You know 'dance like there's no one else in the room' sorta thing."

"Well, I hope I didn't embarrass you or step on you too many times."

"Not at all.", she grabbed his hand and started drawing a small flower on it, "What are you doing tonight?"

"Nothing that I can think of off the top of my head."

"Good, you can meet me at Cup O Joe around eight? Sound like a date?"

"Sounds like a date." Luke grinned. "By the way, how did you know I would be in here and how in the hell did you find me with my hoodie on?"

"Silly boy, we talked about it last night."

"We did?"

"Yes, we couldn't believe how we just met and had a class together the next morning. In fact, I bet Simon you wouldn't show up, and he said, 'there's no way my boy aint showing up to see you'" Candace mocked in her best gruff low bass voice. "You know how Simon does it."

"Wait, you know Simon? Simon LaRue?"

"Of course, he introduced us, silly. Wow, you really don't remember much about last night. Anyway, Simon said you'd be easy to find cause you'd be wearing a gray hoodie pulled over your head and probably sitting alone in a corner, like you were hiding. Voila…here you are." Candace gushed squeezing his hand and doodling on it again.

Luke frowned and rubbed it off.

"Damn…Simon, huh? He said he had to talk to me about something…" Luke mumbled.

"What?"

"Oh, nothing. Just can't believe you know Simon. How do know him?"

"Oh, through a mutual friend." Candace stated dismissively. "Anyway, he's a real sweetheart. A bit uptight at first but a real teddy bear once you get to know him."

"How well do you know him?" Luke inquired through raised eye brows.

"Not like that. Eww gross! Simon's sweet but…no, that's disgusting."

"I agree." Luke laughed. "Hey, did I get your number last night?"

"Yes, but I'm sure you lost it since you can't seem to remember much about last night." Candace added testily.

Luke's flirtatious imploring was interrupted by a loud chorus of laughter. He looked up to the front where Dr. Daniels was smiling atop a long rectangular table answering questions. Luke missed the question but could see the "good doctor" was playfully teasing an overeager student's response.

She quickly pivoted and moved on to the class assignment: write a two-page essay on "The Courageous vs. the Coward: What's Love Got to Do With It?" — Dr. Daniels' sang in her best Tina Turner as the class was dismissed.

Pulling his hoodie lower over his eyes, Luke pondered the assignment. *What's love got to do with it? Damn…nothing. How does love fit into the equation? You're either a fighter or a flighter. You either have guts or you don't. Where's love factor in to it? Geesh, I gotta write a paper on this? It doesn't even make sense.*

"What's the matter, Luke?" Candace tugged on his hand.

"Oh, nothing, really…just that assignment doesn't make much sense."

"Why?"

"Where's love in any of these actions or inactions? I don't get it?"

"Well, I'll have to explain it to you. But, not now. I have to run by the student book store and pick up a few things before my next class. You coming?"

"Sure."

Luke jumped out of his seat and followed Candace up the stairs and out into the lobby. Pushing in and out through a throng of students, Luke was annoyed by the small clusters forming mid-stream that forced the current into a tighter line around them. He marveled at Candace's deftness and ability to navigate swiftly through the clogged artery of the classroom lobby. *I can't believe I'm with a girl like her. She's so easy to talk to. It's been a long time since I could talk this easily to a girl who seems to genuinely be into me. I vaguely remember much about last night, but I do remember her being very forward and interested in me and now...she's so nice. Damn, the last time I felt this good about anything or anyone...no...damn it, no...don't think about her. Get her out of your mind, idiot. I can't allow myself to go down that path. That was a long time ago...time to move on. This girl is...very similar to Janee. Both red-headed beauties with long athletic builds. Both super easy to talk to. Both...okay seriously stop thinking about it. Just enjoy Candace.*

Candace led Luke down the long, wide two-way stairwell split by a blue-painted handrail. Her boundless energy seemed to infect the irascible Luke as she tugged at his hoodie trying to pull it off. Laughing, he adroitly fended off each swipe while playfully slapping her hands. Candace feigned a hurt hand and when Luke showed concern, she quickly swung into action again. Luke secured her wrists and drew her in close.

"You're not getting it down. You're wasting your time, Red." Luke immediately winced remembering that was his tag for Janee.

"Come on Luke. Take that silly thing off."

"No way."

"Why? Do you have bed hair? Is it all flat?"

"Of course. No one should have to see my messy hair."

"Come on, gimme a glimpse." She teased pulling her hands free and reaching futilely for his hood.

"No." Luke snapped grabbing her wrists again. Candace frowned and scanned the front of the student bookstore for a diversionary tactic. Her eyes widened when she recognized a familiar face.

"Oh look, it's my buddy" she called out, pulling her hands free and running away. Candace bear-hugged the well-dressed, light-skinned man beaming with joy toting a large bag. His green eyes matched hers as they gushed over each other's outfits. Bemused, Luke stood with his hands on his hips wondering if she would return. Candace pointed at him and turned back to her friend before lunging at Luke and finally pulling his hoodie down, exposing the flattened mess of tangled light brown hair.

"I told you I would get it down."

"Whoa...not fair. Not cool. My hair looks like shit." Luke teased trying to scramble his hair back into some semblance of order.

"Your hair is a mess...but I like it."

"Really?"

"No. It does look like shit." Candace stated woodenly.

"Oh really? Like shit. I warned you." Luke cried out in defense grabbing her arms and pulling her against his chest. He lowered his head rubbing his bristled face against her soft smooth cheek while her auburn red hair fell across his face. *Damn she feels good...smells good too. I could hold her like this all day...and she's hugging back. Oh man, what a great day.* Luke's eyes fell on a figure moving rapidly down the stairwell that looked vaguely familiar. Within a few seconds, Luke frowned as the emerging figure was his middle brother, Jack.

Bounding down the hillside stairway, darting in and out of southbound traffic, Jack tried to keep his eye on Luke for fear he would lose him—possibly forever. Calling out several times, Jack could see Luke end his embrace of the red-headed girl and grimace. He slowed as he approached the couple. He could see Luke was in no mood for games, so he had to measure his words carefully to avoid coming across as crazy.

"Hey Luke!" Jack said catching his breath.

"Hey Jack." Luke deadpanned.

"Oh, is this your brother, the good dancer?" Candace inserted pulling back from Luke.

"What?"

"Yes, this is one of my brothers, Jack. Jack this is Candace." Luke politely stated. Jack recoiled back as if hit by a sledgehammer to the gut. *Oh no! Dear God...no. Why did her name have to be Candace? Are you serious?* Jack's mind was racing in every direction as he stared at his nightmare come true.

"Jack...Jack...are you okay? What's the matter with you?" Luke inquired. "I guess he's never seen a pretty girl before."

"Hello Jack. You're looking at me weird. Do I know you? Have we met before?"

"No...um...not really."

"Not really, Jack?" Luke said. "You either have or haven't met before."

"Luke, can I talk to you for a second?" Jack asked. "I'm sorry Candace. I just really need to talk to my brother real quick."

"No problem. Luke I'll be in the bookstore. Please stop in before you leave. Nice to have met you, Jack."

"Same, again thanks!" Jack added watching her walk over to the light-skinned man putting her arm in his before disappearing into the crowded bookstore.

"Jack...what the hell's going on? You come running down that hill like a madman. Calling out for me. Embarrassing me in front of everyone."

"That wasn't my intention."

"Well, what is your intention, now that you have my attention?" Luke brooded.

"Luke, listen to me carefully and don't dismiss what I'm about to tell you. I know its going sound crazy and believe me, I understand, I'm not sure I totally believe it."

"What?"

"That girl…Candace. I saw her in my dream last night."

"Okay, now I get it…you want to swoop in and steal her from me. Jack…damn it!"

"No, no…that's not it. I swear. I saw her in my dream or more like nightmare. I'm telling you she looks exactly like the girl and even has the same name."

"Bullshit! You're making it up to make a move on a pretty girl that happens to be interested in me."

"Luke, no I'm not making it up or interested in her that way. I mean she's very pretty but…"

"Ah ha! I knew it. Damn it, Jack. Anytime I seem to find a pretty girl you come sniffing around."

"What the hell are you talking about? I've never done that."

"Oh really? Janee?"

"What! Are you serious? How many times do I have to tell you…there was NOTHING going on between Janee and me and never was. You know that. She was in love with you…always was. You fucking blew that by making shit up that never happened."

"Shut up Jack! I'm serious. Don't talk about her. Never talk about her again."

"You brought her up. I'm just defending myself, as always, against baseless allegations that you know aren't true. It's this attitude of yours that drove a wedge in your relationship." Jack riposted. He instantly regretted it because Luke was fuming. *Damn it Jack! Way to get him riled up. He'll never listen now. Shit he's turning and walking away. I've got to do something to keep him away from Candace!*

"Luke…I'm sorry. Hey, Joseph texted me this morning. He's in from Louisville and wants to play ball at the Seaton Center." Jack offered. "He's expecting you to be there!"

Luke stopped just before entering the bookstore. Paused for several moments as angry students moved around him to enter. *Dang! Joseph's in town and wants to play ball. That's too fun to miss. I love playing a little b-ball with my brothers…even if one of them's being a dick.* Luke shook his head and pivoted back toward Jack.

"Alright…what time?"

"Noon…and Luke" Jack added as he jogged up to him. "Look, I know what I said sounds crazy but its true and there's much, much more to the story than just seeing her. Its bad. Really bad and I need to talk to you when you're more receptive, cause this shit is too crazy and deadly to ignore."

"What? Deadly…Jack, dude you're losing it."

"Okay…meet me and Joseph at Seaton Center at noon. We'll play a little b-ball., kick some ass, and you'll be in a better mood. By the way, that dude— the fancy one she left with…I saw him in my dream, too, and his name is Geoffrey."

"Bull! Whatever, Jack. I'll see you later." Luke waved at him and entered the bookstore. *I don't know what's gotten into Jack but…that's the craziest thing.*

Moving in and out of aisles crowded with eager students holding their schedules in one hand and a basket in the other while loading books, Luke scanned over their heads in search of his red-headed friend. Looking for her, he began to realize how quickly he had become attached to her.

It was unusual for Luke; he prized his independence and ability to stay away from relationships— especially since his high school girlfriend, Janee. It had been three years and he wasn't interested in reacquiring the pain and hurt that relationship had cost him. *Where is she? She must be moving away as soon as I come to where she was. Too many students in here. Good God Candace, you picked the wrong time to pick up your books. Do it after the first week. Make sure you're not dropping the class before you buy the book. The sell back is crap! Why am I even in here? I just met this girl…but dang…she's so easy to talk to…so nice and fun-loving. Her eyes…so easy to stare in to and never want to leave. She's…she's just like…No, dang it! Don't think about her. Get her out of your mind. Don't go there…it hurts too much. But she's…*

"Hey big boy with the messy bed-hair!" Candace joked with her hands over his eyes from behind. "Who are you looking for?"

"Oh…there you are. I was just…um looking for some cute little thing from my Psych. class. She wandered in here and I wanted to stop her and say hi."

"Oh really. She's cute, huh? What's she look like?"

"Well, she's got fiery red hair, buck teeth…oh and missing a few on the bottom and she's a bit plump in the hips with heavy cankles." Luke teased.

"Ugh…sounds horrible. I'll just let you keep looking for her."

Luke grabbed her arm and pulled her in for a hug. She reciprocated by wrapping her arms around his back and playfully mussing his hair. Luke beamed ignoring his flat hair while inhaling her scent of perfume mixed with a cucumber melon body lotion and apple blossom shampoo. *God, she smells good. I can't believe this is happening. What am I doing hugging a girl in public like this? I would never do this. I hate guys that do that. What is she doing to me? Oh man…*

"Hey Luke" Candace said breaking free from the warm embrace. "I want you to meet a dear friend of mine. This is Geoffrey!"

"What?" Luke queried as he fell back a few paces.

"Hello. I'm Geoffrey" the nattily dressed man offered as he stuck out his hand. "Why Luke, you look as if you've seen a ghost."

Chapter 3

"A team is where a boy can prove his courage on his own. A gang is where a coward goes to hide."

— Mickey Mantle

Although Kentucky is renowned for tobacco, bourbon, and horse racing, basketball is majestic. Blue bloods, as they're called, reside throughout the state with a fascination bordering on fanaticism for the roundball. The genesis of this movement was found in the 1930's when a Kansas man moved to the Bluegrass, central Kentucky, to play a different brand of basketball. As originally conceived, the game was stagnant with players spread across the half court taking turns shooting a ball at a hoop. Defense of the hoop was as scant as the offensive movement of the ball— no coordinated effort exerted on either side. It was often a staid contest of shooting— the sport was slow and unentertaining.

However, the "Baron of the Bluegrass", as Rupp would be tagged, conceived of a fast-moving offense that used set plays to get better shots under the basket. These higher percentage shots resulted in a confused defense that had trouble staying with their man. Rupp also innovated the "fast break" as an offensive weapon to score quickly and easily before the opponent had time to set their defense. Getting a rebound and pushing it up court to a breaking teammate, allowed for easy scores. Rupp's half-court offense also required quick ball movements. His motion offense with weaving players near the top of the key, moving the ball like a shell game, fascinated spectators and more importantly allowed the team with "KENTUCKY" stitched to their jersey to win games easily.

With each blow-out victory, more and more Kentuckians began to attend the games. With each collegiate championship, the state of Kentucky could boast of national prominence. Sports in the South are as important as breathing and eating— what's the point of the former if your sports team is terrible. Adolph Rupp's teams at the University of Kentucky created a statewide pride that exuded confidence and entertainment during the Depression and World War II. The radio made it possible for most families to hear the games and experience a commonality that bonded communities. Folks talked about the games at work, discussed tactics with their neighbors and organized basketball associations for their children in their communities. Fathers dreamed of their children wearing a Kentucky jersey, and kids dreamed of playing for "The Man in the Brown Suit", another nickname for Rupp, in a packed gym with a national audience listening.

The basketball phenomenon took hold in a diverse state of Appalachia coal mining in the east and industrialization and manufacture in the northern and western halves. So ingrained was Kentucky basketball that no matter where you traveled in the state, if you wore a "U.K." shirt, you met a friend.

The Miller boys grew up in this highly competitive sport and culture. Though they played other sports such as football and baseball— basketball was king in the royal state. Its fast-paced, intense action that required both athleticism and skill, appealed to their competitive nature. Their father was a good athlete who encouraged their play because it not only built and honed their bodies, but it taught many salient life lessons from successes and failures. Through hard-work, discipline and tactical preparation, Matthew Miller's boys were learning essential life lessons through sports without the abeyant lecture.

Often, he would council his sons on the "lessons of the game" and its applications to life— winning or losing were temporary and resultant of the effort one put into the game. Just like life, sports weren't always fair. Some people were simply born with talents, skills and size that gave them advantages in the game. However, those advantages didn't guarantee victory in the game anymore than success in life. "Never get too high after a victory or too low after a defeat", Matthew would caution his hyperactive sons. "Winning is as fun as losing is awful. Play the game to win, but accept losing, learn from it, and play again— always play."

The Miller's had a basketball goal attached to the roof of their garage. It wasn't the regulation height of ten feet, but an appropriate size for their young age to learn how to be successful shooting the ball. It's too difficult and frustrating for five and six-year olds to shoot basketball on a regulation goal as they aren't strong enough to get it up to the rim. Often resorting to a heaving motion, the child develops bad shooting form and habits. Better to start with a smaller ball learning the correct shooting form, and as the child gets older and stronger, the ball and goal get bigger, but the shooting form remains the same out of reinforced habit.

At least that was Matthew Miller's method to teaching the sport to his sons. He reasoned that, too often, kids who started too soon with the bigger ball and goal, developed bad shooting form and usually quit the sport early from frustration of failure. That was not going to happen to his boys. The shorter goal fueled competitive games as young boys discovered how to shoot the ball with their limited size and strength. They developed good form on their stroke and figured out how to get their shot with a defender hounding them. The Millers played hard and fought constantly for victory. However, beating up on each other grew tiresome, so they took their game to the road to challenge other kids. They found paydirt in the Briar Patch neighborhood, a short bike ride away that housed many kids their age similarly infected with basketball fever.

Joseph and the older boys selected teams and played for hours with mixed results. Joseph cared more about winning than scoring, as too often his teammates did. Frustrated by losses, he constantly argued with his teammates who cared less about defending the goal than shooting at it. Most of the neighborhood kids played selfishly— rarely passing the ball and looking only to score. If you didn't get the rebound or a steal, you rarely touched the ball. This self-interested style of play was boring and unproductive as most players stood and watched the older, bigger players take over. Joseph had trouble getting his team to pass, move around, and play defense. Everyone just wanted to shoot as soon as they ball hit their hands.

Frustrated that his teams lost and wouldn't listen to him, Joseph took matters into his own hands. He decided to create his own team with players who had to listen to him— his brothers. He would mold the team to his will and challenge all comers in the neighborhood. Their three-man team would never be divided up or split and they would play his brand of basketball— team work with an organized offense and tough, hard-nosed defense.

Everyday Joseph drilled his brothers on basketball fundamentals of shooting, dribbling, passing and constantly moving their feet. The brothers developed a style of play that rewarded each player with open shots while placing great emphasis on a physical defense. Jack and Luke initially struggled with defense as they often had to guard older, stronger opponents that hit and beat on them constantly. Joseph exhorted the brothers to suck it up, stop crying and fight back. Joseph never allowed any of the older kids to unfairly attack his brothers. As soon as it happened, Joseph swung into action attacking his brother's assailant.

Jack and Luke felt protected and this gave them the backing to play Joseph's physical style. They adored their older brother and the new-found attention they were receiving. Fearful of disappointing him, the younger brothers accepted his leadership and unquestioned authority. The fact that one of the best players in the neighborhood, or for that matter, the county, turned down other teams to play with them meant everything. They were determined to justify his confidence and make him proud.

The Miller boys, constantly fighting each other, had now bonded as brothers on a team. Joseph's reward was victory. The boys simply beat every team that Briar Patch threw at them. Their motion offense and defensive teamwork set a standard of excellence. Rarely did they lose, and a friendship of mutual respect developed. They still argued and fought, but in the sports arena, they came together as brothers. As they grew older, they would splinter through differences in life-styles, choices and values, but basketball always brought them together.

The University of Kentucky's campus and the Seaton Center was the latest venue for the Miller's game. Although Joseph had already graduated from UK, he often returned in the summer and weekends during the school year from Louisville's Southern Baptist Theological Seminary, a graduate school for Southern Baptist ministers. The outdoor courts, affectionately termed the "Blue Courts", were where some of the most physical games were played in Lexington. Young men gathered early before the lights came on to establish court rights. The five on five games were simple: win and stay on the court— lose and go home or get back in line to play again in an hour or so. Due to the elements of wind, rain and uneven blacktop courts, games on the Blue Courts usually devolved into a rough and tumble, hack and smack affair with outcomes being determined by baskets scored close to the goal. Shooting outside shots on outdoor courts was always tricky with wind changing and effecting ball flight. Therefore, as you got closer to the winning score contests became physical with higher percentage shots around the rim. The ability to drive the ball, absorb contact, and score was at a premium.

The Miller boys loved this style of play and easily adapted. Games were contentious, and many didn't like the physicality and competitive pace the brothers played at, but it was successful, and they usually held court for four or five games. The brothers would either bring two players to the team or pick-up them up at the court. They sought big guys to rebound and play tough defense. They didn't care if the newbies could shoot because the Miller's would provide the offense. As a newcomer to the team, you would get shot opportunities, but you had to be alert because they moved the ball quickly with a deft touch to open players. They demanded you play hard on defense and pass the ball. The reward was simple— win the game and hold the court. Often due to the physical nature of the game, fights broke out— both verbal and occasionally physical. Many resented the Miller's style of play and success on the court and sought to break them. Pushing, shoving and trash talking were standard fare on the Blue Courts.

Jack discovered that his game was fueled by the tense atmosphere. He loved beating opponents off the dribble and elevating over them for a jump shot. He truly believed no one could guard him one on one. Luke had an excellent outside shot, but rarely used it on the outdoor courts. With his increased size and strength, he moved his game under the basket where the action was extremely physical. He often got tangled up with opponents for rebounds and shots. This led to physical altercations that he never backed away from.

Often, Joseph would intervene to prevent a fight, and loss of the court. Jack was as quick in temper as Luke, but less likely to encourage a fight. His was more a bluff than anything else, whereas Luke seemed to want a fight. This drove Joseph crazy because he knew his youngest brother lost his ability to play once blind fury took over. He would often scold and council Luke to "stop looking for a fight and play ball." Inevitably Luke would shut down, lose focus of the game, and seek a fight. Early in Luke's organized basketball years his coach admonished him for his temper exclaiming "You are like a piece of steel. The hotter you get, the easier it is for others to twist and mold you!" Joseph heartily agreed with that assessment, and tried his best calm him saying, "You're better than that guy! Stop letting him get in your head and making you look like a fool." Luke rarely cooled off or backed down. It was a test of one's manhood, and he wasn't about to be bested.

Jack often watched from a distance as the two brothers would argue back and forth. He understood that Joseph was right, but admired Luke's fire, and willingness to fight. It was an attribute Jack wasn't sure he had. He got mad, played hard, talked trash, and got confrontational, but knew he would never take it to the next level and fight. Luke, however, seemed to want to go to the next level. Rarely did his opponent take the challenge. This only emboldened Luke, and it began to drive a wedge through Joseph.

Joseph was the cooler to his hot-headed brothers. He showed a deft diplomatic touch on the court that usually calmed the situation with his reasonable, relaxed approach that often disarmed opponents. They watched him scold his volatile brothers which eased the situation and prevented escalation. He loved his brother's fire and zeal to win, but hated how it could consume them, and cause them to lose focus and the game. He badgered and harangued his brothers to play dispassionately— to ignore the trash talk and physical sparring of their opponents. But his words often fell on deaf ears.

Jack and Luke had become good players in their own right, and usually knew how anger could motivate them to victory. They loved Joseph, but he was no longer the best player, and they still won with their anger, and honor intact. Their game and independence had passed by their older brother. He could no longer dictate and run the team. Jack had emerged as the best player both offensive and defensively. Late in games he would take the shot and guard the toughest players. Luke's physical play set the tone of the games as weaker teams backed down. He became the team's enforcer. Setting hard picks and battling down low for rebounds and put back baskets. Joseph was the steady ball handler, defender and all around good player, but no longer the leader. The problem was he didn't know that.

Checking in at Seaton Center with your student ID should have been a mundane affair. Simply flash your ID showing the current semester sticker on the back to a disinterested student behind the desk. Grab a ball and go play. That was usually the case unless the disinterested student was an upperclassman named Todd.

For some reason, Todd enjoyed the cat and mouse game of dragging out the entrance to the gym. Often there would be a huge line of students waiting to get into the gym because of Todd's meticulous care of insuring the security and sanctity of the use of Seaton Center's facilities. His annoyed persona only made matters worse. He would look up from behind the small narrow table with his eyes just clearing the top of the desk aimed directly at the student's mid-section. He only looked at your face when comparing photo ID. Todd was a tall, thin drink of water with perfect hair and teeth, though you rarely saw the teeth as smiling seemed an uncomfortable burden.

Looking over Jack's ID, Todd sneered "Do you need a ball?"

"Yes." Jack replied slightly annoyed at how long this transaction was taking.

Todd had been checking Jack's student ID for more than a year and a half and still looked it over as if it wasn't valid.

"Here's your ball. It's number 4. Remember to return the ball issued to you, number 4, or you'll lose Seaton Center membership privileges, will be fined for its replacement, and could put a hold on your degree."

"Of course." Jack said after playfully repeating the scripted Todd lines. "Todd, we've been doing this song and dance for over a year and each time you act like you don't know me. You stare at my ID like you've never seen me before. What gives man?"

"It's my job. Have a nice day." Todd retorted dripping of insincerity.

"Yeah…thanks, Todd." Jack laughed.

Opening the door to the gym was an act of great anticipation. You quickly scanned the three full length courts for a good five on five game. Once found, you assembled a squad of those standing around or shooting at a nearby goal, and then checked to see if anyone had the next game. It was extremely important to declare next game, or the following game, so that no one claim-jumped you.

As soon as Jack entered the gym he spotted Joseph shooting jumpers on the opposite end of the center court. For some reason, the five on five game was being played on the farthest court from the entrance.

Walking over to his brother, Jack recognized a large, beefy figure feeding passes to Joseph. Dewayne Beasley was built like an offensive lineman at six foot four and weighing about three hundred pounds. He was bald and sporting a heavy beard. Jack had played with him before in Louisville at the seminary courts when he had visited Joseph. He was a decent player who mostly rebounded and set hard screens. He played at the outset of games, but easily tired, and often late in games, rarely ran down to the offensive end of the court due to fatigue. He was an extremely affable giant who hated confrontation and often served as peacemaker on the Miller teams.

"Hey Dewayne!" Jack called out.

"Hello Jack. Great to see you, friend. You look great."

"Thanks. Is the old man hitting anything?" Jack asked watching Joseph release a jump shot.

"Hasn't missed yet."

"Is that right? Here let me feed him one." Jack smirked retrieving the ball from the net and purposely tossing the ball low on Joseph's feet forcing him out of his rhythm by bending over to catch the ball. Joseph clanged his shot off the rim.

"Wow, I thought you were hitting 'em?"

"I was until a crappy pass on my ankles threw me off!" Joseph laughed as he gave Jack a bro-hug.

"We got next game?"

"Yeah. Where's Luke?" Joseph snapped.

"He's coming…at least he said he was this morning."

"He better get here soon. That game's almost over and its got some good players."

"Yeah, I can see that. Looks like a few guys from Woodford County are back."

"Your boy, Red is eating em up out there. You want me to guard him? You two always fight."

"Nah, I'll be fine. I've been playing against him since seventh grade. I know his moves. He's good, and tough to stay in front of if you've never played him, but I know his moves and where he likes to get his shots. I'll frustrate him." Jack added with a smile.

"Just don't do any trash talking. You and Luke lose your cool talking all that garbage. Just play and keep your head."

"Joseph, talking makes it more fun. You know me, and Luke feed off that stuff. It motivates us."

"Yeah, it makes your opponent play harder and next thing you know a fight has started."

"Ah, we'll be fine. Besides we always have you watching our back!"

"Yeah, well one day…"

"Hey look, its my boy Tater. Tater!" Jack called out waving to his rotund friend entering the gym. Tater ran over like a bowling ball headed for the gutter, fast and aimless. He had just finished his morning workout and his chest and arms were swollen.

Although he was short, Tater was powerfully built with a stout chest and huge calves. He was most comfortable in a weight room slinging around dumbbells and pushing ridiculous size plates off the bench press. The basketball court was not his arena. His movements, like his shots, were stiff and awkward, but he loved the action, and the physical nature of pick-up games.

"Hey Tater, we need a fifth man. You ready?"

"Hell yeah. I'm pumped and primed. Ready to drop that dime!"

"Tater, you can't shoot the ball for shit." Jack cracked.

"Doesn't matter Hollywood. I'll lay the wood on someone so that you drop the dime!" Tater grinned slapping hands with Jack.

"Now you're talking, big boy!" Jack laughed.

"No Jack. We already have five." Joseph inserted.

"What do you mean? You, me, Dewayne, Luke and Tater."

"No. That skinny guy leaning against the wall over there has the next game. We're playing with him."

"Oh…" Jack mumbled looking over at the short, thin man with socks pulled up to his knees and pushing back his glasses. "Okay…well if Luke's a no go, then its Tater."

"Where is he? Man, he's always late. He knows how much this pisses me off!" Joseph snarled.

"Yeah, I'm sure that's why he does it." Jack smirked as he shot the ball with an easy lift.

"Next!" screamed the Woodford County red-head after he drained a jump shot to end the game.

"Crap, where's Luke?" Joseph asked looking toward the gym entrance.

"Come on Tater. Looks like its time for you to drop those dimes!" Jack teased as he jumped on his buddy's back bounding for the next court.

The game started off fast with Red's team scoring the first two baskets off a lazy pass from "Glasses". A third basket was nearly scored, but Tater chased down the opponent and bear-hugged him to prevent an easy lay-up. A confrontation ensued, but Dewayne intervened with the opponent, and talked him down while Jack reminded Tater that this wasn't football or rugby.

Joseph got the team rolling with a steal and a lay-up and a beautiful coast to coast pull up jumper off a rebound. Jack had his hands full containing Red as both players tried to shake each other off the dribble with drives to the basket but resulted in no scores. The game was slowing to a half court battle with back and forth scoring.

The game was tied at ten playing to fifteen with two pointers counting as one point, and three pointers as two. Luke arrived, stretched a few minutes, and then ran onto the court telling "Glasses" to check out. "Glasses" refused stating that it was his game. Luke tensed up and started moving towards him. Joseph darted over and grabbed his younger brother by the shirt.

"Luke, you're too late. It's not your game."

"Bull crap! You guys are out here. Its my game. I'm here to play."

"Look, this is his game. Its his team. He's not leaving." Joseph firmly asserted.

"Fine! Tater, time to go!" Luke barked.

"Bull shit, bro! I aint goin nowhere!"

Jack sensed a real brawl could easily develop as these two never really liked each other— two alpha males searching for a fight to test their strength and mettle.

"Hey, Tater. Look, you don't really like basketball, and besides you knew you were here only cause Luke hadn't arrived yet. Let Luke finish it." Jack pleaded.

"Dude that aint cool. He's late!"

"I know. I know but…"

"I know. He's your brother…damn…alright" Tater lowered his head walking slowly off the court.

"That's a shit move, Luke!" Jack snapped.

"Screw you Jack! Let's play!"

The crowd around the game grew as more people arrived, and watched the heated, tightly contested game. Luke couldn't hit a shot, and started shoving the guy guarding him, and talking smack. His opponent was slightly taller than Luke and played very physical. He never said a word. Just pushed and slapped Luke's hand on his shot. Luke called the foul while the guy guarding him, "Lurch" as Luke called him, never argued. He just looked down and handed the ball back to Luke to check back into play. For some reason, Lurch's demeanor and size bothered Luke as he would get into a shoving match under the basket, and while running down the court, Luke would elbow him.

With the game tied at thirteen, Red brought the ball down the court. Jack knew he would try to win the game with a three-point shot, so he pushed up on him to prevent Red from getting a clean look. Red drove to the basket instead and was hit hard across the arm by Luke. Red quickly called foul.

"Bull shit!" Luke cried. "You're not calling that. Not at the end of the game…little shit touch fouls."

"Screw you! You knocked my arm off!" Red retorted jumping toward Luke.

Luke started marching rapidly toward Red with the ball in his hand. Joseph darted over to intercept his younger brother. He grabbed Luke by the arm and pulled him away.

"Stop it Luke! You fouled him. Damn everyone in the gym heard it. Let's check it up and play better defense. Move your feet and get into better position to draw the charge or block the shot." Luke simply stared down at his older brother contemplating his next move. "Hey, it was a good hard foul, and prevented an easy basket, but it was a foul."

"Maybe Jack should play better defense. I was just cleaning up his mess as usual." Luke offered trying to shift blame and focus.

"What the hell Luke?" Jack offered incredulously.

Luke pulled his arm away from Joseph's grip, walked over to Red, and shoved the ball into his chest. "It's a pussy call! Here you go. Your ball."

"Go fuck yourself, dick!" Red replied under his breath. He handed the ball to Jack to check up.

"Dude, Luke's in no mood to play around. I wouldn't push it with him." Jack warned.

"He's a punk."

Jack smiled and looked back at his younger brother who was staring at Red with an arm leaning against Lurch. Red passed the ball to the wing where Joseph quickly stripped the ball loose from his man. Jack scooped the ball up, and headed down court, but Red's team had quickly retreated preventing an easy lay-up. Jack pulled up near mid court, and surveyed the scene. He slightly nodded toward Dewayne to set a high screen on his left side. Luke shoved off Lurch, and appeared wide open in the corner for a three-point shot. Jack dribbled hard to his right, and then crossed over hard to his left running Red into Dewayne's beefy torso. Jack saw Luke flash open in the corner, but elevated beyond the three-point line to launch the potential game winning shot. Luke called out for the ball, but watched as Jack's shot swished through the net. Red's head dropped in defeat. Jack high-fived Dewayne who enthusiastically lifted him up in triumph. Joseph quickly ran over to fist bump his brother as well. Luke stared at Jack still standing in the corner wide open.

"Hey Jack! What the hell?" Luke called out.

"What?"

"I was wide open! I know you saw me!"

"Luke...seriously? I just hit the game winner. We're playing again." Jack added.

"Are we not hitting the open man? I must have missed that memo cause I was wide open. I guess we're here to glorify Jack. It's Jack's game. Jack's the big hero, and the rest of us are here to make him look good. Is that right Jack? You the big hero" Luke stated as he walked toward Jack becoming more agitated.

"Seriously Luke? You need to slow down and calm yourself. You're getting out of control!"

"Am I...getting out of control...Jack? Is that how it is?"

"Luke, you haven't hit a damn shot all game. You're too busy hitting everyone on the court, and not playing under control. If I had passed you the ball you would have missed, and we might not still be playing. Look we got next. Let's move on." Jack offered feeling himself getting more animated at his little brother's challenge.

The next three games got progressively worse as each new opponent pushed back at Luke's aggressive, physical play, and tried to take him out of his game. Luke still couldn't find his outside shot, but found ways to score under the basket on put backs. Many of the guys tried to match Luke's intensity and physical play but he would always push it to fight level. In the last game of the afternoon, Luke squared off against Lurch again. This time Lurch spoke.

"You push me like that again, I'm knocking you on your ass!"

"I'd love to see you try." Luke warned.

The score was tied at fourteen, when Luke wrestled a rebound away from Lurch, and drove the ball down court. Jack was wide open for the game ending lay-up, but Luke ignored him. Lurch hounded him the whole way to the basket with bumps and hacks to the arm as Luke spun free for an easy shot at the goal. The ball was quickly slammed hard against the backboard as Lurch cleanly blocked it standing over Luke who had tumbled to the ground. A member of Lurch's team scooped up the loose ball raced down court scoring on a three-point shot to end the game. Or so it would appear.

"Foul!" Luke called out.

"What? Bull shit! Game's over. Get off my court!" Lurch yelled in Luke's face. Luke balled up his fist preparing to strike the first blow.

He had learned in middle school that the best, and most effective punch was the first one that caught the opponent off guard. Strike suddenly and fiercely with the first blow aimed at the nose. Pop your man's nose, and it causes instant disorientation as the eyes quickly water up and usually the nose bleeds like a hole in a water hose. Billy Reed, Joshua Morgan, and Lewis Stinnett can attest to this strategy as Luke's middle school guinea pigs. Each kid had pushed Luke to a breaking point, and found out the hard way that Luke didn't bluff. Early successes in fighting at school led to a reputation that prevented fights later in high school. Most kids knew not to test Luke's mettle. He had an easy-going personality up until a point— that point was established his senior year when he met Janee Wheeler. He fell hard for the stunning red-head, and in the process discovered a dark place he called "black ass" — a dangerous mood.

Jack had witnessed "black ass" a few times and worried it would get Luke into serious trouble. Since the end of his senior year of high school, Luke seemed destined for a tragic ending for someone— either himself or the object of his wrath. Joseph had been away at college in Louisville, and had only heard about Luke's outbursts without fully understanding where it came from or why. Jack had noticed that Luke had recently controlled "black ass", but worried it was always on the periphery.

Luke's behavior on the court at Seaton Center was a return to dark days of just two years ago. Jack had to act quickly to prevent his younger brother from doing something destructive that could cost him dearly for the rest of his life. A full fledge fight at the Seaton Center could not only result in a school suspension, possibly expulsion, but an arrest record that would follow him for the rest of his life.

Watching Luke ball up his fists with a determined stare at Lurch, Jack raced over and grabbed Luke by the shirt driving him up against the padded wall off the court.

"Hey Luke! Calm down! Don't do this! It's not worth it!" Jack insisted.

"Get your hands off me punk!"

"Not until you calm down!"

"Jack, you better get up off me now! I'm not playing!"

"No Luke! It's over. Calm down."

Luke pushed Jack's hands away, and delivered a right cross to Jack's jaw. Jack backed off a bit stunned by how quick everything seemed to happen. He stared intently at Luke's face which was contorted in anger. He stood with his fists pulled up preparing for Jack's response.

Jack's mind flashed back to a similar event eight years earlier when his best friend John Paul Wilson punched him over a silly balls and strikes call in a whiffle ball game. Jack screamed at John Paul to swing at the strikes he was throwing in their home run derby contest. John Paul refused to swing at pitches he deemed bad.

"You're a pussy! Those are good pitches!" Jack screamed.

"Say that to my face! I bet you won't come over here and call me that to my face!" John Paul shouted back. Jack calmly walked over to face his bigger best friend, and repeated the insult. John Paul landed a right cross to Jack's face that shut him up. The punch was quick and painful. Jack's head spun as his vision blurred. He could just make out his best friend standing with his fists up rocking back and forth on his heels waiting for Jack's reaction. The pain to his jaw left almost as soon as it hit, but Jack was paralyzed to react. He was both stunned and hurt that his best friend had escalated their verbal fights. He also vividly remembered John Paul getting into a huge brawl, two weeks prior, with his older brother, Jason. The two battled from one room to another before eventually going outside and duking it out. John Paul went toe to toe with a strong, athletic upperclassman in high school fighting with a brave ferocity that Jack didn't know he had. What chance did a skinny middle schooler have? Remembering that fight, Jack rubbed his jaw and walked away. Luke frowned and followed his brother up Third Street.

"Why didn't you hit him back, Jack? You would've killed me for doing that." Luke offered.

"Shut up Luke." Jack mumbled fighting back tears.

Luke's punch hurt, but not physically. He couldn't believe Luke hit him, and was standing there challenging him to a fight in public. He saw the signs that Luke was returning to "black ass", but never believed he would turn on one of his own brothers. *What the hell is Luke thinking? Why would he attack me, especially in public like that? Damn who does he think he is? I'll whip his ass for trying to show me up like this. Hell no…I can't let him get away with this shit!*

Jack could feel his anger rising rapidly. It had been a long time that anyone had gotten him "fighting" mad, and no surprise it was Luke. Being only a year apart in age, and raised in a hyper-competitive family with an older brother that constantly pitted the two against each other for sport; it was only natural that a great rivalry developed. Joseph constantly encouraged Luke to attack, and badger Jack until the two fought. Joseph would quickly side with Luke as soon as Jack got on top. Often Joseph would pull Jack off, sit on top of him while Luke took cheap shots. Jack screamed and twisted to get free, but to no avail. Luke got to hit Jack unabated; Joseph was entertained for the day, and Jack was left angry and hurt.

Today would be different as Jack balled up his fist prepared for an all-out fight at Seaton Center. Joseph watching from midcourt immediately jumped between the two grabbing Luke's shirt, and driving him into the padded wall.

"What the hell are you doing? You just hit Jack! We don't fight each other, you ass!"

"Get your damn hands off me, Joseph. I'll fucking hit you too!"

"No! You're done hitting people! Calm down! Calm down!" Joseph screamed lowering the volume with each admonition.

Luke could feel how strong Joseph was in his grip— the sudden force of the movement took him by surprise.

Luke was firmly pressed against the wall in a way that he couldn't get free. Looking into Joseph's eyes, he saw something he hadn't seen in a long time— real anger. Joseph's face was beet red and his voice was shrill. Luke could feel his own anger recede as Jack continued to stare at him in disbelief. His body slumped giving up his resistance and lowered his head while taking his hands off Joseph's arms.

"Alright…alright. It's over…the game's over…I'm over. It's done. Get your hands off me." Luke offered.

"Alright. Luke…what's going on? Why are you acting like this?" Joseph asked releasing his grip.

"I don't know what you're talking about. Its just a basketball game and those faggots keep calling cheap fouls and then knocking the shit out of me when I have the ball. Don't you see that?"

"No…I don't. What I see is a guy losing his mind over a basketball game, but that's just the effect. My question is…what is the cause? Why are you so angry? You came in here pissed off. In fact, everyone says you walk around pissed off all the time."

"I don't know what you're talking about." Luke mumbled walking away bumping into Todd on his way out. Todd had emerged on the court having heard there was a ruckus requiring his attention.

"Hey you! I need the ball you checked out!" Todd screamed after Luke.

"Its up your ass, Todd!" Luke replied pulling the gym door open to exit.

"Hey!"

"He didn't check out a ball Todd. Check your little clip board." Joseph inserted.

"Here take mine…and put it where Luke's ball is!" Jack added retrieving #4 and shoving it into Todd's chest.

"Jack, where you going? There's still more basketball to be played. I'll get us another game." Joseph implored.

"I've gotta talk to Luke."

"Don't waste your time. Let him cool off."

"Can't. This is too important" Jack called out pulling open the gym door and walking out to the exit.

Luke walked briskly to his car parked several hundred yards away on University Drive. His mind was ablaze reliving the last fifteen minutes—trying to assess why, and what just happened. *Why am I the bad guy here? Joseph gets all mad at me…making me look like the asshole for just trying to win the game…and Jack, Mr. Cocky hot-shot, always trying to be the big hero…shoot the big shot while the rest of us do everything else. Everyone thinks he's the best cause he shoots too much. Does all that fancy dribbling and shit. I'm tired of his ass getting all the credit and praise when I'm the one doing all the hard work of playing tough defense, grabbing rebounds, and holding assholes accountable on the court. He and Joseph act like they don't play dirty or anything. That's bullshit. Then Jack goes over to them and kisses their ass while Joseph screams at me! Its bullshit! Screw them!*

"Luke! Wait up!" Jack called out running down University Drive

"What? You want finish what you started in there?"

"What I started? Luke, you're getting out of control."

"Fuck that!"

"Hey, we seriously need to talk."

"About what? Look, you know I play to win. You do, too. You get just as mad as I do out there. You just are too pussy to act on it."

"Fuck you Luke! Yeah…I get mad out on the court, but I keep my head. I'm not looking to fight anyone like you seem to be trying to do all the time."

"Whatever…I just don't let people push me around, and get away with it."

"Look…that's not what I need to talk to you about." Jack added facing his younger brother. Lowering his head almost ashamed, Jack continued, "Its about that dream I told you about this morning."

"What? Oh shit, Jack. You want to talk about some meaningless dream?"

"Luke this was seriously a scary-ass dream, but I think it was more a premonition than a dream." Jack flatly stated as Luke stared at him in disbelief. "Look, again, I know this sounds crazy but that girl you were with looks just like the one in my dream…even has the same name. When I saw you guys this morning in the Psych. class, I knew exactly what you were going to do because it happened in my dream."

"Bull."

"Luke, its not bull. I'm trying to warn you because what happens later is deadly. She'll invite you to some coffee shop or something like that, and then she'll get a strange phone call that will change everything. She'll be in a hurry to get home, and that's where it gets real crazy. She lives in the Zone, but she'll say she has to pick up her daughter at this other place. She'll lead you deep into the Zone, late at night to some nasty run-down looking apartment complex run by a drug lord."

"Damn, Jack! Do you hear yourself? You sound like some idiot who's been watching too many old gangsta movies…and Candace has a kid? Bull. Where do you get this crap? She doesn't have any kids."

"How do you know? How long have you known her?"

"Long enough to know she doesn't have kids."

"Did you ask her?"

"No, I didn't ask her. Who the hell asks someone they just met if they have kids?"

"Aha! You just met her! So, you don't know if she has a kid."

"No, I don't know…but she doesn't, trust me."

"Look, that's not really even important. The worst part is she'll lead you into this nasty apartment complex to get her daughter back and then she…" Jack hesitated realizing how crazy and improbable this sounded.

"Then she'll what?"

"She'll…be killed…"

"What? What the hell Jack! That's the craziest thing I've heard. 'She'll be killed'. You've lost your freaking mind! Who kills her Jack?" Luke mockingly added.

"I'm not sure?"

"What? Why? I thought this was in your damn dream. You didn't see the 'killer' in your dream?"

"No."

"Why?"

Jack felt a sudden rush of embarrassment as his face turned red. Turning away from his brother, looking off to the distance, Jack meekly proffered, "Because I wasn't there."

"What do you mean 'you weren't there'? You just said she led you into the nasty apartment complex to get her daughter."

"Yes…she led me to the apartment but…I didn't go in?"

"You didn't go in? Why? Did she tell you to stay out?"

"No…I don't think so…she was running to the apartment and then just went in…"

"Why didn't you go in with her?"

"There was this huge black guy. I mean he had to be about 6'8, weighing over three hundred pounds. He...kinda grabbed her at the door and threw her in."

"And you just stood there watching? You didn't go in or try to help her?"

"No."

"What the hell, Jack? Damn...even in your dreams you're a fucking coward!"

Jack had no response. It was true and there was no plausible excuse for his inaction, even in a dream. He stood there staring off while Luke climbed into his car, and sped off. Jack had never felt as much shame as he did in that moment revealing a dark secret to his younger brother that if true, made him the worst type of person on earth, a coward.

Chapter 4

"Yet each man kills the thing he loves
By each let this be heard
Some do it with a bitter look
Some with a flattering word
The coward does it with a kiss
The brace man with a sword"
— Oscar Wilde, The Ballad Of Reading Gaol

Driving home, Luke felt a calm sweep across his body as he scanned the beautiful horse farms adjacent to Harrodsburg Road. He enjoyed driving along this route to Nicholasville with its rolling green hills dotted with large stables, and old tobacco barns. It was a slower two-lane drive into the rural northern boundary of Jessamine County, but much more relaxing compared to the hectic stagnated four lane drive of Nicholasville. Luke's restless spirit yearned for the pastoral vista offered in his hometown.

He saw his days in the urban sprawl of Lexington as a necessary evil to acquire his degree which would allow him to return to his idea of Eden—twenty secluded acres of woodland joined with a stocked pond of large-mouth bass and a log cabin. The frenetic pace of city life dulled his sense of a serene simplicity: few friends, golf, fishing, and family.

His mind drifted aimlessly, and a smile eased across his face as he watched a foursome tee it up at the Golf Course of the Bluegrass. An older duffer held his backswing long before the slow methodical downward arc lifted the ball high in the air and landing softly a hundred yards down the middle of the fairway. *I hope I'm still able to hit it straight at that age. Man, I hope I'm still hitting anything at that age* Luke smirked pushing his long wavy brown hair off his face as a cool breeze dashed through his beat-up Honda Civic.

The tranquility was broken by an Adele song blaring over the radio. Luke's muscles tightened, and he gripped the steering wheel as if he was choking it to death. *Oh man… why did this song have to come on? I don't need this now…I'm just getting over her…It's like… I can't escape what happened. Can't escape the past. Like its haunting me…*

Three years earlier…

The summer leading into Luke's senior year would mark a turning point. He was heading towards a path of lethargy punctuated with drugs and alcohol led by his best friend Simon LaRue when he met Janee Whalen at a party. The five-foot ten-inch red-headed beauty with porcelain skin, and ice-blue eyes reversed Luke's downward

trajectory as she challenged his head, and forever captured his heart.

The Whalen family landed in the trendy neighborhood, The Paddock, on the outskirts of Nicholasville. Janee's father moved his family of four from Chicago having scored a management position with IBM in Lexington.

New students to a rural county high school draw scores of eyes and interest as most teenagers are eager to assess, and categorize the "fresh meat". Simon was quick to the hunt as he, too, lived in The Paddock, and watched the Whalen's move in across the street. Simon alerted all his friends of the two red-headed sisters with text messages and distant photos. He decided to throw a party to celebrate their impending senior year. It would be a huge bash, and a great way to meet the "freshest meat" on the market.

Saturday night parties in The Paddock were already legendary in high school lore— something wild, and outrageous usually occurred as alcohol flowed as freely as clothes coming off young lusting teenagers. Simon played the perfect host by introducing Janee to all his friends, acquaintances, and party-crashers. Janee was overwhelmed by the attention, but not uncomfortable in the spotlight. She had a zest for parties and an energetic zeal for laughter.

She sought the good in everyone, and was at ease in any crowd. Janee instantly hit it off with Lucia Flynn, a rising senior and varsity cheerleader. Janee cheered competitively in Chicago, and wanted to quickly join her new school's cheer squad.

Luke arrived late to the party uncertain how long he would stay. Shy and uneasy around large crowds loaded with fine young ladies, Luke searched for a drink, and a corner to stand in. Simon intercepted his walk to the keg wrapping his beefy arms around Luke's shoulders.

"Dude! So glad you showed up! Thought you were going to be another no show again."

"Yeah, well I'm not sure how long I'm going stay." Luke added backing away looking oddly at his rotund buddy. "Are you high?"

"Hell yeah, just burned one a few minutes ago. You want one? I can get another..."

"Nah... my dad catches a whiff of that and I'm dead."

"Yeah...preacher man... well... hey look at my new girlfriend over there by the kitchen. Aint she hot as hell?"

Luke turned toward the kitchen and locked eyes with the most stunning girl he had ever seen in real life. He felt his mouth open and mutter something.

"Whatcha say Luke?" Simon asked.

"Uh... did I say something?"

"Yeah... you said shit or something like that."

"Couldn't have said anything like that. I don't cuss."

"Yeah... preacher boy!"

"Simon cut it out. You know I hate that stuff."

"Yeah... sorry, anyway...what do you think? Hot, isn't she?"

"You guys are going together? You're dating?"

"Well, not officially. But its definitely happening."

"Oh... another imaginary girlfriend." Luke dismissed with a laugh.

"Fuck off Luke!", Simon scoffed shoving Luke, "Go find a corner and get drunk. I'm going over to talk to my girlfriend."

Janee's head was full of new names and faces. She tried to keep everyone's story and background in her head. Having moved a few times over the years, she understood the importance of meeting the right people and hanging out with the crowd that best fit her outgoing personality.

So far, she really liked Lucia who matched her wit and engaging dynamism. Lucia helped steer her through the intricate web of friendships, relationships, and ongoing high school feuds.

"Okay, Mindy is fun. She's a dancer with lots of energy. Great friend, but going off to college this summer and doing lots of dance stuff. So, you probably won't see her much."

"Who's the guy standing near the fireplace holding court?" Janee inquired.

"Oh yeah. Figured you'd eye him early." Lucia winked.

"He's cute."

"Yeah he's cute and he knows it... if you know what I mean. His name is Jack Miller; besides he's stuck on Heather Mills. They dated on and off last year, but she moved on to Ricky, his best friend."

"Wow... how did that happen?"

"Just did... Ricky's cuter, if you ask me, and his family's really rich and all. Not trying to be a snob or anything but Jack's family isn't really... well off, money wise. Their dad's a minister and they live in town at the church parsonage. They're a good family and all, but not really..." Lucia was searching for the least offensive word.

"I know what you mean. Anyway, he seems pre-occupied." Janee asserted scanning the large open den with a twenty-foot ceiling and several dimly lit large elegant chandeliers.

"Come on. I'll introduce you to him." Lucia insisted as grabbed Janee by the wrist leading her through the dense sea of assorted teens packed in their little cliques.

"Hey Jack!" Lucia called out. "I'd like to introduce you to the new girl in town... Janee Whalen!"

"Oh hey!" Jack nodded in her direction not wanting to stare at her obvious beauty.

He purposely ignored her to make her more interested in him. It was a little game he played that had mixed results. He continued his story about a varsity baseball game the previous spring where he took a bad short hop ball to his testicles at shortstop, and was quickly reminded that he hadn't worn his protective cup. The enrapt circle roared with laughter as Jack demonstrated the destructive shot to the groin.

Janee smiled but was easily bored by Jack's antics. Scanning the room, she spotted a tall figure in the back of the room near the stairwell looking like he wanted to be anywhere, but at a party.

"Who's that? The tall good-looking guy by the stairwell?"

"Where?", Lucia squinted searching through a throng of teenagers. "Oh, that's Luke. You mean the big guy with the beanie, right?"

"Yeah... who is he?"

"That's Luke Miller"

"Related to Jack?"

"Yeah... brothers."

"What's his story?"

"Not really sure... Luke's kind of a mystery cause he's so quiet. He used to play varsity sports at the school like basketball and baseball, but he quit. I'm not really sure why. Heard he got into a real heated argument with the coach and stuff. Anyway, he kinda hangs out with some bad kids."

"What?"

"Not real bad... just smoking a little weed and stuff. Heard he skipped some school and has gotten into trouble. He's always been real nice to me... just real quiet."

"Well maybe someone should pull him out of his shell and find out what he's really like."

"Ha! Good luck with that... he... Janee?"

Dodging and weaving her way through a crowd of laughing teens with an assortment of bottles, cans, and plastic cups in their hands, Janee made it to the stairwell to learn about the mysterious Luke Miller.

"Hi!" Janee shouted over the cacophony of teen partyers.

"Hi" Luke muttered in disbelief as he looked around to see if this beauty was talking to someone else.

"My name is Janee Whalen. I'm new here to Jessamine County. I'm originally from Chicago but my dad moved us cause he got a good job at IBM in Lexington. We live across the street from here.

Umm... I have a younger sister named Teri. She'll be a sophomore. Oh, and two older brothers, but they still live in Chicago... they work up there."

Luke nodded while looking down at the floor. He couldn't fathom that a girl like Janee would be talking to him and show him the least bit of interest. He wondered — if maybe she mistakenly thought he was Jack... the seemingly more accomplished Miller.

Conspiratorially, he imagined that this was a set-up by Jack to embarrass him one last time before going off to college like a big shot. Jack thinks he's so cool talking to the really hot, popular girls but he's not. They don't even like him. They see what a phony he is and talk crap about him behind his back. Yeah, they're all smiles and giggles to his face, but I see their faces when he leaves... he's a joke!

"Anyway... just wanted to say hi. You know, introduce myself... besides Lucia said there was no way I could get you to talk. In fact, we bet that I couldn't get you to say more than two words."

Again, Luke looked down and away. He was ashamed that he couldn't think of anything clever to say or come up with some corny pick-up line he'd heard Simon or Jimmy J. come up with.

"I met your brother earlier... Jack. He seemed nice. Very talkative. Must run in the family, ha, ha. Well, okay... so look I'm going to just leave..."

"You lose." Luke smirked as his eyes fell on hers.

"Excuse me?"

"You lose."

"What does that mean? Oh... oh yeah... okay... ha, ha" Janee fell into her trademark laugh, a hearty cackle. Luke broke into a full smile. He had never heard such a joyous sound— So original and authentic.

"You lose... I get it... no more than two words. That's funny Luke!" Janee proclaimed between laughs. "Actually, I win because you said, 'you lose' twice."

"True... wow. Just lost at my own little game."

"You're funny."

"Not really."

"No, seriously, I think you have a good sense of humor. You're playing the sly game, too. Everyone thinks you're a grouch and moody."

"I am a grouch and moody."

"Ha, ha... see that's funny. Obviously, I don't know you, but I feel like I do know you. Is that weird?"

"Yeah... I guess. What do you mean?"

"I don't know. Just that I get a good vibe... a good sense about

you, Luke. I think you've been underestimated and overshadowed all your life."

"Wow, why would you say that?"

"Well, I met Jack."

"Oh?"

"He seems very confident. Very sure of himself. Has he always been like that?"

"Yep. His whole life... and for no reason. It's not like he's really ever accomplished anything, but you wouldn't know it from the way he acts."

"Oh, sounds like there is some resentment there. Do you have any other brothers or sisters?"

"Another older brother, Joseph. He's in college in Louisville."

"So, you're the baby!" Janee shouted with excitement.

"Yep." Luke grimaced returning his eyes to the floor in shame.

"That totally makes sense! Let me guess, your brothers are smart, good-looking and really good at sports?"

"Wrong. They are ugly, stupid and uncoordinated little nerds."

"Ha! Ha! I love it!" Janee cackled. "Sibling rivalry is the best. I, too, have older brothers. They suck! Give me grief all the time. Used to play tricks on me, tease me until I cried, but I learned to fight back. They actually made me tougher. I really credit them with helping make me strong and independent. Yeah, those big dorks really gave me the business when I was smaller but... wow... I can't believe I'm getting emotional, now. I guess I really miss them. Look, you've got me laughing one minute and crying the next."

"Well... I can't imagine getting emotional over your brothers. You obviously have a much better relationship with them than I have with my brothers."

"I'm sure that's not true. I bet you guys are much closer than you think. Sometimes, moving away from them makes you realize how much you loved them."

"Well... I don't know about that. I guess, I kinda miss Joseph; he's in Louisville but never Jack. We're just too different. He sucks and doesn't know it. At least I'm self-aware. I know I suck."

"Oh, that's not true... Luke you seem much more..."

"Oh wow, look at Simon giving me the evil eye. I'm in trouble."

"Why?"

"Probably because I'm talking to you."

"Why? Were you not supposed to talk to me?"

"I didn't think so, but he thinks you're his girlfriend."

"What? No way! I just met him. He's nice and all but... no way. I'm totally not interested in him that way."

"Oh… well that's going to hurt his fragile ego."

"Oh God… are you serious? I could never hurt anyone. Oh God… I'm so sorry. Maybe I should…"

"Just kidding. Ha! Ha! Simon's fine. He talks a big game about the ladies, but he knows that we know he's just full of it! We laugh about it all the time. He's cool. Probably the nicest, laid-back guy I've ever known. He wouldn't hurt a fly or think twice about helping people. He's just a sweet, easy-going dude I've known since Kindergarten."

"Okay… are you sure?"

"Look at you. You're really concerned about his feelings." Luke stated in amazement.

"Of course. He's a sweet human being. I could never be mean to anyone."

"I believe you." Luke asserted staring into her eyes. He could feel his chest thumping. The world seemingly stopped around him. Those piercing blue eyes stripped down his well-guarded defenses. Luke couldn't believe how stunning she was to the eyes, and how she was just as beautiful in her heart. He never believed he would meet someone that actually took his breath away. She was so real and funny and warm and kind and had an awful laugh, but that could be endearing over time. He felt like he could talk to her forever…tell her anything.

"So, Luke… I promised my parents I wouldn't stay too late, but I loved talking to you."

"Can I get your number?" Luke blurted out thinking how stupid and desperate that sounded. He reasoned that lack of smoothness and finesse was why he didn't go out on many dates.

"Uh, yeah… sure. Of course. Just punch it into your phone."

"I don't have a phone?" Luke slumped in embarrassment.

"Do you have anything for me to write with?"

Panicking as he patted his chest and pants pockets for a pen he knew he didn't have, Luke desperately scoped the crowd of likely suspects who could possibly possess the one thing he needed to make this night a complete success— a pen. He narrowed his focus to girls carrying purses as no guy would randomly have a pen. Fortune smiled on Luke that night as a good friend of Luke's, Olivia, just happened to stroll by with her purse slung across her shoulder.

"Hey Olivia! Any chance you have pen in your purse?"

"Sure thing Luke! Here ya go!" Olivia winked with a knowing smile.

"Thanks Olivia! Okay, Janee what's your number?"

"867-5309"

"8, 6, 7, 5, 3 0... wait a second...okay. You got me! Real funny."

"What were you going to write it down on?"

"Oh yeah...um..."

"Here, give me the pen and your hand. I'll write it down." Janee added with a smirk. "Now don't wash this hand until you've written it down on paper."

"Sure thing. Nice meeting you and talking to you."

"You bet", Janee added with a tight hug as she whispered in his ear, "You're more than you know. You have so much to offer. Don't be afraid to take a chance."

Luke felt a calm and ease in her presence, and embrace that was quickly and abruptly interrupted by his best friend Simon, who happened to crash into him breaking off the farewell hug. Janee checked her watch, and quickly ran out.

"Man, my bad Luke! Damn, I spilled my drink all over you. Let me wipe you off. Look its all over your shirt and hand. I'll just rub that drink right off for you."

"Sure thing Simon...look I'm sorry that I was talking so long to Janee. She's just so easy to talk to and stuff. She really seemed interested in me and my family."

"Yeah, your family is so damn interesting!" Simon interjected sarcastically. "The family of saints and then the little black sheep, Luke. Dude, I'm not mad at ya! I know she's not really into me and all, but you should know she was definitely checking out your brother earlier tonight."

"What? She just met him briefly and then he dashed."

"Yeah and now she, too, is gone and you're stuck here talking to me."

"Yeah...I don't know. She didn't seem like the kind to do something like that."

"Oh well, just stating the facts buddy, just stating the facts." Simon added with a smug satisfaction knowing how to play Luke like a fine fiddle.

The summer had passed as Luke lost contact with Janee having lost her number, and allowing Simon's sordid story about Jack to infect his mind. Many times, he drove to The Paddock to catch a glimpse of her outside hanging out with her friends or family, but he never saw her. He found out through the high school grapevine— social media— that she was playing travel softball during the day and going to gymnastics at night to get ready for cheerleading tryouts. There was simply no time for Luke as he let Simon's story about Jack fester.

Jack was away at UK getting settled into his apartment with his buddies Rick, Mark and Robbie. There was probably no way Jack and Janee could have seen each other, but Simon insisted, several times, he had seen the two together in Lexington.

As the new school year opened, Luke briefly saw Janee at the senior orientation in the gym dressed in a varsity cheerleader uniform passing out pamphlets. His heart sank as he watched her from afar, smile and laugh, talking to seemingly everyone. Luke figured he was just another face in the crowd that Janee had been kind to, flashing her beautiful smile and cackling that awful, yet melodious laugh.

He figured his senior year was destined to be, yet another disappointment and failure compared to his brothers' athletic accomplishments. Joseph and Jack had carved out a fine athletic and academic career that had many of their teachers and coaches scratching their heads wondering why Luke had not followed in their footsteps. Only Luke knew what was holding him back, and he wasn't about to open up to anyone about his doubts and fears or his lost innocence that nearly broke him as he pushed those images to the deep recesses of his brain. He was different from his brothers, and he knew why, but he would never allow himself to think about it.

Often after school he would drive over to Simon or Jimmy J's house to hang out shooting pool, swimming, hitting golf balls, and occasionally smoking pot provided by Simon's mysterious weasel friend, Jeffy. Jeffy wore his pants low and baggy, and his blonde colored hair down over his eyes that caused him to constantly jerk his head to the right to see what he was doing. He was mostly stoned, and rarely attended school, yet he drove a nice sports car, and always had cash.

Simon often joked that Jeffy had the ideal life of leisure and finance stating that no school or college could provide you the kind of happiness, and financial success that Jeffy had. Luke was impressed, but not convinced, as Jeffy seemed content, but stupid as hell. Nevertheless, Luke settled into a pattern of lethargy with a downward drift until one day, lying on his bed at home, he heard the doorbell ring. The clanging bell would forever change his life's trajectory.

"Don't worry Luke, I'll get it! You just lay back and relax. You've had a hard day at school. I've only been working all day at the state unemployment office listening to the most ridiculous hard-luck stories all day, and cooking and cleaning the house since I came home twenty minutes ago!" Melinda added with a full bucket of sarcasm.

Opening the door, Melinda was stunned to see the most beautiful red-head immaculately dressed in her varsity cheerleading uniform, and backpack slung over her shoulder.

"Well, hello." Melinda offered.

"Hello. You must be Mrs. Miller. You're as beautiful as my friends have described."

"Well, who are your friends? I must find them and pay them, ha, ha!"

"Oh no need to pay for the truth...um...I was wondering if Luke was at home?"

"Luke? You mean Jack. He's at college at UK."

"No, ma'am. I meant Luke... your youngest son."

"Oh well, sure! Come on in and I'll round up Luke for you. Just sit on down at the table in the kitchen and help yourself. There's cookies in the jar by the fridge, and lots of snacks and what not in the pantry. Just help yourself as I go find Lou..."

"Hey mom! I'm right here!" Luke hugged his mother and nodded her away. "Hey Janee! What brings you down to this part of town?"

"It's where you live big boy! I've been looking everywhere for you at school, but couldn't seem to find you."

"Well, it is a big school and all, and you're so busy with cheerleading and stuff."

"Not too busy to spend time with my new friend. I thought we got along great at Simon's party?"

"Yeah, I thought so too but..."

"But what? Why didn't you call me? I wrote my number down on your hand. Did you forget it or lose it or just didn't want to call?"

"Actually..."

"I mean, I really thought we hit it off great. I really enjoyed our talk and thought we would hang out during the summer, you know. Maybe I misread everything, but I thought you were opening up, you know. You know really starting to talk to me about what was bothering you and stuff. I know I seem to be going on and on and really just blabbing, you know. But... dang it Luke what happened?"

"I lost your number. Simon accidently spilled a drink on me and trying to clean me up, he must have rubbed your number off. Besides, I heard you were more interested in Jack."

"What? That's crazy! I don't even know him?"

"You haven't been going to Lexington this summer and..."

"And what Luke?" Janee demanded standing up next to Luke looking him straight in his eyes. "Who told you these crazy things?"

"Uh...well...it doesn't matter. I can see that they are not true. I'm so sorry I lost your number and didn't call?"

"Or try to see me at school!"

"Or try to see you at school. Look I just thought..."

"You just thought what? That I was just being nice? That I didn't really like talking to you? That I wasn't really interested in you? Is that what you thought?" Janee beseeched.

"I guess... well. So look, you're here and all. Do you want to go somewhere? Do something?"

"Of course! I came by to see if you wanted to shoot some pictures with me. I love my photography class, and wanted to get some great natural shots out at Waveland. You know the museum out near the Nicholasville and Lexington line."

"Yeah I know the place. Jack and his friends shot a video on the railroad tracks for their English project. It was pretty funny. They were dressed like... oh well, that's not important. I'll grab my hoodie and we can go. I'll drive!"

"Why? My car's fine and I have plenty of gas." Janee added feigning hurt feelings.

"I heard you're a terrible driver!" Luke smirked.

"Who told you that?"

"Who do you think?"

"Look, that was completely Simon's fault. He bolted out of his driveway and crashed in to my backside. Totally his fault!"

"Okay... I'm still driving." Luke grinned grabbing his car keys and telling his mother he was leaving for a while.

Driving up Nicholasville Road was always a challenge, especially during the five o'clock rush hour. Weaving in and out of traffic with the skill of a NASCAR driver, Luke assured Janee he would get her to Waveland before it got too dark for photos.

Again, the two caught up to the relaxed, comfortable conversation that existed at the summer party. It was as if they had picked up where they had left off. Janee related a number of agonizing cheerleading stories of hard practices, gossip, and team backstabbing. Luke was at ease simply listening. Occasionally he grunted in agreement, but mostly kept quiet as Janee rattled on about the latest scandal at school— one of the teachers was smoking weed and possibly having sex with one of her students.

"Its just disgusting! Ms. Roberts is twice his age and... eww... its just gross!" Janee complained.

"Hey, Ms. Roberts is hot! I'm just surprised at who she's supposedly having sex with... Jeffy's a little gross worm. He's been in and out of school so much that they may be closer in age than you think. Besides, she may just be getting weed from him."

"Do you know this Jeffy guy?"

"Yeah... he's really more of a friend of Simon's, but I know him."

"Luke, you don't do drugs, do you? I'm not trying to get in your

business and all, but drugs are really bad, and do horrible things to your mind and body."

"Oh really? What do you know about drugs? See much of that on the mean streets of the Paddock?" Luke mocked.

"No. Not in the Paddock but... it doesn't matter. Just trust me when I say I know what I'm talking about with the destructive effect of drugs, and the dangerous path it takes you down."

"Wow, there's no way you can start that conversation, and not explain what happened."

"Not now Luke... I really don't want to get in to it. Its just..." Janee stared at Luke for a moment and in a serious tone stated, "I've personally seen the destructive nature of a 'harmless' drug, marijuana, and would hate to see it happen to somebody I knew and cared about."

"Oh...I'm sorry. Was it a boyfriend or something?" Luke meekly inquired.

"No..." sensing Luke's unease, Janee added, "It was my oldest brother, Jessee. He started smoking a little pot, but it soon led to other, stronger drugs like cocaine. It became a big deal with my dad. They had a huge fight, and I haven't seen Jessee in about two years now. He's still in Chicago... I guess but... the last time I saw him... he looked awful, and was not the same guy I grew up with and knew and loved. Believe me when I tell you drugs are awful and destructive."

"Okay." Luke said quietly to appease Janee, but he wasn't convinced her sordid tale applied to everyone who smoked a little weed. He and his buddies smoked a little, but it didn't change him or cause him to seek stronger drugs.

Although Simon did seem to hang out with Jeffy a little more in Lexington, and seemed much crazier when they returned, Luke wasn't convinced that marijuana was a gateway drug. He always promised to take Luke with him one day, but only when he was "ready" — whatever that meant.

"Oh Luke, turn it up! I love this song?" Janee insisted.

"What? Adele? Are you serious?"

"Yes, Luke. This song is romantic. Its such a tender message of love, sorrow and regret. It's soulful."

"Soulful? Janee, its just a song. Hello?"

"Ha! Ha! Very funny, Luke... but seriously, listen to the words of regret, broken hearts, and sorrow. Oh. it just makes my heart ache."

"Wow, you're really in to this song."

"Listen... 'Hello from the other side'... its like something tragic happened to two lovers that broke them up or split them apart, and now one is trying to reach the other."

"Maybe they should just pick up a phone and call. Its not that tough. You know hit the call button, send a text or snapchat." Luke inserted sarcastically.

"Ah, you're silly, but no Luke the song says there is some distance. Maybe they live far from each other— like they were tragically separated."

"Tragically? Why is it tragic? Maybe it was a court order. Psychotic girl was stalking the guy, and now she's trying to hunt him down. Poor guy just wanted to get away from a psycho who obviously can't take no for an answer." Luke concluded.

"Ha! Ha! Luke… you're too funny. I know it sounds silly that I'm gushing over this song, but I can't help it. I love this song. It's beautiful in its imagery, and musical timing. Adele's powerful voice and command of regret and loss… its also quite haunting."

"Haunting?"

"Yeah… you know, the lovers have been tragically split up, and she's desperately trying to find him, talk to him, console him— to let him be at peace. She knows she broke his heart and that he's hurting and in so much pain. She wants badly to help and heal him."

"Why doesn't she just go and find him and tell him in person?"

"Maybe she can't."

There was a stillness that settled in the car lingering over those last fateful words. Tears began to well up in Janee's eyes. She stared out the window trying to find the right words. Her mind was racing. She didn't want to scare Luke by coming across as some half-crazed fatalist, but she felt she needed to tell someone what she always believed would happen to her.

"Luke, I believe this song is about a tragic death, and how badly the dead lover wanted to comfort her living lover by reaching out from the other side. In the song, she's tried to call a thousand times, but he can't hear her because he's so consumed with sadness and rage. She can see his restless spirit on Earth, and it saddens her because she loves him so much."

"What is she trying to tell him?"

"That's she's so sorry that he's alone. So sorry that she died. So sorry that they are apart. But she doesn't want him to grieve her anymore. She wants what she had always wanted… for him to be happy— to enjoy and embrace life with gusto. Appreciate every moment you're alive and rejoice in all the wonders of the Earth that God gave us. And… that she is not in pain. She's in heaven and they'll see each other again." Janee ended lowering her head as she quietly wept.

Luke turned left off Nicholasville Road onto the old two-lane Waveland Museum Road. Pulling off the road onto the dirt shoulder, he shifted the car into park.

Sensing the incredible pain that Janee was feeling he wrapped his arms around her and held her tightly. He could feel her body trembling for a few moments and eventually steady into a slow rhythmic pulse. She looked up and gazed at him with her ice blue eyes welled-up in tears and lost in an emotional pain. He sensed her longing and leaned down as they shared their first kiss. Luke's mind was swirling in a confused and excited state. He had never been kissed by a girl with such force of passion. He felt his body warm and tingle in the thrill as they were locked in a moment that seemed to last forever. He lost all sense of his surroundings to a deep and powerful beauty, who seemed, lost herself in the moment. Luke knew this was no ordinary kiss, and Janee was no ordinary girl. In this kiss, and in this moment, he felt truly loved and desired. With each sweet nestle and nuzzle, he could feel his heart beat stronger and stronger. He didn't know what was happening. He had never kissed anyone with such longing and desire. He was with the kindness, most caring girl he had ever met, and she wanted to be with him. In that moment, they fell in love.

A loud and long blaring sound snapped Luke out of the greatest moment of his life. Looking into his rearview mirror, he saw a familiar car and face emerge. Quickly wiping away the tears of a distant memory, Luke rolled down the window.

"Dude, what the hell are you doing?" Simon inquired with a smirk.

"Oh, hey Simon. I was just...pulling off the road to get my head straight."

"Where was your head... up your ass again?"

"No...why?"

"We were supposed to meet at Dearbourne, and get in a few holes. What are you doing parked here in front of Janee's house?"

Luke's eyes darted around to the familiar setting of the Whalen home ensconced in a wooded cul- de-sac. *How in the world did I end up here? The car is in park and the engine is running. Man, I remember nothing about pulling into Janee's old subdivision. Last thing I remember was... the kiss. But what triggered that memory from years ago and had me drive subconsciously to The Paddock?*

"It's kind of creepy, you hanging out at Janee's house. You need to get over it for God's sake! It's over. Time to move on!"

"I know its over Simon." Luke retorted feeling his anger rising. "What's it to you? If I want to stop by Janee's house or go anywhere I want, its none of your business!"

"Alright, alright! My bad Luke. Calm down. Just seems a little creepy you sitting in your car in front of an old girlfriend's house."

"Janee wasn't an old girlfriend. She was… she was… never mind. What did you say about Dearbourne?"

"We were supposed to play this afternoon. I was just stopping by my parent's house to pick up my clubs and meet you over there, you freaking weirdo!"

That last insult snapped Luke out of his emerging funk, and back into the present. Somehow, he had been temporarily transported back to a time, and moment that he had intentionally repressed because it had caused him too much pain. But in that moment, however long it lasted, Luke felt no pain— only joy and unbridled love.

"Okay Simon. I'll meet you there in ten minutes. But I can't play too long. My brother, Joseph, is in town and I'm sure we're going to have a big dinner. Mom loves to cook a huge meal when we are all together, and man I wouldn't miss that for anything."

"Yeah…okay. Can't imagine why you would look forward to that Bible-thumping, moralizing ass you call your brother, but hey that's on you! I don't have to deal with him." Simon snorted.

"He's not that bad, and I would love to see you call him an ass to his face." Luke laughed.

"Shit, he don't scare me! He aint the badass he used to be. Since he's gone up to Louisville and that seminary, he's lost his mojo. Now he's just a Christian pussy!"

"I wouldn't try calling him that to his face."

"Whatever…anyway, see you at Dearbourne in ten."

As Luke pushed down the clutch, and shifted his car into first gear, his mind tried to race back to the memories of Janee, and the fun times they had running around the neighborhood late at night. *No… I can't go back there. It's too painful. The past should remain in the past. I've got to move on!*

Chapter 5

"It takes courage to grow up and become who you really are."
—E.E. Cummings

Luke's spirits were bolstered after beating Simon in nine holes of golf. The pair were once the aces on the varsity golf team until Simon was dismissed, and suspended for possession of marijuana in his golf bag at school. He had been caught by the random high school K-9 drug raids as the dogs circled around his car several times barking. Simon, as well as his classmates, thought it was more comical than serious until his father was notified. A stern man with a volatile temper, and unquenchable thirst for bourbon, James LaRue tried to instill in his son the discipline he lacked. Though he managed to hold down a steady job in construction with the scent of alcohol on his breath every day, he knew he was one accident away from being fired. That fear drove him to ensure that his only child, Simon, would better himself, and not be dependent on his wife's money. However, Simon could never live up to the lofty aspirations of his inebriated father, and instead subconsciously followed his path to drugs to mask the disappointment.

Simon used a disarming charm of self-deprecating humor to win over friends he deemed worthy of his attention. He always admired Luke's grit, and enjoyed toying with his insecurities. He knew how to manipulate people, especially those unsure of themselves. He secretly envied Luke's family life of love, warmth and kinship. Being an only child locked in a large lonely house steeled his resolve to escape his moorings, and find his joy through drugs. However, he wanted others to follow his self-destructive path, and Luke was a prime candidate.

Turning right onto Greenwood Drive, Luke eagerly spied to see if Joseph's old black Renault was parked near his parent's house halfway down the street. As he pulled up, he noticed that both of his brother's cars were there, as well as his parents. *Great, everybody's home. It'll be nice to sit down to a great hot supper and catch up with Joseph and the folks. Hope he's not still mad about the game earlier. He has a tendency to hold onto things much longer than me and Jack. He may be slower to anger than me and Jack, but once he gets mad he never lets it go. It brews and brews to a boiling cauldron that blows up over everyone. Man, he can work himself into a lather! Anyway, it'll be nice to hear what he's learning about in seminary. Besides, I can't wait to see Candace tonight. Hopefully she'll text me cause I forgot to get her phone number…or did I?*

Sitting in the car outside of his parent's home, Luke fumbled through his pockets to find his phone. Pulling it out of his pants pocket, he quickly scanned his contact's list. *Oh crap… nothing under C for Candace. Maybe in my drunken state last night I listed her under another name or tag.*

Bang! Bang! Startled, Luke looked up and saw his oldest brother pounding on his window with a smirk.

"Hey, hot-head… you coming in or are you going to play with yourself in the car?" Joseph cracked.

"Okay, okay. I'm coming. At least I'm getting some action. Not like you monks who flog yourselves for illicit thoughts of pleasure at the monastery!" Luke cracked back.

"It's a seminary, and they haven't used the whip in years!" Joseph mocked giving his younger brother a big hug. "Come on in. Mom's got our favorite meal ready!"

"Let me guess…meatballs and potatoes cooked in a tomato-based broth that's been in the crock pot all day?"

"Yep!"

"That's your favorite meal, not ours!" Luke rebutted with a smile enjoying the embrace of his big brother.

The two climbed the front porch steps and pushed open the door with the sweet smell of dinner emanating throughout the house. *Man, there is nothing better than coming home when the whole family is here!*

"Well look who the cat dragged in! If it isn't my long-lost baby boy returned from the dead!" Melinda quipped in her Southern twang.

Luke darted over to hug his mother hovering over the stove finishing the sides for the big supper. Like his brothers, his size dwarfed his five-foot nothing mother. She loved bragging to her friends about how accomplished her boys were, and took credit for their size with her tongue firmly tucked in her cheek.

"Alright boys let's gather around the table." Matthew ordered entering the dining room. "I see everyone has found their places. You know, you don't always have to sit at the same places you did as children. You can sit anywhere you want."

"Really? I can sit at the head of the table… in your spot dad?" Luke joked.

"Sure, Luke. Is that what you really want to do?" Matthew replied matter-of-factly.

"Nah… just testing you, pops… besides who would want to be at the head of this family with all your other retarded sons. Thank God, you had me to give this family some legitimacy!" Luke mused staring at his disapproving brothers.

"Yes, let's take time now to thank God for our scrumptious food, and blessed family— even if some are a bit slow and dim-witted." Matthew added with a quick grin as the family grasped hands and bowed in prayer.

The familiar clanging of bowls and utensils moving ensued as everyone silently went about gathering their meals on their plates, and digging in to their large portions. Once the first bites were ingested followed by several gulps of their drinks, the family prepared for the initial conversation starter led by the head of the house. It was a Miller tradition to engage in lively discussions, and debates at the dinner table.

It was the best opportunity for Matthew to guide, and instruct his boys on the importance of civic responsibility and being well-informed on all the issues of the day, and more importantly, being able to effectively discuss and debate the merits of their opinions. He wanted his boys to be independent thinkers that carefully and thoroughly thought through their ideas with a cogency that was irrefutable. To do that, they had to debate all sides of a position in their head before taking a stance. This was easier said than done. Much to Matthew's dismay, the boy's debates often turned into heated arguments that usually resulted in a physical altercation. Still Matthew held court at the dinner table hoping one day his boys would mature through age and years in college.

"So, I hear you had a lively game at the Seaton Center this afternoon..." Matthew interposed.

The brothers silently gazed around the table at other trying to figure out who snitched and what did they tell. After a few seconds, Luke noticed Jack lower his eyes back to his plate. *Aha...its Jack. He's the little snitch that ran home telling mom and dad about getting his little feelings and jaw hurt. What a punk!*

"Wow... so quiet. I spend thousands of dollars a year sending you guys to college to learn and engage in discussions and you can't answer a simple question about an event that you all participated in today on campus?"

"How do you know we did anything together?" Luke inquired waiting for confirmation of his suspicions.

"Let's just say I was a bit alarmed by Jack's swollen jaw. I assumed he was clocked by someone. It certainly didn't look like a fall or some accident?" Matthew replied.

"Yeah, well Jack has a tendency to stick his nose or face into places they shouldn't be."

"Oh really? I guess scoring the game winning basket several times in a row, and dominating your opponent on the court counts as 'sticking your face in the wrong place'. Winning can be dangerous business on the courts. But those more interested in fighting, rather than competing, might not understand that."

"Ball-hogging and show-boating can get in you in trouble real fast." Luke retorted.

"Well, my understanding of the games, as it was relayed to me, was that Jack got hit with an errant elbow during one of the games by an opponent. Is that not what happened Luke?" Matthew smirked winking at Melinda.

"Oh... yeah, of course that's what happened." Luke replied looking at Jack with a smiling nod.

"Well, I think all the games were an embarrassment to basketball and our family! These two knuckle-heads are still out of control and haven't grown up at all!" Joseph asserted in a gnawing frustration.

Luke and Jack gazed at their older brother in amazement, and then back at each other prepared for the eruption that was about to spew.

"What do you mean Joseph?" Matthew asked.

"I mean, its getting too embarrassing to play with these two. One 'show boats' and talks trash to his opponent all game, and the other is simply looking to fight someone. I'm trying to play a fun, exciting game without having to referee my own brothers who seem to have different agendas. Yeah, they both want to win, but in different ways. Jack wants all the glory of winning with tough difficult shots while ignoring open shooters. He'd rather lose scoring the most points than win in a TEAM effort!"

"That's bull sh…" Jack started before stopping himself looking over at his mother's disapproving glare.

"No, it's not and I'm tired of trying to explain the importance of TEAM ball to you. Dang it Jack, I've tried your whole life to get that through your head! No one likes to play with a ball hog and glory whore! Sorry mom." Joseph nodded towards his mother.

"Yeah Jack! No one likes playing with you when you do all that one on one crap, and fancy dribbling. You're just showing off and accomplishing nothing!" Luke piled on.

Jack tried to respond, but was abruptly interrupted by the boiling older brother preparing to unload his biggest beef on his youngest sibling.

"And you! Mr. Hothead! Mr. Chip on His Shoulder! Always looking for a fight instead of playing the game I taught you. Why can't you play through a little pushing and shoving without taking it personally? Anytime someone taps you, you explode and want to break into a fist fight! I'm tired of having to break up your fights and intervene on your behalf with our opponents! Not every bump is an attempt on your manhood!"

"I will never back down to those jerks trying to bully or intimidate me."

"No one is trying to bully you. Its in your head. You build up this idiotic conspiracy that everyone wants to fight you or hurt you!"

"No, it's not a conspiracy its just a fact. There are a lot of jerks on the court that hate us because we're good, and win all the time. Since they know they can't beat us skill wise, they try to beat us up."

"Do you even hear yourself? You're making my point. If, and I emphasize if, there is any bullying going on its because they can get in your head. You're right about one thing— teams do envy and resent us at Seaton Center because we often win, but they see you as the weakest link, and the best shot to defeat us because they can easily get in your head."

"That's bull! No one gets in my head. I get in their head, and let them know you're not getting away with excessive physical play. Besides, why aren't you yelling at Jack. He's just as aggressive and physical as I am. He's just not willing to fight when push comes to shove like I am, and his opponents know that. That's why they push up on him."

"They push up on me because they can't guard me straight up. I blow by them easily, so they try to make it physical. I can handle them."

"Yeah because I bump and bruise them for you. You have no idea how many little battles I fight for you in a game. I'm always protecting you."

"Whatever!"

"You're not protecting him. You're looking to provoke a fight! Why? Why are you always trying to fight someone?" Joseph insisted.

Melinda had had enough. These arguments made her nervous and tense. She hated these lively "debates" because they usually turned violent. Looking across the table at her husband, the minister, Melinda tried to get him to intervene, and stop this now before it got out of hand. But Matthew just sat silently bemused by the stirring intercourse.

"Boys I want you to stop this and stop it now! This little 'discussion' has gone too far. Its too upsetting to watch my boys attack each other this way. You're family. Not strangers or enemies. Family. You stick together through thick and thin. Good and bad. Right or wrong. Joseph, you're the oldest, and I've told you a thousand times, you have to watch out for your little brothers. Right or wrong, they are your blood, and as the oldest you're responsible."

"Why? Why do I always have to be responsible for these two? I'm tired of always having to keep them in line. At some point they have to grow up. They are still the little brats they've always been!"

"Screw you Joseph! No one has to look after me! I can take care of myself?"

"You certainly think so. So now you've grown a bit physically, and you think you can take on anybody, anywhere! What you don't know, tough guy, is that I've been covering for you your whole life. Every time you get in trouble or in a fight, I'm the one stopping it, and preventing it from getting out of hand!"

"That's bull crap!"

"Jack? You want to confirm?" Joseph insisted glaring at the middle child.

"Luke, its true."

"What's true?"

"Man, you're so busy blowing your top trying to fight everyone that you don't see the reason most guys are backing down to you is because Joseph has already intervened, and warned them not to mess with you. He quietly tells them, in his own way, they're going to have to go through him if they want a piece of you. Haven't you ever noticed how Joseph breaks into the mix and walks your opponent off to the side? He's getting in their face!"

"That's bull. He's just pushing them away to protect them from me. Besides no one's scared of Joseph. He's too afraid to fight anymore."

"Really? You have no idea how many fights he's been in on your behalf!" Jack stated incredulously.

"That was a long time ago when we were little. Since going off to college and seminary, he became a wussy Christian— either too afraid to fight or too holy. Which is it Joseph?"

"I'm not afraid to fight, and I'm no wuss. Being a Christian does not make you a coward. In fact, it makes you courageous!"

"How's that work? I heard you protesting and whining about the wars in the Persian Gulf, and how wrong it was to fight back against terrorism. How can you possibly be against fighting terrorists to protect our country, our people and way of life?" Luke insisted.

"It's not that simple. This 'War on Terror' is a ruse that's being foisted on the American people as a kick-back to a vast military industrial complex that seems to always profit handsomely every time the U.S. is engaged in overseas activities. Throughout our history, we have waged imperialistic wars that have a more economic justification than a moral cause."

"Really, when the terrorists struck the twin towers in New York and the Pentagon in Washington with a fourth plane downed in Pennsylvania headed for D.C., that was just another 'American Imperialistic' assault to fatten corporate coffers?"

"No. I don't believe that. It was truly an attack by a group of religious zealots who misunderstood the peaceful tenets of Islam to carry out revenge against a country they perceive as an infidel."

"Yeah, they see us as the devil and want to kill us!"

"Yes, from their perspective, we are the enemy. We take their resources and profit mightily while they live in abject poverty. We support a people, the Jews, that they have an ancient animus with, who also enjoy a much higher standard of living than they. Its understandable, from their perspective, why they would lash out."

"Oh, it's understandable? Its okay for them to kill us, is that what you're saying?"

"No. I'm just looking at the complex picture from all sides and trying to make sense of it."

"Have you tried looking at it from OUR point of view? We aren't responsible for their poverty in the Middle East— they're leaders are. Those fat sultans and royal families live greater than kings exploiting and manipulating their only asset— oil, which happens to be the most valuable resource on the planet to the industrialized, advanced world. Those fat sultanates play a duplicitous game of selling us oil while attacking us in their country with their mosques blaming us for their poverty not the evil, greedy pigs living amongst them. These sultanates use their vast profits to sow hatred and discord in their mosques to mask their own evil actions of exploitation and greed."

"There may be some truth in what you're saying, but my greater point is that we should not have gone to war with an impoverished people over the acts of a few. It is not God's will."

"Was it God's will that our nation was innocently attacked on 9-11?"

"Probably. I'm not sure I would say we were 'innocent.'"

"What?! Have you lost your damn mind?"

"Surely you can't blame America for the terrorist attack on 9-11?" Jack interjected in shock.

"I'm not justifying any violence. Those responsible for those horrific attacks were wrong. Killing in any form goes against the Bible and God's word." Joseph insisted feeling he had reached solid moral ground invoking the Bible.

"Are you kidding me? There's lots of killing in the Bible. In fact, in the Old Testament, it seems God is behind a lot of it— pitting people against each other." Luke countered.

"That's certainly man's way of interpreting it?"

"Dad, seriously now is the time for you to intervene. This holy-than-thou novice spends a few semesters in Bible School and pretends to know the Word of God. Tell him he's wrong...he's full of crap and is ignorant of the 'real' meaning of the Bible and the will of God."

Matthew smiled as he watched the debate evolve and devolve into a personal grudge match between two strong-willed young men equally firm in their own righteousness.

"Boys, it would be too easy to intervene and assign a 'right' or 'wrong' interpretation of the Bible and the 'true' meaning of God's will. I taught you to think and develop your arguments as you develop your minds. Part of that development process is to keep my mouth shut and let you two hash it out." Matthew cautiously concluded watching the two combatants eagerly prepare for round two.

"Matthew, no! This has gone too far. This was supposed to be a great night of homecoming for Joseph relaxing with family. Not this incessant arguing that gets more heated with each declaration."

"Mom, I'm sorry but I can't stay quiet while Joseph pretends to be some holy saint that deems the rest of us unworthy heathens. He falsely hides behind a few words in the Bible to hide his own cowardice. Our country had every right to fight back against the terrorists who WRONGLY attacked and KILLED Americans. The War on Terror is to save Americans from future attacks on our soil against these ungodly thugs who falsely kill in the name of God!" Luke thundered.

"I acknowledge that the attack on us was wrong. I'm not defending those terrorists. They were wrong for killing. But our response should not have been to kill back."

"What? Not kill back…what the hell are you talking about? So, we should just let them get away with killing us and take no action?"

"I didn't say that. I said we shouldn't kill as a response. In killing, we are no better than the terrorists. We have to show them a better way… a more Christian response that doesn't invoke violence."

"Don't fight back? Don't kill the killers? What are we supposed to do? Invite them to supper, break bread, sing 'Kumbaya, My Lord', hold hands and ask them why they want to kill us?"

"You're certainly in the right direction. Jesus said we should love those who hate us."

"Love them as they're killing us? That makes no sense. You've been living in the monastery too long. You've forgotten the way the real-world works. You can't sit down and rationalize with those idiots!"

"How do you know? Have you ever tried? Has our government ever tried to understand the perspective of these terrorists we've declared war on? We should sit down and engage in a dialogue."

"How do you engage in a dialogue when they're only interested in a monologue that ends with our death? They're starting and concluding negotiation is our death. They hate and envy our prosperity, our freedoms and liberty. They want to destroy it all with one rule under sharia law."

"That's nonsense. Anyway, in these disturbing and confusing times, its best to consult the Bible and you can't go wrong with 'Love thy neighbor as thyself'. Killing is never justified."

"Never? Someone attacks our mother, you're not going to stop them?"

"Of course, I'll defend our mother. Don't be stupid!" Joseph shouted hopping up out of his chair. Insulted that his brother would think otherwise,

"What if a terrorist or really anyone walked up to you and slapped you in the face? The Bible says you're supposed to turn the other cheek! Are you saying that you'd let yourself get smacked and not fight back?" Luke insisted also jumping up out of his seat approaching his older brother.

"Hey, sit down! You guys are getting out of control!" Jack called out.

"Yes, I would turn the other cheek because its what Jesus said we should do. We, as Christians, are called to a higher cause. We are to live our lives as Jesus taught us. God sent His Son to show us the righteous path to live on Earth."

"Yeah but he wasn't completely human, was he? Jesus is divine and thus not really like us mere mortals. His example is great but unrealistic."

"So, we don't even try? That's no solution! I admit living as a Christian is hard and requires great faith but, that's the point. If it were easy it wouldn't require faith. Faith in God is our hope! It's what separates us from mere mortals. Accepting Christ, his teachings, and his Resurrection ensures our salvation and guarantees or immortality!"

"That sounds great in theory but how does it work in practice?" Luke screamed as he delivered a tremendous blow to Joseph's face. "Are you going to accept that slap and offer me the other cheek, righteous man?"

Joseph reflexively balled up his right fist turned on his heels and grabbed Luke by the throat preparing to deliver his answer.

"Get your hands off me! See I told you! I told you, you would fight back! Look at you! You're fighting mad, ready to attack me. Where is your love and Christian charity?" Luke bellowed.

Matthew grabbed Joseph from behind and forcibly removed his hands from his brother's throat.

"Let him go Joseph! Let him go! You let him goad you into a demonstration you weren't prepared for!"

Hearing his father's words, feeling his strong grip, and looking into Luke's eyes he knew he had failed. All the anger and resentment that he had stored up against his brother began to dissipate. He knew he was right in scripture and verse, but wrong in action. He had failed to show his brother the love that comes from God, and had filled his spirit. He failed to demonstrate God's love and in effect, had failed his brother.

"That's what I thought! You're no better than the rest of us sinners—you just talk a holy game! Sorry mom, I can't be around here now. My heathen soul and violent nature are unwelcomed in the presence of this 'holiness'" Luke stated as he grabbed his keys and walked out of the house.

"Wait, Luke! Don't leave like that!" Jack called out chasing after him.

Pounding on the Luke's car window, Jack motioned for him to roll down the window.

"What?"

"Luke, Joseph didn't mean to come across like that, he…look, its important you stay in tonight. Don't go out?"

"Why?"

"I told you— my dream or rather nightmare."

"Are you going to start that nonsense again?"

"Luke…I'm deadly serious! Everything I saw in that dream last night has come true! I'm telling you to stay away from Candace!"

"Jack, you're an idiot, and your stupid dream is wrong."

"Is it? What was the name of Candace's friend in front of the bookstore?"

"Lucky guess. Besides, looking at the dude I could've guessed that name."

"That's bullshit Luke!"

"I'm in a hurry Jack. I've got no time for your dreams or premonitions!" Luke countered rolling up the window and pulling away.

"Don't chase Candace into the Zone! It's a deadly trap!"

<u>Chapter 6</u>

"No matter how long you train someone to be brave, you never know if they are or not until something real happens,"

—Veronica Roth, Insurgent

Luke had to clear his head. Pulling out of Greenwood Drive, he furiously shifted gears as he sped towards downtown Nicholasville, not sure where he was going or what he was planning to do when he got there. His head was spinning in different directions between the last heated conversation with Joseph, the weird reconnected memory of Janee, and the outrageous premonition of Jack. *What is wrong with me? Why am I always blowing up on people? What is causing these crazy meltdowns? One minute I'm sane and enjoying the normal acts of a college student trying to navigate a tough curriculum while still enjoying life with good buddies like Simon. And the next minute, I'm looking to fight everybody— mostly my brothers. That's it! My brothers…they're the real problem. Always judging and attacking my choices and plans. They don't know what I've gone through or how difficult my life is being connected to them. Joseph sets himself up as some stupid saint that knows more and better than anyone else how to live a holy, righteous life! Well, I showed him what a fake and fraud he is! He's always trying to act like he's morally superior to everyone who has a real, honest and human reaction to facing danger and evil. No one is simply going to let someone else attack them and then 'turn the other cheek'. That's ridiculous! And Jack jumping in saying that Joseph has always had my back my whole life in physical confrontations. I can really only think of a few.* Luke's mind wandered off to one such event many years ago:

Briar Patch was the ideal street for young boys to play every sport year-round. The neighborhood was built in the mid 1980's for young couples seeking to start a family with a wide variety of home styles and price ranges. Once the kids learned how to ride bikes, and their parents were eager for the boisterous boys to play outside; they found the perfect lot to play all the games— Craycraft's field.

Billy Craycraft became a local legend to many of the younger boys through his spectacular success in all sports in the recreation leagues. His home was adjacent to a large, undeveloped lot that would serve as both a baseball field in the spring and summer and a football field in the fall and winter. Many kids would ride their bikes from all over Briar Patch to watch the older kids such as Billy, the Adams boys, the McCuddy's, and the Barnes' brothers play. They would line up their bikes in the outfield to form the fences and watch the older kids play. Once their games were over, usually both sides quit when it got too hot to stay outside, the younger imps jumped in. Joseph started bringing his brothers to the neighborhood when he tired of playing with kids he couldn't control or boss around. He practiced with his siblings at home to get them better for the big games at Briar Patch. Joseph insisted on every contest pitting the Miller boys against any and all comers. Jason Gullett always accepted the challenge, as he thought Joseph was too arrogant. An only child, Jason watch with envy the interaction of the Miller brothers. To Jason, they seemed too cocky and clannish— never wanting to split up, and play on other teams. He also hated their success. No matter what team combination Jason put together, the Miller's seemed to always win. Joseph was obviously the best player on both teams, but his siblings played hard and determined. They had a competitive spirit and esprit de corps that united them to victory. Jason was determined to defeat that camaraderie one way or another.

The baseball game was often played with a Wiffle ball or tennis ball because the Craycraft's would not allow a real baseball to be used on their lot— too loud and dangerous. Because they played three-on-three games, sometimes the Miller's against five, they would close right field since everyone was right-handed. Gloves were used to catch fly balls for outs, but most outs were caused by beaning the runner with the ball. Hard throwing kids could light up runners at close range that would leave a red mark or welt on the runner. In close, highly competitive rivalries, many games resulted in fights.

Jason was pitching in the last inning protecting a one run lead, when Luke ripped a single up the middle. Wanting to stretch a single into a double, Luke took off for second. Jason quickly covered second base to tag out Luke, but the throw was too high. Luke slid safely into second base intent on going to third, but was being held down by Jason who was not only four years older, but twenty pounds heavier. Screaming and twisting under Jason's weight, Luke boiled with rage. Jason pressed his forearm against Luke's throat to shut him up. Suddenly Jason found himself lying on his back with Joseph pounding his face. In a flurry, Jason found out the price of attacking one of the younger Miller boys.

Joseph often cajoled and railed his younger brothers to play harder. Sometimes he even hit them to get a better performance, but he would never tolerate anyone else attacking his brothers. Anytime an older boy tried to attack his brothers, Joseph jumped into the fray to protect them. After each such event, the younger brother's admiration and loyalty to their idol, defender and protector grew stronger. They were a team and family both on and off the field of play.

Luke smiled with tears in his eyes as he merged onto Nicholasville Road at the bypass. That memory set off a cascade of more such events that Luke had forgotten. *Jack was right... Joseph was always watching my back. Even in times when I was wrong, which was a lot, he backed my play. My mouth and hot head got me into many fights with older kids I had no business tangling with, yet for some reason I fought them. Maybe…maybe subconsciously I always knew Joseph would intervene.*

Luke beamed with pride thinking back on those early days of Miller pride when he felt his phone vibrate. Looking down he saw it was message from HOT RED-HEAD CANDACE "Hey Luke meet me at Cup O Joe at 8 😊" *So that's where her number was. She must have put it in my phone last night when I was drunk out of my head and never going to remember her number.* Luke looked down at the car clock and hit the gas pedal with a new excitement.

୶ ୶ ୶ ୶ ୶ ୶ ୶

Jack jogged back into the house eager to assess the damage to the family. Always a pleaser that hated confrontations, Jack wanted to talk to Joseph about several things, but had to be sure he was in the right frame of mind to reveal his ominous premonition. Walking through the front door he watched his mother, pushing back tears, gather the plates and place them in the dishwasher.

"All I wanted was a quiet, peaceful meal with all my boys under the same roof. Its so rare that all my boys are together and now look what happens when you do get together. Fight! Fight! Fight! Just like you did when you were children. When will you ever grow up? When will you ever accept each other and love each other the way your father and I raised you? We raised you in a good Christian home with strong moral values and what do you do? You argue and fight and beat on each other. Why?" Melinda asked in defeat.

"I don't know, mom. I wish I did. I wish we could do what you wanted. The last thing we ever want is to hurt you and dad." Jack offered meekly.

Jack shuffled over to the dining room where he spotted Joseph and his father huddled in a quiet conversation. Their heads were bowed in what appeared to be prayer. Jack urgently needed to talk to his older brother but respected the reverential moment.

"Oh, Jack you're back! Good! Were you able to talk to Luke? Calm him down?" Matthew asked.

"Not really… he's pretty mad right now. I guess he needs a little space to clear his head."

"Well…"

"Dad, I really need to talk to Joseph for a few minutes… if that's okay?"

"Sure, sure… I'll just help your mother clear the dishes and wash up. Let me know if you need me."

Jack motioned for Joseph to follow him downstairs to the basement. He needed complete secrecy and seclusion for what he was about to reveal. Closing the door behind him in Luke's bedroom, Jack took a deep breath knowing what he was about to reveal would sound crazy.

"So, what's up? Why all the secrecy?"

"Joseph... what I'm about to tell is going to sound crazy but believe me its not... I don't think."

"Okay..."

Jack carefully and completely reconstructed every aspect of his horrific dream that he believed was more a fatal premonition about Luke, and not himself. He watched Joseph's expressions during the sordid tale for any sign of disbelief or concern for Jack's sanity. However, with each startling event, told with specificity, Joseph seemed more disturbed by the violent outcomes.

"Jack this whole nightmare could easily just be that... a nightmare."

"I know... believe me, I know. I hoped it was until I started seeing the dream sequence play out earlier today. Candace, the classroom, Geoffrey, everything... its crazy."

"I noticed in your dream the number one twenty-one came up a lot."

"Huh?"

"Yeah... you said the Pysch. class number was 121 and it was located in Whitehall room number 121. Then you specifically mentioned seeing the number again at the drug lord's apartment complex."

"You're right... I never really thought about it."

"Are you absolutely sure you saw that number? Over and over?"

"Yeah."

"Wow... that's really weird... and rare to actually see, vividly, numbers in a dream, much less, the same one intermittingly. It's as if there was a hidden meaning." Joseph pondered rubbing his chin.

"What do you mean?"

"Dreams are your unconscious mind's activity. While your body rests, your mind does not. It continues to function— monitoring your body's systems but also creating a fantasy world full of awe and wonder. And sometimes horror. The mind never stops working. Did you ever notice that you never get hurt or feel pain or ever die in your dream? Whenever you experience an intense scenario in your dream, you somehow survive the fall, or the gunman misses you or the bad guys don't see you."

"Yeah, but Joseph I did experience pain. I felt real sorrow. I distinctly heard Candace scream... twice. The second one sounded like awful physical pain. Like she had been stabbed or something. I saw a big black dude that looked dead-on Denzel Washington, emerge from the apartment with a long bloody knife. I ran, fell, and twisted my ankle. Watched my buddy, Tater, get brutally beaten to death. It was all too real. I even thought I had awakened from that nightmare, only to discover I was in another... running for my life."

"Oh wow... that's crazy. Again, I'm blown away by how vividly you recall details. Usually dreams or nightmares disappear as quickly as they came."

"I know, right…I wish I had forgotten this one." Jack sighed.

"And you came out of this dream just as the big Denzel Washington-looking dude was about to stab you?"

"Yes… Marcus X. If that's a real name or a real person. Its crazy how names and faces I've never seen before, showed up in my dream."

"Yes… really strange. The number thing is what's really puzzling."

"Of everything I've told you about love, romance, murder, terror, running, hiding and fighting for my life, you're stuck on the number? Why?"

"The Bible is full of stories, dreams, and parables in which God used numbers to speak to man. I learned in seminary that on average one in every five scriptural verse contains a number. 'One' is mentioned so often in scripture and 'one', mathematically, is only divisible by itself. It represents the unity of God the Father and His Son, Jesus. Jesus is God's living flesh connection to man." Joseph stated trying to figure out any connections.

"But the number in my dream was one twenty-one." Jack countered.

"Yes… and there's not a 'one twenty-one' in the Bible. There is a 'one-twenty'— it's the number of years between Adam and Eve's exile from the garden of Eden till the flood waters that wiped out man from the Earth in Genesis 6:1-3. Also, one hundred and twenty disciples gathered in Jerusalem to choose a successor to Judas after he killed himself for betraying Christ."

"Wow, I didn't know that. But, again, my number was one twenty-one…"

"Yeah… that one has me stumped. It could be a Bible verse… like Mark or Acts chapter one, verse twenty-one."

"Or LUKE! Luke chapter one, verse twenty-one!" Jack screamed with excitement as having possibly solved the puzzle of the enigmatic number.

"Possibly. I'll check real quick." Joseph stated flatly as he opened the door and walked across the basement to his old bedroom. He grabbed his gym bag and retrieved his Bible.

"You keep a Bible in your gym bag?" Jack inquired having followed him.

"Yeah… don't you?"

"Ha! Ha! No!" Jack nodded his head incredulously.

"Well, you should. The Word of God is always a comfort and always necessary when trying to understand this crazy, complex life we lead. God gave us his Son, so we could better know the righteous path to walk and live. You see…"

"Okay Joseph. Stop the preaching. I'm a Christian. I believe. I just need to know what my dream meant because I think Luke is in real danger."

"Yes… you're right… sorry. Studying God's Word in seminary has really opened my eyes to the world and our understanding of it. But you're right. This dream of yours could be a message or an omen. Yes… an omen."

"An omen? That sounds bad."

"They can be, but not always. Sometimes it can mean a good outcome."

"Well the good outcome would be to stop Luke from doing exactly what I did in the dream because it got me killed. There's no telling where he ran off just now. I tried to call him, texted him several times. Nothing."

"Where would he be in your dream now?"

"Let's see… he already met Candace at class and followed her to the bookstore… oh shit! Shit!"

"What?"

"He's supposed to meet Candace tonight… at a coffee shop and follow her into the Zone where he will witness the bloody attacks! We've got to stop him!"

"We? No, don't include me in this crazy, sordid tale!"

"What? You're not going to help me help Luke?"

"No…I told you. I'm through watching over you guys, pulling you out of jams. I've warned Luke several times he's heading down a dangerous, self-destructive path with the people he associates with and the things they do! Its wrong, immoral and against the Word of God. I will not be pulled into and down Luke's destructive path! I won't!"

"That's bullshit Joseph! All those other times you 'pulled us out of jams' was child's play compared to the jam Luke's about to walk into!"

"Its his problem, his choices and his stubborn refusal to listen to me, dad and especially God!"

"But what if my dream WAS God speaking out to us to help warn and stop Luke?" Jack pleaded.

Joseph lowered his eyes to contemplate that last thought. *Man, that's a tough one. I'm going to need to pray on this. I can't just jump into the fray of something like this without guidance from the Lord. What Jack's asking me to do is extremely dangerous… and possibly deadly. It could cost me my life on Earth and in eternity… no I'm going to need to think this through and seek out God's will.*

"Jack… I'm going to need time to think this through, pray about it…"

"Well, while you're 'thinking' and 'praying' our little brother could be killed."

"That's a bit dramatic! Still, its his choice, his action to make. Not mine. I'm not doing that anymore! If what you dreamed is indeed a premonition or omen, it could condemn us all. We would either kill or be killed by tangling with the type of evil guys you described in your dream. This has nothing to do with me and I'm not going chasing after a guy me and dad have warned a thousand times to change his ways, and the people he hangs out with. As your dream foretold, it leads to death! That's on him, not me! I'm not dying or condemning my soul to eternal hell for that idiot!"

"That 'idiot' is our brother! Fine… screw you Joseph! I'll do it myself."

"No, that's stupid Jack! What are you going to do? You can't stop this! We both know you're too…"

"Too what, Joseph? Scared? Or simply a coward?"

"I'm sorry Jack, but you're not cut out to be courageous. You're just not. I've watched you your whole life and you simply back away from any confrontation that is not on a basketball court or playing field. I'm not trying to be mean, but you are a coward. Its just who you are."

"That may have been true in the past… and I was, and may possibly still be, too immature to know what love is, but something in me just won't allow me to sit by and allow Luke, our brother, to get killed. I don't know exactly what to do, but I do have one advantage over everyone else— I know what's going to happen!"

"Knowing what's going to happen and actually stopping it are totally didn't animals. Jack you're just not…"

"Never mind, Joseph! I'll handle this on my own. My good buddy Tater will help. He knows the Zone pretty well and he's never let me down. You stay here safely praying while I try to save our brother!"

Joseph nodded his head in disapproval and returned his attention to the Bible. After several minutes in deep thought and study, he lifted his head looking across the room at an old clock that hadn't worked in years. Peering closer at the hands on the clock, he was startled to find they were locked in place with the smaller hand on one and the longer hand just past the four. *Oh, dear God… its one twenty-one! One twenty-one! What does that mean? One twenty-one, one twenty-one. One two one… one two one.*

⋙ ⋙ ⋙ ⋙ ⋙ ⋙ ⋙

Luke slid his small compact car into the one remaining empty slot in front of the popular campus bistro, Cup O Joe on the westside of the campus. Before entering, Luke needed to clear his head of everything that had happened already that day. It started confused in Simon's apartment from a wild night before and a chance encounter with a beautiful red-head that seemed promising from yet another surprise meeting with her in class.

However, Luke concluded, everything promising and hopeful about the day changed when Jack decided to intervene. *Wow… Jack basically came in and killed my great day. His stupid story about a nightmare and Candace must have set me off and put me in a dark mood that led to the fight in the basketball game and later at the house with Joseph. Its that idiot egocentric brother of mine that nearly ruined my day… anyway got to stop thinking about all that crap! Candace is the new focus. Man, I can't believe how lucky I am to have scored a date with her and its all thanks to Simon! He's a true friend! I owe him a lot!*

Jumping out of the car with a new hop in his step, Luke pulled the coffee shop door open and quickly scanned the packed dining room for his beautiful new friend. Walking around and poking his head about searching for that familiar face that easily reminded him of another, Luke suddenly felt a pair of soft warm fingers wrap around his eyes. He could smell a strong and powerful fragrance that again, reminded him of another beautiful red-head's favorite perfume.

"Who are you looking for, big boy!" Candace playfully inquired.

"Some hot red-head!"

"Well, I've been here a little while and haven't seen any hot people till now."

"Oh really? Well, I hope you get a chance to talk to him."

"Me too! We may have to stand for a while until a table or booth opens." Candace frowned.

"Ah maybe not too long. Look, the goofy guys in beanies and laptops are moving. Quick, let's grab it!" Luke ordered grabbing her hand leading her to the booth just ahead of several sharp dressed frat boys.

"Wow...Luke to the rescue! Good job big boy!" Candace added sliding into the booth and taking her coat off. "You look nice Luke with your gray hoodie and mussed up hair!"

"Well, I wanted to look nice for our first official date!" Luke laughed.

"Is that what this is... a date?"

"Uhhh... yes... no... I'm not sure." Luke winced not sure if he had overstepped himself.

"Oh, I'm just teasing you Luke! Of course, it is! You'll learn I have a wicked sense of humor!" Candace teased while reaching across the table to hold his hands. "You've got nice, strong hands. Not soft and creamy but firm with a few calluses. Do you do a lot work outdoors like building or construction?"

"No...I'm not the construction type of guy. I wouldn't know which end of the hammer to use. No, my calluses probably come from playing lots of golf... oh yeah and masturbating." Luke deadpanned.

"What?" Candace screamed out loud in a laughing manner. "My God, Luke you have a wicked sense of humor yourself! Oh look, its my dear friend Geoffrey. Hey, Geoffrey over here!"

"Hey girl!" Geoffrey screamed adding a long hug as he plopped down next to Candace. "What are you guys up to? Hey Luke. Good to meet you again." Geoffrey added reaching across the table to shake hands.

"Yeah... good to see you again, too." Luke replied noticing Geoffrey's soft, lotioned hand.

"Have you ordered yet? I really need a drink?"

"No, the waitress hasn't come by yet. Oops, here she is!" Candace smiled.

After ordering drinks and engaging in countless stories about Geoffrey's frustrations with a few classes, professors and in his work at the Gap, Luke noticed how often Geoffrey seemed to be checking his phone.

"You expecting a call or a better offer?" Luke joked.

"I'm so sorry! I know its rude! My mama raised me better. No, I'm waiting on an important call from a friend. He's supposed to be delivering a package."

"Oh… sounds very mysterious. Is that call from someone I know… who causes you to light up all the time?"

"Girl, I have no idea what you're talking about!" Geoffrey mocked. "But yes and… oh wow speak of the devil. There he is now!" Geoffrey jumped out of his seat and ran out of the shop.

"Is he coming back?"

"I wouldn't count on it."

"Ha! Ha!" Luke smirked looking away.

"What's so funny?"

"This whole encounter… I mean with Geoffrey."

"Why?"

"How long have you known him?"

"Oh, about four years. He's a very dear friend that helped me out of a couple of tough situations."

"Oh?"

"I don't really want to talk about that now. Maybe when I get to know you better. But let's just say, my life hasn't always been easy."

"I'm sorry…didn't mean to pry. Its just that Jack…"

"Jack… your brother Jack?"

"Yeah… he told me some crazy things this morning and again later this afternoon…"

"Like what? About me?"

"Yeah."

"He doesn't know me, does he? I mean, I don't recall having seen him before."

"No… he said he saw you in his dream last night."

"Wow, that sounds odd. Tell me more about your brother's dream!" Candace added enthusiastically.

"Well, it's not that kind of dream… I don't think so… well maybe… he didn't say. Anyway, in this dream, he was basically experiencing everything I'm going through now. Like, meeting you at a night club the night before and again in class this morning. He even mentioned Geoffrey by name."

"Wow… that's really weird. What else happened?"

"Well… he said you have a child, a daughter…" Luke winced and looked up at Candace waiting for her immediate denial.

"Oh… that's really strange." Candace countered as she leaned back in her seat looking off at the shop that suddenly seemed half full of customers.

"I laughed at Jack! I told him he was an idiot. That there was no way that you had a kid."

"Luke... I do have a child... a little girl named..."

"Julia?"

"Yes... how did you know? How did Jack know?"

"I have no idea! Its really getting creepy!" Luke stated flatly twisting and turning uncomfortably in his seat. "Look, its..."

"Luke, I'm so sorry I didn't mention Julia. Its just not the kind of thing to bring up, yet. I wanted to get to know you first. See if we meshed. Had a chemistry before telling you about my daughter. She's absolutely beautiful and very sweet. Her biological father is not involved at all in her life. Just so that you know." Candace added.

"Oh...okay. I'm really not upset about this at all. I thought I might, especially after Jack said it... probably because HE said it!" Luke laughed. "Anyway, I'm sorry the father isn't involved. Being a father is a huge and important responsibility. He's really missing out!"

"I'm so glad you feel that way. Not too many guys would look at it that way."

"Its really weird. I'm not upset at all. In fact, I'm kind of cool with it. I mean, wow... a little girl!"

"She's such a sweetheart, Luke!" Candace beamed reaching over holding Luke's hands. "But how in the world did Jack know? There's no way he could've known. I've kept her a close secret. Only a few people know of her existence. You say Jack saw this in his dream?"

"Yeah." Luke mumbled lowering his head.

"Hey, it feels really nice outside. What do say we put these drinks in to-go cups and take a nice stroll through town?"

Luke nodded as they gathered their drinks exiting into a stiff wind as a cold front moved in. Candace wrapped her coat around her shoulders pulling her long auburn red hair out and over the collar. Luke stared in utter disbelief and wonder that a beauty like Candace was interested in him. She tucked her hand into his arm tightly as they walked briskly west from the coffee shop. Both silent and in deep thought about what had just been revealed at Cup O Joe.

"I feel like I should tell you a little something about myself because I want to be as open and honest with you. No games. I went to school here in Lexington at Henry Clay where I played volleyball for two years. My senior year was pretty rough. I went out for the varsity cheerleading team because I was consumed with being popular and running with the 'right crowd'. Though I made the squad, I wasn't really happy. There was already a tight clique and I would always be an outsider. It didn't help that my father..." Candace stopped walking and gathered herself.

"What's the matter? What about your father?"

"My father was arrested for transporting drugs. I hope that's not too shocking for you?"

"No…no… I mean, what kind of drugs was he selling?"

"No, not selling. Transporting. He would never sell or even do drugs. I know that sounds weird…like 'Is there really a difference' but there is. At least a bit of a distinction. I don't know. Maybe I'm being overly defensive of my father. He's a very good and kind man. He just fell into a huge debt trying to pay excessive hospital bills that my mother's poor health had run up. My mother's in and out of hospitals with Acute Kidney Injury— basically, kidney failure that requires a lot of dialysis and hospital visits that ran up a huge bill. Dad didn't have insurance as an independent construction contractor, so he had to come out of pocket. There was simply no way he could stay on top. So, he started looking at other ways to raise the money."

"Illegal ways?"

"Yeah… he knew a few people in construction that put him into contact with others who needed white people to move drugs north out of Miami to Lexington. Next thing you know he's moving drugs, making money and paying mom's hospital bills."

"How'd he get busted?"

"Not sure… he thinks he was ratted out by a local competitor."

"Local… in Miami or Lexington?"

"Oh, Lexington for sure. Some local drug lord must have tipped off the feds because they sprung a trap out on the interstate in Georgia. Though it was out of state, dad always believed a Lexington druggie was responsible. Someone well-connected to the area and law enforcement."

"Whoa… cops are involved?"

"Oh yeah… at least that's what dad says."

"Where is he now?"

"Right now, he's serving out a twenty-year federal sentence in Manchester. He's been approached a few times by prosecutors to narc out his connections or Lexington contacts for a reduced sentence."

"Why doesn't he do it? I mean, prison time has gotta be rough."

"Yeah, I begged him to. He doesn't owe those people anything. I mean they did nothing to protect him. Whenever I try to talk to him about it, he just gets real quiet, lowers his head and says 'there are worse things that can happen than going to prison' if he talks. I'm not sure what that means." Candace stated flatly.

"Yeah…sounds like maybe somebody has gotten to him and threatened him. Like maybe they might do something to him in prison." Luke added but regretted it instantly seeing Candace lower her head. "Of course, I'm probably wrong. What do I know about those kinds of things?"

"No, I think maybe you're right, but I don't think my father's worried about his own safety. He's a real tough guy that can handle himself fairly well. He said he's had a couple of scraps already with inmates trying to mess with him. No… I think he's worried about me and mom."

"You mean if he talks, someone might go after you guys?"

"Maybe…I don't know, the whole thing kinda scares me… Anyway, after dad was arrested I dropped out of school to get a job and pay the bills. Mom was too sick. The waitress job was decent but didn't meet all the expenses. That's when I got another job…" Candace lowered her head in shame not sure if she should go on.

"What's the matter Candace? It's okay, look we all have some crap in our lives that we're not really happy about."

"Really, Luke? I can't imagine you've had hard a time. Simon said your father is a well-respected preacher and your mother is really sweet and everything. That you have a close family and all."

"Ha! That may be what it looks like from the outside and Simon does know me fairly well, but he doesn't know everything about my family. We're not as close and chummy as it may appear."

"Why? Do you all not get along?"

"I get along okay with my parents, its just… I don't know, sometimes I don't think they live in the real world. They have this ideal way of looking at things that I don't think is realistic."

"What do you mean?"

Luke paused to try to catch himself. He wasn't sure how much he could or should tell someone he just met last night. But for some reason, he felt at ease and even comfortable talking to Candace. It was a comfort he hadn't felt since Janee. *My God, she does remind me so much of Janee. She's so full of life and kind. So easy to talk to about anything. But at the same time, I'm not sure how much I should reveal about myself or my family.*

"Let's just say, I think my parents' live in a bubble in Nicholasville and their conception of how the world works and operates is much different than reality."

"Oh, you think they're delusional?"

"Yes, and unrealistic, especially my dad. He's been in the ministry so long that I think I've lost perspective of how things should be to how things really are. Does that make any sense? Sometimes I have trouble expressing myself. I get my thoughts and words jumbled up."

"You're doing fine. I understand you perfectly and you're so adorable." Candace asserted looking up at him in a tender way.

Luke leaned down and kissed her gently on the lips. He was surprised at her eager response. With each long heavy kiss, Luke felt the world spin out of control as he became lost in the moment. The last time he felt this way was with Janee and he feared it would never happen again. He couldn't believe his good fortune to find someone so similar in so many ways to… *I've got to stop thinking of her! I need to let it go… move on… Janee's… This is*

Candace and a new chance at real happiness. Happiness that I thought would only happen with Janee. Janee. Damn it stop thinking about her!

As they pulled back, Candace noticed tears in Luke's eyes.

"Luke… are you okay?"

"What? Oh…uhh… yeah. No, I just… the cold wind and all, kind of messed my eyes up."

"Are you sure? I mean you can tell me anything. Lord knows how much I've told you."

"No, its fine. You're just a really good kisser and I haven't felt like this in a long time."

"Since Janee?"

Luke looked alarmed and pulled away. He wasn't sure how she knew about Janee and wasn't prepared to talk to anyone, much less a stranger about her.

"It's okay Luke. I know about her. Simon told me."

"Simon should have kept his mouth shut! He had no business talking about her to you or anyone. That's very private."

"I'm sorry Luke. Really I am…let's talk about something else." Candace grabbed Luke's arm and led him down another street further and further away from the campus. "Tell me more about your brother's dream. Its really freaking me out how he knew so much about me and everything. I've never seen or met him before this morning and, yet you said he had this crazy dream last night. What else happened in the dream?"

"Oh, nothing really?" Luke cautioned knowing how absurd and alarming it would be to Candace if he revealed too much, especially about her death.

"Are you sure? Jack was pretty crazy this morning running you down in front of the Student Center. He seemed panicked by something— like that dream or was it a nightmare? Luke, are you telling me everything about Jack's dream?"

Luke picked up the pace of the walk. Not sure what to do or say. How much to reveal. *Oh man, I can't start off this relationship by lying or deceiving her. She is asking, and I should tell her everything— even Jack's stupid dream that I'm sure is wrong!*

"Nah…that was pretty much all there was. Just weird stuff about seeing you and Geoffrey, but it was he who met you, not me. It kinda pissed me off because it seemed like just another ploy to try to steal a girl interested in me."

"Had he done that before?"

"Well… anyway. Tell me more about your daughter, Julia. Where is she now?"

"She's with my mother, not far from here. I know this is an awful place, but after dad went to prison we were evicted and, again, I had to take on other jobs to pay the bills for three now. Some of these jobs put me in contact with some really bad people, doing some really bad things…Oh God, Luke… it was awful!" Candace cried lowering her head into his chest. Luke reflexively wrapped his arms around her. "One day, I will tell you what happened but please know, I walked away from all of that. I've cleaned up for my mom, myself and most importantly, Julia. I got my GED, did well enough to get accepted and enrolled at UK where I'm studying to be a pediatric nurse."

"Wow… you are quite amazing! You've taken on a lot of responsibility and really lived a lifetime in a few years." Luke mused.

"Thanks, I'm so glad…hold on my phone's ringing." Candace turned her back recognizing the number. She mumbled and walked away from Luke down a darkened road that looked abandoned by civilization.

Luke followed her slowly wanting to keep a respectful distance as to not intrude on her conversation. He watched her become very agitated and then scream.

"JULIA! JULIA! Listen, you bastard better not harm one hair on her head! I'm coming now!" Candace turned back while starting to run, "Luke, I'm sorry. I need to go! You should go home! Forget this night and forget me!"

Luke stared in disbelief as he watched her long, flowing hair disappear into the darkness. Unsure what to do, he instinctively began following her into the abyss.

ॐ ॐ ॐ ॐ ॐ ॐ ॐ

Simon hated who he had become. His appetite for fast cash, gambling, drugs, and faster women constantly put him into debt with those he could not afford to be in debt to. His growing addiction to stronger, more potent drugs, such as crack cocaine, forced him to delve into a world he couldn't fully comprehend. He placed too much faith in his charismatic easy manner that seemed to endear him to those he couldn't charm. He had first entered the Zone to score drugs for his growing addiction, but later sought opportunities to make easy money brokering sports bets and selling drugs on campus.

As a charming, fast-talking white boy, Simon opened a lucrative market on the Greek system at UK. However, to cover his own losses from bets and drugs, Simon began skimming from his drug supplier and local kingpin, Marcus X. Having accrued a large debt, Marcus warned Simon he risked serious injury if he didn't get clean and pay off his debts. Simon schemed to settle both his debts and some old scores.

Arriving at Candace's apartment in the Zone, Simon rapped on the front door. Within a few seconds the door creaked open with slide lock chain still attached.

"Oh, it's you. Candace isn't here." Cracked an elderly voice from inside the apartment.

"Look, I'm not here to see Candace, per say. She has a package here for me to pick up. Just let me in. I know exactly where it is. I'll grab it real quick and be outta yer hair!" Simon stated firmly trying to calm his rising anger. *That old bat has never liked me! Every time I show up, she gives me the stink eye— like I'm some damn animal or something. I've got no time to play games with her!*

"I'm sorry Simon. Candace didn't tell me about any package or that you were coming by. She knows I don't approve of you being over here especially with Julia here." Candace's mother warned.

Simon turned as if he were leaving and then suddenly drove his body into the door. The force of the blow snapped the chain lock off and dropped the elder lady to the floor in a heap. She tried to scramble to her feet, but Simon kicked her flush in the face drawing blood from the corners of her mouth. Standing over her, Simon grabbed her by the hair a delivered a powerful punch square on the nose. The older lady fell motionless to the floor. Simon grabbed her ankles and dragged her behind the couch. He then hustled down the narrow hallway into Julia's room.

"Come on sweetheart. Come with Uncle Simon" he pleaded in his sweetest voice as he took her small hand and led her towards the front door.

"Where's gammy?'" Julia whined.

"Oh, she's taking a nap back in her bedroom. You wanna go see mommy?"

"Yay! Let's go see mommy!" Julia enthused as Simon scooped her up and carted her quickly out of the apartment and into his car.

"Alright JuJu, be real quiet now. Uncle Simon needs to make a quick call and then we're off to see mommy." Simon added while pulling out his phone and punching his contact number.

"Hey… it's me. I have secured the package and am heading to the drop site. Remember you have to be there at the back entrance and make sure its clear for me to come in. This is a surprise package for Marcus and his goons can't know about it. Okay right… see ya in a few." Simon concluded smiling as he flipped his car lights on and drove into phase one of his master plan.

❧ ❧ ❧ ❧ ❧ ❧ ❧

Luke scanned his surroundings as he jogged after Candace. He couldn't fathom the dark, desolation of the streets he was entering. He could barely make out heaps of rubbish lying about the street and strewn across the walls of vacant store fronts. Every so often the heaps moved about seeming to stir as he ran past them. Occasionally a few would muster the courage to approach him like figures from The Walking Dead. Luke's surreal trek took him across three streets and two abandoned parking lots as he kept sight of his moving target, Candace. Luke had willingly gone after a beautiful girl he hardly knew. It was crazy, but he had started falling for this girl.

He called out for her to slow down but it didn't seem to faze her. *She probably didn't hear me.* He watched her run across another street and then scaled a rusty, rickety stairwell with a wrap-around enclosure that ran straight up. When Luke got to the stairwell, he could see Candace about twenty-five feet above on the last rung. He quickly ran up the old stairwell reaching the top just in time to catch sight of her sprinting across an open field that led to a nasty, two story apartment complex.

Before the Zone earned its putrid reputation, it was once part of an urban renewal project in the late Seventies that promised government assistance for low income tenants. However, it looked as if the city had forgotten all about it once all the local politicians got re-elected and had received their "pat on the backs" for a job well done. Like most government projects, this one failed because there was no follow up; enforcement of rigorous building codes, or even verification of the applicant's backgrounds. Seemingly anyone and everyone of all sketchy backgrounds moved in while law-abiding residents moved out. Luke was staring at the end result of an urban renewal project gone woefully wrong. Catching his breath at the top of the stairwell, he also realized he had run straight into Jack's nightmare. Knowing the outcome of Jack's fatal dream caused Luke to experience something he hadn't felt in a long time— fear.

❧ ❧ ❧ ❧ ❧ ❧ ❧

"Tater! Its me, Jack. Look I really need your help buddy. Are you at the apartment and are doing anything right now?" Jack inquired hopefully.

"Hell yeah! I'm just sitting on the couch now clipping my toenails and sipping a brewski! Might head over to Three Goggles tonight and give the ladies an opportunity at their favorite Tater-Tot!" Tater roared with laughter at his own joke.

"Sounds great… but I really need you to take me to the Zone tonight. Like right now!"

"Hell no! Miller, I told you that place was shit and no place for guys like you. Its too damn dangerous!"

"I know Tater and you're absolutely right but tonight is different. I'm heading over to the apartment right now. I'll tell you everything when I get there. Just don't go anywhere till I get there." Jack added frantically.

"Jack, you okay? You sound like shit! What's going on?"

"I'll explain it when I get there but you need to trust me because what

I'm going to tell you will sound crazy!"

"Does this have anything to do with that stupid dream you had this morning… where I end up dead!"

"Yes… but its not you in danger… at least I don't think. Its Luke."

"Fuck Luke! He pissed me off this afternoon playing ball. What's all this got to do with the Zone?"

"Everything! Maybe we can stop a murder and save my brother's life!"

"Damn! Jack this shit sounds crazy… crazy as hell." Tater stared at the television playing a tape of one of his rugby matches at UK as a club sport. "Okay Jack. You know I trust you but damn…the Zone!"

৵ ৵ ৵ ৵ ৵ ৵ ৵

Anxiously peering out the window, Geoffrey was never comfortable in the Zone and definitely not at apartment 121, nicknamed "the box". Situated squarely in the middle of a large two-story apartment complex, apartment 121 was a dual-purpose front house for residential and illegal drug drops. An assortment of prostitutes, strippers, drug runners and sellers occupied several rooms upstairs while the drug lord's enforcement crew lived downstairs to provide legitimate cover and protection. There was one room, veering off to the right of the front room and down a narrow hallway, that was forbidden for anyone but the boss, Marcus X. Big Jr., first lieutenant to Marcus X and top body guard, had never entered the inner sanctum. However, there was one who had— Geoffrey.

Marcus X had recruited the young man out of one of the night clubs he owned. He liked his style, wit and keen sense of money. It wasn't long before Geoffrey had earned the Boss's trust and a run of his books and drug operations. It was a powerful position for one so young and inexperienced in the violent and brutal world of the Zone. Geoffrey made enough money to ease his conscience and overlook the sins of his boss's brutal business. He despised and feared Big Jr. and his "pack of dogs". On several occasions he had watched Big Jr. turn loose his dogs— Jumpy, Wheels and C.J. on those who didn't pay or "sinned" against the Boss. The brutal beatings with baseball bats were seared into his head and served as a deadly reminder to never betray the unforgiving boss, Marcus X.

Geoffrey had told Marcus X about the planned abduction of Julia in an effort to bring Candace back into the apartment 121 family. Marcus X had allowed Candace to leave to have an abortion but felt betrayed when she had the baby and never returned. Though he had more important business to attend to, he always kept Candace in the back of his mind. It was a bad precedent to allow an employee to leave without permission, especially one he had personally supervised. His ego and reputation could not allow a former stripper and escort to run out on him— bad business and personally insulting.

Seizing on Geoffrey's continued friendship with Candace, the Boss hatched his abduction plan. However, Geoffrey could never abduct or harm a child, especially one he knew so well, Julia. He contacted Simon LaRue, another friend of Candace and part-time employee of Marcus X, to join the scheme. Simon was eager to join the plan as he owed a large debt to the Boss and hoped to clean the slate with his role in the plot.

Geoffrey spotted his rotund associate cautiously approach the back door of apartment 121 with the "package" covered in a large coat. Opening the door, he ordered Simon to take Julia upstairs to unit C, Candace's old room. Simon gave Julia a few coloring books and two dolls he found lying about in the closet and quickly returned downstairs to discuss the completion of the arrangement.

"Okay, where's the sugar?" Simon inquired.

"Hold on, I'll have to get it. Wait here in the front room while I go get it." Geoffrey insisted as he turned on his heels and headed down the darkened hallway.

Simon followed and peered into the inner sanctum watching Geoffrey open a safe to retrieve his powder reward. Nimbly, Simon placed a small cardboard wad into the door latch hole and returned to the front room running into Big Jr.

"What are you doing here and why were you coming from that hallway?" the behemoth bodyguard demanded.

"Oh...uh I was with Geoffrey. He was just getting something for me." Simon replied nervously.

"Oh really?" Big Jr. frowned staring down at the squatty white boy. "Hang on a second. Got a call from the Boss man!"

Simon was sweating profusely in terror when Geoffrey returned with his reward.

"Here. Now go! Its not good for you to be here. The Boss will be here soon to supervise the ensnared runaway rabbit. Besides, I'm sure you won't want Candace to see you here." Geoffrey reasoned.

"Yeah, sure. But first I need a drink. I'll just grab something real quick from the kitchen."

As Simon disappeared toward the kitchen, a frantic knock followed by desperate shouts burst in the air, shattering the solace of the drug den. Big Jr., annoyed by loud noises, angrily walked to the back door grabbing his Hank Aaron edition 44-ounce wooden baseball bat.

Peering through the peep-hole, he smiled and told the Boss on the phone that the "rabbit has returned". Opening the door, Big Jr. grabbed Candace by the back of her head and slung into the front room. Candace, frightened by the brute force of the toss, looked around the front room for her daughter. As she turned back towards her assailant, she felt a powerful backhand across her right cheek. The blow sent chills down her spine and worse— realization that she might never leave again.

ॐ ॐ ॐ ॐ ॐ ॐ ॐ

Tater reminded Jack several times on the drive into the Zone about the danger and idiocy of what he was attempting to do. He reluctantly accepted Jack's story and empathized with his need to protect his little brother, but the Miller boys were simply no match for a drug lord and his minions, especially in the Zone.

"Jack where are we going again? The Zone is a big area and not easy to navigate in the light much less in the dark… which it is now!"

"I know… I know. Just keep going slow while I look for the tall rickety stairwell that leads to the top of a massive hill."

"Wow…that's real definitive. How about we also look for a needle in the street? You get it? Needle in the street…like a syringe needle from a druggie. Not needle in a haystack cause that's not the setting we're in!" Tater laughed at his attempt at humor.

"Yeah…that was good Tater. Sorry I'm a bit distracted trying to save my brother."

"Yeah, sorry bro… looking for a big stairwell…stairwell. Hey, I think I know where that is." Tater spun the car to the right and drove past two streets before heading down a desolate road. Looking up off the right side of the road, Tater grinned at the massive hillside as he put the car in park.

"We're here. Now what?"

"Oh my God! There it is… the huge old stairwell. Right out of my dream. How is this possible? I've never been here before in my life, yet I have a perfect memory of this area."

"Dude, its creepy as hell. What's our plan?"

"Let's climb to the top of the stairwell and hope we're in time to help Luke!"

ॐ ॐ ॐ ॐ ॐ ॐ ॐ

Luke peered anxiously at the beautiful figure running toward the large, seemingly abandoned apartment complex. A cold wind swept across the open expanse of tall grass and weeds blowing against Luke's chiseled chin. Through winced eyes, Luke could make out a large chain linked fence to his far right and a set of metallic garbage cans to the forefront. *That must've been where Jack said he hid when Candace went into the crack house… or whatever he called this dump. This is crazy! Everything Jack predicted has come true… which means. Oh God… there's probably a scream coming and then what do I do? Sit on my ass like Jack and do nothing while Candace gets… murdered? Is this really happening? I can't and*

107

won't do nothing…like Jack. No damn it! I'm not afraid. I'm no coward!

ക്ക ക്ക ക്ക ക്ക ക്ക ക്ക ക്ക

Big Jr. pulled the phone out of his pocket while pushing Candace against a closet door on the back wall of the great room. Candace feared going onto the closet because that was the holding room until Marcus X arrived to administer the punishment— usually a beating, sometimes a murder if you were dispensable. Candace felt extremely exposed and vulnerable knowing the pain and expense she had caused.

"Listen carefully. The Boss has a few things he wants to say." Big Jr. declared holding the phone so that Marcus X could see her.

"Well, well. The little red rabbit has returned! I can't tell you how disappointed I am that you decided to disobey me and then run away. Do you have any idea how much money I've lost these past two years? You were a top money-maker until you fucked up and got pregnant. I had you all set to fix that problem when you decided to run! Who, the fuck, do you think you are, defying me like that?" Marcus screamed.

"A loving mother! I could never abort my baby. No matter what the circumstances were that created her. She is a live human being and MY baby! Give her back now and I promise I will go back to work to pay off whatever debt you think I owe! Please just don't hurt my baby!"

"Don't worry about that little issue. IT… will cease to be a problem after today. You better worry about yourself and your big-mouth daddy in Manchester!"

"What are you talking about?" Candace asked reflexively before realizing the full extent of what "the Boss" was referring to at the beginning of his statement. "Oh my God what have you done to Julia? WHAT HAVE YOU DONE TO MY BABY!"

Luke heard a scream that could only come from a mother in terror. Instinctively, Luke balled up his fists and marched across the field with a murderous intent. As he approached the well-lit back door, he noticed it had a peep-hole. Jamming his thumb across the hole he pounded on the door. Expecting the large black man who threw Candace into the drug compound to come out, Luke braced for a tough battle.

The door was yanked opened from the inside as a tall thin black youth stared at him in disbelief. Just as the youth started to raise the bat in his right hand, Luke landed a solid punch to his face causing him to fall back crashing his head against a small table. Luke was able to catch the bat before it fell to the ground. He spotted the largest man he had ever seen in his life, with his back turned, forcing Candace into a closet. Luke quickly moved on the large target and delivered a cracking head shot that dropped the behemoth to his knees. Sensing the blow was deadly, Luke simply pushed the big man to the floor grabbing Candace's hand.

"Oh, thank God you're here Luke!" Candace grabbed him around the neck. "We have to get Julia! She's somewhere in the complex. Probably upstairs in my old room!"

Running into the kitchen on pure adrenaline, Luke felt a surreal sensation as defender of a maiden in distress and intruder in a deadly domain. With each step further into the drug compound, he had a sickening suspicion he was heading into an abyss of no return. Gripping the bat tighter, he followed Candace up a long narrow stairwell determined to crush anyone who got in their way. Candace bolted down the hallway while Luke hung back scanning the various rooms and keeping an eye on anyone coming up the stairs.

Luke saw several doors left ajar and peeked into the first one on his left. Cautiously opening the door, he could barely make out what appeared to be two objects laying on a bed doing the slow grinding motions of sex but with their clothes on. *Oh God, it's as if they think they're screwing without knowing they aren't. Damn they're fucked up on something!* Luke peered into the second room and saw two young guys scrambling toward the door screaming. He quickly turned the lock on the door knob and slammed it shut as Candace was running out of the far room in the back of the hallway with her daughter safely in her arms.

"Let's get outta here!" Candace frantically announced running past Luke and down the stairs.

The downstairs level had come alive in a bevy of activity as pushers, prostitutes and their clients emerged from rooms previously unseen. Pushing his way through and threatening to bash heads, Luke got in front of Candace as they moved into the large front room. A familiar looking figure with his back turned was attending to the beefy broken bodyguard trying to scramble to his feet. Luke also saw a pair of eyes peering out of a back room down a darkened hallway and then the door suddenly closed when their eyes met. Knowing the immediacy of their situation, Luke bypassed the figures leaning against the closet, grabbed Candace's hand and ran to the door past yet another fallen figure to his hand.

The trio ran out into the frigid night wind that seemed to blow harder and colder against them— as if nature was trying to push them back into the compound because they had cheated certain death. Luke thought he glimpsed two figures disappear behind the set of garbage cans. It happened so quick, and in the darkness, he wasn't even sure it was real. Steadying his left hand on the rickety railing of the stairwell, he watched Candace deftly run down the stairs and sprint across the street hugging her daughter tightly.

Jack looked up from the trash cans and back at Tater in mild amusement.

"Man… that was close! He almost saw us! Oh, thank God he made it out alive with Candace and Julia!"

"You got that right! But I thought you said Candace and her daughter were going to be killed tonight?" Tater inquired pulling his hoodie up over his head.

"They would have… if I had been there instead of Luke." Jack stated flatly staring across the open field at apartment 121.

"You don't know that. Hell, that was just a stupid-ass dream!"

"A stupid-ass dream that had been very accurate up until now. Anyway, at least they are safely down the stairwell. We should see the big dude and his pack of rabid dogs come out soon and when they do we have to go into action!"

"Right! You and me will draw them away from the stairwell and down that big ass hill over there behind the chain link fence."

"That's right! I told you Luke would be wearing his gray hoodie. That's why we are too! They have to believe we are Luke. Once over the fence we'll split up down the hill. Confuse them and hopefully divide them up. You head to the car, get it running while I'm running them away. I'll circle back jump in the car and we gone!"

"I don't know Jack. Sounds kinda stupid that they would chase after us like that. Won't they be looking for Candace and the girl instead of chasing two dudes?"

"It's dark and I'm counting on them being as stupid as they were in my dream. Look! There they are coming out of the house now! Only it looks like the big dude is kinda shaky. Damn, look at his head! He's bleeding. Luke must have hit him pretty good!" Jack marveled. "Okay there's his idiot dogs with baseball bats. Tater jump over the fence now while I throw a few rocks to draw them away from you!"

Tater scrambled over the fence with some trouble causing a clanging, but Jack's rocks had them looking away towards the woods off to their right. As the drug lord's enforcement crew advanced into the open field toward the stairwell. Jack leaped on top of the fence and waited till the flashlights hit him. Jumping down and climbing up over the second fence that overlooked the steep wooded bank, Jack saw Tater flexing and hopping about like a prize-fighter waiting for the bell to ring.

"Dude we're not fighting them! As soon as they hit that first fence we're bolting down that hill. You get to the car and I'll circle back!"

"Yeah! Yeah! But I can easily take those little shits. Why don't you go ahead and run down the hill and I'll hang back and kick some ass!" Tater insisted.

"No Tater! Remember what I told you about what happened to you tonight in my dream. Those guys crush your skull in with those bats! Oh shit, they're on the fence! Go Tater, go!"

Tater started down the far right-side of the hill fast but, not realizing how steep it was in the dark, lost his footing and tumbled. Jack heard the crashing and cussing from his buddy and cautiously stepped down the embankment.

"Hey! There he is! There's the white fucker now trying to get down the hill!" Jumpy called out to his partner.

"Fucking A, I see him! Hey white boy! Your ass is mine now! You better hope you get down that hill first cause we're gonna thump that head in like you tried to do to Big Jr.!" Wheels called out.

"Don't just say it! Get your asses over the fence and get him!" Big Jr. ordered as he struggled to flop his three hundred and eighty pounds over the first fence.

Jack could see that the two-man posse had gotten over the second fence much faster and we're closing the gap. Panicking, Jack quickened his pace with blind leaps down the wooded embankment. Thinking he was near the bottom, Jack jumped expecting the ground to be flat. It wasn't, and he turned his ankle hard causing him to tumble another twenty yards before crashing up against a tree. He immediately grabbed his throbbing ankle and shuffled his body behind the tree to hide. *Damnit! Damnit! Just like in my stupid dream. Busted ankle…only I don't think I can get up on it much less lead a fast chase away from Tater! God… now what? Oh shit, oh shit… I hear them getting close.* Jack tightened his shoe laces to steady and support his injured ankle. Standing gingerly, he could feel the blood rushing to his foot in agonizing pain. Hearing his pursuers off to his left, Jack limped down as the leaves crunched under his feet betraying his location.

"Oh shit there he is! What's the matter big boy? Hurt your foot? Well don't worry, as soon as I catch your ass, you'll forget about that pain!" Jumpy screamed.

"Hell yeah! We're gonna bust you up, boy! Do you hear me? Look at him! He aint running too fast, is he?" Wheels replied.

Jack could feel them very near as he tried to dart and dash to steer clear of a swinging bat. He heard the first swing clang against the tree just behind him and where is head once was. He instantly felt the second blow to his lower back. The blunt force knocked him over and down to the bottom of the hill. Writhing in pain, Jack turned over and glimpsed his assailant raise his bat high above his head. *Oh shit!* Jack thought as he crossed his arms over his face.

A blur removed his assaulter from sight. Leaning up on his elbows, Jack watched Tater scramble to his feet from a powerful tackle and administer a beating. With each punch, Tater released a litany of curses on his downed opponent. Jack smiled, realizing how much better this scenario was than his nightmare. Leaning up to rub is swollen ankle, Jack heard a series of crackled leaves quickly approaching. Before he could alert Tater, the second pursuer had landed a powerful blow across Tater's back knocking him forward. Jack adroitly crawled over and grabbed the youth's legs— easily pulling them up. The jolt brought Jumpy to the ground where Jack punched him several times in the gut and was able to take away the bat. Using the bat to stand up, Jack lifted the bat over his head and dropped it heavy on the young man's legs who screamed out in pain.

"Don't fucking move again or slam you in the head!" Jack yelled. Looking over to his right he could see Tater sitting up and arching his back. "Tater... you alright?"

"Yeah... aint nothing but a thing. My little sister swings the bat harder than that little pussy!" Tater replied.

"Oh thank God. You had me worried for a while there. You know the nightmare coming true with you getting beaten to death by these guys with baseball bats."

"Miller, you're always underestimating my powerful physique and ability to take a hit!" Tater laughed getting to his feet. "Seriously though, we need to get the hell outta here before Marcus X sends reinforcements."

"Marcus X? The drug lord's name is Marcus X? Do you know that for sure or are you just repeating the name I told you from the dream?"

"Dude, you never told me anybody's name. Certainly not his name."

"Then how do you know his name is Marcus X?"

"Anyone who knows anything about the Zone, knows that name. Marcus X runs the largest drug ring in Lexington...hell probably the biggest in all of central Kentucky. I told you, He's a bad dude to mess with!"

"Yeah but you never said his name." Jack stated looking back up the hill. "Actually, I'm glad you didn't because that would have scared the shit out of me and I probably would have chickened out of doing this. Just too damn creepy how accurate that stupid dream was... is. Oh shit, Tater look up! That big dude is coming down the hill. Can you see him?"

"Hell yeah and he's too big and pissed to mess with. Let's get going!"

Tater quickly spun the car around and floored the gas pedal as Jack watched the huge figure reach the bottom of the hill and help his wounded posse to their feet. He turned back toward the road staring off in Jack's direction. Jack felt a chill run down his spine from that glare. He knew he had dodged a massive obstacle and had altered the outcome of his dream, but for how long?

Chapter 7

"Be Brave and Take Risks: You need to have faith in yourself. Be brave and take risks. You don't have to have it all figured out to move forward."
— Roy T. Bennett, The Light in the Heart

Marcus Xavier Williams was his full name listed on the birth certificate issued in 1967 at St. Joseph's hospital in Lexington. He grew up in a tough neighborhood near Bryan Station High School. His only memory of his mother was of her crying from a fight with his father in which he never saw her again. His father, James, told him she ran out on them because "that's what a no-good bitch does". Under the rough, no-nonsense single parent, Marcus learned the manly game of football and how to pass drugs to customers.

Late one night, James was murdered in a drug deal gone badly not long after Marcus had turned seventeen. A once promising middle linebacker with college scouts at every game, Marcus was kicked out of school for trying to unload some of his father's drugs to pay off a debt to the local drug lord, Earl Carruthers, aka "Easy E".

Easy E warned Marcus that he would kill him if the $5,000 debt wasn't paid within six months. Marcus was caught on campus security cameras trying to sell crack cocaine, a schedule II drug, and faced an even tougher judge who sentenced him to five years in a state penitentiary.

The big kid listed at six feet two inches tall and approximately two hundred and twenty pounds entered the prison an angry man looking to take down the first guy that messed with him. He didn't have to wait long as "fresh meat" always attracted the attention of the prison kingpin, Juan Salazar. He sent two Hispanic toughs to test the young man's mettle. The seventeen-year old easily dispensed of his attackers with powerful body blows that couldn't be detected by the guards— just as his father had taught him.

He showed courage by going to the much older prison kingpin and telling him where he could find his boys. Salazar was impressed by the young man's gall, power, intelligence and his remarkable ability to control his acts of violence. He knew Marcus was a "short timer" with great potential to be a drug operator. He took him under his protective wing and made sure he was clean in prison while teaching him the drug trade. Marcus learned how to buy and sell drugs, recruit distributors, run a payroll and most importantly, how to stay out of trouble with the local law enforcement. Salazar taught him which cops to seek out, and how to approach them. He also educated his young apprentice on how to launder or clean your "dirty money" with legitimate businesses.

Juan Salazar was so impressed with Marcus's quick aptitude for numbers and fearless approach to others that he made sure his prison stint was easy.

Once on the outside, Marcus would use Salazar's contacts, but he had to have a base of operations: One in a city large enough to hide in the shadows, but not too big to step on big toes. Marcus wanted to be a big fish in a medium sized pond. This pond also needed a healthy market looking to score his product. Lexington fit the bill. It was his hometown with many high schools and a big college campus nearby. The market in Lexington had been virtually untapped and was ripe for an intelligent, bold, entrepreneur who didn't mind getting his hands dirty with controlled violence assuring his success.

As soon as Marcus left prison, he knew he would have to deal with Easy E immediately as the local drug lord never forgave or forgot a debt. Salazar helped fuel Marcus's fire by telling him that Easy E killed his father because he planned on getting out of the business. According to Salazar's sources, James was trying to go legit because his son was nearing college recruitment, and he didn't want to inhibit his son's chances of big time college football. Salazar had gleaned this information from the plethora of inmates who had been in and out of the state penitentiary from Lexington, and worked intimately with Easy E. Those same informants apparently held no love for Easy E who had turned them over to the cops. Marcus X took the news without any emotion as the two devised a plan that served two purposes: revenge and business opportunity.

Upon returning to Lexington, Marcus quickly recruited a small cadre to carry out his business plans. Instead of waiting for Easy E to strike, Marcus launched his own attack on the unsuspecting drug lord. The murder of Easy E Carruthers shocked no one, and really didn't create much news. Many in law enforcement, as well as the criminal world, welcomed the news of his death. The police did their cursory investigation and simply ruled it a drug hit. No one mourned the demise of Easy E, and Marcus immediately took over his drug operation. He showed amazing business savvy buying legitimate businesses with money fronted by Salazar, and soon discovered a clientele of law enforcement officers from Lexington's finest.

Arriving back at apartment 121, Marcus was not in a good mood. The compound that he had created with lots of rooms for prostitution, drug-running, and an assortment of other illegal activities was nestled in the heart of a community no one wanted to visit, much less reside. Its violent reputation kept "good" citizens away and, therefore, cops at bay. Lexington's finest rarely ventured into the Zone for fear they might discover crimes that could lead to an investigation making many in the hierarchy of law enforcement nervous. As long as Marcus X kept everything relatively quiet, he could conduct his business as usual.

Large campaign contributions to friendly city council candidates, and local judges insured, and protected the operation. But what happened on this night could spiral out of control, and seep into the law-abiding world. Marcus carefully recruited employees from rough backgrounds with little or no family ties. He demanded loyalty and commitment to "his family" with the severing of all ties to the past. Marcus X preached the importance of protecting the family of apartment 121 against all outsiders. He encouraged the use of drugs to create addiction and keep commitments.

Moving through the main room, Marcus noticed no damage to furniture or any disruption of the area. It was a clean hit that simply could not have been a drug raid by a rival, a rogue cop or a federal sting operation by the FBI or DEA.

Walking past his wounded bodyguard in disgust, he walked upstairs to inspect the rooms. Leaving Candace's old room in the back hallway, Marcus, again, noted no damage or disarray of the rooms except the broken lock that Wheels and Jumpy busted getting out. Returning to the main floor, the Boss moved quickly to his back-room office where the door was locked, but not completely shut. Pulling the door shut, Marcus noticed the lock would not go into the door hole completely. Frowning, he pulled out a cardboard wad, and immediately ran into the office checking the safe behind his desk. After a thorough search, the boss determined that a pound of powdered cocaine with a street value of about $9,000 had been stolen.

"Geoffrey! Get your ass in here now!" Marcus called out.

"Yes, boss?" Geoffrey replied meekly.

"You're the only one with a key to this office. I have placed a lot of trust and faith in you. Do you understand the significance of that statement? I don't trust anyone!"

"Yes sir!"

"Why am I missing a pound of coke?"

"What? I don't understand. Where was the coke?"

"In my office."

"Boss, you never keep product in your office. You told me it was too dangerous, and stupid to keep an illegal product in your office… the most obvious place for a theft or drug inspection." Geoffrey stated.

"You're right… but I had stuck a pound in my bottom right hand drawer and now its missing. Were you in my office tonight?"

"Yes… briefly. I paid Simon with 8 balls as per your instructions from the top middle drawer. I had no idea there was more product in the office."

"Simon was here?"

"Not in the office. I don't allow anyone in here. But he was at the compound tonight."

"Ah ha! Old Sugar Booger was here… that makes sense." Marcus reasoned with a curled smile. "Well, our little fat friend thinks he can take from the cookie jar. He'll have to be taught a stern lesson."

"But Boss, you have no way of knowing it was him. Besides, he's a good distributer to the campus… a real rainmaker."

"He's a fucking thief and I can't tolerate a fucking back-stabbing thief in the family, you understand? Now keep this to yourself. Who came in here, and did all this damage to my crew?"

"It was a white kid named Luke?"

"One little white boy did this? Bullshit! Big Jr. get your fat ass in here now!" Marcus demanded watching the large man totter in holding a bandage on his head. "Who the fuck did this to you?"

"Boss man… I have no idea. Whoever it was, they hit me from behind… probably with a bat. Mother fucker. I chased them to the to the bottom of the hill on Spring Street."

"They?"

"I chased two of them and they pounded my crew pretty good."

"You're crew sucks! Two or three white fuckers came into my compound, steal my possessions and beat the fuck out of my bodyguard and crew. Maybe I need to make some upgrades to my security team."

"No sir, Boss man! I'll fix this shit!"

"How? Do you have any idea who did this?" Marcus asked knowing the answer. Big Jr. just stared at him waiting for the answer. "No, I didn't think you would. Anyway, some white boys beat you boys up! Embarrassing as hell! Whatever you have set up for security of the compound has failed. I hold you personally responsible for all this shit, and the loss of a pound of pure coke!"

"What? They stole coke too?"

"Not they. It appears that our boy, Sugar Booger, hit us up. Was he here during the attack?"

"Yeah… in fact I saw him coming from your hallway… he seemed kinda nervous."

"I bet. He probably looted during the attack. The question is, was he in on the attack? Does he know this Luke guy and whoever else you guys chased? Was this part of some bigger scheme?"

"I don't know Boss… Simon doesn't seem bright enough or ballsy enough to pull off a scheme like this." Geoffrey inserted.

"No… he doesn't. But he was in a huge debt to me and may have saw this as an opportunity." Marcus rubbed his chin in deep thought plotting a course of action. "Geoffrey… who's that white boy that stole Candace?"

"Luke… Luke Miller, I believe."

"Okay, I'm gonna make a few calls to the boys in blue and find his white ass. Big Jr. get your fucking crew ready because I'm gonna give you a chance to pay me back for this shit that happened tonight. You owe me big time! Do you understand me?" Marcus sneered grabbing Big Jr. by the shirt and pulling him close. "No more fuck ups!"

"No sir!"

Marcus reached into his pocket pulling out his cell phone as he briskly exited the apartment. Punching up the number of an insider, Marcus stared incredulously out at the open field that just a few minutes ago was the sight of an audacious robbery/ abduction.

"Hey Jeffy, I need you to locate a white rabbit on the run by the name of Luke Miller. He's a student at UK and probably isn't here in town. My bet is he has run home because that's what good little white boys do when they've been bad. This is a major priority and I need location by tomorrow. I'll send my crew in to fix the mess."

"Fuck, this isn't exactly the best time to be calling me?" the voice on the other line whined.

"Why? Some little boy blowing that tiny flute? Look Jeffy, you do, the fuck, what I tell you, and no questions asked! I own your ass!"

"You don't own shit, Marcus! I'll look this kid up for you, but at the standard price!"

"Just do it!" the Boss demanded and hung up.

❦ ❦ ❦ ❦ ❦ ❦ ❦

Jack awoke to the familiar smell of bacon frying as he stretched out in his old bed in the basement of his parent's house. He hoped Luke would have been at the house last night when he arrived at two o'clock in the morning— He wasn't. However, Joseph was there, and that was good because Jack was eager to give him an update on what had happened. *Damn, last night was amazing! I actually helped Luke escape, and fought off a few thugs. Maybe I'm not as much of a coward as I feared from that stupid dream. Maybe last night was a dream... no it definitely happened. My ankle is killing me from that fall down the hill. That damn hill must have been 200 or 300 feet high.*

Leaning up and rubbing his ankle, Jack smiled thinking about his own heroism last night, and the great assistance of his reliable buddy, Tater. *Fucking Tater, stepped up and helped out but not my own brother, Joseph. I simply don't understand how he could let me and Luke face that crap alone. I thought we were brothers. Oh well, no sense bringing it up now. It'll just cause another blow-up, and my poor mother does need that again!* Jack reasoned as he got dressed and hobbled out of his room across the hall to Luke's room. He opened the door and peered into his little brother's empty room with clothes strewn everywhere. *Geesh what a slob! He could be any of those lumps around the bed.* Jack turned the light on and saw no sign of his brother. He could hear plates rattling and footsteps padding across the upstairs dining room. He gingerly limped up the stairwell where he saw a beehive of activity.

"Well, look who just rose from the dead?" Melinda cheerfully posed. "Didn't think you would be here this morning. Don't you have class?"

"Yeah... its first day... not much going on. Besides, I needed to be here this morning. Did Luke come in?"

"I'm not sure. I guess he didn't. It must've been you I heard coming in this morning." Matthew said furrowing his eye brows.

"Yeah, Luke's not here. I'm sure he's blowing off steam somewhere. Did you see that Clint Eastwood movie last night?" Joseph asked cryptically.

"Yeah..."

"Was it any good? Any action? Did it scare you?" Joseph continued.

"It was fine and yeah lots of crazy action but, you know, in the end Clint always wins." Jack responded with a smile.

"I didn't know there was any Clint Eastwood movie on last night. Did you Matthew?" Melinda inquired.

"Oh, it was one we own on DVD. I tried to keep Jack from watching it because of the excessive violence." Joseph smirked.

It had been a Miller brother tradition going back years, to talk secretly in front of their parents using old movie quotes or plot references. Joseph taught the brothers the importance of keeping their parents out of the loop knowing they would only make matters worse. It was much easier to talk in code in front of them rather than whisper.

Jack was beginning to get anxious worrying about his little brother. *He was fine when I last saw him with Candace and her daughter bolting down the stairwell in the Zone. Surely, he got out! Maybe he got nabbed going back to Candace's place. Man, that would be idiotic going back there. That's the first place those thugs would check!*

Looking across the table at Joseph, Jack slowly nodded his head. Joseph stared at him for a few seconds before comprehending the sentiment. While their parents rattled on about the cold snap last night, and the beautiful warm weather this morning, Jack saw the kitchen door knob turn. Luke pushed open the door announcing his presence and desire to eat a large breakfast. Jack lowered his head as if to say a quick prayer. Both Joseph and Matthew looked at Jack and then at each other.

"You okay Jack? You look relieved to see your brother. Was that unexpected?" Matthew inquired.

"With Luke, you never know. Just glad he's here." Jack muttered standing up to greet his younger brother.

After Luke kissed his mother, who quickly scrambled to her feet to cook Luke his big breakfast, he met Joseph coming toward him with a huge bear hug.

"Joseph, I want to apologize for hitting you last night at dinner. It was totally uncalled for and I'm so sorry for being such a dick! Sorry, mom... for using inappropriate behavior." Luke mused.

"Of course, I forgive you. We both have intemperate behavior from time to time. I would like to talk to you though at some point." Joseph insisted hugging his brother again.

"Absolutely… and Jack… man I'm so sorry for what happened yesterday at Seaton Center. Totally out of line. We're brothers, family and we don't fight each other… especially on the basketball court!"

"Thanks Luke! That means a lot. We are brothers and will always have each other's back, through thick and thin!"

"Well, now that that's finally done, get over here son and tell us what you did last night?" Matthew insisted.

Luke obeyed, sat next to his father on the left and Joseph to his left. Jack always sat on his father's right side while the mother sat at the opposite end of the table.

After hemming and hawing about hanging out with a few unidentified friends, Luke introduced Candace to the family as a person of new interest. The parents pursued the standard questions about her background, religion, life goals, etc.

Jack watched in silence not wanting to spill his concerns and spoil the moment. Luke seemed genuinely happy and it had been a long time since a girl had affected him that way. *Good for Luke and Candace! Maybe, they have a legit chance… after all she's alive and that's so much different than my dream. But, I have to know, if anyone in that apartment complex saw him or know him. Is he safe? Is Candace and her daughter safe? Where are they staying? Where did Luke stay last night? I have a ton of questions…can't ask them here.*

"Well, I saw a good movie last night." Joseph inserted. "It's called Gran Torino, you know the tough Clint Eastwood movie about an old man teaching a young boy to stand up to bullies. You know the one?"

"Yeah… it is good movie." Luke nodded picking up on Joseph's cryptic meaning.

"Well, what was your favorite part Luke?" Joseph prodded.

"The part where the old man confronts the drug dealing bullies and kicks their ass. Sorry mom. Kicks their butts."

"Yeah that was certainly the popular part that got a lot of applause at the theater when I saw it a few years ago. But watching it again last night, I found that I really liked the old man's paternal protection for the young boy and his self-sacrifice at the end by boldly confronting the drug dealing thugs with nothing but a lighter and, in front of witnesses, takes the bullets he knew were intended for his young friend. That scene really moved me."

"Oh yes! A truly beautiful moment in the movie." Melinda chimed in.

"What about it Luke? Did you like that scene as well?" Joseph queried.

"Nah… not so much. Seemed a waste. I hated that old Clint died when he probably could have taken most of those thugs out. He just stood there and got killed. He let them kill him and for what? Those punks may have gone off to jail but they're still alive and would probably still cause problems in jail and even get revenge against the boy from prison. I hear many prisoners still have a lot pull on the outside." Luke rationalized.

"So, the confrontation style is your method and you think it works?" Jack quickly inserted sensing Joseph was unfairly provoking Luke again.

"Yeah... yeah... much better to confront face to face your fears than hide from it. It seems to have worked well for me."

Jack nodded in agreement and eyed Joseph hoping he would end this unnecessary line of questioning because he knew where it was leading.

Joseph had an annoying righteousness about many of his discussions. They were rarely innocuous conversations. Since Joseph began seminary, he loved to taunt and lecture his younger brothers for their inattention to their spiritual life and instead focusing too much on the physical present life. He would use the Socratic method, a series of questions, to lead a discussion and conclusion to his perspective. Too often, the younger brothers allowed themselves to be trapped in his moralizing webs. Frustrated, they would often lash out at him, allowing him to assume the high moral ground of non-violent confrontation. Jack didn't need Luke flustered or angry again. Not when he had a ton of questions to ask him and their father seemed uninterested in stopping Joseph's nagging questions.

"Hey guys, it's a beautiful morning, let's play golf at Dearbourne? What do you say Luke?"

"Heck yeah! You know I'm always ready to play. Got my clubs in the trunk now. Beat Simon last night!"

"You still hang out with that loser?" Joseph asked flatly.

"Yeah, he loves you too, big brother. Ha, you're killing me bro. Simon's not a bad guy. He's had some mishaps, stumbles but he's a good guy at heart." Luke countered.

"Well that's not what I heard. I heard..."

"Okay, you don't like Simon. We get it. Move on. Are you playing with us this morning or not?" Jack insisted staring a hole through Joseph's eyes.

"Yes. Absolutely. What about you dad? Make it a foursome?"

"I would love too, but I have too much work to do at the office. Finishing up my sermon for Sunday. You guys go ahead. Maybe will get some golf in tomorrow?" Matthew stated.

❧ ❧ ❧ ❧ ❧ ❧ ❧

Luke arrived first at Dearbourne. After he checked in under his father's family membership, he toted his bag to the putting green. Luke felt at ease and relaxed in the pastoral setting. In golf, he found an extremely challenging sport in an outdoor environment that relied on individuality— no team dynamic forcing you to rely on others. Your score was simply a reflection of your skill and ability— no one else. On the golf course, Luke found the serenity that calmed his troubled soul.

He lined up several putts trying to determine the speed of the greens. The dew had just evaporated so there would be no water trails on each ball roll and the greens would be soft requiring a stronger putting stroke. By mid-afternoon, the heat would firm up the greens requiring a softer, more deft touch to the putt.

"Hey faggot! Aha… rolled it straight by the hole and off the green. You sure didn't putt like that last night!" Simon barked from the parking lot slinging his golf bag over his shoulder.

"I didn't have an ass shouting in the middle of my putt." Luke responded slightly annoyed.

"You by yourself?"

"My brothers are on their way."

"Joseph's coming?"

"Yep. Now would be a great time for you to call him a few names…what did you call him last night?" Luke jested.

"Shit I don't care. I told you, I aint scared." Simon rebutted unconvincingly. "Dude, you're twice his size and you act scared as shit around him. Why?"

"I'm not scared. Just not stupid. Besides, he may be smaller, but he's a hell-cat to tangle with. You'd be wise to remember that. Joseph, when provoked to fight, is every bit as violent as anyone I've ever seen. Trust me, you don't want to mess with him. Size can be deceiving. Look at you… big boy, but gentle as a cat." Luke teased rubbing Simon's blonde mop hair.

"Get off me, boy! I'm a damn tiger when I have to be. Anyway, can I join you guys and make it a foursome?"

"Sure."

"What about Joseph? Think he'll say anything?"

"Oh, I'm sure… in fact why don't you ask him yourself? He and Jack just pulled in." Luke laughed.

Lugging their heavy drop-down golf bags to the pro shop to sign in, Joseph frowned when he spotted Simon with Luke on the practice putting green.

"What's that loser, Simon, doing here?"

"I guess he's playing golf today?" Jack responded.

"Not with us, I don't like that guy. He's bad news… always has been. I don't understand why Luke hangs out with him."

"Probably because he's not judgmental, big brother. Look, you really need to lighten up on Luke. He's been through some crazy shit."

"Yeah… like what? What happened last night? I assume you saw him and obviously he didn't witness anything as horrific as a pair of murders… as per your nightmare."

"Yeah, I saw him. He was in the Zone last night and at the same huge, nasty apartment complex…"

"Apartment 121?"

"Yep… did you ever figure that out?"

"Not yet… still studying on it… anyway what happened?"

"Well, all I saw was him and Candace and her daughter racing across the field to the old rusted stairwell, right out of my dream, and that was it."

"You didn't follow him to make sure he got home okay?"

"No, me and Tater provided a little diversion to make sure he wasn't followed by those drug thugs."

"What? You confronted those guys? Are you crazy? My God, what's wrong with you? Are you trying to get killed?" Joseph loudly asserted.

"Shhh… lower your voice. Luke may come in at any moment and I don't want him to know about this."

"What, that you're stalking him and covering for his stupidity. Jack, you had the ominous dream that I believe. I think God was reaching out to you to warn Luke about his sinful ways and wayward lifestyle. That dream is a gift, not a curse. You've glimpsed the future and have an opportunity to help or even save Luke. Instead of watching him from a distance you should be joining me in condemning his behavior and his awful associations."

"Like Simon?"

"Yes! Like Simon. That dude is a horrible influence. He's never been good for Luke. He's a pothead, probably worse. He doesn't go to school and barely has some construction job his dad gave him that pays crap, but somehow, he drives a really nice sports car and lives in a furnished townhouse on campus. Now explain that?"

"Maybe his parents are giving him some money on the side. Look, I don't know. How do you know all this about Simon?"

"I have friends who know things and try to keep an eye on you guys while I'm at school in Louisville."

"Really…really? That's creepy as hell, Joseph! Who the hell's watching us?"

"Not watching you, per say, just keeping track… look that's not the point. We need to present a united front with Luke to protect him against himself and it starts with Simon."

"I don't know Joseph…"

"Hey, you two retards going to argue all day or are we playing? First tee box is up and Simon's already down there." Luke interrupted.

"Yeah, about Simon. Why is he here? Did you invite him."

"No, no one really invites Simon. He just always shows up!" Luke laughed.

"Come on, let's just play some golf!" Jack insisted grabbing Joseph's arm leading him out of the pro shop.

Detective Jeff Stevens had spent fifteen years on the Lexington police force before being promoted to detective. He had a keen investigative mind and an eye for details, especially at crime scenes. He was thorough and meticulous in scouring crime scenes for clues and any minute objects that could lead the investigation. Though respected for his dedication to his work, Stevens was not liked by many on the force. His arrogance and flamboyant manners turned off most grizzled veterans. He was assigned the only man on the force who could tolerate him, Detective Bob Burris.

Detective Bob, as he was affectionately called, was a twenty-five-year veteran late to promotion as detective. His large six-foot five frame filled with three hundred pounds gave the impression of powerful ogre. But Detective Bob was a teddy bear washed in Christian faith and a love for mankind. Unlike his partner, Detective Bob was a modest humble man who sought the good in everyone. He was the only man in the Lexington police force who could handle Jeff Stevens.

"Hey Bobby. Just got a call about a sexual assault and abduction of a young woman from UK. It appears the perp ran to Nicholasville and may be staying with the victim at his parent's house. Want to ride out this afternoon and check it out?" Stevens asked sitting down across the desk from his partner.

"Sure!" Burris added tearing a big bite out of a glazed donut. "Is it a formal complaint? Let me see the paperwork."

"No paperwork and not a formal complaint. Just one of my C.I.'s called to alert me to a possible assault and abduction. Thought we could get ahead of it before the perp knew he was being hunted."

"One of your informants gave you this tip?"

Stevens nodded.

"Alright, let's saddle up!"

"Oh, not now. Later this afternoon, say around five or six. I'm sure the perp isn't there now but probably will be around dinner time. I have a few errands to run and then I'll swing by and pick you up."

Luke laced a bullet down the middle of the fairway. His low trajectory in the face of the wind allowed his golf ball to race about three hundred yards down the short grass. He was already ahead of his competitors by several strokes starting the back nine holes. Simon launched a high arc shot drawing back to the fairway just ahead of Luke's drive. He was just three shots back. Jack lined his feet up to the left allowing for his harsh slice as he quickly pulled the club back and released a violent swing across the ball shooting it immediately right into the rough. He was five strokes back.

Joseph carefully and methodically lined up his feet, measured his back swing several times before walking back to check his alignment again. This usually took a long time— much to the dismay of his playing partners. Once Joseph swung the club, the ball landed safely in the middle of the fairway but fifty yards short of everyone else. He, too, was five strokes back of Luke.

Joseph had been seething watching Luke and Simon cut up and laugh about seemingly everything. It was obvious the boys had a history and common bond. In Joseph's eyes, they were two immature adolescents in need of growing up— the sooner the better. It wasn't so much that Joseph disliked Simon, he actually found him charming and funny, it was that he was a bad influence, possibly dangerous. He needed to speak to Luke alone. He got his chance when Simon's shot ran deep into the woods. Joseph scrambled over to Luke.

"So, look I know you like Simon and all, but he's not the kind of person you should be hanging out with."

"What? Simon's harmless. Why are you so against him?"

"He's a coke-head, drug dealer and associates with really bad people."

"Simon's not a coke-head. He smokes a little weed from time to time, but I've never seen coke and he's certainly not a drug dealer. Where do you come up with this stuff?"

"Luke, I hear things. I'm told he's working in the Zone dealing drugs, gambling and all sorts of shady stuff. Look you hang out with bad people, then by association, you're seen as a bad person." Joseph stated firmly.

"That's bullshit."

"Ah… add bad language to the mix. You used to never cuss. Now…"

"Oh, okay…you're going there? You've never used bad language? You've never said, 'fuck you Luke'?"

"That was a long time ago. I don't talk like that anymore. At least I try not to. Look, the point I'm trying to make is that you are not the bad ass hombre you're trying to act like. I know you. You're a good person."

"You don't know me, Joseph. You never did. I'm not the little kid you used to pick on and bully. I'm not the preacher's kid who must behave and constantly wear the Christian mask. I'm not the littlest brother always tagging along and seen as the weakest link on the Miller chain. Your idea of who I am is outdated… and old like your philosophy and religion." Luke added smugly lifting his bag back on his shoulder.

"Oh, so now my faith and religion are wrong?"

"I didn't say they were wrong… just not a fit for everyone."

"That's bullsh—"

"Whoa… what were you about to say? A bad word? Can't be because you've 'changed'!" Luke mocked.

"Shut up Luke. I never said I was perfect. I'm always working on improving…trying to do and say the right things which is all I'm saying to you. Being good and doing the right thing is a constant struggle for everyone, especially Christians. We hold mankind to a higher moral standard using Christ as our example. We will fall short, but we must be vigilant in our fight for righteousness sake and hanging out with bad people makes the job that much harder."

"Right things. Wrong things. Good. Bad. Who's to say what is what? What you see as bad others could just as easily see as good."

"Oh, are you trying to make a moral equivalency argument?"

"Sure. Why not. Works for me."

"Luke that's bull and heresy and you know it. You weren't raised that way. You were raised in a good Christian home with loving parents. You were taught right from wrong without this… idiotic moral equivalency nonsense spewed by non-believers to cover their sinful behavior and to justify their bad decisions."

"You call them sinful behaviors and bad decisions…others might say differently."

"Yeah, losers. Look, when you hang out with a bad crowd, you're going to make bad decisions because you have no moral foundation to anchor you. You're like a ship adrift in a stormy sea and if you're not careful you'll drown because you have no moral anchor to steady you from bad decisions and bad people. You're too weak in spirit and morality to stand up for what's right because you won't even recognize what is right. And that's what comes from hanging out with guys like Simon!" Joseph concluded.

"Oh, Simon's harmless. You keep making him out to be more than he is."

"There are none so blind as those who will not see. Luke, you refuse to see what the rest of us see in Simon. He's a bad and troubled person with no intention, other than to drag you down with him. He's a coke-head, drug dealer looking to take you down. I hear he hangs out in the Zone and the loser even comes down here to Shearer's field to sell drugs."

"That's bull. I have no idea where you're getting your info, but it's as flawed as your moral arguments. Simon's a good guy who does things that maybe some uptight religious zealots frown upon…"

"And the law. The law, Luke also frowns on it. Simon's activities are illegal and leads to a dangerous place. Possibly fatal."

"What you talking about? You don't know crap about me or what's going on. I can handle myself. I don't need any help from you!"

"Really? Well that's good because I'm not going to be around anymore to keep saving your butt. My whole life, I've had the onerous burden of watching out for you and Jack and it's too much. You guys are drifting away from everything we were raised on and taught to believe."

"Maybe, it was all wrong. Again, who's to say what dad preached was right. You know it's just possible that all that religious rhetoric is just man-made rules designed to control and manipulate us on Earth. You know, the old saying, 'God didn't create man. Man created God.' It's possible, you, know."

"No, it's not. Sounds like the humanist arguments of the devil. Yet another way of Satan separating man— God's creation— from Him. Just remember Luke, 'Whoever loves his brother lives in the light, and there is nothing in him to make him stumble. But whoever hates his brother is in the darkness and walks in the darkness and does not know where he is going, because the darkness has blinded his eyes.' First John 2:10- 11."

"Joseph... I don't hate you... just disagree with your morality and harsh judgements."

"The brother in that quote refers to Christians who are trying to show them the Light, the righteous path, and what will happen to those who reject the Light."

"That's a beautiful sentiment Joseph. The Bible is full of them. But it was written by men— good and bad, just like thousands of other philosophical texts."

"Yeah, well those were not inspired by God. Luke...I'm not trying to win a debate— that debate has already been won with the resurrection of Christ. That's our victory over death and the promise of everlasting life. The Bible is the Living Word of God and his covenant to mankind. Live by Christ's example and you live forever in the kingdom of God."

"Look, Joseph that all sounds good and it works for some. I'm just not as sure about those kind of things as you are. I guess I need to see more proof of what you and the Bible are saying."

"That's okay. Questioning is healthy, but the intellectual mind that requires proof is weak of faith. Faith is what separates us from the heathen."

"Well, maybe I'm just a heathen. Come on, enough of this moral debate. I'm playing well and hitting it great. I have great faith in the fact that I'm gonna toast you guys on the back nine!" Luke playfully teased his frowning brother.

❧ ❧ ❧ ❧ ❧ ❧ ❧

Looking down at the directions scribbled down on a scrap of paper, Detective Stevens turned his unmarked police cruiser right onto Greenwood Drive with his partner, Detective Burris sitting next to him tackling a big beef and bean burrito. *I hate that the son of a bitch, Marcus X. Fucker treats me like one of his little shit employees. I'm a respected law enforcement official, damn it and should be treated with more respect. I knew it was a mistake to get involved with that uncouth thug... but I just couldn't resist the extra cash and perks. Damn my weakness! Anyway, this has got to be the last favor I do for him. Using my official post in the police department to run his little errands is beneath me and my title. Besides, I'm not sure how long I can fool Bob. He seems suspicious of some of the things I've done... he's too smart to keep fooled for too long.*

"Doesn't look like too many people are here. Didn't you say there was supposed to be five people living here with five automobiles? I only see the one." Burris offered.

"Yeah, my informant said there is actually three people living here— father, mother and our perp, a young male, early twenties about six-foot three, approximately two hundred pounds with sandy brown hair. The informant said there may be other cars here because the perp's brothers are in town."

"Well, maybe we ought to park a little further down the road and just wait for the whole family to get home. This doesn't exactly look like the kinda place you'd hide an abductee... and looking at the address here on my laptop it's a church parsonage! Are you kidding me? The primary resident is a pastor— Reverend Matthew Miller, minister of Nicholasville Baptist Church!" Burris read from his laptop. "Jeff, this has gotta be a mistake. A minister involved in a sexual assault and abduction?"

"I didn't say the minister was involved. Just that possibly his son is. Hell, the minister may not even know there's an abductee in his house."

"I find that hard to believe. Anyway... look here comes the reverend now. Maybe we ought to go ahead and clear this matter up now. I'd hate to embarrass the minister in front of his kids or anything if there's nothing to it. Come on." Burris ordered opening the door and marching across the street.

"Hey Bob, wait!" Stevens insisted grabbing him by the elbow. "Look, this is my hot tip. Let me do all the talking. I've got the intel on this caper."

"Caper, Jeff? Is this a caper? Geesh, Jeff sometimes I don't know about you. Caper? How old are you again? Seventy?" Burris roared with laughter. "Alright, you can ask all the questions, but as soon as I see this is going nowhere, we're walking."

"Yeah, yeah!" Stevens assented as he climbed the Miller's front porch steps and pushed the doorbell.

An attractive lady with a pleasant countenance opened the door.

"May I help you?" Melinda smiled at the two strangers oddly paired in different styles of suits. The largest man in an ill-fitted sports coat with a pair of mismatched polyester stretch pants and the thin, small man dressed like Tubbs from the 1980's hit detective show, Miami Vice.

"Yes ma'am. Does a Luke Miller live here?" Stevens cackled in a high-pitched voice as if puberty had just hit him. Clearing his throat several times, he continued, "Does a Luke Miller live here?"

"Why yes. He's my son. Who's asking?"

"Ma'am, my partner, Detective Burris and I, Detective Stevens of the LPD are here to ask your son a few questions if you don't mind?"

"Well...I'm sure that's fine. Come on in and make yourself comfortable in the front parlor while I get my husband."

Both men immediately pushed forward to enter but hit the threshold at the same time. Burris being the bigger and senior officer shoved himself ahead of Stevens looking back in disdain.

There had been an unspoken competition for leadership in their confederacy. Stevens assumed he was lead detective purely from intelligence, embrace of technological innovations and rapid advancement. Burris, too, saw himself as lead dog through seniority, age and experience as a detective. Both resented the failure of the other to recognize their obvious place in the partnership.

Pushing through, Burris began looking about the large front room for any signs of hairs, nails, jewelry or anything else that might seem out of place. Lifting several figurines on the fireplace mantel, Burris recoiled at the high-pitched voice that mocked his efforts.

"I'm certain our missing girl won't be found lying about the fireplace mantel. Unless, of course, the Miller's shrunk her to a 6-inch doll. I swear, Mary never should have allowed you to see that god-awful movie, Sack Lunch." Stevens smirked.

"That was a very funny movie... very underrated and underappreciated. Anyway, I was looking for female fibers, you snooty ass." Burris replied.

"I'm certain you'll find several female strands as one of them let us in the house."

"Well, why are you just sitting on the sofa resting your delicate ass. Shouldn't you be investigating...detective?"

"I don't need to skulk about searching for clues. I'm doing it all in my head through thorough observation of the room. Besides, I'm more interested in what the family says than what they're possibly hiding. Much more can be discerned through informal conversation. Speaking of which..." Stevens rose from the sofa as Mrs. Miller returned with a tall, distinguished-looking man.

"Detectives, I would like you to meet my husband, Reverend Matthew Miller." Melinda offered timidly.

"Good evening sir. Sorry to disturb you before dinner." Burris replied beating Stevens to the handshake.

"Not at all. How can we help you? Usually, when I meet the fine men and women in law enforcement it's to ride out and talk to bereaved families of an accident or some sort of tragedy. I hope no such event as occurred."

"No sir, we ..."

"We are here to ask you and your family, specifically Luke, about the disappearance or possible abduction of a young lady from UK last night." Stevens averred.

"Oh, my…what does this have to do with our Luke?" Melinda asked.

"Well, we're not sure but there were several witnesses who spoke on anonymity, that your son was seen with her last night prior to her going missing." Stevens again answered ahead of Burris.

"If this happened last night, why is it seen as a missing person or abduction case? Did someone also see her grabbed or forcefully removed?" Matthew quickly retorted.

"Well… not exactly." Burris replied looking to his partner who suddenly remained silent. "You see, a C.I. or informant, notified us about some suspicious activities in a known drug den in which your son, Luke, and this missing girl were involved."

"Known drug den? Where?" Matthew inquired.

"The Zone."

"The Zone. I'm afraid you're mistaken. My sons have never and would never visit such a place."

"What's the Zone?" Melinda asked innocently.

The detectives briefly looked at each other, annoyed that the minister and his wife had turned the tables by asking most of the questions.

"Ma'am, the Zone is an unpleasant area in Lexington known for street gang violence, drugs and a history of other illegal activities." Stevens stated flatly.

"Well if its known for all these illegal activities, why don't you guys just arrest everyone and shut it down?" Melinda countered with a slight annoyance.

"That's a bit tricky and more complex than you think thanks to the Bill of Rights and their aggressive attorneys." Burris chimed in beginning of one of his infectious roaring laughs. Both parties laughed uncomfortably over the jest and awkward situation.

"Anyway, we're looking for a young lady named Candace Echols." Stevens stated resuming the lead.

"Candace Echols? Candace Echols?" Matthew repeated. "The name doesn't ring a bell. Certainly not one of our church members." Matthew added looking at his wife. "Do you have a picture of her?"

"Uhh… well not exactly…" Stevens replied lowering his eyes.

"You don't have a picture of the girl suspected of being missing?" Matthew stated incredulously.

"No, again its very early in the investigation… I mean probe. Look, do you mind if we look around a bit until your son gets home?"

"Do you have a search warrant?" Matthew quickly countered.

"Do I need one? I mean, if you don't know this girl, then there's nothing to hide. You should have no problem with us looking around a bit." Stevens sniveled staring back at Matthew.

The uneasy situation grew more intense as a long stare began. The detectives presented a united front against the equally unified parents. Melinda hated these types of confrontations and sought an armistice.

"Matthew, I don't see any harm in them looking around. There's nothing here that would be of interest to them."

Matthew continued to stare at Stevens in a battle of wills but saw that the detectives weren't going to back down and there really was no need to block their path. *Better to let them snoop about unhindered. If we don't fully cooperate it could be perceived as us hiding something and that's crazy... but they don't know us and they're just doing their job... but still there's, something about this younger guy and the way this whole thing is unfolding that's very weird... kinda unnerving. Can't quite put my finger on it...*

"Sure. Why not? Look wherever you need. Our house is at your disposal, detectives." Matthew offered.

"Thanks Reverend... for your cooperation. We won't be too long or invasive." Stevens sneered walking past Matthew. "By the way, when do you expect Luke to return? I smell dinner cooking and looking at the place settings, you're expecting a large crew. Perhaps all your sons will be here shortly?"

"Yes, that's right." Melinda answered. "The boys should be home soon. They're at Dearbourne playing golf."

"Is that right? I love that course!" Burris joined in trying to break the frigid atmosphere while his partner moved about the upstairs, ducking in and out of rooms. "Why just last week I shot a 72. Had four birdies and nearly dropped an eagle but the darn ball rimmed out on number 15. You know the par five on the back nine, Reverend?"

"Oh, I know it well. One of my favorite holes on the course. Not a long par 5... very reachable, but the green is treacherous." Matthew added as Burris roared with laughter.

"Say Reverend, which room is Luke's?" Stevens asked.

"He's downstairs in the basement. You can reach it from the basement door... there on the right side of the hallway. I'm afraid his room is a pig's sty." Melinda stated with embarrassment.

"Oh, that's alright ma'am. Not too many teens keep a clean bedroom." Stevens mused as opened the basement door ignoring the scornful frown of his partner.

"Oh look, here come the boys now!" Melinda cheered looking outside watching Joseph and Jack unload their golf bags and head toward the front door.

Jack lagged behind his older brother as he noticed the exact same unmarked car from his dream. He motioned Joseph's attention to the car and mentioned its place in his dream. Joseph nodded his head in awe.

"Are you sure?"

"Oh yeah. I bet there are two Laurel and Hardy detectives bumbling around the house now asking strange questions about Candace. Not sure how, but I believe they are connected to Marcus X... or at least one of them is. The thin one I would see later in the barn and..."

"And what? What happens?"

"Uhh... I don't remember. Come on. Let's go in and get this over with." Jack pushed by his brother entering the house.

After the cursory introduction and questions from the detectives, the scene moved to the front room as everyone was waiting for Luke to come home.

"He shouldn't be too long. He was right behind us, detective..." Jack paused.

"Stevens. Do I know you? You seem familiar for some reason."

"Oh no! You don't know me. I'm too old and I'm into girls." Jack laughed.

"Excuse me..."

"Hey here's Luke now!" Melinda shouted breaking an embarrassing accusation. "Luke, honey there are a few detectives that would like to ask you a few questions." Melinda added hugging her youngest as if he were being hauled off to jail.

"Really? What about?"

"The disappearance of a young lady from UK last night." Burris replied just ahead of his partner firmly establishing his lead in the investigation.

"Who disappeared?"

"Candace Echols." Stevens chimed in watching Luke's reaction.

"Candace Echols? Really Candace Echols?"

"Do you know her, honey?" Melinda asked looking up at Luke.

"Yeah I know her. When did she go missing?"

"Late last night."

"Who says she's missing?"

"An informant."

"What did this informant say?"

"Just that they..." Burris replied.

"We're asking the questions here. When did you last see Miss Echols?" Stevens interrupted.

Looking around the room at the assortment of people, Luke saw Jack smile at him from the fireplace mantel. Joseph's look was hard to read near the front door, but his father's stare from the recliner was unmistakable in disappointment and his mother's face was worried. The two detectives were comical in their opposite appearance. The bigger, older man had a kind face whereas the younger, painfully thin man in front of him, had a severe look pocked with acne scars.

"Early this morning." Luke answered avoiding the inevitable stare of disbelief from his mother.

"Approximately, what time?" Burris asked empathizing with the young man's parental dilemma.

Nodding his head back and forth and twisting with unease, Luke answered, "Between three and four."

Looking over at his partner confused, Burris added, "Where was she?"

"Uhh... Luke told me he dropped her off at her car near Cup O Joe. Isn't that right, Luke?" Jack interjected causing the detectives to turn around back and forth between the two responders. Joseph cracked up at the comical spectacle as Matthew flashed a brief smile followed by a rebuking nod.

"Ye...es. That's right, Jack. I did tell you that. She got in her car at Cup O Joe and I assumed drove home. Did you check for her at her apartment?"

"Well...thanks so much for your cooperation and I'm sure we'll wrap this thing up real soon. Reverend, ma'am, again thank you so much for your kindness in opening up your home. We'll just let ourselves out." Stevens rushed and nodded at his confused partner. Burris exited the door first as Stevens held the door and then popped his head back in, "Oh Luke, you will be around here tonight if I have any further questions?"

"Yeah, sure."

Stevens thanked the family again and quickly walked across the street to his unmarked car. Luke watched as Burris and Stevens appeared to argue over who was driving until the larger man shoved the car keys into the thin man's chest and ambled over to the passenger side.

"Whoa... that was weird?" Luke stated turning back to the family.

"But not unexpected." Joseph added.

"What do you mean?" Melinda asked.

"Oh, nothing mom. Joseph's being dramatic as always. Aren't you Joseph?" Jack insisted staring a hole through his older brother.

"Yeah."

"Well, I have more questions for you Luke than those detectives." Matthew inserted. "Who, for some reason, didn't ask a lot, especially after your crack about checking her apartment."

"I know, that was really weird and then they abruptly left." Luke countered.

"Mom, can we eat now? I'm starving. Losing golf balls and the match to these two idiots really takes it out of ya!" Jack laughed trying to get the family at the table where food would occupy their mouths, not probing questions.

Gathered at the table again for dinner, it was decided that this meal would not be interrupted by any mention of what just happened. Melinda insisted on a peaceful meal with her family. Jack was relieved, but he sensed his father's unease was filled with tons of questions about Luke's nocturnal activities. Jack knew Luke would stonewall the father's questions and would create a big blow up. *There's no way this will end well and could set Luke off again. I have to speak to him before dad. I need to know if anyone saw him last night. This thing may not be over. There is some connection between Stevens and Marcus X. I think... at least that's what it seemed like in the dream.*

After a peaceful dinner, the boys helped their mother gather the plates and load the dishwasher. Joseph pulled Jack aside.

"So, what's going on?"

"What do you mean?" Jack replied.

"Don't play dumb. You knew those detectives would be here. You even described them to a tee and you didn't seem worried about their presence or their questions. What happened in the dream?"

"Pretty much the same thing, except they were asking me about the murder of Tater. Remember in my dream, Candace and Tater were killed because I didn't act. They asked a bunch of questions about Tater because he was my friend, but I sensed they were there for other reasons, especially the thin pizza-faced detective."

"Yeah, I got a weird vibe from him, too. So, Luke saved Candace and her daughter last night?"

"Apparently."

"So, why are the Lexington cops down here investigating a missing person who apparently isn't missing?"

"Good question. Probably because that wasn't the real reason they were here."

"Whoa...what was the reason?" Joseph asked intently.

Suddenly, loud angry voices burst out of the front room, as Luke stormed out with Matthew trailing behind him.

"Son, I just asked you a simple question about what you were doing in the Zone last night."

"And I told you. I don't know. I didn't know I was in the Zone until... it doesn't matter. No matter what I tell you, you won't believe me."

"Probably because you've lied before."

"I had to because you and mom get all crazy about everything I do. It's never the right thing or the 'Christian' thing, so I have to hear a lecture or a sermon about what a horrible person I am."

"Look, we're just trying to keep you out of trouble which you obviously have a penchant for. If you listened more to my 'sermons' maybe you wouldn't constantly find yourself in these bad situations."

"Hey, they're MY situations to get out of! Not yours! Just leave it be."

"They're not YOUR situations when they come into my home and search it."

"That's not my fault. I have no idea why they were here."

"But they were here, son. And I have to know why. You owe me that as long as you're living under my roof."

"Well, maybe I shouldn't be living under YOUR roof any longer!" Luke argued closing the basement door behind him.

"Luke?"

"Dad… let him cool off for now. You guys are killing him with these questions and driving him further away." Jack offered.

"Jack, don't interfere. When I get through with him, you're next!"

"What do you mean?"

"I have a ton of questions for you and Joseph, as well!"

❧ ❧ ❧ ❧ ❧ ❧ ❧

After a series of phone calls, an embarrassed Detective Stevens discovered that Candace Echols was indeed, not missing, but at the hospital with her mother. Apparently, the mother had accidentally fallen at home and was presently in a coma. Not wanting to pursue the matter further, Stevens informed his partner they should just drop the matter altogether as the informant's "hot tip" was off base and cold as ice.

Eager to avoid a fight with Burris over the wasted evening, Stevens suggested they get dinner at his partner's favorite restaurant in Lexington, The Pork Belly Palace. While they were waiting for their food, Stevens excused himself and headed to the restroom. Closing the stall door, he pulled out his cell phone and punched a coded contact.

"Hey, it's me…Stevens! Damn, you do that all the time. You damn well know it's me, every time I call but insist on me saying my name!" Stevens frowned listening to a hearty laugh from his receiver. "Look, the perp lives in Nicholasville. 116 Greenwood Drive."

"Is he going to be there tonight?"

"I'm sure. I told him we may need to get back in touch."

"Yeah and we know how persuasive you are with little boys, Jeffy!" Marcus X laughed.

"Shut the fuck up! You can't talk to me that way!"

"Listen to me very carefully, Jeffy, cause I don't want to have to explain this again. I own you! You're a dirty cop waist deep in debt to me, not to mention other illegal and immoral acts you constantly engage in. So, you best shut your damn mouth, talk less and listen more for your orders. Do I make myself clear or do I need to find a replacement, Jeffy?" Marcus ended in an ominous tone.

"It's Jeff or Stevens. Not Jeffy." Stevens snapped defiantly. Listening for a response as several seconds passed without comment. "Alright… you don't need to find a replacement."

Stevens' fretted as he heard a long buzzing tone from the other end of the phone. Great, now he's pissed. I have got stop provoking him until I can bust him or kill him myself and I can't do that till I find his proof of my illegal activities. Until then, I have to suck it up and play up to him as the Boss!

ᭌ ᭌ ᭌ ᭌ ᭌ ᭌ ᭌ

Matthew stormed down the basement steps as he approached his youngest son's room. Matthew knew and dreaded the long overdue conversation he felt he had to have with Luke. For years now, Luke had been drifting listlessly away from the church and its righteous values. It was time to confront this eroding moral descent before it was too late.

"Luke, open up son!"

"No!"

"Son, I sense you're hurting. We need to talk."

"There's no talking to you dad. Just lectures and sermons."

"Look, you're mad and angry. I want to help." Matthew stated waiting several seconds for a response. The longer he waited, the angrier he got. "Open the door now or else!" Matthew shouted.

"I choose 'or else!'"

The tense air was suddenly filled with the boom of the bedroom door bursting open. The sound startled Luke who was laying on his bed. Seeing his father rubbing his shoulder as he advanced toward the bed, Luke sat up and prepared for a scrape. He wasn't sure if it was going to be physical or verbal or both, but he was prepared for either.

"Congratulations, Superman! You popped the lock on a seven-pound door. How did you do it?" Luke sneered sarcastically.

"Yeah, well you guys used to think I was Superman." Matthew stated trying to calm himself.

"Yeah… well I grew up and learned about a lot of your myths and illusions."

"What are you talking about? Myths and illusions?"

"Drop it. It doesn't matter anyway?"

"Look Luke, you seem to be mad all the time. You skulk around here with a huge chip on your shoulder. Ready to snap off someone's head over the slightest things. What's wrong?"

"Nothing… drop it."

"Luke, I'm your father. I love you and care about you. What's eating at you?"

"Look, I can't talk to you. You'll start lecturing with sermons and parables."

"Well, I am your minister, too. Some would find it convenient to have both."

"I don't." Luke replied quickly. Seeing how much that retort had wounded his father, he added "Look, it's too weird talking to two different people. Can't you be normal and just be my father."

"Yes…I promise to hear you out as a father. Now what's got you so angry?"

"I don't know… people just seem to piss me off all the time."

"Luke…language."

"I thought I was talking to my dad, not my minister?"

"You're right, son…I'm sorry. Please continue." Matthew pleaded.

Foul language was a constant burr in Reverend Miller's saddle. It had always bothered him that intelligent people chose to use bad language. To him, it was part of the moral decay of society and, that if allowed, would lead humanity into an immoral abyss. Once bad language was accepted in societal lexicon, soon bad behavior would follow— leading mankind spiraling out of control into an undisciplined immoral world.

He tried to instill this moral discipline into his sons and it took root in Joseph and to a lesser extent, Luke. However, Jack was another story. He found popularity and acceptance with his peers using foul language. Luke, too, enjoyed that peer acceptance, occasionally spewing the sinful language, especially in the competitive atmosphere of sports. Matthew tempered his young son's tongues with whippings from his belt; while Melinda employed less violent, more logical measures of washing their mouths out with soap. The boys hated both methods— vowing to never utter such garbage but it never seemed to cure their affliction or appetite for the salty language.

They simply found a way to curse out of the earshot of their parents. Luke cared less about impressing his classmates and stopped cussing. However, Jack delighted in the attention a 'preacher's kid' received employing the colorful verbiage. Over time, he found creative new ways to hone this craft. Joseph, however, understood the reverend's logic and reasoning and employed it as a code of discipline for his behavior. Jack couldn't understand this discipline as it stunted a perfect opportunity to entertain others with the foul but fanciful art of wordplay.

Nonetheless, Jack learned to keep his criticisms of Joseph's prude behavior to himself and his crafty language out of his earshot, as well, because Joseph would hit him for being undisciplined.

"I don't know dad… you wouldn't understand."

"What wouldn't I understand?" Matthew asked softly as Luke lowered his head in silence. "Look, I've lived a pretty long time and have seen and experienced many things. I'm pretty sure there's not much in your twenty years that I haven't come across."

"That's right dad… you've seen it all, experienced it all and made perfect, moral decisions every time. You're the greatest man since Christ to walk this earth." Luke thundered, once again, feeling his pulse rise.

"Hey, hey… there's no need to shout, son. I'm right here. Now, why are you so angry? You flare up over innocuous statements for no reason. What's eating at you?"

"You wouldn't understand." Luke replied lowering his voice.

"What wouldn't I understand? Son, you seem to be carrying around some kind of awful hate for everything and everybody…" Matthew reasoned looking around Luke's room before fixing his eyes on a photo next to Luke's bed. "Ever since her death."

The statement sent Luke into a blind fury as he snapped his head up, "What are you talking about? Who's her?"

"You know who… Janee."

"Dad, I'm warning you to stop there!"

Sensing he had finally hit the nail on the head, Matthew delved deeper.

"Why? Look, I understand you cared deeply about her and her death was truly tragic. But that's been years now and sadly death is part of the natural way of things."

"Dad, I LOVED her and there was nothing natural about the way she died! It was my fault! My fault! Don't you understand? The most caring, loving, kindest person I have ever met or known was killed at my hands!"

"No son! Her death was not your fault. That's not what the police report stated and it's certainly not what the toxicology report said about her condition at the time of the accident. Accident, son. It was an accident… a tragic accident but one you didn't cause! You've got to stop beating yourself up over this!"

"That's easy for you to say. You didn't kill the love of your life! Janee was so beautiful and kind and gentle. She was filled with joy and laughter. She was so fun to be around. Life was so much more enjoyable around her. She made me a better person by making me WANT to be a better person… and now she's gone and it's my fault!" Luke raged with tears welling up.

"I understand, Luke…"

"No! You don't understand! I've heard enough of your sermons at funerals talking about the 'mysterious ways' or 'nature of God' that we mere mortals wouldn't ever understand. That's bullshit! It's simply bullshit, dad. You, religious types, make up shit to cloak the nature of God because you don't know shit about God or even if there is a God!"

"Luke! Watch yourself! What do you mean, there is no God?"

"I mean, there is no God. Certainly not the caring, loving God you preach about. If there were, how could He allow a beautiful, innocent, good person, like Janee, to die? Huh? Explain that, Reverend Miller!"

"Calm down Luke. As I told you before, God didn't kill Janee and neither did you or anyone else, for that matter. It was simply and accident that occurred. It's no different than others that have happened over time, all around the world, because God gave us, humans, free will. We, humans, make decisions and choices every day that have consequences— some good, some bad. But they are OUR decisions to make and we have to live with the consequences or results or that, too, will kill us. Janee made the tragic decision to get in the car after having drank too much and swerved off the road into a tree."

"Yeah, but I caused her to swerve. I was the other car on the road!"

"Yes you were, but you weren't drunk. You hadn't been drinking like her."

"I still don't believe that stupid police report. Janee never drank to excess. It wasn't like her. She drank a little, but I never saw her drunk and I just don't believe it possible." Luke added staring at her bedside photo. "And now she's dead!"

"She's not dead, Luke. That's the point! She's alive!"

"Oh, don't give me that hocus-pocus bullshit about heaven!"

"Son, it's not hocus-pocus or magic. It's real."

"How do you know? Huh? How do you know? Have you been there? Have you seen it?"

"Son, don't start with that humanist garbage, again?"

"Humanist garbage? You mean, the argument that makes sense— if you can't see it, smell it, hear it, feel it or taste it— it's not real. That garbage? Well that garbage, as you call it, makes a hell of a lot more sense than the bullshit story you ministers have been selling for centuries!"

"To the non-believer, yes! To the secularist, yes! To the humanist, who arrogantly believes in the superiority of man, yes! Son, I've told you a million times to beware of the humanist argument— it's the devil's voice. Satan is a persuasive influence that wants to drive a wedge between you and God. He will employ all types of methods and tactics to lead you away from God and toward himself. The devil was driven from heaven because he envied God's power and creation— mankind, and he wanted to drive God's creation away from Him. Satan envied God's love for mankind and constantly disobeyed Him by meddling in man's affairs on Earth. God cast Satan out of Heaven as a fallen angel because of his envy and disobedience, and ever since, he has plotted to come between us and God. Life without God is a dark, desolate path to eternal damnation in Hell. Janee was a Christian who believed in God and His son, Jesus, and His Resurrection from death and Satan. Through Christ's Resurrection, we who believe, are saved! That's the good news and what I mean when I say Janee isn't dead. She's alive and in no pain. You have to believe that, son. I know it's a leap of faith— you can't prove it through man's scientific method, but it's real! Look at Christ's disciples after His death. They were afraid. Certainly, an understandable emotion after witnessing Christ's brutal death and knowing that all his disciples were, also, being sought for a similar fate as their master. They hid in fear until they WITNESSED his return. When Christ visited them after His death, they no longer feared death because they knew, they too, would follow Him into Heaven. They were believers that came out of their hiding, boldly proclaiming the Resurrection, and starting the Church that would become a worldwide phenomenon. Now let's use some logic and reason. Do you really believe that those disciples, who feared their own deaths, and hid their association to Christ, would come out of hiding and fearlessly proclaim Christ's victory over death, if they hadn't seen Him, touched Him, smelled Him, and heard Him? Death is, probably, the greatest fear to man, but not to the Christian because they KNOW Christ saved them— just as much as those disciples stepped out of hiding, knowing their bodies on earth would perish but not their souls— that would live forever with God in Heaven, Amen."

"I don't know, dad. That's…that's a lot to think about. What you're saying about the disciples and all, does make sense. I get that. They would have definitely been terrified to be associated with a guy who was just executed for doing nothing more than being deemed a threat to some religious leaders. The fear is real and the disciples coming out and preaching…I mean that's crazy brave and courageous…" Luke conceded. Staring at Janee's picture, his eyes narrowed in on the cross draped across her neck. His mind pored over everything his father said and tried to make sense of it. "I just… I just need some time dad, to think it through."

Matthew leaned over and hugged his son. "Yes, think it through and remember well what we talked about tonight and what you've learned your whole life through the Bible. It's natural for intelligent people to question that which they can't prove but what sets us apart is our faith… and belief in God. He loves us all the time. Just as a parent loves their child. Its ever-consuming and never ends. You may stop loving and believing in Him, but He never stops loving and believing in you. I know because, as a parent, that's how I feel about you!" Matthew added with a kiss to his son's head.

Luke grabbed his car keys and left the house out of the back door of the basement. His mind was racing, and he needed to get away… away from a loving home.

Chapter 8

"A man with outward courage dares to die; a man with inner courage dares to live."
— Lao Tzu, Tao Te Ching

The drive to Nicholasville was a mixture of calm and anxiety. Big Jr. enjoyed the serenity of rural settings with the lazy sway of hardwoods in the breeze and the baying of farm animals strewn across the rolling bluegrass hills of central Kentucky. Driving down Harrodsburg Road, he turned off the radio, opened the windows, and gazed at the graceful strides and gait of the thoroughbreds ensconced behind the long black fences about both sides of the road. A peaceful calm settled over him from the rural lea on the outskirts of Nicholasville. However, that tranquility would be disrupted by the task at hand in a town he was unfamiliar with.

Born and raised on the streets of Lexington in a tough neighborhood littered with low rent apartments, Big Jr., Elijah Lovejoy Washington, Jr., never knew his birth parents. His paternal grandmother used a strict Baptist adherence to God and the church's teachings to stay clear of the sinful environment that engulfed his neighborhood with drugs, fast cash and faster women. Much bigger than all the kids in his school, he was never bullied or hounded by local gangs— though many tried to recruit him.

Encouraged by high school coaches to play football, Big Jr. developed into a four-star D-1 offensive tackle recruited heavily by Ohio State, Michigan, Notre Dame and his home state school, UK. However, during the last regular season game of his senior year at Henry Clay High, Big Jr. tore the ACL in his right knee scaring away most of the big schools, except UK. The university believed that through hard-work in rehab, he would not only recover, but flourish as an SEC lineman. Big Jr. rebuilt his knee as a walk-on, joined the practice squad and was on his way to earning a full scholarship until he re-injured the same knee.

The recovery was slow and painful and a new coaching staff at UK seemed uninterested. They dropped him from the active practice squad list. Depressed and angry, Big Jr. stopped his therapy workouts and lost access to the pain medication. Marcus X swooped in to ease his pain with OxyContin, and other controlled prescription drugs.

Once Big Jr accepted the "helping hand" of the local drug lord, he was hooked. The lifestyle of big money and power was as addicting as the pain medication, and Big Jr earned his slice of the pie for doing little more than being big. Occasionally he had to get rough and use violence, but he was used to that on the football field where you fought hard in five second bursts, and then returned to normal. His football background and even temper served him well as body guard to Marcus X.

Dragging deep on a Pall Mall, Big Jr. felt the need to go over, once again, the simple plan of a "stop, pop and drop" with his young, volatile crew. He was a powerful big brother figure to his posse of three high school drop-outs. He needed them for their speed and demanded absolute obedience to his authority.

He taught them the hierarchy of authority with Marcus X at the top, and himself just below— everyone else, except Geoffrey, figured at the bottom. However, by working with Big Jr., you could advance up the short ladder as lieutenants in his special forces operation. Being part of Big Jr.'s posse allowed more access to drugs, women and cash through the use of unbridled violence. Big Jr. didn't carry a large posse because he hated being around loud, obnoxious, stupid teenage boys. His crew knew to remain silent while on the job. Less talking and more observing was the mantra as Big Jr. insisted that a wise man learns more watching than talking. Those who violated this rule were severely reprimanded with Big Jr.'s fist to the head as a 'bell ringer'.

"Alright young idiots listen carefully as I go over the 'stop, pop and drop' so that there will be no mistakes."

"Hey Big Jr., why you gotta always call us idiots. Damn, so disrespectful." Jumpy queried.

"Because you are idiots! Now, shut-up and listen."

"Yeah Jumpy, stop interrupting Big J. You always cutting in like you offended or something. Like you are really smart or something." Wheels insisted.

"I got farther than you in school. You didn't ever make it out the 9th grade, you stupid nigg…"

"No! Damn it, I told you boys we aint using the N-word! I swear to God if I hear one of you use that degrading word, I'll crush your damn skull in! Do you hear me? Now, shut the fuck up and listen to the plan. Damn, why can't you be more like C.J. there and listen?"

"Ah damn, there you go propping up Dark Chocolate again!" Jumpy

"Hey, what did I tell you about that name?" C.J. alerted.

"Who the hell said that? I can't see them, but I heard a voice back there in the dark!" Wheels joined in from the front seat.

"Alright shut the hell up!" Big Jr. shouted reaching back and grabbing Jumpy's inner thigh with a powerful squeeze. Jumpy screamed, Wheels got quiet and C.J. smiled.

"Now, once again, uninterrupted. When we arrive, if the target is at home, C.J. will lure him outside where you two idiots will be waiting behind bushes or beside the front door and snag him with short pop of the bat and drag him quickly back to the car."

"I'll hit 'em, cause last time Jumpy popped 'em, he split their damn head open." Wheels laughed.

"Well shit, the fucker was huge!" Jumpy rejoined.

"Yeah, I remember. I had to haul his fat ass to a construction dumpster. Boss man wasn't happy that night cause he needed that guy alive… anyway, yeah Wheels you got the bat. Now, if the target's not at the house, C.J. and I'll wait in the car, watching for target, while you two wait in the back yard by his bedroom door. The info I got said, the target's bedroom is in the basement, and if he's coming in late, he'll probably enter from backdoor to his bedroom."

"How will we know if he's home? Do you know what car he drives?"

"Yeah…banged up little Honda Civic."

"Honda Civic? Damn white boys drive the stupidest, ugly-ass cars on the planet. Now, if I was sitting pretty like these little white fuckers, I'd drive a damn Humvee! Fuck! Those bastards are HUGE and plow over shit!" Wheels enthused.

"And get horrible gas mileage and pollute the earth." C.J. retorted.

"Who the fuck cares about the gas mileage and pollution shit. Look how badass that son of a bitch is!" Wheels insisted pulling out a worn car magazine featuring Humvees traversing over a mountainous incline.

"When would you ever be driving off road in the mountains where this type of vehicle would be of better use?" C.J. asked.

"Damn, I wouldn't need it for mountains. Just driving through the Zone has enough obstacles!" Wheels laughed.

"I heard that!" Jumpy rejoined slapping hands with Wheels.

"Alright, enough of the chatter. Time to get quiet, get focused. We're nearing the target." Big Jr. demanded as he weaved his charcoal Gran Torino through Main Street in Nicholasville.

Turning right onto Greenwood Drive, Big Jr. slowed to a crawl looking for 116. Once spotted, he frowned as he saw several cars, but not the Honda Civic.

"Alright boys, you know the procedure. I'll park over here on Melrose, which gives me a great view of the house while not appearing to be staking it out. You two sprint down and around back of the house. Call me when you get in place."

The boys hopped out of the car and scrambled down the street into the backyard. It appeared one of them fell but quickly recovered as they turned the corner of the house. Big Jr nodded his head and laughed in disgust at the idea that he put too much trust in these two. *Damn, I'm getting too old for this shit. Hanging out at night on a stop, pop and drop with those two… that's alright, I've saved up a ton of money and will be able to walk away from all this nonsense soon enough. Just a few more years and I'll be able to buy that little farm in Keene and grow some tobacco. Still, Boss man needs to find some better-quality workers cause Wheels and Jumpy are the cream of the crop out of apartment 121. Thank God, I got C.J.! Boy's bright and got a good head with an even temper. Almost too docile. Boy aint got a mean streak at all in him. Probably shouldn't have him on this posse cause of what it requires but... just no other quality candidates. Besides, he's interesting to talk to. Doesn't fill my head with bullshit about cars and drugs and girls. Damn, he's never ever talked about girls. All teenage boys brag about the ladies but not C.J....*

"Big Jr., can I ask you something and you promise to keep it to yourself? Not saying anything around the guys?" C.J. asked softly from the back seat.

"Sure. What's on your mind?"

"Do you like girls?"

"What the fuck kinda question is that? Of course, I like girls! Why the hell would you ask me that?"

"Easy Big Jr., I meant no offense. Just a question cause I never see you around any at the apartment complex and they're everywhere, but you don't seem interested."

"That's cause at the box, you have ho's and street pros, not exactly my kinda ladies. I'm sure most of them have s.t.d.'s and shit." Big Jr. insisted. After a long pause he added, "For your information I have a lady I'm seeing. No one knows about her cause she doesn't know the line of work I'm in. She's a sweet, refined lady who doesn't need to know, and no one else needs to know, either. If you know what I mean."

"Absolutely! I would never divulge anything you and I ever talked about. I feel like you're the only guy, adult, I can talk to. I'm surrounded by adolescent inferiors and though I chose this line of work, you and I both know, I'm not cut out for this kind of thing. I'm only doing it for the money to pay for my granny's rent, prescriptions and bills. Anyhow...I don't think I like girls the way I'm supposed to..."

"What the fuck are you saying C.J.? You a damn faggot?"

"No! No... I don't think so. I mean, I watch the way the guys are around the girls at the complex and I just don't feel the same inclination."

"Have you ever tried? Did you go up to any of the girls and talk to them?"

"Yeah, several times and... it just... its nothing. I feel nothing for them, other than empathy for their plight, lack of education and, in many cases, lack of feminine hygiene."

"Damn, boy! That don't mean nothing. Half those girls are skanks anyway. You just need to get out a bit and see real girls. One day, I'll drive you out of the Zone and show you around town to some nice spots with real ladies."

"Yeah that would be nice... but..."

"But what?"

"I kinda have feelings for someone, and I think, no I'm pretty sure, they have feelings for me, too?"

"A dude? You talking about a fucking dude?"

"Yes."

"What the fuck C.J.? No, no… oh hell no! You aint no damn faggot, boy. You can't be no damn faggot cause if you are, you can't be in this car!"

"Big Jr. are you serious? I came to you in confidence. I thought you might understand."

"What, the fuck, would I understand about homosexuality? Huh? What makes you think I would understand a damn thing about fucking fudge-packing?"

"I'm sorry I brought it up. I thought you were more mature and could help me in this confusing time." C.J. stated flatly while pausing to gather his thoughts. "I'm not saying that I am a homosexual and I have never acted on it or anything like that. It's just that I feel very much the same way Jumpy and Wheels feel when they describe being around girls, except around a certain guy."

The atmosphere in the Gran Torino was thick with resentment and angry thoughts. Big Jr. remained quiet for several minutes trying to make sense of this revelation and contemplate how to proceed. He always knew that C.J. was different— sensitive, caring, kind-hearted with a sharp sense of fashion— but being a homosexual never crossed his mind. He had never really known a gay person on a personal level. In school, they were picked-on, bullied and ridiculed. He never joined in, but never defended them, either. He, upon reflection, was indifferent to them. He couldn't care less one way or the other, but now, one worked with him and conversed with him and wanted advice from him. He liked the boy but would never understand him.

"Look, I aint mad at ya! Like you said, maybe you're just confused or something. Maybe it's just a passing fad with just this one dude. By the way, is it someone at the box?"

"Yes…its Geoffrey."

"Damn, that fucking faggot done infected one of my crew!"

"I would hardly call it an infection… maybe a bit of the love bug." C.J. mused at his own pun.

"Hey this shit aint no joke. You can't talk about his around anybody, especially the boys at the box. They find out about you and your ass is dead and there aint a damn thing I can do about it. You understand? This shit gets out and you're on your own."

"I understand." C.J. replied despondently. Shaking his head tears welled up in his eyes as he stared out the window. He had reached out to the only male role model in his life about the most confusing time, and he suddenly felt ashamed. Not about the way he felt towards Geoffrey, that he reasoned was natural, but that he had disappointed his idol.

"Look kid, I'm not trying to be mean or anything, it's just that… well hell, in our world of drugs and thugs you can commit just about any sin, but not that one. If you're a damn fag… you'll get cured of it real quick! And the cure will be permanent. If you know what I mean."

"I understand. I'll keep all this as quiet as before."

"Yeah and be real careful around Geoffrey. I mean everybody assumed he was a fag, but because he makes us so much money, and he's the Boss man's ace, aint nobody gonna touch his ass. I mean… you know what I mean. I wasn't making a fag joke!" Big Jr. laughed. "Anyway, look I didn't mean to come down on you like that. I don't really know any fags, so I have…"

"Well, first of all, stop referring to them as fags. They are human beings and that's as derisive and demeaning a term as the N-word that you have rightly banned."

"Yeah…okay. It's gonna be tough but I'll try. Anyway… I better check on those two numb-nuts out there and make sure they're where they're supposed to be." Big Jr. said looking back at C.J. in the mirror shaking his head.

❧ ❧ ❧ ❧ ❧ ❧ ❧

Matthew Miller marched up the stairs with a renewed determination to get to the bottom of what had transpired and what role his sons had played in it. Turning the corner to the dining room he saw the boys huddled up at the table talking softly.

"Alright, I need to know what's going on and I need to know, right now."

"What are you talking about dad? You know everything we know." Jack offered unconvincingly.

"That's bull and you know it. I know about the whole Clint Eastwood movie talk."

"What are you talking about… Clint" Jack inserted.

"Don't play dumb. I know that you boys communicate with each other around me and your mother by referencing Clint Eastwood movies, especially when you're discussing bad stuff. I've known about that tactic for years but didn't say anything because I wanted to know what you guys were talking about. If you knew that I knew, you'd leave the room and make it harder for me to know what you guys were up to!"

The brothers looked at each other in mocked wonder— stunned by the accusation.

"Come on, what happened last night?"

"Well, Jack can tell you better than I because I was here all night."

"Luke's seeing a girl that lives in the Zone— a kind of dangerous place in Lexington."

"I know about the Zone. Go on… so he's dating a young lady who lives in a bad area, He mentioned her earlier this morning and?"

"And…let's just say her daughter was kidnapped, Luke followed her to the drug lord's compound, they retrieved the girl and he came home."

"And that's it? Sounds too simple for that kind of place. Did Luke run into trouble? Was there a physical confrontation? Some sort of deal made that released the girl?"

"I don't know."

"How do you know what happened? Were you there?"

"Yes." Jack admitted not wanting to lie to his father, but not wanting to tell him too much.

"And? What did you see?"

"I saw the three of them leave the apartment complex…"

"Apartment 121." Joseph added.

"Apartment 121, yes… thank you." Jack repeated staring at Joseph incredulously. "And they got in Luke's car and, I guess, he took them home. We saw Luke arrive this morning…end of story."

"Not end of story. There's more there than you're telling. Why were you there?"

"I thought it wouldn't be safe, so I trailed him with Tater."

"Tater went with you? Well, he's a good guy to have with you in a scrape."

"Dad, it was fine. I probably overreacted. Where is he? Is he still in his room?"

"No, he left."

"He did? Did he say where he was going?" Jack shot up out his chair.

"No, he was still a little upset and needed to clear his head. I assume he went for a drive somewhere. Where are you going?"

"I have to go back to my apartment. Supposed to meet Tater there. See ya dad!"

Jack grabbed his keys and darted out the front door. His eyes instantly fell on the dark Gran Torino with tinted windows parked on Melrose but thought nothing of it. He had to find Luke and fast because tonight was the night of the deadly attack in his dream. Starting the engine, he saw Joseph at his door signaling to roll down the window.

"Hey where are you going?"

"To get Luke. This is the night of the deadly assault. You want to come with me? I have an idea where they are and, more importantly, where they are going."

"No. I came out here to stop you. This is madness. You're following Luke into an extremely dangerous situation that could get, not only Luke killed, but you, as well! This is stupid! We can't keep watching over him and taking the hit for his stupid mistakes!"

"He's our brother."

"He's our stupid brother whose stupid decisions are now becoming deadly. Look, God gave you a vision of what was going to happen. You warned him and he, like always, ignored it and decided to run headstrong into the fire and now you're going chasing after him! Why?"

"He's our brother and…"

"And what?"

"That dream gave me a crazy review of my whole life with him and it showed me how often I've failed him. Any time there was a physical confrontation with someone, I backed down and allowed him to get hurt. It happened over and over again, and I have failed him Joseph! Failed him! Not again. I see the dream differently. It was God's way of telling me, 'you've got a chance to save him, now do it!'"

"How? How are going to do it? You going to fight someone? We both know, you don't do that. You going to kill someone? Do you have a gun or any weapon?" Joseph reasoned.

"I'll figure it out. I have the prophetic dream on my side and the Lord watching over me."

"Don't count on the Lord to sanction your violence or even killing. He doesn't go for that."

"This is a special case. I'd be protecting my brother."

"Yeah, I'd like to see that defense when you face Him at your judgement! You'll be condemning your soul to hell for taking the life of another. That's why I'm pleading with you now! Luke's gone! He won't listen, but you… you I can still save. Don't do this!"

"What are you saying? Luke is NOT gone! He's still alive and he's still our brother and I'm going to try and save him. Now, you can get in this car now and help me or you can stay here like a COWARD!"

"Fine! Get yourself killed and condemn your soul, as well. I'm tired of protecting you guys. I will not lose my soul for this!" Joseph cried out as he pulled away from the window.

Jack floored the gas pedal and turned right onto Weil Lane. Joseph stood at the curb as tears welled up in his eyes and prayed *Dear Heavenly Father, place Your loving hands around my brothers and steer them in the right direction. Help them see the light and avoid the darkness of the path away from You. I can't serve You and protect them at the same time. Give me strength to know Your will and to follow Your way, not mine. I pray that Your will be done. Amen.*

❧ ❧ ❧ ❧ ❧ ❧ ❧

Luke's mind was racing as he pored over everything his father had said about God, faith and religion. He wanted to believe what his father had taught him his whole life and he loved and respected his father. But did that mean he was right. *Is there a God and a Heaven and a Hell? Is there a Satan who is trying to come between me and God? It makes sense in the literary world. I mean it makes for a good story— good versus evil— God versus the fallen angel. But is it real or fiction and… Janee. Damn, why did he have to bring her up? Oh man, he hit harder with that statement than any punch I've ever felt. Janee…her death… was my fault!*

He turned left onto Waveland Museum Road and slowed his car as he approached the stately Greek Revival mansion on the right. Pulling into the U-shaped driveway, Luke shifted the car into park but left the car running as his mind drifted back to his second kiss with Janee.

They had just finished another photo shoot for her photography class, when it started to rain. They sprinted back to his Honda Civic and laughed at how hard and fast the storm had fallen on them.

"I can't remember the last time I saw it rain so sudden and hard. Phew, glad I was able to get some more shots of the cellar and the slave quarters. I think I'll print them in black and white to create the right image. You know— stark, desolate, hopelessness." Janee intimated.

"Sounds right." Luke added with a grin.

"Sounds right." Janee mocked. "Anything else you want to add? It would really help if you weren't so agreeable. You know sometimes I'm wrong."

"Really? I never noticed." Luke frowned as Janee playfully shoved him.

"Seriously Luke, it's okay to tell me when I'm wrong or if you disagree. I won't flip out or anything."

"I think you're beautiful. I think the camera could never truly capture your beauty or the essence of your goodness. I think the best image I saw all day was when the sun appeared out from behind a lazy cloud and hit the highlights of your gorgeous hair turning the tips to a shimmering auburn hue as you knelt to photograph a rabbit bounding down the tilled field."

"Oh, wow Luke…" Janee gasped as she stared into Luke's hazel-green eyes. Her heart was beating faster as he leaned down to kiss her.

Though it was just their second kiss, Luke felt like it was even better than the first. Again, his mind swirled as he kissed her with a yearning that this moment would never end. He cupped her face in his big hands and gently stroked her cheek and whispered in her ear "I was born when you kissed me, and I died when you left me."

"Oh, Luke that's beautiful and haunting. Did you just make that up or what?"

"Uhh… actually that's a quote from an old Bogart movie, 'In A Lonely Place'"

"Oh, you Miller's and your love of old movies. Do you guys memorize all the lines?"

"Just the good ones. I remember thinking that was the corniest, most God-awful line I had ever heard. There was no way a sane man would have said that. But just now... in this moment... I really understood it." Luke offered as he leaned down and kissed her again.

A man stood banging on Luke's window indicating that he had to move his vehicle or go park in the side lot reserved for paying guests. He nodded and shifted the car into gear merging right onto Waveland Museum Road and to the sight of his worst nightmare. Just as he reached the railroad tracks, Adele's haunting song, "Hello", broke the eerie silence as Luke wheeled off the road. *Why did this song, of all songs, have to come on now? It's an old, tired song that they should retire from the airwaves. It's, its's...* Luke's mind couldn't escape the song's strong connection to an unresolved past. A past that beckoned a second look from the repressed recesses of a restless conscience. Staring out the window at a large, gnarled oak, Luke revisited his high school senior year.

West Jessamine High School was beginning to emerge as a real threat in sports trapped in the Lexington region with perennial powers such as Henry Clay, Lafayette and Dunbar. The football team had its first winning season in fifteen years and there was great anticipation in their basketball team's chances to improve on the previous year's breakthrough. Luke, encouraged by Janee, made the varsity basketball team and she won a spot on the varsity cheerleading squad— the pair became the "it" couple. Luke earned a starting position and played well at the beginning of the season. He loved making eye contact with Janee during the games— it made him play harder. Everything changed in January when Luke tore ligaments in his ankle forcing him to miss the rest of the season.

Watching games from the bench was excruciating. However, watching his girlfriend cheer for his replacement, Josh Spaulding, was unbearable. Spaulding was a tall, athletic sophomore with great promise as a D-1 scholarship player. Moved up from the junior varsity to replace Luke, Spaulding quickly emerged as the team's leading scorer. Luke ached worse than his throbbing ankle at the sight of Janee cheering for his handsome, successful replacement. His low self-esteem fed a growing concern that Janee was interested in Spaulding off the court. Often, Janee enthused about how much better the team seemed to be playing since Luke's injury, and how it looked like the team may make the playoffs. At parties, Luke was alarmed at how quickly Janee would rush over to greet Spaulding when he arrived and gush over his play like an adoring roadie.

Simon, too, watched this love triangle develop, and did everything he could to encourage it. He had held a long, simmering grudge against Luke for stealing his girlfriend. Though Janee never saw him that way, Simon persisted in the belief that had Luke not been at the party, he would be her boyfriend. Luke never knew about the grudge because Simon wanted to punish him. To exact his revenge, he had to stay close to Luke as a trusted friend and confidant. As an insider, he fed Luke's insecurities and jealousies with vicious rumors of Janee's infidelities with many guys— Spaulding being the latest.

In February, Simon held his birthday party at the Morgan House Inn off Nicholasville Road in Lexington. He invited mostly seniors and Josh Spaulding, in hopes of breaking up the "it" couple, and then swoop in to win Janee's affection. The rebound plan took root after Simon informed Luke, at the party, that Janee had insisted he invite Spaulding. Once the seed of deception was planted in Luke's head, Simon watered it with more comments about seeing Janee and Spaulding talking privately. Luke erupted.

Limping through the Morgan House Inn lobby, Luke searched for his cheating girlfriend. Unsuccessful in his quest, he returned to the ballroom where the birthday bash took place. He ladled a large cup of punch as Simon approached with a flask of Jack Daniels. Luke refused the whiskey saying he needed a clear head for his confrontation. Simon, seeking to help his best friend, informed him that he saw the missing couple talking in the back hallway near the ladies' restroom. He failed to mention that he had sent Spaulding on an errand to deliver a message to her for him. The trap was set for a fight.

Luke entered the back hallway and instantly spied the couple talking amicably. He balled his fist and moved decisively on the pair.

"Oh, hey Luke." Spaulding called out.

"Get the hell outta here, Josh." Luke demanded.

"Luke! What's wrong with you? Why are you acting like this?" Janee implored.

"He doesn't need to be out here with you... bothering you."

"He's not bothering me. Calm down. My God, you look insane!"

"Hey, Josh... dude, why are you still here? Get out before I lose my temper."

"Easy Luke. I'm not doing anything wrong. Just delivering a message."

"What message? Who sent you?" Luke insisted.

"None of your damn business." Spaulding indignantly retorted.

The two alpha males began the fighting ritual of puffing out their chests and staring hard at each other waiting for the other to start the party.

"Luke, stop this! You're acting crazy!" Janee cried out.

"Josh... you can leave now. I need to talk to MY girlfriend!"

Spaulding glanced over at Janee. She nodded emphatically for him to leave and avoid a fight. Staring eye to eye with his senior teammate, Spaulding brushed past Luke.

"Okay, Luke he's gone. You happy? Now, why are acting this way?"

"No, I'm not. I'm not happy and really haven't been since my injury."

"Luke, I know and I'm so sorry. It must be painful to watch the games from the bench."

"Yes, it is… but its more painful watching you fawn all over my replacement."

"What are you talking about? I don't…"

"Yes, you do. I see it with my own eyes and I hear people come up to me all the time saying, 'why is Janee always talking to Josh?' And I have no answer…well?"

"I'm not always with Josh. That's crazy and who is telling you this?"

"Lots of people. Look, ever since I got hurt and Coach brought up that scrub, Spaulding, you've been all goo-goo eyes over him."

"What are you talking about? And Josh is no scrub. He's already getting scholarship interest."

"Oh really? How do you know that? You two been talking?"

"Yes, I talk to Josh. Big deal. There's nothing wrong with talking to him or anyone, for that matter. You don't own me and can't talk to me like that!"

"Oh, I guess Spaulding talks nice to you. Treats you real nice, huh?"

"As a matter of fact, he does."

"Yeah, what else does he do?"

"What does that mean?"

"You know what it means. I hear you guys have been messing around. It's not just talking, but hugging, kissing and …"

"And what? Who's telling you all this? It's crazy. I've never kissed Josh. I've hugged him a few times, like after a game to congratulate him but that's it."

"Yeah, I'm sure. Look, all I know is that ever since my injury, my replacement seems to see you more than I do. We don't go out or really see each other much."

"First, I happen to have several advanced classes with Josh and we have study groups. Second, I've been so busy with cheerleading and preparing applications and resumes for colleges. It's a really busy time and…"

"Oh yeah and those study groups meet at the mall? Heard you

were hanging out with Spaulding at the mall."

"I saw him there a few times with other people. We weren't together! Who's telling you this?"

"It doesn't matter. Obviously, it's the truth. Basically, you're admitting that you're seeing Spaulding."

"Luke William Miller, I'm not going to stand here and be wrongly accused of nefarious insinuations. You've lost your mind in an obsessive jealous born from your own insecurities. You got hurt. You miss playing and now you're taking it out on me. That's not fair. I'm outta here!"

"Fine! Go back to your boy, Spaulding! I'm sure you know exactly where he is!"

Janee stomped off towards the ballroom and flipping him the middle finger after his last accusation. Luke threw his cup against the wall and followed her. He knew he couldn't talk to her now in her present mood, but he wanted to make sure she didn't fall into the arms of his rival. Word spread quickly about an impending fight between the teammates and romantic rivals.

The locker room was initially divided by class over the teammate feud— upperclassmen with Luke; the rest with Josh. But as the team progressed in Luke's absence, they, too, seemed to side with the new leading man, Josh. The winning atmosphere of a successful basketball season trumped personal loyalty as Luke felt the sting of yet another betrayal.

By the time Luke trailed Janee into the massive ballroom, several team members had gathered around Spaulding in a show of support. He had hoped for a one on one confrontation to end the "Spaulding Affair" as it came to be known in school. Instead, he witnessed the solidarity of his teammates to protect their star, and the gathering of the rest of the party to see a fight. Convinced that a physical confrontation would resolve none of his problems, Luke lowered his head and limped out of the Inn. He had lost everything: his playing time, his teammates and, more importantly, his girlfriend.

He drove around Lexington to cool his ire and restore his senses. The blind fury that had enveloped him when he entered the car, had begun to ebb as he approached Waveland Museum Road.

Turning right, he drove down the twisted winding path lined by ancient oaks whose voices sang through the wind tales of sorrow and tragedy. The road was notorious for automobile accidents with many blind rises and sharp turns. It was difficult to navigate in the daylight but deadly at night. Easing past the railroad tracks, Luke was heartened by the opening on both sides of the road that led to a four-way stop at Winthrop. However, the road returned to its dark, ominous past as it narrowed through large, overhanging trees. He carefully steered through the twists and the turns eventually veering right over a small bridge. Turning left, Luke pulled into Willow Oak Park ignoring the entrance sign that read "Residents Only".

Parking in front of a terraced gazebo, he took several deep breaths. Staring at the ornate white octagonal structure, Luke felt at ease as he remembered the times he spent laughing, teasing and embracing Janee in the gazebo.

Janee was furious when she learned where the rumors and fantastic stories about Spaulding had originated— Simon. She was not a confrontational person, but this had gone too far and needlessly hurt too many. She determined the time had come to demand answers from Simon.

"Why did you send Josh to tell me about a Chemistry test on Monday?"

"What? I don't know what you're talking about?" Simon pleaded innocently.

"Oh really? Okay, I'll get Josh over here."

"No, no, no… don't do that! Ha! Ha! I was just kidding! It was a joke! I thought it would cause you to panic if you thought we had a Chemistry test Monday morning." Simon laughed.

"That's not funny Simon and you told Luke that Josh and I were hanging out together in the mall, hugging and kissing and doing all sorts of things— knowing none of that was true!"

"Hold on. Everything I told Luke was true. You did see him at the mall. You did go into several stores with him. You did hug and kiss him on the cheek goodbye."

"How do you know all of that? Were you there… spying on me for Luke?"

"Of course… why else would I be there?" Simon coughed nervously before taking a sip of his cup.

"Look, nothing I did at the mall was wrong or could be seen as 'cheating' on Luke. If you were there, you know that. By telling Luke what you saw, you had to know it would feed into his insecurities and drive him crazy with jealousy."

"No, I didn't. I was just being a good friend. Luke begged me to watch you. I told him it was a bad idea and tried to talk him out of it. He insisted… you know how he can be?"

Janee nodded as her temper receded.

"Look, if you want I'll call the lunatic and explain everything to him. You know, try to get him to see the innocence of the whole misunderstanding."

"Would you really? That would be great, but this can't be done on

the phone. It has to be done in person. Would you ride with me to go find him?"

"Sure, do you know where he is?"

"I have a pretty good idea. Let's go!"

"Yeah sure. I'll meet you at your car in the parking lot. I just need to grab a few things first."

Janee felt better as she unlocked the passenger side door for Simon. He was carrying two water bottles wrapped under his coat as he slid into the seat.

"Why two water bottles?" Janee inquired shifting her blue Mustang into second gear.

"One for me, one for you, silly. Here, I heard you coughing all night. You need to clear your throat."

"Oh, thanks Simon. My throat is raw. Guess I'm coming down with something." Janee added with two quick gulps.

"Hey… Janee, I just want to say how sorry I am about everything. You know 'spying on you and all'. It really wasn't my idea and like I said, I tried to talk Luke out of it but… well you know how he can get."

"Yeah, unfortunately that's a side of him I could do without. He's such a sweet, easy-going guy most of the time. He has a real romantic side to him that just…" Janee paused in reflection. "He's a lot different than you would expect. He seems all gruff and moody but he's really not. There's a soft, gentle side. He has a vulnerability that makes you want to take care of him. Like he's been grievously wounded or something."

"Wounded? Well he does have two older brother's that beat on him all the time." Simon joked as he took a large swig from his bottle.

"Ha! Ha! Yeah, but that's like brother stuff. It's all done in fun. I have brothers, I know. No, it's like something really weird or strange happened to him a long time ago and he's really never gotten over it."

"I can't imagine anything too weird. After all, he's been raised in the church and his pastor lives with him." Simon jested taking another hard hit on his bottle. "I wouldn't know about brothers. I'm an only child. It can be real lonely growing up without any siblings. But, it also has its advantages."

"Oh? Like what?" Janee inquired before taking another sip of her bottle and driving south past the Fayette Mall.

"Well, you don't have to share your parents, for one. You get tons of gifts on the holidays!"

"Yeah, I bet!" Janee laughed.

"But, again it would have been nice to have a brother or sister

around the house to talk to or do stuff with. My dad was never really around much, and mom was too involved in her charity work, and an assortment of women's associations that she belonged to."

"Oh, Simon. I'm so sorry. I never knew."

"Yeah, well I don't talk about it much. Anyway, Luke is my best friend and like a brother to me. I've known him since elementary school when I used to protect his scrawny ass every day from getting beat up."

"Oh? Why? Did Luke get in a lot of fights?"

"Hell yeah! You wouldn't know it today, but Luke was a little punk, always trying to fight bigger kids to prove how tough he was. I had to protect him all the time."

"That's funny… he used to tell me he got into some fights in school but his older brother, Joseph, was always stepping in and defending him against bigger kids that were bullying him."

"Is that what he said? Ha! Joseph didn't do shit! He was never around when the fights started. I was! I did a lot for him… still do and what do I get in return for it? Betrayal…" Simon mumbled as he took a deep swig off his bottle.

"Betrayal? What are talking about?"

"Nothing."

"Come on, Simon. How did Luke betray you?"

Simon looked out the window. He wasn't sure how much to reveal but he was getting a bit woozy from the vodka in his water bottle and it seemed to steel his nerves. Now was as a good a time as ever to let Janee know how he really felt about her.

"Janee… I'm pissed that Luke swooped in and stole you away from me!"

"What?"

"Yeah, you know at my party last summer that I threw for you. You and I were supposed to be together, but he took you away. I didn't get a chance all night to talk to you or anything. He hogged all your time. If it weren't for him, you and I would be together." Simon proclaimed as he stroked her cheek with the back of his hand.

"Stop, Simon!" Janee protested with a quick slap of his hand. "That's pure nonsense. Luke didn't steal me away from you. I wasn't 'supposed' to be with you or anyone else for that matter. I think for myself and do for myself. No one controls me. I'm no one's property!" Janee insisted slurring the last word prompting Simon to laugh.

Janee turned right onto Waveland Museum Road. Instinctively slowing the car, she had trouble seeing the road. Everything was becoming blurred. Her eyes felt heavy as she looked over at Simon *who seemed to be smiling.*

"Are you smiling? Why are you smiling?"

"Look, you better pull over. You don't look so good." Simon cracked.

"Yeah, okay." Janee meekly replied pulling off the road onto the arced driveway in front of the stately mansion. "What kinda wadder... did... you give me?"

"Wadder? Ha! Ha! You mean water? It appears to be working and faster than advertised."

"Wad are you talking about?"

"Rohypnol. It's better known as a roofie. I slipped one in your water, so you would be more receptive to my advances. You see this?" Simon asked as he pulled a sparkling diamond necklace out of his coat pocket. "This was the necklace I was going to give you last summer at my party. But the opportunity was squandered when Luke cornered you all night. I've been waiting for the right time to give it to you and, well, no time like the present." Simon leaned over and clasped it around her neck.

Janee tried to push him away but her arms felt heavy and her effort was weak. She could feel his breath warm on her neck as he began kissing her and rubbing his hands across her chest. In her mind she could hear herself screaming but it had no effect in the car. His hands hungrily clawed about her clothing as he tore open her blouse. Her upper body felt numb as her mind raced to find a solution. It was as if she were trapped in her body paralyzed in fear and anguish. He leaned up and kissed her in the mouth probing his tongue against her teeth. Instantly, she bit down furiously on his tongue forcing him back against the passenger door. In that moment, she was able to grab the steering wheel and floor the gas pedal.

Turning right onto Waveland Museum Road, she felt she was losing control of the steering wheel, as well as her sight. She knew Luke was probably nearby at Willow Oak Park. She had to get there and quick while she was still conscience.

The road seemed to fly by in a blur and she knew she had to slow down for the deadly turns, but she couldn't feel her legs. The car hopped over the railroad tracks as she caught a brief glance at Luke's Honda Civic. She ran directly into his headlights but didn't hit his car. Instead she crashed headlong into a gnarled oak tree as her head slammed against the wind shield causing her sight to go dark. Her body fell back hard against her seat. The impact had thrown Simon out of the car and into a ditch along the road. His shoulder was badly bruised from the rough landing, but he was conscience and able to walk back to the car. The front end of Janee's Mustang was bent into the tree and crumpled back to the front seats.

Looking in through the passenger side door, Simon saw Janee's eyes wide open with a large gash above her head and blood streaming down her face. Seeing headlights approaching slowly down the road, Simon grabbed his vodka water bottle and splashed the remains about her mouth. Using his coat, he carefully wiped off his fingerprints from the bottle and placed it beneath her feet. He retrieved her water bottle and yanked the necklace off. Crouching low, he backed up the embankment and disappeared into the woods.

Luke pulled up cautiously fearing that the car smashed into the tree was indeed Janee. He thought he had glimpsed her face as her car raced towards him. He had swerved hard to his right and avoided the head-on collision but drove down into a side embankment. He smashed his head into the steering wheel and could feel a cut oozing warm blood, but he was conscience and his car was still running. Wheeling the car around, he feared the worst as he approached the accident.

The car's lights were still on and he quickly recognized the rear license plate and bumper stickers. Walking slowly to the driver's side door, he could see Janee's beautiful red hair tousled about. He grabbed the door handle and tugged franticly to open it. When the door finally gave way, Janee's lifeless body spilled out into his arms. Luke stared into her icy blue eyes in shock. Holding and stroking her hair Luke screamed for help and prayed for God's divine intervention.

"Janee! No! No! Don't leave me! I'm sorry! I'm sorry! I'm so sorry! Please God, don't take her! Don't take her. I will do anything and everything you ask! Just please don't take her! Take me, dear Lord! I'm the one at fault not her! She's an innocent angel who never did anything wrong! Oh God, please no!!"

Luke's eyes were red as tears streamed down his face. He had returned to the scene of his greatest living nightmare and his body was trembling uncontrollably in sorrow. He hadn't felt this kind of intense pain since the accident years ago. He thought he had it under control lost deep in the recesses of his troubled mind. He heard a familiar buzzing coming from his coat pocket. Pulling out his phone he saw a text message from Simon—"Dude meet me @ Shearer's field now! Need your help!"

❦ ❦ ❦ ❦ ❦ ❦ ❦

Big Jr. took a hard drag on his Pall Mall and blew a large cloud of smoke through the driver's side window. With his thick arm resting atop the rolled down window, he flicked a long ash into a tray under the dashboard. Pulling his phone out of his pocket, he punched Jumpy's phone number.

"Hey Big Jr.! What up?" Jumpy replied.

"You guys seen anything? Heard anything?"

"Nah... not inside the house anyway. There was this crazy-ass cat that snuck up on us. We wuz just hanging down in this hole-like stairwell by white boy's back door, when all the sudden this fat-ass cat jumps out of the bush. Scared the fuck out of me, and Wheels fucking chased the damn thing all over the yard. Stupidest thing I ever saw. I mean, Wheels is fast and all, but damn that fat cat just took off. He darted all over the back yard. He must have chased that fat ass for a good ten minutes. I was laughing my ass off!"

"Glad to know you guys are having fun. Did he make a lot of noise?"

"Nah...that's the craziest thing. That stupid nigg... I mean, negro, was flying about like a damn bat outta hell but made no sound. I guess, the only sound made was me cracking up. When he came back and saw me laughing he got mad. I told him, 'Negro what was you planning to do with that damn cat once you caught his ass?' and you know what he said?" Jumpy asked waiting for Big Jr.'s response but never hearing it. "He says 'Damn Jumpy, I don't know. Never really thought about it.' Can you believe that shit?"

"Yeah, that sounds about right. You idiots going off half-cocked without any thought about consequences."

"Damn, Big Jr., I only told you cause you asked and I thought you'd think it was funny." Jumpy added with a wounded ego.

"Look, I was just checking on you guys. One of the brothers, left a few minutes ago. He may be trying to locate our boy. Who knows. Looked like him and possibly the other brother got in a pretty heated argument. One of the brother's peeled out of the neighborhood. Anyway, we could be here a while. Keep alert and close to the phone, in case I see anything. If you guys see anything of interest, and not some stupid-ass fat cat, call me. Otherwise sit tight and don't make a sound or a scene. Tell Wheels to stop spooking out over little things!"

Nodding his head in disgust and drawing hard on the last drag of his smoke, Big Jr. pulled out another cigarette and lit it with the butt. Looking in the rearview mirror at C.J., he tried to lighten the mood in the car with an easy target.

"Those fucking idiots would shit themselves if you didn't tell them to drop their pants!" Big Jr. scoffed. "I mean, damn, you have to explain everything to them. There's no common sense between the two. Kinda like that movie, 'Dumb and Dumber' and I don't really know which is which."

"What they lack in intelligence, manners, ethics, civility, education and basic human decency, they certainly have an abundance of courage. Those nimrods fearlessly go into battle and attack. I've seen them take on guys twice their size and whip them to a pulp with sheer audacity and will. They may be as a dumb as a box of rocks, but their courage can never be challenged." C.J. averred.

"That's bullshit, C.J.. What they do is not courageous because they don't know any better. They're so damn stupid, they don't realize they should be afraid because they never think of the consequence of their actions." Big Jr. countered.

"What do you mean?"

"I mean, they go off half-cocked all the time without thinking, 'damn what might happen if x, y, or z occur. So many different scenarios can happen in a scrape. Just stupidly running in headlong into a fight or confrontation isn't brave or courageous, if you don't understand what could occur. You see, it's the brave or courageous dude that KNOWS his ass could or probably will get kicked or even killed that stills goes in. You see? Its knowing the dire or fatal consequence in advance and still going in to the fight that makes one courageous. Anyone can thoughtlessly attack another. It's the intelligence of understanding our mortality...our humanness... our weaknesses... that produces real courage."

"Wow... that was nice Big Jr. I never really thought about it like that, but it makes sense. Still, I could never do that. Show that kind of courage." C. J. frowned.

"Dude, are you kidding me? You just did earlier when you told me about your sexuality... might have been the bravest thing I'd ever seen."

C.J. grinned from ear to ear. It brought joy to his heart and spirit to hear his idol and mentor say that. Earlier, he felt shame at having confessed his homosexuality. Now he swelled with pride knowing that maybe he was courageous after all.

However, the serene moment was abruptly ended when they saw the front porch light flash on. The door opened and a middle-age man in decent shape emerged staring at them. He was gripping a baseball bat.

"Oh shit! It's the Reverend Miller! Fuck, we got to get the hell outta here!" Big Jr. screamed starting the engine.

"We running, Big Jr.?" C.J. inquired incredulously.

"Damn right, we running! I don't mess with a minster! A man of God! Call the boys and tell them to haul ass out of the back yard and to run to the street behind them. I'll pick them up!"

The Gran Torino screeched rubber pulling out of Melrose and making a hard left onto Weil Lane. C.J. looked back at the figure standing in the middle of the road pointing his bat at them. *Damn, I think he's screaming at us! I can't believe the balls on that white dude to walk out of his comfortable, suburban home to physically confront strangers in a car clearly not from around here. Why wouldn't he just call the cops like most rational guys at his age and his background? Is he really stupid or really brave?*

"Big Jr., would you say that white dude was stupid or brave?"

"Fuck, you kidding me, that preacher has HUGE stones! Look, don't ever mess with men or women of God!"

"Why? What makes them so special?"

"Because they don't fear death! Know what I mean? They know this life on Earth is temporary and they'll be rewarded with a rich, beautiful afterlife for standing up to evil in righteousness!"

"Damn, Big Jr., you sound religious."

"I don't know about all of that, but my grandmamma taught me the Bible and shit, and from what she told me, what I've read… shit, those men and women of God, of the faith, brave as hell!"

Big Jr. turned left onto Hickory Hill and spotted two figures running in the street toward them. Slowing the car, the boys quickly scampered in. Settling back in their seats and breathing heavily, the two looked in wonder at the big man gripping the wheel.

"Big Jr., what the hell? What happened? You look like you seen a damn ghost!" Jumpy blurted out.

"Maybe I did… maybe I did. More like the Holy Ghost." Big Jr. mumbled.

"What the hell you talking about?" Wheels joined in.

"Guys we were visited by God!" C.J. exclaimed in merriment.

"What?" Jumpy shouted in confusion.

"Never mind about all that! Let's just say, we've had a change in plans. An audible to the original plan. I'm calling the informant to see if there might be another place in town that our white rabbit may have hopped off to." Big Jr. replied punching the phone number of Detective Stevens.

"Hey C.J. what's all this shit about seeing God?" Jumpy whispered.

"Well it appears that the father of our white rabbit is man of the cloth, a minister and Big Jr. fears those guys like a pedophile on Judgement Day!"

"Why? They just weak-ass talkers. Don't none of them fight. Least not any I know."

"How many ministers do you know? I mean, real preachers, not some talk-show hucksters we occasionally see trolling around the Zone looking for 'spiritual healing' through our drugs."

"They the only preachers I know. You know those two faggot guys that claim they are men of God, but they suck your damn dick to get a damn eight ball, am I right, Wheels?"

"Fucking straight. Nobody's afraid of those homo's! Hell, only thing I would fear from them is that they may give me some damn disease!" Wheels laughed.

"Yeah, what kind of disease would that be?"

"Fucking AIDS, man!" Wheels retorted.

"How would that happen? You plan on fucking them?" C.J. countered with a smirk.

"Hey, you better watch your ass, C.J.! Don't give me none of that homo shit! I fuck the ladies left and right back home!"

"Yes, I'm sure they're thrilled by your two-minute pump-action performance." C.J. stated tersely prompting Jumpy to crack up laughing.

"Hey, shut the fuck up, back there! The ladies love me, and you know it! You two faggots are just jealous!"

"You're absolutely correct, Wheels. I do wish I could win over the affection of 'One Tooth Sarah' or 'Milk-Duds Mikayla' who hasn't worn a bra in forty years. Those two exquisite beauties are the envy of Apartment 121." C.J. added sarcastically.

"Damn, Wheels, Dark Chocolate done toasted your ass!" Jumpy mocked.

"Oh yeah, well as soon as Big Jr. stops this damn car, I'm going to pound the dark chocolate outta Dark Chocolate!"

"Nobody's doing shit! I just got off the phone with our informant, and he says, our boy is most likely at a place called Shearer's Field. It's north west and about ten miles from here… in a little area called Keene. Boys you're about to enter a whole other type of world… rural America." Big Jr. smiled.

"Strangers in a strange land…" C.J. muttered staring out the window.

Chapter 9

"Success is not final, failure is not fatal: it is the courage to continue that counts."
— Winston Churchill

The drive to Sean Shearer's farm took about fifteen minutes from the Miller house in Nicholasville. The farm lay just on the outskirts of town about eight miles due west toward Woodford County. Sean Shearer had been a local legendary football player about twenty years ago at Jessamine County High School. During his reign in school, his parents held bonfires out on the back fifty, of a two-hundred-acre farm. It was a quasi-school event that was just for the students. No parents, faculty or administration were allowed. It was organized and run by the senior class with the cooperation of Sean's parents, David and Martha, who parked at the entrance to the field and checked for alcohol or any other drugs. They were determined to have a good clean party especially since David was a deacon at First Baptist Church of Nicholasville. School pride and spirit filled the air with the roar of the fire, cheers, chants and the fight song. Sean's parents patrolled the field just outside the clearing perimeter with their lights on as a reminder of their presence. The party began just as it got dark and lasted until midnight when David flashed his headlights and ran a hose to put out the bonfire. All who attended thought it was the best way to kick off the football season and passed the tradition and torch on to each new senior class for the next ten years.

The trek to Shearer's Field, as it came to be known, became a tradition and rite of passage. Many kids looked forward to high school just, so they could attend this storied event. The Shearer's enjoyed playing host to such a prestigious affair as each year the party got bigger and the tales about what happened got crazier. However, tragedy struck when Sean was killed by a drunk driver. Devastated by the death of their son, the Shearer's tried to continue the annual affair but their heart wasn't in it and they stopped hosting the event. Months later, David died from a stroke and Martha shut herself off from the world. The tradition was too important to die out and each year the students returned both past and present with the party becoming more raucous without any supervision.

Jack drove down Route 169 and then turned left onto Keene Troy Pike. Slowing his speed, he remembered how crazy and dangerous this road was on a Friday night as drunk teenagers hit the road. Surprisingly, law enforcement rarely ventured out to patrol for drunk drivers. It would have been an easy jack-pot. However, since it had become a county tradition and many of the local politician's children often attended these soirees, it would have been an unnecessary source of embarrassment for everyone.

Tragically, the sheriff's department only showed up when the inevitable car crash occurred on Keene Troy Pike. Jack certainly had his fair share of wobbly rides home from Shearer Field. *Man, if roads could speak, there's no telling what sad, sordid tales would come from this place* Jack smiled. *Too many rough but very memorable nights out here. Seems like, every Friday night something wild happens out here. Must be the free flow of booze, drugs, music and loss of inhibition. One thing's for sure, you'll never catch Joseph out here! Can't believe he won't help!* Jack frowned.

Turning left onto an unmarked dirt road, the deep-rutted path slowed low riding cars. Winding down the narrow one-way trail was difficult to navigate when large numbers arrived. Fortunately for traffic sake, visitors usually arrived around eight and trickled out around two in the morning. There were a few carved out shoulders along the rustic path allowing for head on traffic to proceed. Rarely was it an issue as most people arrived and left at the same time.

Working his way through the wooded trek, Jack merged into a vast open expanse. To his right, he spotted fierce flames flickering upward to attack the darkness evincing scores of youth packed beneath its sensual glow. A gentle slope ran towards a lofty peak that opened to, yet another lea surrounded by woods. Jack knew his small car could never traverse the slope, so he veered to the right side where scores of vehicles dotted the field.

He arrived much later than he intended. A phone call from Tater forced him to drive to UK's campus to settle a dispute with their Korean neighbors about a mail mix up. Unfortunately, Rick was in Louisville attending a funeral and unavailable to calm the turbulent relationship between Tater and the Asians. Tater instigated most of the encounters as he had a low tolerance for their broken English and cooking that filtered throughout the apartments.

However, many of Tater's clashes with the "Asian Three" — as Tater ascribed them— came from his drinking binges that left him disoriented and banging on their door late at night. When they opened the door, Tater barged in angrily cursing them for changing the locks on the door before crashing in a corner to fall asleep. He would apologize profusely the next day, but his bullied neighbors harbored resentment at this weekly occurrence. Usually either Jack or Rick would help Tater back to the right apartment to avoid the misunderstanding.

The latest dispute erupted around seven o'clock as Tater accused the "Asian Three" of stealing his mail. Jack arrived as the Asians were threatening to call the police. Fortunately, the missing mail was located under the stairwell in the hall— likely left from another debauched encounter from a previous night. The Lexington diversion pushed back Jack's timeline. He had hoped to find Bobby Joe Bradley before he left for a repo— at least that's what his nightmare had forecasted.

Jumping out of his car and weaving through the maze of assorted cars and trucks, Jack noticed a dark sports car with tinted windows parked away from the others. He glimpsed smoke circling out of the driver's side window. The car had an eerie familiarity that Jack couldn't quite place. His mind shot back to the present as a teenage girl bumped into him fleeing and giggling from another eager teen.

The back area of the field was the sight of many sexual rendezvouses mostly in cars but sometimes just on blankets. *Oh wow, those two are really going at it! They are either really drunk or hopped up on something cause they are oblivious to me walking past them. Kids these days!* Jack mused repeating the oft heard phrase of his grandmother. Scaling the sloped hill, Jack felt the warmth of the blazing bonfire. He watched as a handful of boys tossed more wooden pallets into the fire. Coming into the light he recognized many familiar faces from his high school days. He made the cursory stop and catch-up with each clique that was somehow still intact.

Old wounds and bruised egos were still in play. Jack marveled at the intensity of each re-telling of a high school clash that continued to engage the crowd. *My God, these guys really need to move on with their lives! That happened years ago. They need to leave Nicholasville and meet other people that they can piss off!* Jack thought to himself. He knew it was better to stay silent lest he be sucked into the high school vortex.

Scanning the crowd, Jack spotted the Barnes twins, Todd and Scott, drinking cold beer out of their truck. He loved hanging out with the brothers as varsity baseball teammates. Like most of his high school friends, he had known them since elementary school but hadn't seen them since high school. He was eager to catch-up with old war stories on the diamond; hear what they were presently doing and hopefully find out if Bobby Joe was there.

"What's up guys!" Jack screamed approaching the brothers and receiving the obligatory bro hugs.

"Not a damn thing, Hollywood!" Todd responded.

"Oh damn, hadn't heard that name in a while!" Jack laughed.

"Hey Hollywood, we heard some crazy shit about your brother Luke in the Zone last night." Scott offered.

"You did? Like what?" Jack frowned. He could feel his body tense up with a nervousness that caused him to start visibly shaking. It was an embarrassing tic Jack hoped he had outgrown.

"Oh, some stupid crap that he was selling some wild shit and got into a little trouble."

"Oh wow… hadn't heard that. Where did you hear that?"

"From that idiot, Four-Square!" Todd countered with a laugh.

"Oh well… Four Square…damn that's a reliable source!" Jack cracked instantly feeling the tension ebb. "That little fucker hears drug raids every time the wood on the fire cracks. He shits his pants and runs around telling everyone to swallow their shit or…"

"They'll get busted and do twenty years!" the Barnes boys echoed that last phrase in laughter as it was a well-known joke at Shearer Field.

William Basil Eugene Hawthorne, aka "Four Square", was a small bodied, big-headed toad that was constantly in the elementary school principal's office for fighting. Due to his lack of size, Four Square felt the need to challenge every boy to a fight to avoid being picked on. His scruffy appearance and large head made him an easy target for schoolyard bullies. To avoid the inevitable encounters, Four Square initiated fights and established a fearless reputation. But the nickname came from his intense affection for the playground game. He was an enthusiastic player who quickly achieved the coveted first square that served the ball. Once entrenched, he rarely relinquished his spot. He had quick hands and a fearless spike that won him his title. Sadly, Four Square peaked in sixth grade and never grew physically, emotionally or intellectually. He struggled to find his way in high school, eventually turning to drugs before being expelled for selling on campus. He became a permanent fixture at Shearer Field with an open market of eager teens.

"So, Four Square's still here?" Jack inquired.

"Hell yeah, he's out back by the woods plying his trade." Scott scoffed taking a big swig from his beer.

"Did he say anything else? Like what Luke was supposedly selling and what he was doing in the Zone?"

"Nah…nobody believes any of the shit that comes out of that dumbass's mouth!" Todd added. "But I have to admit, he tells some funny-ass stories and cracks me up!"

"Oh, dude is stupid as shit…always high as hell, but damn… so funny!" Scott inserted. "Hell, there he goes now stumbling and bumbling around selling his shit!"

"Wow…that's crazy!" Jack marveled as Todd tossed him a beer out of his cooler. "Thanks buddy! You guys seen Luke here tonight?"

"Uhh… yeah I saw him here a while ago. He was with Simon. Fat fuck is selling Eight Balls!" Scott warned.

"What? Are you serious? He's selling coke around here?"

"Hell yeah, and for eighty bucks! Dude this place is going to, for real, get raided and ultimately shut down if we don't get rid of dumbasses like Simon and Four Square! I'm serious, I work my ass off all week and rarely get a chance to come out here and, you know, drink a few beers, shoot the shit, just hang with the boys and damn if those two don't ruin it!"

"They're not the only ones. Bobby Joe and his crew are always here as well!" Todd added.

"Bobby Joe's here? Where?"

"Back in the woods where all those big-ass trucks are. Robbie and, your boy, Conrad are usually with him."

"Yeah… my boy Conrad." Jack mumbled thinking of his old grade school nemesis and rival. "Where did you last see Luke and Simon?"

"Dude, I'm pretty sure they were walking back to the woods where Bobby Joe's set up!"

"Alright, thanks for the brew. I'm going head over there and see if I can't find Luke. Later guys!" Jack pivoted and headed out towards the dark open expanse.

Squinting his eyes, he could see a small fire encircled by several large off-road trucks. However, as he got closer, he heard many voices and saw figures standing near the fire or sitting in the back of the trucks.

The back wooded area of Shearer Field had always been reserved for the older crowd. High schoolers rarely ventured this far back for fear of what would happen. For years, the older kids spread stories that teenagers got lost coming back to this side of the farm. The fables kept the field segregated— though not free of trouble. It was not unusual for the older kids, inebriated, to trek back to the bonfire and mingle with the teenage girls.

This is eerily familiar. I think I recognize that little shit Conrad sitting on a cooler on the back of a huge truck… and looks like long neck Robbie skulking around another truck. There's more people back here than I thought. So many dark figures moving about. This is just about the time to DUCK! Jack quickly lowered his head as an empty beer can flew over. A chorus of laughter ensued as Jack lifted his head back up and eyed Conrad.

"Wow Jack…pretty impressive for a little punk college boy. What are you doing back here?" Conrad sneered.

"I see you're still hiding in the dark throwing stuff at people. That's weak, Connie!" Jack retorted feeling his temper rise.

"Look bitch, you know not to call me that!" Conrad called out as he stood atop the truck's tailgate.

"Dude, calm down… just came back here looking for Bobby Joe." Jack stated flatly trying not to escalate the scene. *I didn't come back here to settle old scores with that little jerk. Think bigger picture Jack!* "The Barnes boys said he was back here. Relax."

"Sit down, Conrad! Damn, you two kill me. It's been years since you guys have seen each other, and you go right back to your school day shit. You guys kill me!" Bobby Joe laughed as he stepped out of his truck. "Get over here Jack!" Bobby Joe smiled and bear-hugged his former basketball teammate.

"Damn Bobby Joe, look at you… you're huge! I'm mean shit, you look like a pro wrestler. You hitting the 'roids?" Jack cracked. *Damn… right out of my dream! I haven't seen this big joker in years and he looks exactly as I imagined.*

"Nah, no 'roids Mill. Just a healthy lifestyle with plenty of twelve-ounce curls!" Bobby Joe motioned with a beer in his fist. "Whatcha up to brother? Looks like you've put on a few pounds!" He added slapping Jack's abs.

"Shit… been working out, too!"

"Still looks like a pussy to me!" Conrad insisted still standing on the truck.

"Why are you still standing up there? Don't want to have to look up at me from the ground?"

"Fuck you Jack!"

"Alright, I see some things never change. Come on Jack, let's talk." Bobby Joe swung his arm around Jack's shoulders leading him towards the woods. "What's up bro? Why are you out here? You haven't been here in years."

"Yeah, I know… damn it's good to see you!" Jack stalled not sure how to proceed. *I can't put my finger on it, but there's something different about him. He's not quite how I imagined him in the nightmare… not sure what it is… but, what the hell, everything in that damn nightmare has come true. I have to trust the premonition Bobby Joe. Besides, there's no time.* "Look, this is all going to sound really weird and I know we haven't seen each other in years, but you know me. You know I'm not some flakey dude or hopped up on drugs or anything like that. I… I had a crazy dream a couple of nights ago about witnessing a few murders in the Zone and this huge black drug lord, named Marcus X, sent a posse of thugs after me and you helped me…" Jack unloaded feeling a large burden had been lifted.

He looked at Bobby Joe but couldn't get a feel for his reaction. After a few more seconds passed in silence, Jack added, "Did you hear me Bobby Joe?"

"Yeah… yeah I heard ya! Just trying to make sense of it all. Shit Jack, you're messing with me aren't ya!" Bobby Joe smiled and playfully shoved Jack.

"No, Bobby Joe… I'm not joking. Look, the dream happened a few nights ago and instead of me witnessing a few murders, it was Luke!"

"Luke witnessed murders in the Zone?"

"No… there were no murders. He did things different than I did in the dream, so no one got killed…"

"Wait, you had a dream about murders in the Zone, but it wasn't you, it was Luke?"

"In the dream it was me, but in reality, the guy who would experience everything I did, was my brother, Luke, not me."

"How do you know?"

"Cause in reality, the guy flirting with this beautiful red-head, who gets murdered, was not me. It was Luke. Everything that I dreamed has occurred exactly as I saw it...just with Luke, not me."

"Is the hot red-head dead?"

"No."

"I thought you said everything happened exactly as you dreamed it?"

"Well, not exactly. Turns out Luke and I are pretty different."

"I'll say. Like night and day."

"What's that mean?" Jack asked defensively.

"Easy Jack. No offense, but you guys react differently to things. In sports you all are similar. Both hot heads that blow up quickly, but you calm down... don't take things personally or even hold a grudge after the game. But Luke... damn that boy's looking to take someone down. He wants to fight. He wants to prove he's the better man or some shit like that. You two are just wired differently. Just curious, why did the hottie die in your dream, but she didn't with Luke?"

"I'm not sure...well, let's just say we had different approaches to the same event. His worked out better."

"Okay... so what's the problem. No murder, no problem."

"Not exactly. Those guys are after him. They chased after him, but he got away."

"Do they know who he is?"

"I'm sure they saw him going in and out of apartment 121 in the Zone. They must know..."

"Did you say apartment 121?"

"Yeah, why?"

"Oh... nothing. Just weird that you mentioned the specific number."

"Yeah, well that's another weird thing. That number seemed to come up a lot in my dream."

"You saw a specific number several times in a dream?" Bobby Joe asked warily. "Hey, speak of the devil. There's your brother now. Over by those trucks to the right."

"Hang on Bobby Joe, I've got to go talk to him real quick."

Jack sprinted across the open field and off to the tree-lined woods near a creek. He could see that Luke was with a smaller stout guy. *Simon! Shit, why is Luke with that dude all the time. I've got to convince him that Simon is a loser. He's a problem not a solution.*

"Hey Luke!" Jack called out slowing to a trot.

"Jack... what the hell are you doing out here?" Luke asked in annoyance.

"Yeah, Jack this isn't your kind of place?" Simon added with a twisted smile.

"Yeah well... Luke I need to talk to you alone."

"Oh, some Miller secrets?"

"Yeah something like that. Luke?"

"Sure." Luke grudgingly allowed and walked over towards the creek with Jack for privacy. "What's up? Dad send you? I've already had a long talk with him and we're cool."

"Great. But dad didn't send me. I have to warn you…"

"Oh, shit Jack, not the damn dream again."

"Yeah, the damn dream that has come true. Luke, I know you were in the Zone last night and some crazy stuff happened. Just as I said it would."

"How do you know I was in the Zone?"

"Not important. Look, tonight's the night that everything bad happens!"

"For you… in the dream! Not me! Hey, I'll admit a lot of what you predicted, did happen. I can't explain how you knew. It's bizarre to say the least, but in your dream, Candace died. She didn't. I took her home last night and she is presently in the hospital with her mother."

"She's in the hospital? What happened to her mother?"

"Someone broke in their apartment an attacked her… anyway not relevant. Candace is okay."

"I'm glad about that but those guys are not going to let you get away with taking Candace and her daughter out like that. They're going to chase after you."

"How did know about her daughter?"

"It was in the dream. Anyway, they're probably sniffing around town now looking for you. Did you attack anyone or… kill anyone last night?"

"This is so weird that you know any of this…damn." Luke scratched his head looking at an impatient Simon signaling him to leave. "Look, I did hit a few guys. I busted a huge black dude with a bat and another tall kid near the door, but no one was killed and I'm pretty sure no one saw my face and they sure wouldn't know who I am."

"Luke there were cops at the house earlier tonight, remember? That means they know who you are?"

"You're saying the cops are dirty? That they're in on this?"

"They were in the dream."

"Look, I gotta go. Simon needs me to help him do a few things tonight?"

"What? Sell more drugs?"

"I'm not, but… yeah he's in a pinch financially to some guys and came into a stash of coke that he needs to drop and turn real quick. It's just a one-time thing."

"Yeah right! Damn Luke, look at who you're hanging out with… a fucking druggie loser!"

"He's my friend and I won't desert him just because he does things differently. You and Joseph are too judgmental!"

"We don't want you hanging out with the wrong guys that will lead you into trouble!" Jack pleaded as Luke turned and walked away. "Hold up!

Look I obviously can't stop you from doing this but… tonight you will arrive at an ugly rundown laundromat in a scuzzy area of Lexington. The big boss himself, dude named Marcus X, will be there. You'll know its him because he looks exactly like Denzel Washington. Luke, you can't be there! You must run! It's a trap! Trust me!" Jack called out as Luke turned his back again and waved off his hand at his brother's warning.

"He looks like Denzel Washington? Really, Jack? You've been watching too many movies. It's gone to your damn head!" Luke called back.

"Have any of my dreams and predictions been wrong? Huh, Luke? I'm telling you, the worst of the dream occurs tonight! Don't get trapped in the laundromat!" Jack shouted in frustration. *Damn that kid's stubborn! Won't listen to anything I tell him. Gotta go get Bobby Joe to help me.*

❧ ❧ ❧ ❧ ❧ ❧ ❧

Big Jr. continued to drag heavily on his Pall Mall enjoying the serenity of the rustic rural setting. Inhaling the fresh cut grass of the field, listening to the chirping of cicadas as a cool gentle breeze swept across his face, he knew it couldn't get better than this. The piece of land he had in mind was only a few miles west of this field. He had no idea that the local teens used this area as a modern-day Gomorrah. *Damn, aint it just like white people to destroy a black man's dream! I just want a nice piece of the American pie to grow a few crops and make a decent living while living out here in this beautiful place and now this. Stupid-ass kids getting their minds fucked up and banging each other in my rural dream. Ha, ha… look at me acting all moral. White rich kids are no different from other kids their age… looking for different ways to get fucked up and get laid!* Big Jr. nodded his head at the absurdity of his moralization. The pastoral setting took him temporarily away from the mission to his utopian fantasy.

"Big Jr.? Can you explain to me again, why we ran from an old white man back in town?" Jumpy implored breaking the silence of the car with his high-pitched voice.

"No."

"Why?"

"Because you're a moron! You'd never understand, and I don't feel like wasting my breath."

"Damn, Big Jr. that's harsh. Jumpy's just asking a question. You aint gotta insult him like that." Wheels meekly responded.

"It's not an insult. It's a fact. You guys are simply ignorant. You talk all the time and never listen. You should close your mouth more often and open your eyes and ears instead."

"What… like Dark Chocolate back here? He doesn't talk much because he aint got nothing to say and knows he'd get his ass kicked if he did say something! Aint that right Dark Chocolate? Damn, is he back there, cause I can't see shit!" Wheels added with a laugh.

"Hey cut the chatter. Keep your eyes on the beat-up Civic."

"Big Jr. we've been out here a long time and seen no one. We've seen several cars exit recently. Is it possible that our guy has left in another car?" C.J. inquired ignoring the insults.

"Now that's an intelligent observation. Yes, it is entirely possible that our target has left. To make sure, you guys need to walk around the parking area here looking for him. If you need to, ask a few people if they've seen Luke Miller, but don't start anything and for God's sake keep your cool. C.J. go with them. I'll stay back and watch the car."

"You aint coming?"

"Hell no! Nothing scares little white kids more than a three hundred pound, grown-ass black man skulking around in the dark."

"Good point. Let's work our way through the parking lot towards the bonfire."

"Good point!" Jumpy mocked slamming the door. "Look Dark Chocolate, you aint in charge."

"Yes, he is! Shut the hell up and listen to him!" Big Jr. warned with a serious expression that the boys knew not to challenge.

❧ ❧ ❧ ❧ ❧ ❧ ❧

"Jack, I'd love to help you. Even though that dream of yours is pretty fucked up. But I gotta standby in case a repo call comes in. You know I've got a pretty successful towing service here in town."

"Yeah, it's called Five Star." Jack retorted.

"How the hell did you know that? I just changed the name a few months ago to avoid some debts and such."

"The dream. I told you. That stuff is real…"

The roar of a motorcycle broke through the night air as a pink clad figure raced to the top of the upper field and ran a few loops encircling the older crowd. A long blonde pony-tail bounced underneath the helmet as the cyclist pulled up in front of Bobby Joe revving the engine. Dropping the kick stand down, Jack saw a beautiful face emerge from beneath the helmet.

"Who's that?" Jack asked.

"That Jack old boy, is Nikki Wolfe."

"She from around here?"

"Yep, you wouldn't know it but she's a senior at the high school!"

"Yeah, Conrad's old girlfriend!" Robbie announced looking back at the truck.

"Shut the hell up Robbie!"

"Oh, that's right, you guys never dated cause she kicked your ass!" Robbie continued.

"Bullshit!"

"What they're talking about, Jack, was an unfortunate misunderstanding. Our boy, Conrad, made the mistake of assuming our badass motorcyclist was some little bimbo high schooler he could mess with...our girl here, showed him differently."

"Damn straight! Conrad got on the bike with her and tried one of his patented breast grabs and she busted him!" Robbie laughed.

"What did she do?"

"None of your damn business, Jack!" Conrad called out jumping down off the truck.

"She grabbed his balls and twisted them." Bobby Joe stated flatly.

"Oh my God the funniest thing I ever saw. He fucking squealed like a pig!" Robbie roared with laughter.

"And I'll do it again, if he tries to get fresh!" Nikki joined in staring at Conrad who lowered his head.

"Nikki Wolfe, meet Jack Miller." Bobby Joe introduced.

"I know who Jack is." Nikki stated shaking Jack's hand. "He once dated my big sister, Rebecca, in high school."

"Uhh... it was one date and it was seventh grade. Rebecca transferred to another school and I never saw her again. Wow, you're her sister. Didn't know she had a sister."

"Yeah, I'm sure she wouldn't have mentioned me. We don't always see eye to eye on things." Nikki winked.

"Nikki occasionally helps me at the shop and sometimes on a few repos." Bobby Joe said.

"You take a high school girl on a repo?"

"She's eighteen and, as you can see, fearless as hell and great on a motorcycle. She's easy on the eyes and a great distraction while the boys are hooking up a repo. Hell, by the time she's done with them, they don't care about losing the car. They just want her to come back!" Bobby Joe laughed.

"Craziest thing I ever saw!" Robbie added. "Conrad and me, have their car hooked up and dudes don't even care. Just watch her riding off on her Harley! Screaming at her to come back!"

"A real badass, huh!" Jack gaped.

"You wanna take a ride Jack? Or does a lady in charge scare ya?"

"No... I mean, yes. I'll ride with you." Jack allowed as he followed her over to her bike.

Sliding her helmet over her silky blonde hair and straddling the big hog, Jack stared in awe at this beautiful confident teenager. Climbing on behind her, Jack nervously fidgeted his hands about not knowing exactly how to hold on without offending. Nikki grabbed his hands and wrapped them tightly around her waist.

"Don't worry Jack, I don't bite! At least not on the first date!" Nikki cracked as she revved the engine and spun out into the open field.

ఆ ఆ ఆ ఆ ఆ ఆ ఆ

C.J. and his compadres felt strangely out of place in this exotic rural backdrop. The stillness of the night air in tranquility spooked the boys who were raised on noisy streets of the city. The hustle and bustle of the urban milieu soothed their youthful vigor as it was a familiar voice they had known since birth. Walking late at night in the city was natural and easy, but strolling through the fields in the dark, evoked an eerie sense of foreboding.

"Man, this place gives me the willies! Too damn quiet and dark." Wheels stated breaking the silence as they strolled through and around various people engaging in nocturnal activities. "Did you hear me C.J.? Damn where'd he go? Smile C.J. so I can see ya?"

"Shut up Wheels! That's getting old real quick and for once I agree with you… this place is eerie. Can't quite put my finger on it but…"

"It's like, I don't know, too damn peaceful. Like something crazy's gonna jump up on you any minute!" Jumpy added.

"Yeah… fuck all this quiet shit. Wait… listen… I hear a damn motorcycle. Now that's more like it! Love the rumble of a Harley sportster with a 1200 engine!" Wheels exclaimed.

"How the hell do you know that?" C.J. implored slightly impressed.

"I know things Dark Chocolate. You aint the only guy who reads shit. One day I'm gonna buy one of those big hogs!"

"Wow… I'm blown away by all these kids fucking outside! I didn't realize white kids were this crazy!" Jumpy stated incredulously.

"You didn't think white people liked sex?" C.J. replied.

"No, I didn't mean that. I meant that they got their freak on outside and in the grass and shit. Crazy wild."

"Look, all these white dudes look the same. Anyone of them could be our boy. Why don't we just ask around and cut to the chase?" Wheels asked.

"Now that's an intelligent observation." C.J. stated in an obvious reference to Big Jr.

"Good. Now who do we ask?"

"Well, we probably shouldn't bother the ones rolling around on the grass. Let's go up the hill to the bonfire. There's a lot people and our boy could be one of them." C.J. directed.

The boys lumbered up the hill following C.J.'s lead. They hated to acknowledge him as a leader because he wasn't a fighter. In their rough world, leaders were uninhibited brawlers— guys who fearlessly attacked and never asked questions— never worried about the consequences or risks involved. C.J. was different— a sensitive, reflective boy with a keen intellect and an inquisitive nature. His meekness in a scrap made him disliked and distrusted in the feral pack. However, he was Big Jr.'s favorite and therefore off limits to abuse. Though the boys envied his position with Big Jr., they grudgingly acknowledged his intelligence, and often deferred to his decisions when Big Jr. wasn't around.

The tall thin figure strolled confidently to the bonfire site trailed by his two hyperactive companions. Scanning the raucous horde of teens, C.J. searched for a tall white boy roughly matching Luke's description. *Wow... this is going to be tougher than I thought. All these kids kinda fit Big Jr's description of Luke Miller. I hate to be stereotypical, but for once Jumpy may be right... all white kids DO look alike! Need to walk around, blend in and try to hear someone mention his name.*

"Guys, we need to circulate around the fire. Kind of blend in and try to hear what people are saying. Maybe his name will come up." C.J. instructed.

"How the hell do three street negroes blend into this country fuck crowd?" Jumpy implored.

"Well, first we need to split up. I think the sight of the three of us together will scare this crowd. Besides its dark and they've been drinking. I'm sure their cognitive abilities are quite inhibited." C.J. responded flatly.

"Cog-ni-tities? What the hell you talking about C.J.?" Jumpy frowned.

"Cognitive... their ability to think and reason. You know...well I take that back, you wouldn't know. Anyway, spread out, circulate, listen in on conversations but don't engage. We don't want to draw attention or cause a scene. Just locate Luke and follow him."

The boys broke out into different directions trying to keep a low profile. Wheels was drawn to the sound of the motorcycle and walked toward the vast expanse catching glimpses of two figures astride a Harley darting about. He could just make out the driver in splashes of pink with a blonde ponytail whipping about. The second figure holding on appeared to be much larger. He heard screams of laughter and terror bounding about in the dark. He wanted to be riding that bike. For a moment, he escaped the present to imagine himself driving that motorcycle.

Jumpy nervously poked his head in and out of conversations occasionally drawing strange looks. It was difficult for him to stay inconspicuous. He had a quick temper that flared over any slight— especially from white boys.

As a poor child sent to a predominately white public school, Jumpy felt isolated and bullied by white boys who teased him about his worn and tattered clothes. Often in and out of the principal's office for fighting, Jumpy developed a hatred for all white kids based on his interactions with them in school. He refused to be a bullied victim, so he terrorized them. When he played games on the playground, he sought opportunities to embarrass the white kids. Gifted athletically, he could defeat them in every game that required speed and agility. However, any games that involved cognition, he struggled and was teased relentlessly. He knew he could best them in the athletic arena, but there seemed to be no lasting reward for that feat as he was never academically eligible for school sport's teams.

Dropping out of school was easy because he never fit in, and his aunt couldn't care less. She was his only living relative and struggled with her own addictions. Caught up in the dizzying drug dens of the Zone, she resorted to prostitution to put food on the table. She introduced her nephew to Big Jr. to pay off a drug debt. His athletic abilities finally paid dividends as courier and runner. Once entangled in the Zone, Jumpy found the family and acceptance he had so sorely needed. He would fight to defend them and their lifestyle as it was the only one he knew that accepted him.

"Hey, what's up?" Jumpy asked a mixed group of teens gathered around the blazing bonfire.

The teens stared at him and returned to their conversations. Jumpy shook his head and moved around to another more boisterous group. The center of attention had a large head atop a small frame and flitted about in an animated story. Small in stature, the mop top youth had a big personality and would be the perfect person to ask about Luke Miller. Leaning in to the group dynamic, Jumpy laughed and smiled with each gesture. Hoping he had sufficiently joined the group, Jumpy plunged forward with his mission.

"What's up guys? How y'all doing?" Jumpy asked in his best country accent.

"Y'all? Do you live around here?" the mop top, aka Four Square, mocked.

"Nah... I'm from Bryan Station. Name's Larry White...ey" Jumpy improvised.

"White...ey. That's a strange name for you isn't it?" Four Square added to a chorus of laughter. "Hi! My name's Poon." Stretching his hand out to shake.

"Poon? Is that your first or last name?" Jumpy asked shaking the jester's hand.

"Yes."

"Yes? How do you spell it?"

"Like spoon."

"Oh... except without the 's'."

"No, it still has the 's'. It's silent." Four Square deadpanned as a large crowd encircled them eager for something to happen.

"What? That's crazy!" Jumpy smiled trying to follow the conversation. "What's the ethnic origin of Poon?"

"Comanche."

"You don't look Indian."

"You don't look white?"

"I'm not white."

"Exactly."

Jumpy felt the increased crowd's presence and was embarrassed by the roar of laughter. Looking around, he saw scores of white kids about him with grinning faces. Instantly he had returned to the schoolyard taunts and teases. Feeling his temper rise, he swung Four Square around by the shoulders to face him.

"Hey funny boy, do you know Luke Miller?"

"Luke Milner?" Four Square laughed. "Nah... never heard of anybody by that name. What about it guys? Anyone here heard of Luke Milner?"

"Miller, ass wipe! I said, Miller!"

"Oh...Miller. Miller Milner? Strange name... anyone heard of Miller Milner?"

"Okay bobblehead, I gave you a chance to be cool... but you couldn't do that, could you?" Jumpy growled as he grabbed Four Square's arm and twisted it behind his back. Pulling his arm up, Jumpy heard a slight yelp, but not the scream he had expected. *This fucking little white dude's pretty tough or stoned out of his mind cause I've got a tight grip on him. Little shit isn't screaming or squirming like most white boys! May have to work him over a bit.*

Several teens pleaded with the intruder to let their friend go. C.J. and Wheels quickly ran over to the melee to help their comrade. Leaning over the crowd of teens, C.J. called out for calm. He tried to reassure the high schoolers that they just wanted to talk to Luke and nothing more.

"If that's true, why is that idiot breaking Four Square's arm? Seems pretty damn drastic action for just a 'talk'" Matt Foley called out in defense of his large-headed friend.

"Look, apparently your friend, insulted my friend. Not a wise thing to do. He will let him go if someone would just tell us where Luke is?"

"That's bullshit! That animal's probably looking to do worse to Luke!" Matt insisted.

Wheels ran over to Matt and spun him around before delivering a powerful punch across his face. Blood shot out of Matt's nose as Wheels slugged him again in the abdomen forcing Matt to double over to the ground. The crowd screamed obscenities at the trio of invaders and inched toward them. Jumpy twisted Four Square's arm harder forcing him to the ground, while Wheels grabbed a burning log from the raging bonfire and began swinging wildly at the crowd.

A voice from the throng cried out that Luke was behind the trio, followed by another claiming Luke was in front of them, "No!" cried out another, "He's the one on the ground!" Before long, the entire mass was chanting Luke's name over and over in mock assistance.

Nikki immediately stopped the joyride and removed her helmet to hear what she was seeing.

"Uhh…Jack, I think the kids down there are chanting your brother's name…why would they be doing that?"

"Oh shit! That's the guys from the Zone. I didn't see that coming!" Jack exclaimed.

"What do you mean, you didn't see that coming? Do you know those guys?"

"Not really. I mean…I don't know them at all, but they are chasing after my brother for something he did last night?"

"Luke? Luke did something in the Zone?"

"Yeah… I tried to warn him not to go there but… he's so damn hard-headed."

"Is Luke still here?" Nikki asked.

"No, left about 15 minutes ago. He needs more time because his meeting with Marcus X will happen…hey Nikki, I got an idea. I need to stall these thugs a little bit. They're after my brother and will be heading back to Lexington to trap him. But before all that, maybe we can buy him some time. Would you be willing to play rabbit while the wolves chase us for a while?"

"Why Jack, you're asking a Wolfe to play prey. We're predators!" Nikki laughed.

"I can see that, but tonight, let them chase you for a while. I'm sure you're used to guys chasing you around." Jack cracked.

"Oh yeah, and like these boys, they'll never catch me!" Nikki winked slamming her helmet back on and revving the engine. "Hold on tight, Jack! This is about to get crazy!"

The Harley sportster roared and raced across the upper field before circling the crowd gathered around the bonfire. Everyone stopped and stared at the biking duo that ran several laps before halting on an incline. Looking down over the crowd, Jack stood up and called out to the trio.

"Hey, you assholes looking for me? I'm Luke Miller!"

"Bullshit! Every fucking white boy here claims to be him!" Jumpy replied grabbing Four Square by the hair and pulling him up. "Hey, funny boy… is that Luke Miller?"

Squinting through watery eyes and writhing in pain, Four Square nodded yes. Wheels lowered the burning branch to Matt's face.

"Hey, country cracker, is that Luke Miller? Don't lie to me, cause if you do, I'll burn your fucking eye off!" Wheels threatened.

Before he could answer, a loud booming voice cried out from behind. A behemoth emerged from the crowd toting a forty-four ounce baseball bat. Spinning the bat like a toothpick in his hand, Big Jr. walked over to Wheels pushing him aside and swung down on Matt Foley's leg making a sickening crack. Matt screamed out in pain as Big Jr. silenced him with another crack to the head.

"If you're really Luke Miller, I suggest you come down here now so that no one else gets hurt. Like my friend said, we just want to talk, and I have something special to give back to you from last night." Big Jr. grinned.

"You want Luke Miller?" Nikki screamed. "Then you're going to have to catch him, you fat fuck!"

She raced down the incline directly at the big man. Veering hard to the right, they spun past a swinging bat. Jack looked back as the Zone figures raced after them. Nikki toyed with the men as a cat plays with a mouse as she sped up and slowed down to allow them to stay close. The big man called out to the trio to follow him to the parking lot. Nikki pulled over near the tree line that ran adjacent to the only road entrance.

"Alright Jack, you've got their attention. What now?" Nikki asked looking back.

"They're getting in that big black roadster. Think you can outrun that?"

"There aint a car made that can catch me on my sportster."

"Alright, get out in front of them and let's do some circles around Shearer Field. There's some pretty rough ground out here that might tear up or at least slowdown that beast-mobile!"

"Okay Jack, but you need to hold on real tight and lean into the turns as I do. We're going to be moving fast and you've got to anticipate my moves by feeling the motion of my body. Got it?"

"Yes…" Jack replied meekly not sure how this would play out.

Tonight, was just the second time in his life he had been on a motorcycle and wasn't thrilled with the "bunny ride" on a small field. Gripping tightly, Jack said a small pray, *Dear God please help me hang on and give Nikki guidance!*

The motorcycle's 1200 engine roared to life as Nikki sprinted across the parking lot mocking the black roadster to follow. Big Jr. cursed, gripped the wheel tight, and floored the gas pedal in hot pursuit.

"Aint no fucking way some pink chick and a little white rabbit are going to fuck me like that. I'll chase her little ass all over this country!" Big Jr. screamed.

"Damn, Big Jr.! You can't possibly catch her out here! Look how she's darting and dashing all over the field. That Harley roadster in the hands of a damn pro can't be caught out here!" Wheels called out.

"Bullshit! Look… she's heading toward that tree line. I'll pin her little ass. She's trapping herself!"

Nikki looked back briefly to make sure the roadster was still tailing her.

"Okay, Jack…lean hard right…NOW!"

The motorcycle duo drove into the woods and veered right down a narrow dirt path. The roadster stopped at the tree line and slowly entered the narrow pass. Nikki had stopped near a creek watching for the two big yellow orbs. Once the lights streaked across the arched trees, she gripped the throttle turning it down and then back up shifting gears as she crossed the dry creek bed. She led the Zone intruders through a wooded labyrinth about a quarter of a mile before circling back out and towards the upper field where Bobby Joe was leaning against his Ford 250 diesel truck.

"Hey. I'm going to lead these idiots out of the main entrance. You want to follow, and we can do that repo in Lexington? I'll lose these guys here in Keene and meet you downtown across from Rupp Arena. Don't you have a repo near there tonight?"

"Sure thing. You lead them down the entrance road and I'll box them in from behind!" Bobby Joe replied opening his driver side door.

"We don't have a repo tonight? I thought we were making a drop?" Conrad asked strapping on his seat belt.

"We do, but she doesn't know that and she aint going…neither are you."

"What? I thought…"

"Things changed. I'm taking Jack with me and you… can ride back home with your girlfriend." Bobby Joe laughed.

"She aint gonna like that!" Conrad frowned watching her lead the Zone car down the open field toward the narrow entrance.

The teenage crowd roared its approval at the epic chase of the pink biker and black roadster. Somehow the Zone car was able to stay within a hundred yards of the bike while bouncing up and down traversing the fields.

"Damn Big Jr., she's leading back to that scary-ass entrance. Aint no way we can catch her on that tiny raggedy little road." Wheels screamed.

"For once, I agree with Wheels. It's a big mistake to speed down that road in this big car. What if someone's coming in?" C.J. queried.

"They'll hit her first and will pick up Luke and drive his ass back to the Zone! Like I said, I owe his ass a beating for blindsiding me at the Box!" Big Jr. snapped.

Nikki slowed her bike through the twists and turns of the narrow, gnarled dirt road. She stopped at the top of a steep incline and saw the headlights of an incoming car. Looking back at the black Gran Torino that had sped up to catch her, she gripped down on the throttle and drove straight at the incoming lights. At the last second, she darted hard right. Caught off guard while looking back, Jack was thrown headlong into an embankment. The large car in hot pursuit quickly veered to the left but was T-boned by the oncoming pick-up truck.

Aching in pain, Jack grimaced as he rotated his arm several times to loosen the muscles. He pulled himself up to his knees and looked back toward the loud crash. Standing up and walking back a few yards, he could see a huge figure in the darkness scream at the truck driver. The truck driver screamed back with animated gestures. The large figure closed in quickly and brutally beat the man to the ground. Jack could hear the screams and pleads for mercy.

Suddenly another large truck emerged from behind the wreckage using the embankment to pass. The truck slowly approached Jack as the passenger side window eased down.

"Are you alright Jack?" Bobby Joe asked.

"Yeah…my arm's banged up a little and my head's screaming but…I'll live."

Nikki returned and spun in toward Jack.

"You should have held on tighter. Didn't you see me veering right?" Nikki asked.

"To be honest, I was looking back just as you made that move. Totally my fault!"

"Well hop on! We need to get out of here."

"Jack's riding with me Nikki. He and I need to talk. Take Conrad as your consolation prize!"

"Are you serious Bobby Joe?" Nikki barked.

"Yep. Get in Jack. See ya later Conrad. You two don't stay out too late!" Bobby Joe chuckled.

"Fuck you Bobby Joe!" Nikki growled as Conrad approached. "What the hell are you looking at? You make one false move and I'm dumping your ass on the road!"

Chapter 10

"Everyone has talent. What's rare is the courage to follow it to the dark places where it leads."

— Erica Jong

Simon needed to leave sooner rather than later. The sale of his stolen booty, cocaine, was netting too little at the teenage soiree in Keene. To make matters worse, he spotted Big Jr.'s Gran Torino at the outskirts of the parking lot in Shearer Field. In his paranoia, he assumed the top lieutenant to Marcus X was there to find and extract him back to the Zone for severe punishment.

Though he hadn't heard from Geoffrey or Marcus X about the missing cocaine the previous night, seeing Big Jr. sent his mind racing. *Oh God, they must know. They must know. Why else would Big Jr. be here. He never goes anywhere unless ordered by Marcus. I'm sure he knows I was there from that faggot Geoffrey, and Big Jr.…. he's also probably discovered that he's missing some coke from his office. And connecting two and two, he has his big-ass bear chasing me! Shit! Shit! This was not supposed to go down like this! Luke! Fucking Luke was supposed to come to apartment 121, rescue Candy and get his ass beat by Marcus X. I was just a shadow that would slip in and out with some coke; make some quick sales and pay back my debt to Marcus. Simple plan that was ruined… by Luke! Damn him! He seems to be the bane of my existence. Everything that I've wanted or loved from Janee to Candy to scoring some quick cash, he seems to have ruined. He's lived too charmed a life and must pay. I'm keeping his big butt close, so he can take the hits coming my way.*

The air in the car was as thick as the tension between the childhood friends. Simon resented Luke's family, athletic ability and rugged good looks. Luke's quiet demeanor and firm conviction bothered the unsettled, tempestuous man who had no moral compass or guidepost. His absentee parents allowed him to find his own way in the world with liberal financing until the till broke. With his father's finances in ruin, Simon sought the quick and easy road to riches ignoring all portents.

Luke resented his role as bodyguard and connection to a drug dealer. His brother's words of "guilt by association" put him a difficult position. He wanted to be a good friend without a condemning harsh judgement, but at the same time, he understood that what Simon was doing was not only wrong, but illegal, and jeopardized him as well. It was unfair for a friend to put another in this position, especially knowing how it put him at odds with his own family.

"Look Simon, I don't know if I can go with you to Lexington. Selling this shit here to teens was wrong and…"

"Dude, don't fucking preach to me. I'm not a Miller boy who has to hear his father's sermons. I get to sleep in on Sundays. Besides, we didn't sell much… I never should have come down here anyway. The risk/ reward rarely pays off. Dude… don't bail on me. I need you. As I told you before, I'm in a big debt to a bad hombre who means to hurt me. I just need to make some quick scores, so I can pay it back."

"How did you come into all that coke anyway?" Luke queried.

"I told you, I found it."

"You found all that coke… just sitting around."

"Actually, yeah. Someone must have left in a hurry and dropped a pound of coke."

"Where?"

"I told you, outside of some apartments in the Zone. I was doing a few drops and noticed this tightly wrapped brown bag near a dumpster and grabbed it. Probably a drug bust, and some dudes had to ditch the shit quick. Their loss, my gain."

"Yeah… where are we going now?" Luke asked skeptically.

"Got a couple of stops to make. Won't take long. I've already got the shit cut up into Eight Balls, so they'll be easy to sell and distribute on the street. First stop is the Red Mile. I got a distributor over there waiting on me. He called me a few minutes ago. Shouldn't take long."

Turning left off Keene Road onto Harrodsburg Road, Simon knew this would not be an easy drop. His distributor at the Red Mile, Little Billy, was difficult to deal with— demanded high quantity for little pay. He always had enough muscle around to get his price and, as a result, Simon stopped using him. With Luke at his side, he figured he could unload some of his coke at a better price. At this late hour and with Big Jr. looming, he couldn't afford to be particular.

Turning left onto Red Mile Road and then right onto Winbak Way, Simon slowed past the racetrack and back to the north parking lot.

The drop off was usually conducted by parking a few rows away from the car that had flashed their lights. Though the price had always been agreed upon in advance, Little Billy liked to shake you down for much less because he could— he had plenty of "associates" to insure his rate.

"Alright there's our boy… see that light flash? We're going to park over by that huge truck and leave the car running…"

"What? Why?"

"Just in case…Look, I'll do all the talking. You need to stand by my right side… a little behind me. Scan the area thoroughly. Sometimes Little Billy has some of his friends parked in other cars watching. They may even get out. If, and only if, that happens, you need to show them this…" Simon added pulling out a gun.

"What the hell is this?" Luke exclaimed.

"It's a Glock pistol. This is a G42 .380 AUTO. Very lightweight and dependable."

"Yeah, I get that it's a gun, and thanks for the sales pitch, but why are you handing it to me?"

"Because you're my muscle and you can't hustle unless you have muscle... and my muscle has to be armed." Simon grinned. "I just made that up. I like playing with words."

"That's cute. I'm glad you enjoyed your play on words but...man, toting a gun... that's taking everything to another level."

"Dude, that's all these guys respect...guns. Every time I made a drop here, Little Billy was armed, and I didn't have shit. But tonight, will be different... I have an armed escort and should get my price. He won't be expecting that. Just keep an alert eye to everything and anything that moves."

Luke nodded though he was unsure what to do or how to react. He shoved the gun in his back waistband, exited the car and followed Simon's lead to an old pick-up truck parked behind the car that flashed its lights. He noticed only two figures, and both were relatively short. The lead man was stout and sported a thick goatee with a wide grin beneath it. His perpetual smile betrayed a sense of overconfidence and eagerness to toy with an opponent. The man behind him was portly with an oversized neck ringed with thick skin carrying a small head and a short-cropped hair cut. The obese Weeble sat back on his heels making him slow footed, Luke observed.

"So... Simon says he needs to make a dump. I assume you need to quick cash." Little Billy smiled.

"Yeah sure, you know how it is. Money transfers quickly around to buy other things." Simon responded.

"Okay." Little Billy nodded looking at Luke trying to assess his abilities. "I see you didn't come alone. You know I don't like that... especially with guys I don't know. Who's the little shit with a snarl?"

"His name is Brad and I wouldn't disrespect him." Simon cautioned.

"Oh really... what about it 'Brad'? You a tough guy?"

Luke stared intently at Little Billy and again at his fat buddy who seemed preoccupied with cleaning his fingernails. Scanning the parking lot and seeing no unusual movements, Luke refused to be baited into a confrontation. His goal was to get the money and go. Avoid confrontation.

"What's the matter, can't your monkey talk? He likes to look, but doesn't answer when spoken to, is that it?" Little Billy taunted stepping toward Luke.

"Hey, we're here to make a drop. Let's do this shit quick so we can both go back to what we were doing. I got a half pound of Eight Balls in my jacket. Just gimme the forty-five hundred and we're out." Simon insisted.

"Forty-five hundred my ass! Your shit aint worth three thousand. I'll give you two."

"What the fuck you talking about Little Billy? We talked on the phone just thirty minutes ago and agreed on forty-five hundred."

"That was before you brought your little monkey to the show. Now the price has dropped and if you don't take two, it'll drop to one." Little Billy grinned taking his eyes off Luke.

The first blow was a vicious right cross to Little Billy's nose causing blood to shoot like a geyser. Luke followed with a second blow on top of his head. Caught flat-footed, the thick-necked associate was late to block Luke's backhand across his face. Grabbing and tossing the fat man to the ground wasn't as difficult as Luke anticipated.

Simon scrambled over to Little Billy, who was screaming about his bloody nose, and snatched a wad of bills out of his coat pocket. Counting out five thousand dollars, Simon tossed the rest of the money and his bag of Eight Balls on Little Billy's head before adding a swift kick to his ribs.

"Now what do you think? Huh? I can't hear you...too much blood all over your face. Simon says, 'you shouldn't insult his friend'. Simon says, 'that insult cost you a bloody nose and another five hundred dollars'. Come on, Brad."

Luke's adrenaline was flowing, and his spirits were soaring as he hopped about like a prize fighter hovering over his defeated foes. He never saw himself as some muscled bodyguard type, but he hated when people went back on their word and tried to bully others. He understood this was an immoral occupation with unethical thugs, but he wouldn't allow it to happen to his friend.

Assessing the damage that he had inflicted in such a short time, Luke beamed with confidence. Flexing the fingers of his right hand, he was surprised that there was no pain. Walking back to the car, Luke scanned the parking lot to make sure no surprise visitors popped up. Seeing no movements, he backed into the passenger seat.

"Damn, Luke that was AWESOME!! Fuck, I need you around more often. Word of this shit gets out and I'll have zero problems on drops. Look, dude I scored five thousand. Here's five hundred for a quick night's work!"

"Keep your money. I didn't do it to get paid."

"Shit Luke, you kill me! Fucking kill me... alright. But damn, that was sweet how quick you nailed Little Billy and that smug face of his. You fucking broke his nose! He won't have the shit-eating grin on his face anymore after tonight! That's for damn sure!" Simon exulted circling out of the back parking lot and onto Winbak Way.

Simon followed Luke's lead and kept silent. Luke wasn't the brash talker and extrovert like Simon. Whether he was scoring baskets, rebounding, blocking shots or knocking someone down a few pegs, Luke was never boastful or gloried in his successes. Unlike Jack, he was never self-assured, even when he was successful. The dynamic drug duo drove deeper into Lexington as Simon assured him he had just one more stop to make. He turned right onto Maxwell Street.

"There's a fraternity house on campus that we need to hit real quick. Dude's going to take the rest of my Eight Balls."

"Will there be any need for this?" Luke asked as he pulled the Glock out of his waistband.

"Nah… these guys are little rich pussies. You won't need a gun, especially with that quick right hand. Damn, I can't believe how fast you put those two on their asses!"

"Yeah, well…let's hope I won't have to do that again." Luke frowned looking out the window at Memorial Coliseum.

❧ ❧ ❧ ❧ ❧ ❧ ❧

Rolling out of Keene at a fast pace in Bobby Joe's F-250, Jack felt an inexplicable foreboding sweep across his body. The Bobby Joe in his dream/ premonition seemed more congenial and assuring. This Bobby Joe said the right things, but there was something different about him. Jack couldn't quite put his finger on it, but he needed to know if he could trust this Bobby Joe. The stakes were too high tonight to misjudge anyone.

"So… whatcha been doing since high school?" Jack inquired to break the silence.

"Oh… not too much." Bobby Joe replied without any sense of amplification.

"I heard you lost your scholarship at Sue Bennett? What happened?"

"What did you hear?"

"Oh, just that you got into a fight with the head coach who caught you using and selling drugs."

"Ha… that's funny. Not exactly how it happened but… whatever."

"Care to expound?" Jack asked.

"Not really… no point, really. Shit happened a long time ago and I've moved on. Why do you want to know?"

"Well…I'm not trying to pry or get into your business but… you know…I'm out with you now, and as I told you, I gotta help Luke. Did you use and sell drugs and, if so, are you still doing it?"

"Look, preacher boy. I've done some things I aint proud of and would certainly fill your father's sermons, but it aint contagious. You won't get infected with my bad influence." Bobby Joe laughed.

Jack stared out the window watching the truck turn left onto Harrodsburg Road. There was palpable tension in the king cab and Jack had to know why without trying to offend and make matters worse.

There seems to be something eating at Bobby Joe...like maybe I did something to him. He seems annoyed by my presence yet he's the one who told me to get in. Why did he want me to go with him if he's mad at me? Jack's mind was racing to every conceivable scenario before landing on the paranoia. In my dream, Bobby Joe knew Marcus X... hell he worked with him...they did deals. This is the night all that shit happens and now he's probably driving me to meet him! He was supposed to do a repo, as Nikki suggested, but he called that off. Robbie and Conrad aren't following either. Damn, damn what have I gotten myself into? Things from the dream are happening but... differently. Probably because its Luke reacting to the events and doing things differently and causing an unpredictable result. Great! The only edge or advantage I had in this nightmare was knowing the next step...now I'm not so sure.

"Don't look so worried Jack. I aint busting your balls or anything. Just wanted some company on a stop I need to make and wanted to catch up a little bit. I haven't heard a damn thing from your brother Joseph since he went off to college in Louisville. We used to be pretty close...now nothing." Bobby Joe frowned driving past Southland Christian Church. "And you, Jack. You and I got close during my senior year. Hell, I even got you out of that Michael Westbrook fight!" He added with a laugh.

"Yeah... that was pretty intense...to say the least. I really haven't much to catch you up on except that I'm in my senior at UK and still haven't a clue what I want to do with my life!"

"Ha, ha... you college boys... you go to school with all these dreams of making great grades, scoring with tons of chicks, and walking away with a diploma and a job with a fortune 500 company. It's all a big lie. They take your parent's money; tell you shit that won't work or apply in the real world; hand you a parchment worth a buck fifty and convince you that you can do anything now. Conquer the world because that little worthless paper has your name on it with their school logo. It's a fucking money-making scam foisted on the naïve to save their children from working as hard as they do. What a joke!"

"You have a diploma, don't you?"

"Yeah... in communications. Ha, I think it's still rolled up and sitting in a box in my parent's attic. I drive a tow truck and run my own business. Lot of fucking good that rolled up parchment did for me."

"How did you know how to run your own business? I mean, make a payroll, purchase equipment, shoot off invoices, collect fees, file taxes. Damn, the crazy different tax codes and laws for small businesses change so much. Where did learn how to do all that?"?

"Ah... smart boy! I see what you're driving at. Didn't I learn some of those accounting practices and business methods in school? No. Most everything in those schools is theoretical. They don't work at all in the real world. Most of those fucking professors wouldn't make a dime in the real world running off their theories. I make money mostly through cash only transactions and reporting very little in income— keeping me in a low tax bracket. I move money around and occasionally launder it through other money-making ventures."

"Selling drugs."

"No. I don't sell drugs or anything really. At least nothing tangible that could be nabbed in a crime."

"I don't get it?"

"Look, it's like this, and I'm telling you cause you're a friend and I still think highly of your family, I need powerful pain medication for my knees. As you know, I fucked them up pretty bad at Sue Bennett and my asshole coach got me hooked on them, and then took them away when he revoked my scholarship. I'm not a dope head or anything like that, but the medical staff at Sue Bennett didn't finish my rehab properly, and my knees never properly healed. I'm in constant pain without certain drugs, like OxyContin… and you can't get that shit without a prescription, and I can't afford the health care coverage for that because its seen as a 'precondition' ailment. Too damn costly. So, I barter for the meds."

"What do you barter?"

"Information. Simple as that. I know things that are important to my 'pharmacist' and in return he fills my prescription."

"Who's your pharmacist?"

"Ha, ha… you're going to meet him tonight. I need to make a quick stop." Bobby Joe laughed as he swung right onto New Circle Road heading east.

❧ ❧ ❧ ❧ ❧ ❧ ❧

Simon gripped the steering wheel tight with a heighten sense of relief and excitement. The toughest part of the night sales was handled without loss of money or body parts. Luke's quick, no-nonsense approach eased Simon's anxiety about paying off his debt.

Turning right onto Woodland Avenue, his mind raced to his campus distributor, Andy Smith, a youth director at the campus Baptist outreach mission. The former lineman at UK was an imposing figure at six-feet eight inches tall and weighing three hundred and fifty pounds. Students simply called him "The Mountain".

Okay the hardest part of the night is over…now swing by the campus near fraternity row and drop off the rest of my stash, Simon reasoned as he turned right onto Woodland Avenue driving past Euclid Avenue and slowly turning right onto Rose Lane.

The street was packed with cars and students milling about in various states of drunken euphoria and hedonistic desire. It was late at night and the fraternities were the sight of many festive engagements rarely confined inside the Greek houses. The Greek system banned drugs and any illegal behavior with minors. Many of the Greek houses had started employing bodyguards at their doors to prevent trouble inside.

"Man, this place is packed and looking at those frat houses across the street, it's going to be hell getting in. Look at that crowd around the door." Luke pointed at a mob of rowdy students reveling in the cool night air.

"We're not going in. Come on. Our boy is over there behind that huge frat house. There's a construction site… building another massive frat house. Our guy will be over there." Simon stated as he double parked next to several cars on the road.

"Hey ass-wipe! You can't just park your shitty car like that…blocking someone in!" shouted a tall thin frat boy dressed in a button-down striped collared shirt with a sweater tied about his neck wearing deck shorts and loafers.

"Go fuck yourself!" Simon replied walking briskly across the street toting a large paper bag.

"Bet you won't say that to my face, fat ass!" the boy retorted.

"I told your mother and then fucked her again!" Simon shouted back.

The crowd roared with laughter and taunted the young frat lad to take umbrage and challenge the party intruder. However, the frat boy decided it wasn't worth it when Luke stopped and started walking back towards him. Staring back at the boy in the crowd from across the street, Luke heard the jeers and taunts of the Greeks urging their brother to accept the gladiatorial challenge. However, the tall thin lad downed another mouthful from his red Solo cup and decided he didn't want to cross the Rubicon. Luke figured as much, wheeled around and followed Simon to the construction site.

"How the hell are you going to find your guy out here in the dark with thousands of kids running around?" Luke inquired.

"Easy. He's a fucking landmass. Will probably be the biggest dude you've ever seen… ah ha! See there, by that ridge above the construction area?" Simon pointed.

"That big dark mass. That's a pile of dirt…"

"No that's The Mountain! He's fucking huge! Come on!" Simon smiled as he jogged over to his campus distributor. "Hey Andy, what's up?" Simon greeted the giant with the obligatory bro hug.

Luke watched in disbelief as his fat rotund friend seemed to disappear in the large mass called The Mountain.

"Hey Simon! Not much… just getting along feeling blessed by God for His gift of each day on His beautiful creation." The big man added with a smile through an enormous beard that reached out about seven inches and rested on his massive chest. Looking back at Luke and extending his hand, "Hello, my name is Andy Smith. Youth counselor at the Christian Student Center here on campus."

"Hello yourself." Luke added in disbelief as the man's hand swallowed his own. Staring up at The Mountain, Luke added "So you're a youth minister who buys and sells drugs to kids?"

"Luke… not important. Leave it alone." Simon warned.

"Nah, that's okay Simon. I get that a lot though usually not from the drug supplier." Andy added with a laugh.

"I'm not a supplier… just here to make sure nothing happens to my friend." Luke replied as the two stared at each other for several uncomfortable seconds.

"Okay, well anyhow this is my unique outreach program. Christianity shouldn't be confined to churches. You need to go where the sin is… you know what I mean? Beat the devil in his own lair."

"Okay?" Luke added with a raised eye brow.

"You look skeptical. I get that…anyway… though I sell them drugs, I also counsel them and use it as an opportunity to be a witness for Christ."

"You counsel them? How?"

"You know, tell them they don't need drugs, and things of nature or man-made products, to feel good 'or to be high on life. That only a one-to-one relationship with Christ can fulfill that empty void. I tell them my story…you know…testify about my journey to Christ."

"You talk about Jesus after you sell them dangerous, addictive drugs?" Luke added in further disbelief.

"Yes…I try to convince them to stop buying, using and abusing drugs."

"I'm confused. You take their money; witness to them about Christ to prevent them from becoming a future client? You're working to kill your own sales?"

"Bingo! Simon, this boy is bright!" Andy beamed.

"Bullshit! He thinks too much and talks even more!" Simon winced as he handed the paper bag to The Mountain who quickly opened it and scanned its contents.

"Good…Eight Balls! They sell quickly!"

"What do you do with the dirty money from the sinful drugs?" Luke asked sarcastically.

"Goes to the church and our mission work overseas."

"All of it?"

"Well, there are a few administrative costs. Like this… having to pay for product."

"You don't take a cut?"

"Oh Lordy no! That wouldn't be right…unethical and would put me in a precarious position with the Big Man!"

"There's a bigger dude than you that you have to answer to? Damn, I'd like to meet him!" Simon inserted in awe.

"Then go to church, you idiot." Luke retorted staring incredulously at

Simon, who still didn't understand. "He's referring to God." Luke added as Andy smiled widely.

"Oh, oh…yeah… of course. Well anyway it's all there. Did you bring the money?"

"Yep" The Mountain replied reaching into his coat pocket retrieving a wadded white envelope and handing it to Simon.

"Well buddy, thanks for the business!" Simon stated flatly shaking his hand and walking away.

"Not gonna count it?" The Mountain asked playfully.

"Nope. You never cheated me before. You're the only honest guy I know."

"So you really preach and testify the good news to these kids as you sell them drugs? You don't see a moral dilemma in this? You take their money and give them hell." Luke stated.

"The way I see it, these dudes are going to buy the drugs anyway from someone— most likely a scuzzy slime ball that will use the money for more sinful behavior. I'm taking the dirty money and cleaning it— giving it to God. That way dirty money, like sinful souls, can be saved and converted to a good cause, you know?"

"I guess that's one way to look at it. So, God's getting a cut of the devil's action?"

"Ha! Ha! I like that, Luke. That's real clever. You're different, Luke… not like some of the clowns I deal with out here. You have a good head."

"Thanks! If I had a good head, I guess I wouldn't be out here doing this kind of thing." Luke added with irony.

"Maybe, but God has a plan for all of us and its different for each person. You just have to recognize it. It's usually based on your unique gifts and talents. Mine is simple. I'm big and scary looking but as gentle as a church mouse. I have the gift of gab and put people at ease. That makes them more receptive to my message."

"And your message is… buy drugs and don't do them?"

"Ha! Ha! No, Luke…its real simple— God loves you. He knows where you are and how you're hurting and wants you to turn to Him for guidance and direction."

"Sounds good Andy, but I wonder if that message ever resonates with these buyers. Do you know any success stories? Any kids you turned around?"

"Oh yeah…dozens over the years. Many have gone on to productive careers. I don't really keep an exact total because the numbers would be skewed against doing what I do. I figure if I convert just one person to the righteous path that God has laid out then it's all been worth it." Andy smiled.

"Come on, Luke its Friday night, not Sunday morning. I got another stop to make." Simon called out.

The two strolled back across the wild outdoor party as people were darting about playfully slapping each other and throwing cups. The pair nimbly moved in and out of groups of loud obnoxious students trying to be heard over each other. Each group telling the better story filled with more exaggerated lies. Simon reached the car and saw a filthy film strewn across his windshield.

"Ah shit! Damn it! Some faggoty-frat boy has spit up all over my car! Look at this shit! Its running down the side!" Simon growled.

"Ha, I guess the frat boy in the stripe shirt didn't like you referencing his mother that way and showed you how it made him feel!" Luke kidded with a laugh.

"Hey fat-ass! I told you not to talk about my mother and then run away." the tall thin frat boy exhorted ambling and stumbling across the street as if he were walking on a tightrope.

"Why you little shit! I'll fucking kill your ass!" Simon screamed lurching out after the drunken sot.

Luke deftly stepped in front of Simon and forced him back against the car keeping space between the two combatants.

"Look you better get out of here or I'll let him loose and he'll beat your drunken ass!" Luke advised. Seeing more of the frat boy's friends join the melee, Luke admonished the crowd to take the boy away. They simply stared at Luke and jeered their buddy into action.

"Look fat-ass, I'm going to kick your…" the thin man stopped in mid-sentence, made a distorted face and felt a surge of nausea that spewed directly at Luke. Luke saw it coming and quickly stepped aside as the spewed mass hit Simon's chest and splattered on his face.

"What the…damn it, I'm going to kill you!" Simon screamed wiping bits from his lips and eyes. He lunged forward but again Luke pinned him against the car and warned the students to grab their buddy instantly or he would kick everyone's butt tonight. The stunned and amused crowd heeded Luke's warning and retrieved their sick friend from the road. He was still spewing as they pulled him away.

"Damn it Luke, you should have let me kill that idiot!" Simon screamed.

"Nope, you don't have time to be getting in a drunken frat fight and face problems with campus police, or worse, the cops after you just made a drug drop. Now, wipe yourself off and let's go. You said you had one more stop. Fine. Let's do it quick so I can get home. This night has already lasted too long."

<u>Chapter 11</u>

"I learned that courage was not the absence of fear, but the triumph over it. The brave man is not he who does not feel afraid, but he who conquers that fear."

— Nelson Mandela

Jack couldn't shake that gnawing feeling that there was something different about this Bobby Joe than the one from his dream. Though the one sitting next to him in the truck did pretty much everything he had done in his dream, there was an edge or uneasiness about him— a resentment. *Yes! That's it! He seems resentful of me and being put in this position. Its weird because he didn't know I was coming… couldn't have and volunteered to take me on some errands after I revealed my stupid dream…. Damn that's it! Right after I told him about my dream and the thugs in the Zone, he got quiet… almost uneasy as if I were onto him, somehow… man if he is somehow connected to Marcus X, I am screwed… trapped.*

Jack sat quietly staring out the window as Bobby Joe turned left off New Circle Road heading north on Tates Creek Road. The silence in the King cab was eerie in that Jack sensed he was being escorted to his destined doom. *Wait a minute, I remember feeling this way as we approached that seedy little laundromat in the dream. Bobby Joe was on his way to pick up pain pills from his pharmacist at the laundromat… and the pharmacist was Marcus X! Damn… he's taking me to Marcus X! Jack felt his body tense up as his mind raced to every possible scenario but invariably they all ended in his death. Okay, wait a second… in the dream Bobby Joe took me there but had no idea about Marcus X and about him looking for me… but he knows now cause I told him at Shearer's Field… but… they're looking for Luke, not me! Jack's body relaxed at the revelation that he was not the target for the crime boss in the Zone. Phew! Its Luke, not me! What the hell's wrong with you Jack? Stop worrying about your own worthless life… focus on protecting your little brother. I wonder if he's driving to that crappy little laundromat?* Jack reached back behind his seat and felt a large duffel bag stuffed full.

"Whatcha doing, Jack?"

"Is this a laundry bag?"

"Yeah… how did you know?" Bobby Joe asked incredulously as he wheeled his diesel truck left onto Cooper Drive.

"Just came to me… are we going to a laundromat tonight?"

"Yeah, how did you know?"

"It's going to sound crazy but… its all kinda happening like that dream I told you about?"

"Are you serious? How in the hell would you dream about a laundry bag in my truck? I haven't seen you in years and you sure as hell haven't been in this truck cause I just bought it a few months ago."

"Bobby Joe, did you think I was kidding when I told you about the dream? That I was making shit up?"

"Well… yeah I guess you could say I was a little skeptical."

"Then why did you take me with you? Why am I riding with you to a drug pick-up?"

The cab got quiet for a few minutes as Bobby Joe looked out of his side window and at the rearview mirror. It was obvious he was uncomfortable with what he was about to say.

"I had to… I had to… get you away from Nikki?"

"What?"

"Nikki."

"Why?"

"Cause I really like her and… and I could see she was really crushing on you."

"I don't think so, Bobby Joe. She was just being a friend and helping out. Hell, you encouraged her to."

"Yeah… that was so she wouldn't think it bothered me… but it did. Sorry bro, had to get her away from you."

"Hey, no problem. I mean, Nikki's really hot and all, but I'm not really thinking about anything except surviving that damn dream… and making sure Luke does too!"

"I hear ya. I hear ya. So, in this dream what happens?"

"Well, you pick-up your prescription at some seedy little laundromat and we run into some criminal kingpin, named Marcus X?"

"Whoa… that's crazy! How could you know shit like that?" Bobby Joe stared in disbelief at Jack and turned left onto Romany Road. Slowing the truck to a crawl, he pulled into the poorly lit gravel parking lot.

The powerful headlights streamed across the front of a run-down looking business with a large white sign that read LAUNDROMAT. Backing the truck up, Bobby Joe shoved it into park and turned the engine off. Jack squinted to see into the large windows of the laundromat and could barely make out a few figures milling about on the inside. The interior lighting was dim but there were a large number of security cameras blinking red lights on the corners of the one-story concrete block building.

"Well… does it look the same as in the dream?"

"No… not really… is this place even open for business? It looks more deserted than anything. Kind of a crappy cover business for a drug lord."

"Ha! Ha! That's just the way the Boss likes it. He hated doing actual business. Too many complaints about the washers and dryers not working properly and people saying the machines ate their money… you know stupid, annoying shit like that. So, he decided to make it look scary in hopes no one would really use it."

"Isn't he afraid the cops will stake out the place. You know bust him on deals going down here. I mean, it looks like the ideal drug drop. Look, you got a lot of weird people walking around here late at night. Can't be up to anything good or legal." Jack added.

"I don't think the Boss really cares about getting busted, if you know what I mean?"

"He's got connections with the cops?"

"Oh yeah, but much higher than that. Alright, time to go in."

"Aren't you going to grab your duffel bag?"

"Why?"

"To do your laundry... keep your cover?"

"Dude I would never do my laundry here. The machines are shit and they eat your money. Boss won't even give you your damn money back!" Bobby Joe laughed exiting the truck. "You coming? Want to see if more of your dream is accurate?"

"Yeah, sure... why not. Looks a helluva lot worse out here in the parking lot." Jack replied with a curt laugh. He ran his hand under his seat and felt a small cardboard box. He pulled it out and smiled, "Bobby Joe's laundry detergent."

Jack jogged over to catch up with his large beefy friend. He noticed several odd figures approach and then back off. Bobby Joe swung the glass door open as if he owned the place. Walking in, Jack felt a weird sensation of deja vu— the machines, benches and folding tables were arranged exactly as he envisioned them. There were even a few bums dry-humping each other in the corner. Working their way to the back of the building, they came to a large metal door. Bobby Joe promptly banged three times followed with a single bang— coded. A slotted window opened followed by a muffled voice.

"Open up Scarecrow." Bobby Joe said with irritation.

"What's the password?" came the voice from the other side.

"I'll bust your fucking ass if you don't open the damn door!" Bobby Joe quickly responded.

After a few seconds, the sounds of deadbolts unlocking broke the silence. The door opened slowly as a tall thin black man sporting mirrored sunglasses emerged.

"Damn it Scarecrow, you can see who it is when you slide open the fucking window slot. Why the hell do you always ask for a fucking password? There's no password, dude! Never has been!"

"You should show more respect for your elders and my name is Leroy. Leroy Bass and I used to be..."

"Yeah, yeah you used to be a badass. I've heard it all before. Look, is the Boss in?"

"Yes... if you would wait here while I see if he's available for visitors." Leroy added in defiance as he strolled across the beautifully furnished anteroom.

Large stuffed leather chairs and couches encircled an exquisite mahogany coffee table with an assortment of business magazines strewn on top. In the corner, Jack could see what had to be the Scarecrow's desk with neatly arranged office supplies. Looking back at Bobby Joe, Jack sensed an uneasy agitation— like Bobby Joe shouldn't have to follow the rules of "ordinary" clients or employees. *Its like he thinks he is above these formalities of the Boss. Does that mean he's closer and more involved in this criminal underworld than he's let on? If so, I'm in real danger and that stupid dream has led me right into a deadly trap. Damn… why am I so stupidly following that horrible dream… but much of it has been remarkably true. Can't discount that… still… I've walked right out of a hot spot and into a cauldron.*

"Hey Jack, dude lighten up. You look like you're about to walk into your own funeral. Dude this won't take that long. I promise. Anyway, you said you would meet a criminal kingpin named Marcus X here tonight. That's crazy. How did you know his name?"

"I told you, that stupid nightmare I had… its been fairly accurate about a lot of things. Like us being here."

"That's seriously creepy dude. What does Marcus look like in the dream? Do you remember?"

"Oh yeah… I'll never forget that face or what he does…"

"Well… what does he look like and what do you mean, 'what he does'?"

"He… looks exactly like Denzel Washington with a goatee… powerfully built upper body and a cool customer, an almost serpentine personality. You know, he says the right things but gives you the creeps."

"Damn, Miller… that's really, really accurate. And you've never met or seen him before?"

"No. Not at all. We don't run in the same circle of friends." Jack added with a laugh to ease the tension.

"Yeah… I'm certain of that except here you are with me… the common denominator to another world."

"Yes… and the longer I'm here, the scarier it seems to get…"

"Don't worry, Jack, you've got nothing to fear here. You've done nothing to Marcus or any of his associates."

"No… not me, but what about Luke? As I told you before…"

Suddenly the large mahogany door opened as the tall thin man appeared sliding through. Closing the door behind him, he adjusted his mirrored glasses and clasped his hands in the front as if an important announcement was in the offing.

"Well, Leroy? Is the Boss in or not?" Bobby Joe queried in growing agitation. "Damn it, just say something!"

"The Boss will see you now. You may proceed." Leroy reported in his slow deliberate cadence.

"Well, glory be! What the hell's wrong with you, Scarecrow?" Bobby Joe added as he pushed the elder gatekeeper aside and walked briskly into the darkened room. "Come on Jack!"

Jack felt his body respond to Bobby Joe's command as he moved slowly towards the door, but it was as if he were on a moving walkway at the airport. He was moving but not conscientiously doing it. He felt as if he were experiencing an "out of body" phenomenon— seeing himself move without trying to. His mind was screaming caution and "don't enter" and yet his body was moving toward the open door and past the tall thin gatekeeper. His senses were alive as he could smell the combination of cigarette smoke and Dorito's on the gatekeeper's breath walking beneath him.

He entered a room that was poorly lit and revealed very little about the size or scope of the place. Looking at the source of the light, a green banker's lamp sitting atop a vast ebony desk, Jack could make out a few features that was taking him back to the images of his nightmare— pictures on the walls, ornate book case lining the two adjacent walls, and a large leather stuffed chair turned away. He could hear a soft muffled voice behind the chair finishing up a conversation. He looked over at Bobby Joe who was sporting the same goofy expression as in the dream.

Jack started to feel the room spin as his eyes darted about. He could barely make out what Bobby Joe was saying but it was followed by a laugh. Bobby Joe turned him around and mumbled an introduction to his boss. Jack turned slowly back to the desk and immediately felt his heart pounding through his chest like a wrecking ball attacking a condemned building. To his horror, Jack was now staring at the face that haunted him in his nightmare— Marcus X was not a figment of an overactive nightmare. He was flesh and blood and real. Standing behind his desk in a perfectly tailored three-piece Brooks Brother suit, Marcus X smiled with his prefect white teeth and extended his hand.

"Well, it's nice to meet you Jack. You must be a real good friend of Bobby Joe's because he never introduces me to any of his friends or associates." Marcus X stated with an easy grace.

"Thank you..." Jack heard himself reply as he shook the cold, lotioned hand of pure evil.

"Why Jack, you need to work on that handshake. Very limp. A man learns a lot about another man from their handshake. A firm grip and pump shows great confidence and ability. Let's the other man know he's strong, self-assured, ready to do business or battle. However, a weak, almost effeminate grip that just sits in the other man's hand... well that tells something very different."

"Yeah... like what?" Jack meekly offered.

"Like he's weak, unsure and already beaten. You don't look like that kind of person Jack. You're tall, well-built and fairly handsome...but you're giving off the wrong vibe and impression of a weakling. You won't last long around here like that." Marcus X finished with a smirk and a laugh.

"Oh, you need to cut him some slack Boss. You see, he saw all this before in a dream. This very scene that's happening right now… and its freaking him out!" Bobby Joe inserted with his own laugh.

"Oh really?" Marcus stated as his facial expression instantly changed matching the darkened room. Jack felt it as if a cold breeze had whipped through the room leaving him shaking uncontrollably. "What exactly did you dream about Jack?"

It was the way he said "Jack" that seemed so evil and accusatory that Jack was feeling his legs wobble as the room blurred. He was asked a direct question from his nightmare come to life and he couldn't make himself answer. He stared at the cold brown eyes of the tall dark figure across from him as the image of the man standing at the doorway of apartment 121 holding a bloody knife flashed before his eyes.

"Ha, he knew your name and said you looked like Denzel Washington… I never really thought about it before but damn if he aint right… you do kinda look like him!" Bobby Joe tried to break the tension and help answer the question.

"That's pretty good. I've been told that before by many people but never from someone who I've never met or seen. Have you seen me before Jack?"

"No… not ever."

"So, what about this dream of yours? You look terrified, Jack? What is it you think we do here?"

"Um… I'm not sure. Bobby Joe said he had to pick up some medicine for his bad knees." Jack responded on cue as if reading it directly from his nightmare. He heard his voice saying the words but was unaware he was talking. "I assume this is some sorta after-hours pharmacy."

The room erupted in laughter as Marcus X's face lightened and he turned toward Bobby Joe smiling from ear to ear. The two continued to laugh for several minutes occasionally repeating the "after-hours pharmacy" line.

The lightened atmosphere should have eased Jack's mind and allowed him to steel his nerves, but it made him more nervous because Bobby Joe and Marcus X seemed too close… too affable around each other. In Jack's nightmare, Bobby Joe was merely an acquaintance or a reluctant client to Marcus X. However, in reality, they seemed chummy— like partners. That thought ran through Jack's mind like a semi-truck racing across the interstate highway without breaks and posed just as deadly an outcome for all oncoming cars like Jack.

"Yes… yes Jack. That's exactly what I do here. I provide an excellent pharmaceutical service that helps folks get the kind of medicine their body needs but the government denies them and deems it illegal. You see Jack, the government is the creation of man's desire to control and tame the baser nature of mankind. To try to bring law and order to the natural jungle of mankind. If left alone, man would descend to the lower beasts of the jungle and fight and kill each other over anything and everything. He constructed a government to function as security and protection to those who have stuff to protect against those who want it. The government is a legal entity paid for by the people, ostensibly to protect them, but at the behest and benefit of the rich and powerful. There are really only a few rich and powerful entities on the planet, but they run everything and manipulate the masses, the people, to do what they need them to do which is protect their possessions on earth and allow them to pass it on to their legacies. The rest of us just scramble like squirrels trying to grab a few nuts for our own survival. Drugs, like the ones I provide, allow people to escape the harsh realities of this existence and even embolden some to challenge the system. And shit... the government can't allow that... can't allow free thought and expression that calls the whole system into question. If people actually knew how this world worked, and was manipulated by a few, there would be revolutions all over the world. Law and order would descend into chaos and confusion."

"And you would want that?" Jack boldly inquired.

"Hell no! That shit would be devastating to my business. In that chaotic world, nobody would pay for anything and I'd have to build an army to protect my turf and possessions. That's why I benefit from the very instrument that deems me illegal— government. The government says my 'business' is illegal, and I should be locked up... but I aint and haven't been in jail for a long time. You know why? Because I do business with the government. I keep a low profile, sell my drugs to lots of people in both the criminal world and the legal business world. I provide services deemed immoral by society, yet many of those same people keep me rich purchasing those damnable drugs and prostitutes. As long as I keep the noise quiet in the Zone, with few interactions between the two societies, I stay in business. You think the Lexington city council or local government doesn't know about me or this place? Ha! They need me here and won't touch me as long as people from the other world don't come into MY world and try to rock the boat. Ever so often, some little shit from one of the colleges comes into my world and causes problems. They run out and try to expose the problems to an unaware public that could cause an uproar and shake the whole system. Trust me when I tell you, the system is protected by many government officials and many law enforcement officers." Marcus X emphasized with a threatening menace that once again shook Jack to his core. "Now, what was the prophetic dream about, Jack?"

Jack stared at his nightmare in shock and disbelief. *Oh my God! Oh my*

God! This is really happening! This guy is also really crazy! What is talking about? The government and the police are in cahoots with drug lords like himself to maintain society! That makes no sense! Or does it? Shit I can't focus on that… he's demanding to know about my dream. It's as if he believes in dreams, premonitions or omens. Lord knows I can't tell him anything close to the truth or Luke is dead and me too! Shit… keep it together… he's staring at you demanding an answer. God, he is scarier than the dream. You gotta give him something…

"Jack? What was your dream about? How did you know about me? What I looked like? What happened?"

"Well… it was really just a weird dream that happened after I had watched American Gangster." Jack replied tepidly. Jack was astonished that he gave a logical response. Again, it was as if he wasn't conscientiously acting in this nightmare scenario. It was becoming too surreal.

"That's real cute, Jack! A lot of white America's understanding of black America is through the movies. Hollywood makes more racist films and creates so many myths about what's really happening. They're supposed to be the bastion of tolerance and liberal understanding but they're the ones perpetuating the stereotypical images of the black man as a sinful, lusting criminal incapable of governance. What a damn joke! Anyway, I'm not sure I believe you Jack. What's your last name, boy?" Marcus X asked with a menacing glare.

"Uh…"

"Why are you asking about his last name? That shit's not important around here. He's my buddy and he doesn't need a last name." Bobby Joe defended.

"He does when he comes into my world and sniffs around here. I already had one white boy come into my world yesterday and cause quite a disturbance and could, if not properly disposed of, cause a great deal of damage to the operation. I won't allow that shit to happen and neither should you. We're both heavily invested here." Marcus X warned.

Jack turned quickly toward Bobby Joe as the truth of Marcus' words stung like a death sentence. Bobby Joe refused to look at Jack as he lowered his head in thought. *No! No! This can't be happening! Bobby Joe is not in cahoots with Marcus X… can't be. Damn, he was so different in the dream, so trustworthy and my protector… but then again… I was being hunted by Marcus X in my dream but not in reality. Instead its Luke, he's after, not me. He just confirmed that he's after Luke… damn… if he knows my last name… he might put two and two together and force me to turn on Luke! No way in hell would I turn on Luke! Don't do it Bobby Joe! Don't give up my last name! Jack's thoughts so terrified him as he stared at Bobby Joe waiting for his answer.*

"What do you want from me, here?" Bobby Joe weakly answered.

"I want the fucking truth about this white boy who had a dream or premonition about me that seems to be true. I take dreams very seriously.

Much truth is revealed in the unconscious mind and this boy may have stumbled upon a truth that could threaten everything!"

"Do you know how crazy you sound right now? Hell, I only told you about that stupid dream because its absurd and funny... not real, and certainly not threatening! Jack doesn't know shit about anything, at least not before you went on a fucking rant about government, society, and the criminal underworld."

"What's the boy's fu...." Was the last thing Jack heard before the room spun out of control and his fear encompassed his whole body as his mind determined it was time to shut everything down. Jack collapsed in a heap falling back against the wall.

"Oh shit! What the hell, Jack!" Bobby Joe screamed as he ran over to try and rouse his friend from his unconscious state. He scooped Jack under his right arm and tried awakening him with a few slaps.

"Ha! Ha! Your boy is one scared little white rabbit. That boy couldn't harm a damn fly without feeling guilty." Marcus X laughed. "Hell, get that weak piece of shit out of my office. His presence leaves a putrid odor of a damn coward around here."

"Well shit, Marcus! You scared the hell outta the guy. He's never been around this kind of environment. He told me about his crazy dream and I brought him here as kind of a joke to see this place was nothing like his dream and then you go all crazy, scary Hollywood-like on him and scare the living shit out of him."

"He had every reason to be scared Bobby Joe. Cause if he is related or connected to that other white boy... he won't be around very long."

"What other white boy are you talking about? I thought you just made that shit up to scare Jack. You know, playing along like some Hollywood gangsta to fuck with his head."

"That was no joke and I'm deadly serious. A stupid-ass white boy named Luke Miller came into my world last night and fucked up. He took something very dear to me and may have stolen some drugs... but more importantly, he got away unharmed and that shit doesn't happen! You don't waltz into MY WORLD AND STEAL MY SHIT!" Marcus X screamed. "Now, I'm asking you for the last time Bobby Joe. What's this white boy's last name?"

Bobby Joe lifted Jack up and cradled him in his arms. He defiantly stared at Marcus X for several seconds before stating flatly, "Singleton. His fucking name is Jack Thomas Singleton. He's one of the few childhood friends I have that isn't a fuck-up and he knows nothing about this or this goddamn world we exist in!" Bobby Joe turned toward the door, opened it as he pushed past Scarecrow.

"Let them go. They're not the white ones I'm looking for. They will be coming by very soon. Let me know when they arrive." Marcus X stated sitting down behind his desk as a grin curled up from his lips.

❦ ❦ ❦ ❦ ❦ ❦ ❦

Simon opened the trunk of his car and retrieved a blue UK pullover. He yanked his soiled shirt off in disgust and threw it on the ground. He was already in an agitated state from the earlier drug drops, but his last stop tonight was the one he was genuinely concerned about— the Boss. He had texted Geoffrey earlier, inquiring about where the Boss would be tonight.

Marcus X was a careful man who rarely did anything routinely as to never become predictable to his enemies and rivals. He stayed alive by doing things spontaneously. He owned several legitimate businesses such as a laundromat, an arcade, a bar and a strip club. Simon remembered Marcus telling him that any successful business man needed to diversify his portfolio and have a hand in multiple operations to draw an income and, more importantly, that sin businesses were always recession proof— "people will always pay for tits and alcohol no matter what the economy is like."

Simon smiled thinking about his earlier days with the Boss as he was once seen as the "golden boy". *Marcus took me under his wing and showed me the ropes of this business because he thought I had great potential. I reached a clientele— college students and the upper middle classes in suburbia— that had been out of his reach. He showered affection and attention on me in those early days… but I blew it… damn it, I blew it. He warned me not to ever use the product we sold— it was dangerously addictive and ruined lives. Man… was he right!*

"That's so random that you have clothes in your trunk, Simon." Luke teased trying to break the quiet tension in the car.

"Why's that?" Simon retorted.

"Ha, just is… you still pissed about the puking frat boy?"

"Nah… not really. You were right to keep me from kicking the little shit's ass. It would've started all kinds of bad things in motion that you can't control and, if there's one thing I learned from the Boss, its that you should always avoid areas and things you can't control." Simon added with a chuckle.

"Boss? Who's this Boss you mention from time to time?"

"You don't want to know, and you don't need to know. Best for everyone involved."

"Alright. Where are we going?"

"Last stop tonight Luke, my boy, last stop. It's a little laundromat off Romany Road."

"Say what? Did you seriously say it was a laundromat and that's where you're going to meet your boss?" Luke inquired incredulously.

"Yeah… what's the big deal? Lots of drug lords use legitimate businesses as fronts. Its great cover. Damn Luke, you look white as a ghost.

I don't think I've ever seen you like this... you spooked?"

"I just can't... damn it, Jack!" Luke mumbled to himself. "Why are you right again?"

"What are you mumbling about? Did you just curse Jack?" Simon demanded as Luke nodded affirmatively. "What's Jack got to do with anything?"

"Well... its going sound crazy... hell, I'm not sure I believe it but... Jack had this weird dream a couple of nights ago about some crazy shit happening in the Zone and witnessing murders, being chased by a drug kingpin and his minions and, hell just saying it out loud now sounds even crazier." Luke laughed.

"Damn, your brother has an active imagination." Simon chuckled.

"Yeah... that's just it... Jack doesn't have an active imagination. He's straight down the middle. I mean, he's never really done anything outrageous or unpredictable in his life. He's a pleaser... an ass-kisser who would never do or even dream of something as wild and dangerous as what I've experienced the last two nights and yet..."

"And yet, what?"

"He's pretty much predicted all of it... just the outcome was a bit different."

"What do you mean he predicted everything?"

"His nightmare a few nights ago has been pretty accurate... except in his dream, it was himself doing what I'm doing now... including the trip to a seedy laundromat tonight."

"He predicted the laundromat?"

"Yep."

"You're fucking shitting me!" Simon stated in stunned awe.

"I shit you not. You're my favorite turd and I would never shit you." Luke offered with the oft told reply.

"Damn, that is crazy strange and you're right about Jack. His ass would never go or do anything as adventurous and daring as what we've been doing tonight. Still... what did he say happened at the laundromat?" Simon probed as he turned onto Romany Road.

"Nothing really specific... I really don't remember because he was shouting stuff at me as I was leaving the bonfire tonight. Just something like 'beware of going to a scuzzy laundromat' and 'tonight's the night that is the worst part of the dream'... whatever that means." Luke remembered staring out the window as they pulled into a vacant parking lot as the wheels crunched across the gravel.

Simon drove past a large pick-up truck and drove behind the cinder block laundromat. He spotted the Boss's dark Lincoln Town Car parked beneath a large oak tree facing the building. Pulling the car's stick shift into reverse, Simon backed out and parked about fifty yards from the pick-up truck.

"Well, this is definitely a 'scuzzy' laundromat. You coming in or did Jack's dream freak you out?" Simon asked with a laugh trying to goad Luke into the building.

"Do you need me? I mean… you said you had some quick business with the Boss. You won't tell me his name and …"

"You don't need to know his name, is what I said, because you don't. It's better for everyone involved that you don't. Damn it Luke, you look and talk like Jack now… where's the adventurous ass-kicker who knew what he was doing at the Red Mile earlier and saved my ass with the frat boys? Where's that confident ass-kicker who punched the hell out of Little Billy and his stumpy side-kick?"

"I don't know… Jack's been right about a lot of things and …"

"And Jack's a little pussy and a coward. He's scared of his own shadow?" Simon responded in agitation.

"Wow, you talk so much crap about my brothers to me but never to them…"

"That's because they're not worth arguing with. They've always hated me and hate that you hang out with me."

"They haven't always hated you… just said you changed a lot after your dad died and you went bad… turned to drugs and stuff… dropped out of school…"

"Yeah, yeah same old shit out of the preacher's home. Simon's dad was shit and his son is shit because he wasn't raised properly in the church. Well, I got news for ya preacher boy, there's lot of sinners in that church of yours and a lot of its coming some of the leaders!"

"What the hell are you talking about? Which leaders? What are they doing?"

"Never mind… let's just say I hear things from my crooked side of town. You coming in or not?"

Luke tried to process the accusations that Simon had made about his family and their church. He had heard a few rumblings about some of the church members, such as harmless flirting in the choir, some drinking and gambling but nothing criminal as Simon was suggesting. *Simon doesn't know shit! He's just making excuses for his own poor decisions by deflecting on church members. He's desperately trying to establish moral equivalency! Damn… did I just use the word equivalency? College must be working if I'm thinking in terms of "equivalency" … anyway, I can't let Simon make punks out of the Millers. Jack wouldn't go in and Joseph would never even be in an area like this. So, I got to show Simon that not all the Millers are soft.*

"Yeah, I'm coming." Luke mumbled as he pulled the door handle.

As they crossed the parking lot, Luke stared back at the large black pick-up truck facing the building. The tinted windows made it impossible to see if anyone was in there. Simon looked back and said he didn't know whose truck it was as he opened the front door of the laundromat. Luke followed him in and instantly felt a wave of fear shudder down his body.

The interior had the requisite washing and drying machines placed in rows across the large front room, however, none of the machines were in operation though there were many people milling about in the darkened corners. The main panel of fluorescent lights above began flickering creating a surreal stop-action motion. Luke's eyes fell on two objects moving about under a large folding table. They seemed engaged in some sort of sexual act yet fully clothed and moving slowly.

Simon grabbed Luke's arm and led him to the back wall where a large metal door was framed by two security cameras with a blinking red light. Simon pounded the door once and waited. After a few seconds a slot opened, and a deep voice asked for the password.

"Oh damn… what did Geoffrey say… umm… 'Epcot'" Simon called out.

"Epcot? That's the password to a drug lord's lair?" Luke asked in jest.

"Yeah… it's the Boss's favorite place on earth."

Suddenly the sound of several deadbolt locks clanged, and the door opened. A tall thin black man with mirrored glasses appeared from behind the door and led them into a beautiful ornate room that seemed to Luke out of place in this desolate, deserted building. They were instructed to wait as the tall man with polite, proper manners would check to see if the Boss was available. He slipped seamlessly out of the room through another large door. Within seconds he returned with instructions for them to enter the Boss's realm.

Luke tensed up as he crossed through the threshold of reality into Jack's nightmare. The dimly lit room limited Luke's ability to look for signs of danger or escape. He had always relied on his senses, especially his eyes, to alert him to perilous threats. The only sense working at the moment was a gut feeling of alarm and Jack's ominous admonition. *Man, what did Jack say? He kept saying something… like… damn, what was it? Oh… he said the Boss looked like Denzel Washington with a goatee… that's right because I remember thinking that sounded too much like a movie stereotype. But, he's been right about so much so far. The Boss must be sitting in that big chair turned away from us. My God, if he looks like Denzel… Why is Simon looking so nervous? I thought this was a routine drop or visit but he looks nervous as hell.*

"Gentlemen, please take a seat." said the voice from behind the large chair.

"Thanks Boss! I brought you a gift… you know the payment." Simon offered meekly.

"Yes, just place it on my desk…" the voice replied as the chair swiveled around.

"Okay, there it is Boss… you can see its all there. Go ahead and count it. It's all there."

"I'm sure it is Simon. How about you introduce me to your little friend over there who's looking at me as if he's seen a ghost or something. Damn, I seem to frighten a lot of white boys tonight?"

"Oh, don't mind him. He's just reacting to a stupid-ass dream his brother had about this type of place."

"Is that right? Your brother had a dream? About this place?" Marcus X asked.

Luke stared at the menacing Denzel Washington face looking back at him. He was asked a probing question and waited for a response. Luke was unsure how to proceed when the tension was broken by a cell phone ring. Marcus looked down at his phone and spun his chair back around.

Luke looked over at Simon who avoided his eye contact. He listened intently to the muffled voice behind the chair. He could make out a few phrases such as "hurry back" and "I think I got the package I sent you to pick up". *Oh dear God… what have I walked into? Jack tried to warn me… why didn't I listen. The dude DOES look like Denzel. Jack was right. What else did he say? He kept saying something else… oh yeah "it's a trap" and "run". Shit!*

Marcus swiveled his chair back to face the front when he saw a large man standing over him. Luke delivered a powerful punch to the nose causing Marcus's eyes to blur in a watery pool. The second blow, rapidly delivered, came across the left eye leaving the large boss dazed as he slumped over.

Luke scrambled out of the room into the ornate anteroom where the tall thin man moved to block his exit. Luke lowered his shoulder and drove the gatekeeper's body into the wall like a professional linebacker attacking a blocking sled on the football field. The impact left the elder man crumpled on the floor. Luke twisted several deadbolts off and pulled the large metallic door open. Shoving his way past a few coke addicts at the entrance, he flung open the glass door and darted out into the darkness.

Instantly he heard a voice from the big black pick-up truck calling out his name. He turned back and recognized the familiar face of Bobby Joe Bradley leaning out of the driver side window beckoning him over. Luke stopped, hesitated, and then ran to the passenger side door yanking it open as Jack fell into his arms.

"What's Jack doing here and what's wrong with him?" Luke demanded.

"He's fine… just a little groggy from his encounter with the Boss." Bobby Joe stated flatly. "Come on, get in. We need to get you guys out of here. I don't know what you did, but the way you ran outta that building can't be good."

"No… you're right. We need to get outta here fast!" Luke cried as he pushed Jack towards the middle of the front seat.

Bobby Joe turned the ignition as the pick-up truck roared to life. He floored the gas pedal shooting gravel off the back tires as he turned onto Romany Road and then exited left onto Cooper Drive.

Luke shook Jack several times to revive him. Jack stared at Luke for a few seconds as he regained conscientiousness. Looking around and confused, Jack sat up as he turned toward Bobby Joe.

"What happened in there?"

"You... passed out." Bobby Joe replied trying to soften the revelation in front of Jack's younger brother.

"I did what? Passed out... seriously?"

"I'm afraid so. I carried you out and put you in the truck. Was about to take you home when Luke and Simon showed up. I remembered what you said about your crazy dream and waited to see what would happen. Sure enough, Luke comes flying out of the laundromat and here we are."

Jack turned back towards his brother, "What happened? What did you do?"

Luke lowered his head and stared out the window. He nodded his head several times trying to acknowledge that Jack was right without coming across as an idiot.

"Well... just as you predicted. I walked into a trap with a nasty drug lord who did look like Denzel Washington."

"Yep, that's Marcus X." Bobby Joe piped in.

"Yeah, Bobby Joe knows everything." Jack reassured Luke who hesitated to say more. "It's okay. He knows Marcus X but doesn't work for him. He's kind of an independent contractor that does some occasional jobs for him."

"That's a great way to put it, Jack." Bobby Joe grinned.

"Now, what exactly happened in there?" Jack asked as he turned back toward Luke.

"I was in his office with Simon... damn, I just left Simon behind." Luke realized as he tried to piece everything together. "Anyway, the Marcus dude was talking on the phone to someone about having found a 'package' and to 'hurry back'... I assumed I was the package after I remembered you told me that the laundromat was a trap."

"Oh thank God, you listened to me and remembered."

"Yeah, no doubt. Anyway, when he turned around I clocked him several times and may have knocked him out. Then I ran out and saw Bobby Joe."

"Wow... wow! You punched Marcus X in the face? You punched a damn drug lord in the face? Shit, Luke you have balls!" Jack marveled in awe.

"Yeah you do! Fuck, I can't imagine hitting the Boss in the face. I know a lot of people who would love to have the balls to try something like that but damn, Luke!" Bobby Joe smiled in admiration.

A chill ran through Luke's body as he looked strangely at Bobby Joe. Jack picked up on his brother's unease and silently nodded at him. Luke nodded back that it was nothing. *He called Marcus X the Boss… just like Simon did. Why would an occasional acquaintance or business associate refer to him that way? Seemed too familiar and like an underling working for Marcus X, not with him… I could be wrong. Just a gut feeling and I'm in no position to say anything now while the guy is rescuing us.*

"Anyway, you're going to need to disappear for a while cause this shit aint over. It aint over by a long shot." Bobby Joe warned.

"I'm afraid he's right. You have any ideas Bobby Joe about where he should go and hide for a while?"

"Hell, he can stay with me out at the farm for a while… till things settle down."

"No! No, just get me back to my car at Shearer's Field. I've got an idea where I should go."

"What? Are you crazy? Stay at Bobby Joe's. It'll be safe. Marcus doesn't know where Bobby Joe lives and he'll keep you safe. You can't go back to Lexington or on campus and you can't go home to Nicholasville. They got that place staked out." Jack reasoned.

"You're right about all of that. Just drop me off at my car and I'll disappear for a while. It's safer for me if no one knows where I am. Besides, didn't you say this was the dangerous night… the night where everything bad happens? Well, all I have to do is survive the night, right?"

"Right… I guess… I mean that's according to the dream."

"And the dream has been right most of the time hasn't it?"

Jack nodded affirmatively.

"Then it's settled. Take me back to my car and I'll disappear for a while. I'll contact you to let you know I'm safe." Luke reassured his brother while staring at Bobby Joe.

Chapter 12

"Confront the dark parts of yourself, and work to banish them with illumination and forgiveness. Your willingness to wrestle with your demons will cause your angels to sing."

— August Wilson

Jack had a fitful night trying to sleep and reconcile the truths revealed by his nightmare. So much of the dream had been accurate to a point— they revealed how he would react in the dangerous underworld. He couldn't account for his brother's reactions to the same encounters and thus he lost the ability to predict the future outcome. Tonight, was the fatal night in his dream, and so far, Luke had survived, at least he was when they dropped him off at his car earlier. Luke seemed confident and unafraid. He seemed to have a plan, but did he fully grasp the seriousness and gravity of the situation?

Jack feared Luke's casualness in alarming events, and yet, he had survived each deadly encounter. Maybe boldness and daring and a willingness to face mortal danger were the true key to courage. *My timidity and constant fear leaves me vulnerable to harm. Luke's reactions to the same perils I faced in the dream make him... courageous!* Jack concluded. Still, he worried his little brother was in harm's way and that this was far from over. What was more alarming to Jack was the knowledge that much of what remained was now out of his hands and outside of his ability to prevent the fatal event portended in his omen.

Jack returned to his apartment in Lexington hoping this nightmare would end where it had begun. He felt fairly safe in the apartment as he figured Marcus X wasn't targeting him and didn't know he was Luke's brother— Bobby Joe reassured him the secret was still safe.

However, the peaceful night's sleep at the campus apartment was not to be as Tater was throwing an open-door party that seemingly involved everyone on Maxwell Street. Jack pushed and elbowed his way through the labyrinth of alcohol sotted students to the backroom beds. Seeing several co-eds lying on his bed in an inebriated state, he decided to have a few drinks and wait for the party to conclude.

"Jack! Jack! Buddy, I'm glad you're here. Look I sent you two girls... they're waiting for you on your bed." Tater screamed with delight as he bear-hugged Jack.

"Thanks buddy, but they're passed out. When did you decide to throw this huge party and where did you get the keg?" Jack inquired slightly annoyed.

"Shit, Jack these things just sorta happen. You know they're organic and you can't question orgasms… I mean organics!" Tater cracked in his high shrill drunk voice. "Relax buddy! You're too uptight… drink some more and find a girl who hasn't passed out!"

"No, Tater! I not in the mood to party!"

"Why? Shit, is it about that stupid-ass dream you had the other night? Look, I'm alive and well and partying my ass off! Do I look dead to you?"

"Not yet, but if you keep drinking that crazy concoction in your cup, you might be!" Jack joked.

"Fucking A!! That would be a helluva way to go! Damn, look at that chick's ass… I need to go investigate a little further." Tater mumbled as he pushed Jack away heading toward a crowd of girls.

The party helped keep Jack's mind off the nightmare and the Zone as he mingled with several people he knew from campus, some from classes and others from earlier parties. He hoped that Heather would show up. He enjoyed talking to her and rekindling a past flame, but she was a no-show. *Not the kind of party she would attend. Too many people she didn't know, drinking too much and acting stupidly… that's the Heather I remember from high school, and though she said she had changed, it was still not likely she would show up, even though the party was across the street from her sorority house. Oh great, there's Rick. I'll go shoot the shit with him. He might be the only drunk guy here who can converse.*

As Jack was strolling back towards the kitchen, three hooded guys grabbed him from behind and started to drag him out of the apartment. Jack whirled around and swung wildly at his assailants. He could hear screams mixed with laughter from the crowded room as he pushed and shoved the figures off him. Rick pulled one of the hooded men off and joined the laughter as it was one of Tater's friends. Jack landed a solid punch to one of the men's throat. The sickening thud left the hooded warrior screaming in pain.

Jack was amazed at how easily he was able to dispatch the lightweight attackers. Finally, Rick grabbed and showed him that the "assailants" were not from the Zone, but instead were some of Tater's buddy's playing a prank on him. Jack was furious and started to go after Tater when Rick intervened.

"Look, I know you're pissed and want to cuss out Tater, but it'll do you no good. He's too drunk to talk to now and he'll never remember it tomorrow. You know how he gets on those damn Long Island Teas… he's sloppy and stupid. You know he means no harm." Rick reassured.

"Yeah, but that shit went too far. He knows how terrified that damn dream has me and sending those dudes in wearing hoodies… man someone could've gotten hurt just for a laugh!"

"Someone did get hurt. You throat-punched Mario and look at him… he's still holding his neck."

"Hey Mario! Dude, I'm sorry! I thought you were… well anyway, I'm really sorry. Tater's an asshole!"

Mario looked up and nodded in agreement.

"I can't stay here tonight. This party is not even close to winding down."

"Where are you going?" Rick asked.

"To the only place I know where I can get some sleep."

⇔ ⇔ ⇔ ⇔ ⇔ ⇔ ⇔

Jack awoke to the delicious aroma of bacon frying, coffee brewing and biscuits baking. It was as familiar a scent as the surroundings of his room in his parent's home in Nicholasville. Yawning and stretching, he ambled out of bed, and hit the upstairs bathroom for his morning relief before following the enticing smell emanating from the kitchen. He saw Joseph sitting at the table with his father who was reading the newspaper. Joseph seemed eager to talk.

"Where were you last night?" Joseph asked.

"I'm sorry, you're not my father." Jack retorted.

"Where were you last night?" Matthew responded looking up from the newspaper.

"Oh wow… did you two work on that all morning?"

"Don't get smart Jack. It's a simple question." Matthew stated firmly.

"I was several places… started out at Shearer's Field where I hoped Joseph would've joined me." Jack added staring at his older brother who simply nodded his head. "Then I went back to my apartment. It was a bit crowded there so I came home. End of story."

"Why was your apartment crowded, Jack?" Melinda called out as she turned the bacon over.

"Uh… well there was an unannounced party going on and I wasn't going to get any sleep."

"What sort of party, honey? One of your roommates celebrating something?" Melinda asked innocently.

"Not exactly."

"It was a kegger, mom. There were probably tons of people there getting drunk and making out and doing lots of other things." Joseph enjoined with an accusatory glare at Jack.

"Oh my, Jack you were right to leave. That's not the kind a place a good Christian boy should be. I bet it was that boy Tater. He seems a little wild. You need to be a better Christian role model for him, Jack. Show him the errors of that loose and wild way." Melinda added.

"Oh, I try mom, but Tater seems hell bent on partying with the devil and consorting with his minions." Jack sarcastically replied.

"Oh, you're teasing me Jack, but I'm serious. Tater needs a good friend and role model."

210

"Well, he aint going to get it from Jack, mom. Your middle son seems just as 'hell bent to party with the devil's minions' as his buddy Tater. Isn't that right, Jack?" Joseph goaded.

"Well, you certainly can't find the sinners sitting at home reading the Bible and judging them as doomed heathens, eh Joseph?" Jack retorted.

"All right, enough of that nonsense. That spiritual debate can wait for another time. My greater concern now, is where's Luke?" Matthew demanded.

"I don't know. Is he not here?"

"No... at least he wasn't when I went to bed last night around one o'clock and I checked his bedroom again this morning. Did you see him last night... at Shearer's?"

"Yes."

"Well?"

"He was there."

"Was he with anyone?"

"Yes... Simon."

"Man, that pot-head! I've warned Luke to stay away from that kid... he's trouble and trouble follows him." Joseph called out.

"Okay, so he was with Simon. Anything happen at Shearer's?" Matthew grilled.

Jack looked at Joseph who stared back at him.

"Look, I know about your dream and everything. Don't be mad at Joseph. He's very concerned about Luke and thinks your dream is an ominous wake up call for him. I happen to agree. Dreams are often God's ways of communicating with us, if we're willing to listen and heed them. Your dream was a gift from God."

"I would hardly call that nightmare a gift." Jack replied.

"It is and it's given you an opportunity to save your brother, now what happened?"

"Uhh...there were these guys, from a bad area in Lexington..."

"The Zone?" Matthew asked.

"Yeah... how do you know about the Zone?"

"I'm not that naïve and unknowing of the ways of our surroundings. I don't stay shut in at the church and ignore the sinfulness of the world nearby... now go on...what about these guys from the Zone?"

"Well, they were looking for him."

"Why? Because of what had happened the previous night in the Zone? What did Luke do?"

"Look, I'm not sure what he did in the Zone. As I told Joseph, who apparently told you, I saw Luke running from an apartment complex and, me and Tater ran a distraction to take the predators off the prey. He was fine the next day and somehow they knew he was at Shearer's."

"I'm sure it was the gang in that dark car parked across the street last night. I ran them off, but they must have found out that Luke was at Shearer's. Wonder how they knew that? Must be someone on the inside, someone that knows Luke and this area that would lead them to Shearer's…" Matthew contemplated.

"Wow, dad… you seriously confronted those guys?" Jack marveled at yet another Miller who faced peril without fear.

"I wouldn't say I confronted them exactly… I walked out toward them with good ole Ted Williams in my hand and then they just drove off."

"What would you have done if they hadn't driven off?" Jack asked in awe.

"I'm not sure… I was too mad and worried about you guys to stop and think…"

"You just reacted… that's what seems to be the difference… no real forethought, just a visceral reaction."

"Love, Jack. Love is what made me react. Unconditional love for my children in danger caused me to take up arms."

"Would you have attacked them? Used violence to resolve the conflict?" Joseph asked incredulously.

Matthew lowered his head and paused for several seconds, "Yes, I believe I would have. I'm not proud of that revelation but…"

"You would quickly and easily have forgotten all your knowledge of the Bible, God's word, and His rebuke of violence in resolving conflicts? Dad… you're a minster of God… his servant on earth as a moral guide and an example of His teachings! How could you so easily forget Him to take up arms against your fellow man? Reject everything you've learned and taught others as a man of God!" Joseph barked.

"You're right, Joseph… it's not something I'm proud of… but my family… my children mean the world to me and their protection is paramount. It's not really anything I can explain to those who don't have children, but in a way, I think it shows us mortals, the way God views us… as His children and He wants desperately to protect us, but He often doesn't directly intervene because he gave man the gift of free will. Free will allows us to make up our own minds and make mistakes. Once we make mistakes, we must acknowledge it, pray for God's forgiveness and He returns us to the fold. God's love is all-encompassing and forever, but we must acknowledge our sinful ways and pray for His guidance."

"But you're saying that you will act out violently if you perceive a danger to your family. Isn't that premeditated sin? You know in advance that if your children are threatened, you're choosing to disobey God's word and sin against another. Its not some visceral reaction, as Jack suggested, but instead a preconceived rationale for vigilante justice. Is that taught in the Bible? Was there a chapter about this that I missed? Where do you get the right or moral authority to take that kind of murderous action of your fellow man?" Joseph insisted.

Matthew stared at his oldest son for several seconds then looked over at his middle son. Both children awaited his reply with bated breath. Matthew's eyes darted to Melinda, who had stopped tending the stove to hear his reply.

"What can I tell you, son? I am but a mortal man whose chief mission in life was to save lives for God, but when I became a father... my children and their safety trumped all that. I can't explain to you that love until you experience it yourself... I'm not making excuses or hiding from the truth... it's how I feel... I can't imagine God would punish a man for protecting those he loved. I love you boys more than you'll ever know and if protecting you through the use of violence is wrong, I'll accept the consequences from God. His judgement is righteous, not mankind's." Matthew concluded with tears in his eyes. "Jack... you said they knew he was at Shearer's... did they find him?"

"No, sir. He had left before they arrived."

"Where did he go?"

"He went with Simon to Lexington."

"And... anything happen in Lexington?"

"Well, I'm not sure exactly what happened but he came running out of a laundromat and into Bobby Joe's truck with me."

"How did you happen to be at that particular laundromat when your brother ran out?"

"The dream... I knew he would be at a laundromat... Bobby Joe drove us there... he was making a visit..."

"Bobby Joe was doing his laundry that late at night?" Melinda asked the obvious.

"Not exactly... he was picking up a prescription."

"A prescription at a laundromat, Jack what are you talking about?" Melinda admonished.

"Bobby Joe was picking up drugs, Melinda. Go ahead Jack, what happened next?"

"Uhh... we went in, picked up the prescriptions and left... Luke and Simon soon went in after."

"You saw Luke and Simon go in?" Joseph interrupted.

"No... not exactly."

"What does that mean? Weren't you there? You said he came running out to the truck. I assume you were still there. Why didn't you stop him from going in?" Joseph argued.

"Because... because I had passed out."

"What?"

"I passed out."

"What caused you to pass out? What happened in the laundromat that caused you to pass out?"

Jack looked around the room and it was intensely quiet as all eyes were squarely on him. Admitting you were weak and cowardly to yourself was one thing. Stating it as a fact to your family was extremely difficult under any circumstance, but especially harsh when it affects another, your little brother.

"I passed out because I was really scared... I saw the evil face of my nightmare and the realization of the moment must have hit me. All I know is that Bobby Joe brought me out to his truck and that he said he saw Luke come running out. He climbed in the truck and we left. We took Luke back to his car at Shearer's and that was it."

"What do you mean that was it? Where did he go? What did he do?" Matthew insisted.

"I don't know dad. He wouldn't tell us. I insisted he stay with Bobby Joe because I knew they would be coming after him and he wouldn't be safe here."

"Oh my God... Luke's in real danger... he might be..."

Suddenly the kitchen door flung open as Luke entered.

"Good morning family! Boy, does it smell great in here. Momma make me three scrambled cheese eggs and half a dozen slices of bacon. I could eat a horse!" Luke announced.

The stunned family stared at him in disbelief before erupting in joy. They ran over to the prodigal son and "Miller-hugged" him in a familiar group embrace.

❧ ❧ ❧ ❧ ❧ ❧ ❧

Luke ravenously ate his mother's breakfast while fielding a ton of questions from his worried family. He was evasive about where he stayed overnight reasoning that the less they knew the safer it was for them. He assured them he was in no present danger and that this whole misunderstanding would pass over time. Matthew pressed for details about the action the previous night in the Zone and what had occurred in the laundromat in Lexington last night.

Again, Luke downplayed the events as "being in the wrong place at the wrong time" and that Jack was overstating a simple mistaken identity to connect it to a silly nightmare. Matthew watched quietly as Joseph took the reins as chief prosecutor.

"So, everything that's happened over the past two nights is 'mistaken identity' and 'wrong place, wrong time'. Is that your contention?" Joseph inquired in a shrill voice.

"Yeah... really that's it. Why are you getting so mad? It's not your problem. Not your issue?"

"It is! It's affecting all of us because you are family and we care about you, you idiot!"

"Yeah that sounds really touching, especially that last part. Look, I'm not in any real danger. I parked the car over on Hickory Hill so that those guys wouldn't bother or harass you all."

"They were here last night, you know?" Joseph informed.

"Were they?" Luke asked nonchalantly. *Damn, so they do know who I am... only one way they could've found out... Simon. He must be in a huge debt to his 'boss' that they pressured him to give up my name. I must be the package the 'boss' was referring to on the phone. He was probably talking to the guys that he sent to Nicholasville last night looking for me... damn this is really getting crazy! I need to get away from my family. Can't expose them again to that violent gang again... but I'm so damn tired from sleeping restlessly in my car last night. I'll take a quick nap downstairs in my room and then head out. Can't stay too long... just so damn tired.*

"Luke? Luke! What's wrong with you? I've been asking you about those guys from the Zone that were here last night?" Joseph insisted.

"Oh yeah... sorry. Umm, again, it's just a little misunderstanding with Simon, not me. He has run into some debt with these guys and because I was with him so often, they must have thought he was hanging out with me at my parent's place. A simple misunderstanding, really. I'm not the target of their inquiry."

"Inquiry? You think this is an inquiry... as if these thugs from the Zone are associates from a business firm that found some accounting errors from one of their employees?" Joseph insisted, "and are simply conducting a probe? Are you really that naïve, stupid or..."

"Joseph! Enough! There's no need for further insults. Your brother's home. He's safe and we're not getting anywhere with these inflammatory accusations and unverified statements. Luke, you look tired. Why don't you go downstairs and get some sleep?" Matthew implored.

"Yes! That's a great idea pops! I do need to catch up on my zee's. Mama, as always, great breakfast! Jack, thanks brother for your help. But again, I'm fine... all is well. Joseph... I know you mean well, but... I'm not your responsibility and your watch is over. You've been watching over us your whole life and I'm telling you now, you can retire. I can handle my own business. Good night, guys... enjoy the day, I'm sleeping."

The room was silent as the youngest departed downstairs. Melinda resumed to her work in the kitchen cleaning up the breakfast skillets and pans as Matthew gathered the dishes. Jack jumped to his feet and announced he was returning to Lexington to work on a research paper in the Young Center library. Joseph groused about the need to keep a vigilant watch out for Luke but didn't seem interested in taking on the task.

"Look, I know you're concerned. I am too, but grilling him like you did will not get the desired result. You know Luke. When pressed, he gets stubborn and downright obstinate. His explanation about Simon actually made sense. He would be the target of those thugs from the Zone… not Luke. Luke didn't do anything." Matthew rationalized.

"Are you serious? He was deflecting… like he always does when he's guilty of something or lying to cover something up. He's the target, or are you simply going to ignore Jack's dream?"

"I'm not ignoring or discounting Jack's dream. It's very important but it did end last night. Luke survived the end of Jack's nightmare and he's here now. Maybe the worst is over, and the outcome was changed because it was Luke, not Jack experiencing it. I don't know. Jack, is there anything else to your dream that we can work with?"

"Umm… it's hard to say because, like you said, the terrifying conclusion happened last night and because Luke escaped the laundromat, whatever followed must not occur…"

"Okay, see Joseph… the path was altered, and the outcome changed. Look, I have to be in Lexington this morning. You guys have fun doing your research. Joseph, don't you have a sermon to work on? Here's the keys to my office at the church. Use all my books, papers and anything else you need. Melinda, I love you dear. I have my cell phone if you need me." Matthew announced as he scooped up his briefcase and left out the side kitchen door.

"You and I both know this isn't over and there is much more to follow. I'm still puzzled by the 1-2-1 that kept popping up in your dream. I'm going to the church to do more research on it. You did a great job watching out for Luke last night. He's safe because of you… you know that, right? I'm not sorry for staying home. It was the right thing to do. Luke has to grow up and face the consequences of his ill-conceived actions and associations with questionable characters, like Simon. But it was your dream and, really, you're the only one who knows the whole truth of the matter. I don't think you've told us everything… for whatever reason and I'm trusting you… keep an eye out on Luke. He acts like he knows what he's doing and he's tough as nails. May be the strongest, and best of all of us, but his confidence in his strength and abilities could also be his weakness. You know what I mean?" Joseph offered in quiet voice to keep his mother out of earshot.

"Yeah… he's a badass and he's successfully run through this gauntlet. Let's just hope nothing else comes up and maybe this thing will pass as Luke said. Anyway, I need to get outta here. Have fun crunching the numbers at the church." Jack mocked. "I can't think of anything more boring than spending a perfectly good Saturday researching my stupid dreams' numbers at the church!"

Matthew Mitchell didn't make many demands on his sons, such as household chores, high academic grades, or even civic responsibilities like missionary outreach. He even stopped requiring them to attend church regularly. Once they graduated high school, he believed they were mature enough to make those decisions for themselves. Coerced religion appealed to few and usually didn't stick, Matthew reasoned. He took a more liberal approach with his boys— raise them to love and obey God, respect adults and societal institutions, and treat others as you would want others to treat you. He believed that Christian core values equipped a child to face any societal challenges or evil acts.

Because of Matthew's liberal approach, only Joseph attended church regularly. In fact, he decided to make a vocation in the church following his father's footsteps. However, the younger siblings felt liberated from the Sunday shackled ritual. They enjoyed the benefits of a full weekend with late-night Saturday parties and sleep-in Sundays. Matthew knew his recalcitrant sons would eventually return to the church, but it had to be on their terms and at their behest.

Matthew was running the day's schedule through his head, when he realized he had forgotten to drop off some Sunday school training materials off with Deacon Wilkins. He also remembered that he needed Melinda to join him on a difficult hospital visit with one of his church member's daughter who had attempted suicide. Melinda knew the mother well and was a great source of strength and comfort. Turning the car around, he headed back home.

On his return, he noticed that the oldest boys had already left while Melinda was straightening the closet in their bedroom. Matthew reminded her about the Dawson girl and she readily agreed to join him but needed a few minutes to get ready. Matthew knew he wouldn't have time to drop off the Sunday school materials to Deacon Wilkins without being trapped into a long theological discussion about anything that happened to pop into the postman's head.

He often found that many of his deacons and church officials wanted to engage in a dialogue about church affairs and theology, but really just wanted to vent into a monologue. These monologues could be quite tiresome as the members didn't want spiritual or biblical advice, just the minister's affirmation. Matthew nodded his head, *Wilkins is a good man but too talkative and I don't have the time for his stories. Hate to wake Luke but I really need his help this morning. Won't take any time for him to do this simple task* Matthew reasoned as he descended the carpeted steps into the fully finished basement complete with three bedrooms and a den.

The downstairs den was a popular hangout for the boys and their friends and was replete with a stocked refrigerator and microwave oven. The relaxed atmosphere of the basement was a teenage haven compared to the stuffy upstairs parlor and sitting room Melinda used to entertain various church clubs.

As Matthew walked across the den, he noticed several articles of clothing lying about the floor and furniture as well as many dishes and glasses left dirty on tables and trays. Matthew shook his head in disgust. *That boy lives like a pig with no regard for this house or its rules. I will definitely have to address this. Can't let him turn our home into his lazy pig sty. But I can't get caught up in that now. I need Luke to do something very important and simple. Giving him the business about the den could create a whole scene that could keep him from doing what I need him to do. He seems to always be on the edge... even before this latest garbage from the Zone. He's not the same easy-going, carefree teen... at least not since the Janee accident. He's a boiling teapot ready to explode at the slightest incident. He's got to learn to get over events that are out of his control... that he had no hand in. It's consuming him. I know it. He's good at masking it occasionally, but you sense there's a rage boiling and ready to vent at any moment.*

Matthew knocked softly on Luke's bedroom door but heard nothing. He knocked several more times before turning the door knob allowing a beam of light to shoot through the room. *Man, he keeps it dark in here. Need to turn the light on... but that might freak him out. Too bright, too soon. I'll just ease the window shade up and let a little light in.* The outside sun streamed across Luke's face causing him to wince. Luke frowned and rubbed his eyes before pulling the comforter over his head.

"Luke... Luke" Matthew called out more firmly the second time.

"What?" Luke replied in mild agitation.

"Sit up, son. I need your full attention. I need you to do something important for me today."

"Yes, sir... what is it?"

"I'm going to be in Lexington all day with your mother. We have hospital visits and several other things to attend to that will keep us out all day. I need you to drop off the Sunday school training materials for Mr. Wilkins."

"Mr. Wilkins? The mailman?"

"Yes... he's also a deacon at the church and head of the Sunday school department. You know him... he taught you guys, I believe, when you were nine or ten years old."

"Oh yeah... he taught us about Hell. Scared us pretty good. In fact, he didn't scare the hell out of us; he put the fear of hell in us."

"Not a bad idea. Some people need that jolt."

"Yeah, but dad, we were what... ten years old? That's kind a creepy." Luke added sitting up in bed. "Now that you mention it, I always thought there was something creepy about him... can't quite put my finger on it..."

"Really? That's odd. He always plays games with kids, especially when he sees them on his mail route. I know it makes the mail run late, but people really like him and don't seem to mind too much."

"Yeah, but… I don't know. It just seems weird that he plays games like 'Duck, Duck, Goose' and 'Hide and Seek' when he's supposed to be working."

"He played Hide and Seek with you guys?"

"Not us, but with other kids in the neighborhood."

"That does seem weird… I do believe, now that you mention it, some parents did complain, but nothing really came about from it…" Matthew paused in thought. "Anyway, I need you to drop off the materials to him sometime today… preferably in the morning."

"Why not give it to him when he stops by to deliver the mail?"

"He's off today."

"Mailmen get days off?"

"Sure."

"But they only work a couple of days a week and sometimes on Saturday…"

"This is his Saturday off, I guess. In any case, just swing by his house, drop off the materials that are sitting on the kitchen table upstairs… and he's got some papers to give you."

"Papers to give me?"

"Not you, me. They're church papers… financial reports."

"Oh, okay. Yeah, I can do that. What time do I need to make the drop?"

"The drop? Oh yeah, that's street lingo." Matthew mocked.

"Yeah… whatever. Dad, I don't do drugs or anything like that. I've told you before." Luke asserted a bit animated.

"All right. All right. Thanks for doing this."

"Where does he live?"

"Oh yeah… 121 Pinewood Drive."

"Pinewood Drive… Pinewood Drive…" Luke muttered.

"What about Pinewood Drive?"

"Oh nothing… just haven't been to that neighborhood in a long time."

"Well, that's where he lives. He's been there as long as I've known him… almost thirty years. See ya later son." Matthew added patting Luke on the leg as he left.

"Bye dad." Luke replied walking over to the window and raising the shade. Staring at the neighbor's backyard towards Pinewood Drive, Luke was locked in a deep thought. *Mr. Wilkins lives in Pinewood… Pinewood… haven't thought of that place in a while. Man, he sure scared us all with that freaky story about hell.*

Luke's mind drifted to that Sunday morning eleven years ago—

The Miller boys were dragging their feet in the education building of Nicholasville Baptist Church. They hated Sunday school because it was too much like real school— reading, writing, sitting still, and behaving. Joseph walked his younger brothers to their assigned classes making sure they got there. The few times he didn't walk them in, they ran off to Hemphill's Drug store to wait until church started. After dropping his brothers off on the first-floor classroom, Joseph hopped up the steps to his class for young teens.

Jack and Luke slumped into their seats like prisoners assigned to their fate among seven other unlucky inmates equally enthused about Mr. Wilkins' class.

Mr. Wilkins strolled in whistling in an ill-fitted suit and tie from a bygone era. His hair was slicked back with enough oil to resolve the energy crisis of the 1970's. He reeked of after-shave and hair tonic. Squatting down in the small wooden chairs for children, he welcomed the class.

"Well kids, I'm awfully glad you could make it this morning. I just flew in from Cincinnati and boy are my arms tired!" Alvin canned with a forced chuckle cueing the kids to laugh. Often, they politely acquiesced his corny humor though they rarely understood.

"Kids... what I'm about to talk to you about today brings me no pleasure. No sir, no pleasure at all but you need to hear it because you're old enough to know about these sorta things." Alvin added wiping his forehead with his beefy hand clutching a handkerchief, he proceeded cautiously. "Today we're gonna talk about Hell." Pausing for dramatic effect and waiting for an outpour of gasping. Instead the kids simply stared at him in eager anticipation.

"Again, this isn't an easy topic to talk about but... you gotta know." Alvin added while lowering his head into his calloused hands. "Boys... have you ever been hot. I mean real hot from being outside in the middle of the day in July or August and you were sweating so bad it seemed like you had been swimming?"

"Oh yeah!" came a cacophony of voices from the kids as they easily imagined what Mr. Wilkins had described. "One day, I got so hot..." Mason tried to insert.

"Well Hell is a thousand times hotter. It's a burning lake of fire that torches your soul all day and night without ever letting up or getting cooler. Your soul burns forever!" Mr. Wilkins screamed silencing the boys to open-mouthed shock. Like any good orator, he allowed that image to sink in for a second while he lowered his head back into his hands.

"Boys... you ever cut your finger? Slice it with a knife or cut it with some sharp object and it hurt really bad?" Wilkins proceeded

with his rhetorical question while twisting the ruby ring on his pinky finger.

The students nodded in agreement as a plump red-headed boy named Rusty started in on his tale of woe from an old nail when Wilkins blared, "Hell's like being cut and stabbed a thousand times more painful than anything you've felt on Earth. The devil pokes and prods and stabs you with his pitchfork and you're in pain forever!"

Lowering his head once more, Mr. Wilkins allowed that image to meld in the boys' active imagination. For greater dramatic effect, he continued in a whispered voice, "Boys... you ever been thirsty? So parched and dry-mouthed that it felt like you had cotton balls wadded up in your mouth? So thirsty for an ice-cold lemonade, or a sweet tea or a Coca Cola? Well Hell makes you so thirsty that your body shakes violently in need of hydration... it so thirsts for water. But the devil denies you that cold water. He taunts and teases you with a glass of ice-cold water and just as you reach for it, he yanks it away!"

The class was completely absorbed in Mr. Wilkins' animated story as some sobbed quietly in fear of damnation. Jack and Luke sat in awed silence awaiting the next horrific revelation of Hell. Mr. Wilkins playing the young audience to his theatrical performance, lowered his head once again while rubbing his eyes with is left hand and tightly gripping his knee with his right hand to demonstrate his anguish.

"Boys... I don't tell you this merely to frighten you. No sir, that's not the point... I want you to be aware that there are consequences to your actions and behavior on Earth... there is a loving God willing to forgive us our hateful sins, but we have to acknowledge it, ask for His loving forgiveness. For without it, we will all go to Hell... and boys I'm here to tell you it's a very real place and its eternal— forever. Your soul, as we discussed two weeks ago, is what makes you who you are. It's your core of essence. These bodies of ours are mere suits, like temporary clothes for our souls. They are of the Earth and will stay of the Earth. But our soul is from God and will return to Him in heaven if we obey Him on Earth. If you don't... if you choose the devil's earthly pleasures and sinful desires, you separate yourself from God and separation from God," Wilkins demonstrated by stretching his hands wide apart, "is like denying His existence and as Christ said in Matthew 10:33 'But whoever denies me before men, I will also deny him before my Father who is in Heaven'... boys let's pray."

Luke shook his head in wonder at the thought of a grown man, respected mailman, and Sunday school teacher, telling little kids such a terrifying story. *Man, I can't believe he told us a story like that about Hell. Didn't he think we were a bit young to fully understand such a complex concept as Hell. I can't believe dad let him do it. Maybe dad didn't know... oh well, he always seemed a bit weird.*

Luke's phone hummed from the night stand. It was Simon. Luke hesitated to answer, not sure how he felt about Simon's role in last night's encounter with the "Boss" at the laundromat. He needed to know whose side Simon was really on and what the repercussions were for his attack on the "Boss".

"Hey"

"Hey yourself, Luke. Damn son, I've been trying to get a hold of you all night and morning. Where the hell are you?" Simon implored.

"Nowhere. Why the hell did you take me to that damn laundromat and why didn't you leave with me? Did you set me up?" Luke demanded.

"Hold up, buddy! I'm the one who should be pissed, not you! I told you I wanted you to meet the Boss and see he was not some gangster-thug Jack imagined from a dumbass dream. Jack had you all spooked and I thought you needed to see the truth. Not some judgmental image created by your judgmental family. Then just as things were going well, you punch him several times and then bolt... leaving me sitting there looking like an ass to the Boss. He was pissed but not for the reasons you concocted. He damn near chewed my ass out for an hour. I was able to calm him down cause he wanted to send you a strong message last night at your parent's house."

"He better never step one foot near my parent's house again! I swear to God, I'll finish his ass if he does!"

"Alright, easy Rocky! Damn, you knock a few heads around and you think you're fucking invincible! Look, as I said, I calmed him down and got him to agree to let matters go if you do something for him. You know, a peace offering for an unprovoked attack."

"I thought he was talking about me on the phone as the 'package' and it felt like a trap. It followed everything Jack had warned me about in his dream."

"Alright, Jack's dream is shit and its gonna get you in real trouble if you keep spewing about it. Now do you want to get clean and off the hook with the Boss or not, cause I put my ass on the line for you!"

"Yeah... alright. What's the 'peace offering' that I have to do?"

"Its real simple... he wants you to go on a repo with me today. You'll play clown or muscle to distract or hold off the client while I hook up the repo."

"I thought Bobby Joe did that sort of thing for the Boss?"

"He did. Not anymore."

"Why?"

"I'm not sure, but I'm sure it has something to do with what happened last night. Anyway, you need to do this with me. What do you say?"

Luke stared out the window weighing his options and trying to make sense of the latest revelation about what happened at the laundromat after he left and why Bobby Joe was now on the outs with the Boss. *Damn this is happening too fast… too much to think about in such a short time… man its beautiful outside. The perfect day for golf.*

"Hey, meet me at Dearbourne. Let's get some golf in." Luke entreated.

"Are you serious? You want to play golf today?"

"Absolutely! Meet me there in an hour. I have an errand to run first and then I'll meet you there."

"Alright… don't be late cause we'll have just enough time to squeeze in nine holes and then we need to do that repo."

Luke slid on a pair of khaki trousers and flung a red polo over his shoulders. Running his hands through his sandy brown tussled hair, he decided it looked fine without a hat. He grabbed his car keys and bolted up the stairs from the basement. The house was empty and comfortably quiet from several days of argument and debate. Popping the fridge door open, he looked for some kind of fruit that he could easily eat on the way to the golf course. *Yes… mom has apples! Okay off to the golf course! Oh wait, I've gotta drop off that Sunday school crap to Mr. Wilkins.*

Luke walked over to the kitchen table and found a large box labeled "NBC- Sunday School Training Material" with a note from his father— "Mr. Wilkins, 121 Pinewood Drive". He shoved the apple in his pants pocket and hauled the box out to his car. Starting up the car set his mind in motion. *Mr. Wilkins… Mr. Wilkins… man that dude is odd. There's something about him… like… damn, can't wrap my head around why he seems really odd to me… like something happened but I only had him a few times for Sunday school and then he suddenly started teaching another class. Wonder what happened that caused him to move to another class… damn, turning onto Pinewood Drive… haven't been here in a long time. Not since that fucked up Halloween…*

Luke pulled up to 121 Pinewood Drive. Eased out of the car and pulled the big box of Sunday school material out of his trunk. Looking around as he crossed the street he felt an eerie sensation— as if he had been here before. He walked up to the front door and rapped the lion's head knocker. After the second knock he could here movement towards the front door.

Alvin Wilkins was excited. His favorite time of the year was fast approaching— Halloween. He had pulled his life-size dummy clown, Sparkles, out of the attic and set it on his wife's Dante chair in the front parlor. Delores complained about the annual frightful event but knew it was useless to argue about it as Alvin insisted it was good, clean fun.

"Oh Alvin! Why do you always have to haul that ugly old clown down for Halloween? It's too creepy and scares the little ones and why is it sitting in my beautiful chair in the parlor?" Delores implored.

"That's the point…it's scary. I want it to stay in the front parlor and see what kind of reaction it gets from your stuffy old Women's Circle crowd." Alvin replied from the bathroom with a chuckle.

"Oh, that's great. It's tough enough explaining your eccentricities to many of the ladies of the church without you fueling their concerns with this type of behavior. Look if you're using the restroom, I wish you wouldn't reply. It's in poor taste to engage in a conversation while you're conducting nature's business."

"You mean taking a shit!"

"Alvin J. Wilkins, such language!"

"Ha, ha! You old Puritan ninny, I'm not 'conducting nature's business'" Alvin mocked in his wife's voice. "I'm working on a surprise for this year's Halloween. But first I gotta get into character."

"Oh dear, tell me you're not putting on that dreadful clown make-up."

"Now what have I told you about that Delores? Stop badgering me about my hobbies and what I like to do on my free time. I work hard during the week, walking all over Nicholasville delivering mail, entertaining the public, that clamors for my stories, and then on the weekends, I'm often preparing for my Sunday school class and making sure all my teachers are well-prepared for their classes. By the way, did Reverend Miller drop off the training materials? He said he was going to at some time today."

"No, not yet. Dear, I'm not scolding you. It's just… oh wait I hear someone at the door."

Delores gathered herself, straightened her dress, and checked her hair in the hallway mirror. As she opened the door, her heart skipped a beat as she gasped. *Oh dear God, Oh dear God! What is he doing here? Oh, I just knew this day was coming… play it cool Delores. He looks like he's delivering Alvin's Sunday school materials.*

"Good morning… or afternoon, Mrs. Wilkins. I'm not really sure if its morning or afternoon." Luke shrugged innocently. "My dad wanted me to drop this huge box off for your husband."

"Oh… yes… Mr. Wilkins was expecting it. I'll take that off your hands."

"Oh no, Mrs. Wilkins, this box is way too heavy for you. I'll just bring it in, if you don't mind."

"Oh… well… sure. Come on in. Here just follow me to the kitchen." Delores grabbed Luke's elbow and guided him away from the front parlor. "Here, you can just put it down on the table."

"Great. Well, I better be heading out. Oh wait, dad said he needed me to pick up some financial reports from Mr. Wilkins."

"Financial reports? Oh. I'm not sure Alvin has those ready yet…"

"Yes, I do, Delores. They're down in the office in the basement. They're sitting on the desk in a red folder." a voice from the back hallway replied.

"Oh… well, I guess I can retrieve them. Just wait here Luke in the kitchen. I won't be but a second."

Luke nodded while Mrs. Wilkins dashed down the basement stairwell. He could hear her rummaging about frantically searching for the red folder. Always curious about the dwellings and keepsakes of others, Luke wandered into the den looking at an assortment of service awards, framed certificates of appreciation, and family portraits of the pair. *No children… that's odd. They seem like ideal parent-types. I wonder why they never had kids. Oh well, he probably couldn't rise to the occasion. Wonder what's in that other room that Mrs. Wilkins steered me away from?*

Luke poked his head into the front parlor. The room was dark with the front shades pulled down. He could make out an elegant room with a piano surrounded by an assortment of chairs and a small love seat. He squinted his eyes to try to make out what was in the far corner. It looked as if someone was sitting in a chair in the dark. Luke could feel an odd sensation take hold of his body. A sensation he hadn't felt in a long time.

The room began to move about and blur as he stumbled in the dark to find a light source. His shin hit the coffee table and he dropped to his knees in anguish. Rubbing his shin, he looked up at the figure in the corner chair. He could feel his heart beating faster as if it would explode out of his chest. Slowly rising he reached for a lamp sitting on a side table. He pulled the lamp cord as the light instantly streaked across the clown's face. Luke's mouth opened wide as images began to flash in his head— evil clown eyes opening from a coffin— the clown face smiling at him— grabbing his arm— rising from the coffin. The room swirled rapidly as Luke tried to keep his balance. More graphic images flashed— red-painted lips of the clown moving— yellow sharpened teeth gleaming— evil piercing eyes with dark high arching eye-brows and vertical lines running down through the eyelids— Luke was transformed back in time to that horrific Halloween and in the garage that he had hoped he had repressed.

He was backing away from the coffin and watching in stunned fright as the dead clown climbed out. Through the small slits of the Transformer mask, Luke spied the clown rise to full height grinning with bright red lips from ear to ear revealing sharp yellow teeth surrounded by pale white skin. His hair seemed to be ablaze in red and orange flames flickering in the dull garage lights.

"Relax, relax… big boy. Did you come here to get candy from Sparkles? Well, did you?" Sparkles demanded as he crept closer.

Luke was paralyzed in fear. He couldn't move a limb as he stared into the red demonic eyes of the possessed clown come to life.

"Not a talker eh, big boy? Well that's okay because Sparkles will do all the talking. You want Sparkles' candy, you're going to have to give him some candy, too! Do you understand what I'm saying big boy? Sparkles likes candy... especially from big boys like yourself! Now to get Sparkles' candy, you need to unzip your pants. You heard me, big boy, unzip now!" the demonic clown commanded the terrified Transformer.

Sensing that the youth would not accede to his demands, Sparkles pulled off the glove of his left hand and slowly unzipped the boy's pants. He dropped down to his knees and began to tug on the boy's pants. Luke was screaming on the inside but could hear no sound emit from the mask. The room began spinning, lights glared in a dizzying array as images of red and orange flickered. Suddenly the garage was filled with a burst of screams and shouts.

"No! No! Stop it this instant! Stop it now!" cried the voice filling the den of iniquity. Luke's eyes batted about picking up brief glimpses of the clown's head turning back towards the door. He fell forward and lost consciousness. The spinning, cataclysmic world went dark.

Luke heard a distant voice calling out his name from the dark world and with each cry he felt a stinging sensation to his cheek. Trying to gather his thoughts and make sense of his befuddled environment, he opened his eyes in terror as he saw the same haunting specter from eleven years ago sitting atop his chest— the flaming red and orange hair flickering in the light. The yellow sharp teeth encased in wide red lips and the eyes— demonic red- hot coals searing into his soul the fear and horror of his lost youth.

"Well now big boy, seems like you fainted. Did old Sparkles give you a fright?" the clown queried in laughter grinning from ear to ear.

Luke raged as he regained full consciousness and drove his right fist into the ample gut of the clown. Sparkles doubled over groaning as Luke scrambled to his feet. He grabbed the clown from behind and threw another powerful punch into the back of the head. Sparkles screamed and squealed as he crawled on all fours trying to escape his fate. Luke kicked the clown several times in the rear end, like a cat toying with his prey before the fatal blows. However, Sparkles got to his feet and ran into the kitchen crying out for help and begging for mercy.

"Mercy! Mercy! You want mercy, you fuck-faced nightmare!" Luke replied as he cornered the clown and delivered a devastating right cross to the clown's jaw, followed quickly by two more blows to the left eye and ear.

He grabbed the clown's frilled high-collared blouse and drove him into the refrigerator twice. Each blow seemed to knock the wind out of the clown's lungs.

"Stop! Stop it this instant Luke! You're going to kill him!" Delores screamed as she emerged from the side basement door of the kitchen.

"He deserves to die!" Luke barked and threw the clown down on the floor.

Sitting atop the crumbled clown, Luke repeatedly punched the clown's painted face until he felt a powerful pang on his head and his world went dark. He fell forward and slumped against the sink cabinets. Delores put the iron skillet down on the counter and called the sheriff's department.

"Yes, I want to report an attack on my husband, Alvin Wilkins! Yes, that's right… it's at our home…121 Pinewood Drive. Please hurry! I've knocked the attacker down but he's stirring and I'm not sure I can keep him down! Please hurry! Tell Sheriff Walker I need him now! Oh God! Oh God, he's getting up! He's getting up! Please Luke stop this madness! No more! No more!" Delores screamed as Luke rose to his feet and grabbed the phone out of her hand. He slammed the phone down and grabbed her by the arm leading her down the hallway. He shoved her into a bedroom and locked the door.

Luke's head hurt, and his eyes were blurry as he returned to the kitchen. Rubbing his eyes to clear his vision, he was shocked at what he saw or didn't see— the clown was missing. *Great! Where the hell did that demonic shit-face go? It's not a big house but… wait there's blood over by that side door.* Luke cautiously approached the opened basement door and peered down the lighted stairwell. Slowly inching his way down each creaking, cracking wooden step, he reached the bottom. The floor was dotted with red droplets leading a trail toward the back wall.

The room itself was dark, as the only light came from the stairwell. Looking from one side to another, he saw an office space complete with a desk, roller chair and two tall metal file cabinets in the foreground. Squinting his eyes, he could see a large overstuffed sofa and coffee table against the back wall and another door. Drawn to the mysterious and seemingly inexplicable door adjacent to the back wall, Luke slowly padded past the coffee table and stared for a few seconds at the protruding door on the right-side wall. He reached for the door knob, grabbed it and tried several times to turn the locked door.

"Looking for something, big boy? Maybe you want some candy? Sparkles has all sorts of different candies. He loves all kinds of candy!" growled the voice from the past followed by an eerie shrill laugh.

Luke spun on his heels and saw the squat pale demonic clown. Much smaller and less intimidating than he remembered, nonetheless, the clown curled his red-painted lips, narrowed his beady red-tinted contacts, and shoved a snubbed-nose pistol into Luke's abdomen.

"I guess the wheels of fortune have turned and …" Sparkles intoned just before his face exploded in pain as Luke punched him squarely on the rubber red nose that squeaked.

Sparkles fell backwards. Luke pursued his prey and shoved him to the floor. The gun dangled in the clown's right hand. Luke kicked it away. Filled with the rage of a tormented soul, he dropped down on the clown's chest executing a series of powerful blows to the face. With each stroke, Luke was haunted by flashbacks. Images that he had repressed had re-emerged in a flurry— red and orange flaming hair, sharpened yellow teeth, red devil eyes with dissecting black lines— the raspy, authoritative voice demanding and laughing at the innocence and terror of a child. Each image provoked a new, volatile attack on the face that no longer smiled.

The grisly sound of a fist hitting a motionless, misshapen face was abruptly broken by a powerful swift tackle driving Luke to the ground. The stunning force found Luke lying pinned against the desk with a two-hundred-pound man pulling his arms behind his back. He was swarmed by an additional three uniformed men sporting tan cowboy hats.

"Calm down, Luke! Calm down! It's over! It's over!" screamed Sheriff Joe Walker as he wrestled mightily with Luke's arms. "I don't know what this is all about but it's over! Calm down!"

Luke looked into the sheriff's eyes and saw true grit and determination— the kind of characteristics that Luke had always admired in the Walker brothers. Though were many years older than the Miller brothers, they very similar in demeanor and competitive spirit. The brothers had often competed against each other in recreational sports of basketball and softball. The Miller's, like most in Nicholasville, admired the talented Walker brothers. Joe had recently won the sheriff's seat after his older brother, Steve, had retired from fifteen years of service.

Luke lowered his head and gave up the fight. He could feel the rage subside and was drained of all energy. As the deputies pulled him up to his feet, he heard the sheriff frantically try to revive the battered clown and then call for an ambulance into his shoulder walkie-talkie. Luke was rapidly walked up the stairs and past a weeping woman sitting at the kitchen table.

"Luke, you went too far! You went too far! Why didn't you stop? I tried to stop you! I tried to stop it! But I couldn't! I'm too weak! Too weak…" Delores wailed.

With a deputy at each side and one in front leading him out the front door, Luke lowered his head as the bright sunshine beamed in his face. He could feel his body moving to the cadence of the perp-walk as neighbors lined the street to witness the shocking event of a minister's son being arrested for an assault on a beloved postman and community leader.

Once inside the sheriff's cruiser, Luke watched the ambulance drive into the front yard as EMT's scrambled into the house. Luke stared numbly at the front house and then transfixed his eyes to the large metallic garage door— site of his tormented childhood and repressed until a horrific image sparked the haunted memory from the recesses of his brain. He recognized many of the street features such as painted house numbers on the curbs and cracked asphalt streaking across the road that made bike riding difficult. Nothing had changed in the eleven years since the Halloween assault, and yet, here was Luke sitting in a sheriff's car handcuffed.

The EMT's returned with a gurney carrying a lumped, red-headed clown out of the front door as his wife held his hand and spoke to him hysterically. Sheriff Walker helped her into the back of the ambulance and marched back to his car.

"I have no idea what just happened, but my God Luke, you may have killed the man. His face is so distorted, and his breathing is so tortured... the EMT's don't seem to like his chances. Luke, you better pray that man doesn't die!" Sheriff Walker stated forcefully looking back at the assailant in the rearview mirror.

Wrong! I pray the fucker dies and meets his Maker today! He'll learn what Hell is really all about! He scared us as children with vivid details of damnation, now he'll get a chance to experience it for real and FOREVER! Luke reasoned in silence.

Chapter 13

"Courage is resistance to fear, mastery of fear — not absence of fear."
— Mark Twain

The drive to the Jessamine County Detention Center didn't take long—down Shun Pike and onto West Maple Street. Cruising through downtown Nicholasville and past the courthouse, Sheriff Walker had tried to engage Luke in a conversation to try to make sense of a senseless assault. Each attempt resulted in silence. Luke refused to talk to defend or explain his actions. He had an absent stare out the cruiser window that the sheriff recognized as shock.

He had seen it many times from some of the assailants he had encountered over the ten years of service on the county force. He reasoned it was useless to try to get them to talk in their present state of shock. He couldn't believe what he saw down in Wilkins basement just a few moments ago. *What the hell was Wilkins doing dressed as that creepy clown? Why was Luke there? What was the dispute that drove Luke into a blind rage? My God, I've never seen such anger and blunt force trauma like Luke was giving to Wilkins. The pounding he took! What caused this and what was Mrs. Wilkins getting at when she kept mumbling "I knew this day was coming! I knew this day was coming!" I asked her several times in the house what that meant, and she refused to answer... just looked at me blankly.*

The brown and tan sheriff's car turned left off East Maple Street to the county detention center and entered through a large security gate for law enforcement personnel only. Pulling into the sally port, Sheriff Walker parked and exited the car to retrieve his prisoner.

"Come on Luke, we gotta process you."

Luke stared at the multitude of cameras mounted all over the garage-like building. He was escorted to a table where a deputy thoroughly searched him for hidden weapons. Sheriff Walker checked his side-arm in to another official who registered the number and placed it in a bin with a locked door.

After a few minutes of playful banter with law enforcement personnel, Walker led Luke into the detention facility where he would be booked and fingerprinted. The highly skilled officers swiftly processed Luke like a well-oiled machine. Within twenty minutes, Luke was sitting in a holding cage waiting for Sheriff Walker who had disappeared into his office.

"Reverend Miller, I hate to make this call and trust me, I'm as stunned as you're going to be to hear what I'm about to tell you, but its not a joke or some crazy prank. I just arrested your son, Luke, on a second-degree assault and possible murder of Mr. Alvin Wilkins."

"What? Assault... murder... Alvin Wilkins? What's going on Joe? Where's Luke now?"

"He's here in the detention center. He was arrested and processed and is presently sitting in a holding cell now. Do you have an attorney you can get a hold of and do you wish to post bail?"

"Wow... this is so crazy...I'm having a hard time processing all of this. You said possible murder. How is Alvin? Where is he now?"

"He was taken by ambulance immediately to Lexington. Probably Central Baptist Hospital. His wife, Delores, said he had a heart condition... Reverend Miller what I saw of him... it will truly be a miracle if he survived the beating he took from your son, Luke,"

"My God! My God... look I'm in Lexington now and will swing by and visit Delores and try to get some answers about what happened... as far as Luke's concerned... he can sit and ponder what he's done while I try to make sense of all this. Thanks, Joe!"

∽ ∽ ∽ ∽ ∽ ∽ ∽

Matthew struggled to reconcile the actions of his temperamental youngest son and the seemingly mild-mannered Sunday School teacher and church deacon. Having spent the last half hour explaining, dissecting, and discussing Luke's incarceration with his wife, Melinda, the reverend was at a loss to understand what had transpired over the last forty-eight hours. From Jack's ominous dream of fatal collisions in the Zone to Luke's erratic behavior and association with questionable characters, Matthew had reached the limits of his secular reasoning.

He knew there was a spiritual answer and he had prayed for several hours at Central Baptist Hospital awaiting the opportunity to meet with Delores Wilkins. She had refused his requests insisting that it was too soon to talk about what had transpired and what she had witnessed. She sent her plea on a note explaining that she was also in prayer and needed to be near Alvin has he prepared to go into surgery. Matthew readily agreed and took Melinda's hand and exited the hospital.

"It's just surreal what has happened with Luke today. This morning we were so thankful he was alive and well and had survived Jack's dire portent. He assured us that he was not the target of any aggression or retribution from the Zone. And then I, like an idiot, send him out on a stupid errand and then all of this..." Matthew moaned.

"You couldn't have known what would happen sending him to see Alvin? No one could have. It's a mystery and nightmare what would have possessed our baby boy to viciously attack a man of God. Has he lost his mind? Has he wandered so far away from God that he would attack his servants?" Melinda reasoned.

"No. I don't believe that and neither do you. Luke has his doubts... questions about God. Not unlike many kids his age, but he would never attack, unprovoked, anyone, much less a gentle spirit like Alvin… but its funny. Luke was mentioning this morning that he thought Alvin was odd, kind of a weirdo… especially around little kids. He mentioned how strange it was that Alvin played a lot with the children on his mail route. I didn't think anything of it until he said so… which got me to thinking… there have been a few complaints over the years about Alvin's eccentric behavior around the kids at church."

"Like what? I don't recall hearing anything."

"Not likely you would as Delores is head of just about every women's club or association in the church. Anyway, several years ago there was an incident on a camping trip at High Bridge with the RA's. One of the parents said his son felt uneasy around Alvin when they went swimming and changed their clothes. The father dismissed the whole ordeal as simply his son's shyness about undressing around adults."

"Matthew, that's awful. You should have had a talk with that young boy and a serious talk with Alvin. There's no excuse for dismissing a child's cry for help. He turned to his father and … dear God, you men!" Melinda scolded.

"I know, I know… its awful and totally irresponsible and, in hindsight. I should have taken an active role and investigated."

"You said there were a few. What were the others and when?"

"I don't recall the specifics of the others because they happened before I became minister at the church. They were really rumors that cropped up when Alvin was nominated for church deacon. Similar allegations but no evidence and no one really wanting to testify or be interviewed. So, we passed him. Now… "

"Now the past has reared its ugly head in the form of our son attacking him."

"Yes… he attacked Alvin… I wonder… You know Alvin was Luke's Sunday School teacher years ago… he then asked to move up the building to teach older kids. I didn't think anything of it at the time and he was chairman of the Sunday Schools… no need to question it…"

"What are driving at Matthew? You have that serious, pensive stare going. What's going on?"

"I'm not sure but I need to talk to Luke. I've let him sit and stew in the jail cell long enough. Its time to call Matthew McCord and bring our son home. I'll drop you off at the house. If Joseph or Jack is at the house, tell them to stay there. I will need them."

ᨀ ᨀ ᨀ ᨀ ᨀ ᨀ ᨀ

Matthew pulled into the Jessamine County Detention Center and saw his attorney and lead church soprano, Matthew McCord's car in the parking lot. Matthew entered the detention center surrendering his cell phone, car keys, and coins in a small bowl before walking past several county deputies observing the metal detector. Once through the high glass double doors he spied his attorney sitting on a bench with his brief case. The two shook hands, exchanged pleasantries and proceeded into the merits of the case and what had occurred at the Pre-Trial interview.

"Everything went fine. The Pretrial Service Officer assigned to Luke is a good guy, Brandon Whitaker. He tried to get Luke to talk. Asked him basic questions about his background, risk to run and then informed him of how the pretrial services work while you're released on bond. Once bond is met there would be scheduled visits and interviews that had to be met in order to stay out of jail before trial."

"Oh, man… I've been here a few times with church members and others from the community, but never figured I would be here for one of my own." Matthew allowed lowering his head.

"Couldn't agree more, Reverend. It's a good thing you sent me here because Luke said nothing to Mr. Whitaker. Normally I advise my clients to stay silent and let me do all the talking, but at a pretrial interview, the client needs to talk and assure the officer that he's no risk to run, jump bail or any kind of threat to the community. Its his recommendation to the judge that allows a bond to be posted and then the judge sets it at a reasonable rate… based on that risk assessment. I told Luke he needed to plead his case to the Mr. Whitaker that he was no risk… he just sat there in stone-cold silence."

"He said nothing in his defense? Not even to you about what happened or why he attacked or how he wasn't a risk or threat to the community?"

"Nothing. I gotta be honest with you Reverend, if I were in Mr. Whitaker's shoes looking at Luke and the condition he was in, both physically and emotionally, I would have denied bond. No question about it."

"Really? That bad, huh?"

"That bad. Look, Mr. Whitaker recommended bond… more as a favor to me, and your sterling reputation in the community, and the judge agreed. I posted the bond and the paperwork is complete."

"You posted bond?"

"Yeah, don't worry it will be itemized in my bill." McCord added with a laugh.

"Yes, I'm sure. Matthew thank you so much! I can never repay your kindness, thoughtfulness, and thoroughness. Is Luke able to leave now?"

"Yep. He's waiting in the holding cell. Look, Reverend you might want to give it a day or two before you talk to him about all of this. He seems to be in a state of shock… like he's not all there. Its gonna take some time to recover from whatever state of mind or place he went to, but based on what I heard from Sheriff Walker... man, we need to pray that Alvin Wilkins recovers... cause Luke could be put away for a long time..."

"You're absolutely right, Matthew. I will be praying and will try to follow your advice about giving Luke some time and space."

"Not too much space, Reverend. I need him to meet all of his pretrial scheduled meetings or I'm out twenty thousand dollars!" McCord joked.

◈ ◈ ◈ ◈ ◈ ◈ ◈

The drive back to the house was quiet save the scant questions Matthew posed to get a response from his youngest son. Simple instructions about the pretrial process, hearing date, and scheduled visits were empty statements left lingering in the air adrift among the rancor and seething anger still present coming from the passenger seat. Luke stared out the window trying to avoid any eye contact and conversation from his father.

During the hours he spent sitting in the detention center, Luke ran the whole affair repeatedly in his mind and concluded that everything that occurred today was the result of a failed system that had let him down as a child. He figured he was too frightened to tell his parents about the Halloween assault because he feared nothing would happen. *No one's going to believe the word of a child against an adult. I'm sure I was afraid of being accused of being a liar and, worse, tagged a freak by all the kids for talking about that kinda stuff. Too heavy for a small child of nine years to face... sexual assault of a minor... so silence was the only option and I must have really repressed the event to the point I completely forgot about it... though it would explain my fear of clowns and instinctual desire to stay away from Pinewood Drive. I have no regrets about beating the hell outta that fucking pedophile. He had no right to attack me... a child, defenseless... well he saw first-hand what this child could do when grown up. His ass won't be hurting anyone else for some time... wonder how many other kids were assaulted by that ass-wipe? My God... he was a "man of God"... a trusted, revered leader of the church and community... He got what he had coming, and I regret none of it...*

"Luke, son I've been thinking... really poring over what has happened today and tried to reconcile it in my head. Alvin Wilkins... you mentioned earlier this morning that you thought he was weird, kind of strange for playing so often with children. What did you mean? Did you witness something? Something that was improper?"

Silence.

"Look... I know it's probably too soon to talk about this. McCord advised me to let it be for a few days... but I can't stop thinking about that statement this morning and how others had raised similar concerns over the years about Alvin..."

Luke abruptly turned to stare in anger and disbelief at his father's outrageous admission but said nothing as he returned his gaze to the window.

"Did something happen to you in the past? Something involving Mr. Wilkins?"

Silence.

"My mind is racing back to about ten or eleven years ago… that Halloween when you got separated from Jack. I remember you coming home late and very upset… but you said nothing and really refused to talk about it again. Is there a correlation to that night and what happened today? Did Mr. Wilkins do something to you that night, years ago?"

Silence.

Matthew pulled into the driveway and decided not to press it. He could tell his son was in a bad emotional state and he wanted to do nothing to push him back to that mental state. His son had reached a point in the human mind that had him act out so violently, so viciously, and so savagely that he possibly killed a man with his bare hands. Matthew needed to treat the patient with kid gloves until he was ready to talk calmly and reasonably about this horrific series of events. He offered a silent prayer before he turned off the car.

"Just go in the house and get some rest. I see that Joseph's here. I'll get him to follow me over and pick up your car. You gonna be alright?"

Luke exited the car slamming the door behind him. He opened the front door walking past his mother who tried to hug him and talk to him. He retreated to his basement lair.

On the drive back to Pinewood Drive, Matthew told Joseph to do nothing to cause Luke to explode. He wanted him to avoid him as much as possible given his propensity to rile his younger brother. Joseph agreed, jumped out of the car and followed him back home in Luke's Civic.

ର ର ର ର ର ର ର

Turning the house key into the side kitchen door, Matthew announced, "Melinda, I'm home."

"Oh thank heavens, you're back." Melinda said as she hugged and kissed her husband.

"Anything from the boy?"

"No. He stormed past me and went downstairs to his room."

"Okay, that's fine. Look, we need to be extremely patient with him. He's in a very fragile state and needs all the love and support this family can give him."

"Did he say anything to you at the jail or on the way home?"

"No… and to be honest with you, that kind of scares me. His silence and the stare he gave me when I mentioned Alvin's name… and if possibly something had happened in the past… man, it ran shivers down my spine.

We've got to give the boy time and space. No arguments or inquiries… nothing."

"I understand. Did you tell that to Joseph?"

"Yes. Speak of the devil, hey Joseph remember, say nothing to your brother."

"I know." Joseph replied tossing Luke's keys on the counter.

The basement door flew open as Luke marched across the hall toward his family in the kitchen.

"Dad, I need my phone." Luke stated firmly extending his hand.

"I'm not sure that's a good idea son… given all that's happened in the last few hours. Really, the last couple of days have been chaotic and its probably best that you not have any contact with the outside world for a while."

"That's not right, dad. Its my phone. Bought and paid for on my dime, not yours. I'm not a child. You have no right to hold that from me."

The silence was deafening as the two alpha males stared at each other in a game of wills. Neither male showing weakness nor sign of backing down.

"Luke, why do you want your phone? Who are you wanting to contact? What's so important about that phone that has you on edge?" Joseph insisted.

Luke turned his glare onto his older brother as a fit of rage was rising like boiling water in a teapot about to explode hot air.

Ring… ring… ring… Matthew's phone cut the tense standoff. Stepping out of the kitchen to talk privately, Matthew glanced at his youngest son who was still staring at his oldest son. After a few minutes, Matthew returned to the kitchen.

"That was Delores Wilkins. She says she's ready to talk and insisted I come talk to her immediately at the hospital. Luke, I can only imagine what's behind your rage and will not push you further to talk about it. I don't think it's a good idea that you have your phone… but… as you correctly stated, it is yours and I'm giving it back to you. Please, son, use it wisely and remain here until I get back. You're under my protective custody and I'm responsible for not only your safety, but the safety of the community at large, since you're on bail."

"I'm no threat to anyone in the community. You know that."

"I do. Please, listen to me. Stay home. Rest. Relax. I'll be back as soon as I can."

ह ह ह ह ह ह ह

Luke felt caged in. He was restless and needed to get out of the house to think. His basement bedroom felt more like the jail cell he had sat in for hours. He needed to talk, not text, Candace. He wanted to hear her voice.

Seek her consul, but mostly, hear her voice as it reminded him of another— a voice and image from the past that wouldn't let go of him— that seemed to always be on the precipice of every thought recently. In Candace he saw Janee. She was a beautiful, kind, caring, loving, passionate soul that reached out to him and connected. She was strong and vulnerable. Her mother was in the hospital and needed his support. Though he was in plenty of hot water himself, he needed to save someone— Candace. He was determined to rectify his past failure and to do that he couldn't be holed up in the basement.

Racing up the stairs and opening the door, Luke peered into the kitchen and saw his car keys on the counter. He quietly walked over and scooped them off the counter. He could hear the television blaring a comedy in the other room. Peeking in, he spied Joseph poring over a few books splayed across his lap and deeply engrossed in thought.

Easing the door knob and exiting the house, Luke felt an air of excitement in his release from his "house arrest". *Wow, fresh air and ... damn, Joseph! Seriously, you park your car behind me! Well that's not stopping me! I'll back into the yard... I don't give a damn!*

Luke's car roared to life as he maneuvered it back and forth to avoid hitting Joseph's car and driving over his mother's azaleas. Joseph popped open the front door and tried desperately to hold Luke's car in place. Frantically pounding on the car, Joseph screamed at his brother to stop or he would call the police. Luke ignored him and reversed the car over the azaleas and onto the road. Shoving the car into first gear he sped down Greenwood Drive. He needed to think and there was only one place he truly felt at peace— Waveland Museum Lane.

❧ ❧ ❧ ❧ ❧ ❧ ❧

The phone rang at the Miller house as both Joseph and his mother jumped up and raced over to the kitchen. Joseph grabbed the receiver hoping it wasn't the police or his father— neither option seemed the answer to his prayer.

"Joseph, I've got fantastic news! Alvin survived surgery and the doctors expect a full recovery!"

"Oh, thank God! Wow... that takes murder off the table." Joseph remarked.

"Yes... and there's more... much more. I had a long talk with his wife, Delores. She revealed a lot! Turns out Alvin has a dark past... that he did have an encounter with Luke years ago on Halloween. You remember, that crazy Halloween that Luke came home late, alone, scared and unwilling or, probably, unable to talk about what happened?"

"Yeah... it was a freaky night that Luke never talked about."

"Well, there's a very good reason. Delores said she opened the garage door that night and saw her husband, bent over in front of Luke. She couldn't really tell what was happening but instinctively knew it wasn't good. She screamed, and Luke passed out. She scolded Alvin for what it looked like he was doing but he denied it all and said she was crazy. She scooped up Luke and drove him back to Greenwood Drive after she had pulled off his mask and discovered, in horror, who it was. Luke was a bit groggy, but able to walk back to his house. Delores said she stayed at the end of the road to make sure he safely made it back."

"Unbelievable! Simply unbelievable! So Alvin, a trusted deacon and Sunday School teacher, molested my little brother?"

"Well, she didn't say for sure what happened but… yeah… that asshole sexually assaulted my son!"

"Why did she tell you all this now? Why didn't she say or do anything when it happened? There's no way Luke is the only kid that he molested. That creep probably attacked a lot of kids. He was so freaking creepy… always hanging out with kids when he was supposed to be working— delivering mail or running the Sunday school departments. Just always around kids. Man, this crap is making me mad! Poor Luke… he's carried that burden and shame his whole life. That damn asshole. Wilkins has ruined him!"

"I know. I know. Calm down, Joseph. Delores told me she always feared there was something wrong with Alvin and his need to be surrounded by children. She had hoped it just his need to fill the emptiness of not having children of his own and, naturally, she blamed herself. As a result, she ignored all the little warning signs of living with a pedophile— like being banned from his basement lair. The few times she ventured down there, she discovered a locked door. When she asked him about it, he screamed at her and vowed to leave her if she ever went down there again without his permission. Today, when she went down to the basement to retrieve the church's financial reports, she found some horrible magazines of naked children. She nearly fainted until she heard the banging noises upstairs of Luke attacking Alvin."

"Why was she telling you all this?"

"She said when Alvin went into surgery, she prayed, like she had never prayed before, for Alvin's recovery… and that if he recovered, she would rectify everything. She would call Sheriff Walker and make a full confession of what she had witnessed over the years and what she had discovered in the basement as well as give them permission to open the secret locked door."

"Does Alvin know about all of this?"

"Yes… that's really what prompted this! This is the part of the story that is absolutely fascinating! After his surgery, Delores was at his bedside in the recovery room and told him about her prayer and how it was answered by God and that she would keep her end of the bargain. Alvin immediately agreed and would fully cooperate. Turns out he had an after-life experience in Hell."

"What?"

"Yeah… Delores was in tears recounting Alvin's tale of his spirit drifting away from a powerful light and into a cold, dark abyss. He couldn't tell if he was in a nightmare or simply dying, but he was alert and aware of his surroundings. He told her he fell into a pit of cold, wet sinking mud. He tried to pull himself out of the mire, but each handful of slimy muck, revealed the face of a child he had harmed. The experience horrified him as he knew he was either in Hell or on his way there. His sins had caught up to him and he was dying of terror with each fist full of evil— his damnation was revealed."

"My God! That's awful…"

"Horrifying… Alvin said that just as he had thought he could stand it no longer and his slide into Hell would not stop, he suddenly felt a powerful hand grab his arm and yank him out! That's when he woke up after surgery and heard his wife crying and clinging to his hand. He knew in an instant his wife's prayers had delivered him from damnation. God had given him a second chance— a chance of absolution. He begged her forgiveness and they prayed together. He vowed to fully cooperate with the authorities and accept the consequences. He said the punishment on earth was nothing compared to what he had experienced in death. He wanted to try to save his soul from eternal damnation… a powerful testimony!"

"Absolutely. I'm stunned."

"Let me talk to Luke. I need to relay this to him. I'm sure it won't resolve everything but it's a start."

"Uh… dad. Luke's not here."

"What? What do you mean, 'Luke's not here?' Where is he?"

"I'm not sure."

"You're not sure? What happened? Did you get a fight? I told you to leave him alone. Don't rile him. He's in a dark place and very fragile and hurt."

"Dad, stop. I didn't get in a fight with him. He sneaked out of the house. I forgot that I had thrown his keys on the counter. I had him blocked in with my car in the driveway and he drove around it."

"He drove into the yard? Over your mother's azaleas? She's gonna freak out. Joseph call Jack and tell him what's happened. Luke needs to know he's not wanted for murder or even in any trouble criminally with Alvin. He needs to know before he does something stupid. He's in a bad place and must be found."

❧ ❧ ❧ ❧ ❧ ❧ ❧

Luke turned left off Nicholasville Road and onto Waveland Museum Lane. The beauty and majesty of the mansion at Waveland had always impressed him. Its connection to Janee inspired him. It had become his sanctuary. He rolled down the window and eased back the driver's seat. Closing his eyes, his mind drifted back to Janee as his pulse slowed and the tension ebbed from his body. He saw the beautiful soft features of her face— the small mole above her upper lip; the crinkle in her smile; the penetrating ice blue eyes. Those eyes seemed to be pleading with him… imploring him. *What is it Janee? What are you telling me? Are you okay? Are you in trouble? I'm so sorry… I'm so sorry I let you down. I'm so sorry I killed you. I should have listened to you. I was an idiot enraged in stupid jealousy. I knew you would never cheat on me and hurt me. I was just too… too prideful. Janee, please forgive me. Please forgive me. I want nothing more than to be with you again. To see you… touch you… hold you… Damn it Luke! Stop torturing yourself. She's gone. She's not coming back… Candace… I need to call her.*

"Hello? Luke is that you?" Candace stated softly into her cell phone.

"Yes. How are you? How's your mother doing?"

"No change, really. She's stabilized but still in a coma. Luke, Julia told me something really odd and maybe frightening."

"Yeah?"

"She said that Simon took her to the Zone and the apartment a few nights ago. She claimed it was Simon who came to the house and told her she was going to see her mommy. I asked her several times if she was certain it was Simon. Each time she said yes and got mad that I didn't believe her. So I called Simon."

"Really? Wow… what did he say?"

"He denied it. Said it wasn't him. He said he wasn't even in the Zone that day. He got mad at me for even suggesting that he would ever do anything like that… blah, blah, blah. Then he tried to say it was probably Geoffrey who snatched up Julia and took her to the apartment. I'm really confused Luke and don't know who or what to believe. Julia has gotten people mixed up before. I mean, she is just two years old, and could've been wrong about Simon. One thing I'm certain of… whoever grabbed Julia nearly beat my mother to death and I honestly don't think Geoffrey has an ounce of violence in him… certainly not the kind that savagely beat my mother."

"No… he doesn't seem the type to brutally beat someone into a coma… especially an older lady. Damn… Julia said it was Simon. I can't imagine he would ever do anything like that to anyone, much less, a child and her grandmother… but he is in debt out his ass to the 'Boss'."

"Simon owes a lot money to Marcus X?"

"That's what he told me last night. I helped him do a few drops to pay off the debt. He took me to see the Boss man and it was beyond weird… it was pretty scary."

"You met the Boss, Marcus?"

"Yeah, Simon took me to see him at some dumpy laundromat."

"Oh my God…"

"What? Oh wait, I'm getting more calls from my brother, Joseph, and my dad. Don't feel like dealing with their condemnation and crap. Candace are you okay? You sound weird… like scared or something."

"I can't believe Simon took you to see Marcus. That's a huge no no. There's never a good reason for an outsider to meet Marcus X. Luke, you could be in real danger."

"Well, strangely that may be the least of my problems right now. Well speak of the devil. I just got a text message from Simon… and Jack. Wow, they both hit my phone at the same time. Look, Candace I need to talk to Simon. Clear some things up with him. I'll get back to you soon. Stay safe. By the way where is…"

"Julia? She's playing… wait… she was in the chair by the door. Julia? Julia?" Candace called out as she ran out into the hospital hallway. "Luke, I can't find Julia… talk to you later!"

Oh crap! Now where's little Julia run off to? I hope to God it's just a two-year old being a two-year old and wandering aimlessly away from the room and not something else. Damn, poor Candace… she's facing a lot crap from so many different sides. She doesn't deserve this. Her whole life has been one crisis and disaster after another, and she has managed to survive every one of them. The birth of Julia seemed to be the wakeup call she needed to re-direct her life, and now that she's on her feet and pushing forward, the past is beckoning her back… trying to exact some sort of vendetta or punishment. Why? Hey God, if You're listening and truly exist, maybe you can explain why an angel like Candace, whose whole life has been nothing but shit, has to be dragged back down after she— no help from You— fought to escape her past indiscretions to make a better life for herself and Julia? She is a beautiful example of human triumph from a horrible and tragic environment— through sheer force of will and true love she escaped and now nature, karma, some unknown universal force… or You are going to send her back? Why? Why is this Your will? Why would You allow this? You're supposed to be all good and have no evil in You and yet… how could this be anything but evil? No righteous god would ever allow this to happen. Well… if You exist and if You allow this to happen… know this— I WILL STOP IT! Candace will not suffer any more if I have anything to do about it! She won't… Luke averred as he wiped tears from his eyes. *Oh wow… Bobby Joe's calling. Wonder what he wants?*

"Bobby Joe, what's up?"

"Too much! Look dude, you're in some serious shit and, so am I, but we can help each other?"

"What trouble are you in?"

"Dude, the Boss is after my ass because I helped you last night. He's staging a repo of my wrecker as a pretext for a hit. I still owe him quite a bit of money, but none of that shit matters compared to my disloyalty in helping you escape."

"Wait, how do you know this?"

"Let's just say I have an informant in the right places that told me a huge sting operation was coming my way and that both, you and me, were the targets."

"Oh shit! Damn… is Simon part of this?"

"Oh yeah. He's gonna try to get you to do a repo with him tonight on my wrecker at my farm. It's a trap. Once I come out to challenge the repo, the Boss and his goons are gonna bust us up pretty good. Luke… this is serious shit. People are going to die tonight. I'd prefer it not be us."

"No shit! Who's this informant? Are you sure about this info?"

"Oh yeah… let's just say it's a Lexington cop who doesn't like the Boss any more than we do, and he wants us to come out on top. In fact, he said he would even help get rid of the bodies."

"Shit! My God… this is crazy. Do you have a plan?"

"Hell yeah, I have a plan! Are you in?"

"I guess I have no choice. Yes, I'm definitely in! Fuck Simon! Son of a bitch, he's… never mind. What's your plan?"

"Alright, look, meet me at my farm but don't come to the house in the front. Meet me at the old service road off Brannon. Do you know where that is?"

"Is it that old dirt road on the left off Brannon about two miles down if I'm coming in from Nicholasville Road?"

"Yeah that's it. Used to be a utility access road but its hardly ever used. I'll be back there in my truck parked near the edge of the woods."

"Where's the wrecker going to be?"

"It'll be parked in the barn like it always is. Don't want to change anything up that might alarm our rats from our trap. I'm going to place dynamite all along the inside of the barn. I'll run a wire all the way out to the woods and connect it to a blasting box. Once the rats have entered the barn, I'll blow their ass to hell! My informant will get a clean-up crew in and quickly remove all the human debris. It'll be quick and resolve all our issues at once."

"Damn, Bobby Joe! Dynamite? Where the hell did you get your hands on dynamite?"

"I've got a buddy in construction that was able to acquire the necessary explosives to do the job. Look, are you in?"

"Uhh… yeah I guess. Like I said, I really don't have many choices… oh wow… Simon just sent a text telling me its urgent that I call him now. Look, what time do you want me to meet you at your truck?"

"Nine o'clock… and tell Simon you'll meet him at my farm in the front on the street."

"But I won't be there. I'll be with you in the back near the woods. Won't that be a problem? Make him suspicious?"

"Damn, you're right Luke. Didn't think about that. Okay, meet Simon at nine in front of the house." Bobby Joe's mind quickly recalibrated the new ruse. "Yes… much better… you can make sure to lead Simon into the barn. Marcus and his gang of thugs will likely get there a bit early to set their trap for you and me. His crew will be in the barn waiting while Marcus sits in the car. Big Jr. will signal him to come once you and Simon start up the wrecker. Make sure Simon starts up the wrecker. You need to be near the door. Marcus will see me darting towards the barn and will follow."

"You're coming into the barn?"

"No. It'll look like I am in the dark from the front street. Marcus will only see me running to the back of the barn. Instead, I'll run to the blasting box in the woods."

"Man, there's a lot of moving parts and wild variables in that plan."

"You think? Damn son, I don't work at the Pentagon or some think tank in Washington on strategy and tactics. I'm just a country boy trying survive and stay one step ahead of the vultures in a dog-eat-dog world."

"Okay, nine o'clock."

"Hey Luke, when you enter the barn look up at the big cross beam near the entrance. You'll see a red bandana. That's your signal to get the hell outta the barn cause the dynamite is set. Once Marcus enters the barn, you casually step out, close the door. There's a drop handle latch on the outside door. Drop it and run. You'll have about fifteen seconds. Run towards the woods— it's about a hundred yards from the barn. You can run a hundred yards in fifteen seconds can't ya?"

"Fifteen seconds! Damn, that's kinda cutting close, isn't it?"

"Hey, I got no time to mess around. Once the rats enter the trap, I have to drop the hammer. If you know what I mean, son."

Luke gathered his thoughts as he stared at the urgent text message from Simon and two new text message alerts from Jack. *What the hell does Jack want? He's sent several text messages. I'm sure he's talked to Joseph and dad and they're trying to get him to talk to me or get me to come home… sorry Jack, can't do it… or maybe he has some more insight about the nightmare… maybe he's giving me a heads up about what's going to happen tonight. Can't think about the uncertainty of an omen or dream. Gotta stay in the real world and right now that means talking to Simon and setting the trap for Bobby Joe.*

"Hey Simon, what's up?"

"What's up? Are you fucking serious man? What's up? You're in fucking deep shit buddy! I just talked to Jack."

"You just talked to my brother? Like recently?"

"You're damn right, recently son! Like a few minutes ago. He's desperately trying to reach you. Hell, the whole damn family is. He just told me that Alvin Wilkins died in the hospital and that you were the one who killed him. The whole police department is after you and they are alerting all the cops in the metro area to be on the look-out for your ass!"

"Oh shit! Seriously?"

"Seriously, Luke! Look, I know I weirded out on you last night taking you to meet the Boss and everything... and shit, a lot of this trouble you have with the Boss is my fault. I probably never should have taken you to meet him at the laundromat. But there's a clean way out of your trouble with the Boss and your current trouble with the cops."

"I'm listening."

"You need to do that repo with me tonight. The Boss insists on this peace offering and he really needs it done tonight. Can you meet me at my apartment in an hour?"

"No. I have too many things I have to do. But I can meet you at the repo site. Where is it?"

"440 Calloway Drive. It's a couple miles off Brannon Road. It's an old farm. We have to repo a wrecker."

"Are you kidding? We're going to hook up a wrecker to another wrecker?"

"No, idiot I have the keys. It'll be parked in a barn. The barn is never locked. You and I will go to the property at night, say around nine o'clock. I'll enter the barn and start up the wrecker. You'll be on look out in case the owner wakes up or something. Distract him; fight him, do whatever, while I drive it out. Then you'll need to meet me at that old tobacco warehouse off Preston Street around midnight. You know the warehouse I'm talking about?"

"Yeah. Simon... you sure this is the only way for me to get out this mess with your boss?"

"Absolutely and if you do well tonight, he'll help you with that murder rap. He's got big connections in law enforcement circles all over the area, and he's connected to a ton of judges on the take. If you know what I mean?"

"Yeah, I guess. It's comforting to know the scales of the justice system are easily manipulated by the criminal world."

"Hey, don't be a smartass, Luke. You're a fucking criminal now, and if you play your cards right, the Boss will tip the scales in your favor."

"I guess. Okay, I'll meet you at 440 Calloway Drive at nine."

❧ ❧ ❧ ❧ ❧ ❧ ❧

Jack was extremely anxious and frustrated. He received great news from his father about Luke's predicament in Nicholasville with Alvin Wilkins but was unable to get in touch or locate Luke. Contacting Simon should have made him feel better, knowing how close he was to Luke, and the likelihood that he would be able to get the message to Luke.

But the conversation with Simon was odd. *It was as if Simon was happy that Luke was on the run thinking he had possibly murdered someone, and then seemed saddened when I told him that Luke was not in trouble, and all the assault charges had been dropped. I always thought Simon envied Luke, but I also believed he was a real friend to him. I can't imagine why he would envy Luke or want anything bad to happen to him.* Jack dialed his home number hoping to talk to Joseph.

"Hello?"

"Joseph! Good, glad I got you and not dad. Look, I got in touch with Simon and told him to tell Luke the good news."

"Simon? Are you sure he'll tell him the good news?"

"Why wouldn't he?"

"Simon's a punk. He only cares about himself and, from what Luke said this morning, Simon's in trouble with some bad dudes. I wouldn't put it past him to use his friendship with Luke to get out of his mess with these guys from the Zone."

"Yeah… you might be right. I hope you're wrong… but I can't count on that. Okay, let's assume Luke reaches out to Simon… he's in trouble and doesn't trust any of us right now, but for some reason he's always trusted Simon. Simon finds Luke… what will he do with the good news I gave him?"

"He'll turn it bad. Simon won't let Luke think he's not in trouble. He'll somehow turn the good news into something to his benefit. Simon's in debt to the Zone and will get Luke to help him in some way by convincing him that it will also get him out of trouble. Simon is a user. I never trusted his friendship to Luke. He's used Luke his whole life and Luke's been too stupid to see it."

"That's interesting you say that cause I got the same impression just a few minutes ago when I talked to him. Damn… he's probably setting Luke up for some dangerous scheme or plot… but what?"

"What about your dream? Was there anything in there about this?"

"No… not really cause Luke did things differently and survived the second night… he changed it."

"What happened to you after the laundromat in your dream?"

"Well… Bobby Joe and I went to his farm and set a trap for the Zone thugs chasing us…"

"Is it possible that same scenario could be happening tonight?"

"Oh my God! Oh my God! Joseph you're right! Damn it you're right! Shit! Shit! This fucking nightmare isn't over! Luke's walking into a trap in the barn and Simon is probably leading him there. Damn it, this whole thing could be stopped if Luke would answer the damn phone or look at my text messages!"

"I'm not sure Luke wouldn't still go just being an obstinate hard-ass. He doesn't listen to anyone. But still what he went through as a child with Wilkins… kind of explains a lot and… I don't know…"

"Look, this thing's going down at Bobby Joe's farm and that old barn in the back. In the dream, I used the old access road off Brannon. The woods provide a good cover for sneaking up to the barn. Can you meet me there… say around nine o'clock? Maybe we can stop him from going into the barn."

"No. Absolutely not."

"What? Are you crazy? Luke's our brother. We've got to stop him."

"We've tried already and each time he ignored our advice or attacked us for it. He simply doesn't listen and won't listen now."

"Joseph, if my dream is correct and, its been pretty damn accurate thus far, tonight's the huge night where he may get killed. You can't sit at home on your holy ass and let this happen!"

"Yes I can, and as I told him, I'm not fighting y'all's fight anymore. You hot-heads have to start taking responsibility for your actions. This is not MY fight. Not MY stupid entanglement with thugs from the criminal underworld. I'm not fighting for you guys anymore. Besides, the Bible says…"

"The hell with the Bible Joseph! This is our brother! My God, he needs us."

"No he doesn't. Didn't you hear him last night and, again, this morning. He doesn't need anyone and I'm tired of coming to the rescue! You should do the same. Let it be Jack. Let it be. Maybe its providential that this happens. His whole life really seems to be leading him down this doomed path… maybe its best…"

"Don't say it, Joseph! Don't you fucking say it!"

"Jack, I'm not risking my soul's salvation and eternal damnation for Luke's stupidity! I'm not! You can't save him!"

"Yes I can! I've got to try! Damn it… I've let him down his whole life. I've been nothing but a damn coward. If I hadn't left him that Halloween at Wilkins' house, he wouldn't have been hurt and molested. Its stunted him his whole life and now, maybe, I have a chance to fix that! I can't let him down. Not again, damn it! I'm not a coward and I've got a chance to save him and I will. With or without you!"

"No Jack! Don't! You'll condemn your soul!"

"Well at least Luke will have a friend with him in Hell!"

<u>Chapter 14</u>

"Being deeply loved by someone gives you strength, while loving someone deeply gives you courage."

— Lao Tzu

Love is a powerful force that beckons mankind to act in unpredictable, illogical, and inexplicable ways. It can bring out the best in humans or the worst— in fits of rage and jealousy. Pages of history are documented, and novels penned with acts of love where powerful forces stirred the human soul to fight for a loved one. While love for your children is instinctual, as in many species, love for your fellow man is acquired, developed, and tested. To fight and possibly die for another is a love like no other.

Jack loved his parents and believed he loved his brothers. Though he never told them, he acknowledged the sentiment in passing to his mother, who insisted they love each other. But did he love them? He liked doing things with them— sports, movies, games and parties, but was that love. Jack's nightmare revealed the weakness of his understanding of love and forced him to reflect on his life with his brothers.

Visiting the past was not a pleasant journey. In many instances, he discovered that he had failed his brother Luke through fear and inaction— cowardice. As he learned more about love and its powerful relationship to courage, he wondered if fear was the absence of love. *It can't be. Fear can't be the absence of love. Some people do love others but still get scared and fail to act. Is that failure a lack of love or simply an instinctual or innate inability to act? Dad has said many times in his sermons that fear stems from the unknown and the inability to control events and that comes from not knowing God or not trusting in Him. He said, "No man who loves God and has faith in Him knows fear because your faith puts Him in control.' Joseph believes my nightmare was a revelation from God… if so, I shouldn't be afraid to act, and the unknown is actually known— I know how, where and when this horrific confrontation is going to happen. Dear Lord, I place my life in Your hands to do Your will* Jack prayed as he gripped the steering wheel firmly with a renewed sense of faith and determination.

Turning right onto Brannon Road, he punched Bobby Joe's number on his cell phone. *This thing is going down at his farm and I need to get him on board with what has to be done, but I don't seem to be able to get in touch with him— can't get in touch with Luke or Bobby Joe.*

After a few miles on Brannon, Jack slowed the car down for a left turn on the unmarked service road. The one-way path marked with heavy wide tracks was not easy to navigate in the dark as Jack's tires settled into the deep grooves. The twisting dark road leading to Jack's fate seemed an eerie and appropriately symbolic backdrop. The vivid accuracy of the dream's imagery of this road with its enormous cluttered trees and low hanging branches that arched across the road sent chills down his spine.

Once again, he felt a foreboding creep into his head. *The dream doesn't have to be a nightmare but instead a warning… maybe a divine warning to change our ways before it's too late. Though much of the dream has come true, it is malleable and changeable… Luke has proved that and if he can change it, so can I. I will change the outcome because I do love my brother!* Jack argued pushing down the gas pedal in resolution.

Winding down the access road, Jack saw headlights flash about two hundred yards ahead. It seemed to be a signal. As he slowed down, he saw Bobby Joe's huge truck parked off the road in an embankment. The headlights flashed again revealing another truck with two people sitting in the front. Jack parked behind Bobby Joe's truck and hesitantly opened the door. Walking toward the unknown truck, he could hear familiar voices taunting him.

"What the hell are you doing here Jack?" said the driver.

"I could ask you the same thing, Conrad?"

"None of your damn business."

"You're just sitting in a truck late at night with Robbie in the front seat? Seems a bit cozy, guys."

"Fuck you Jack! We're here waiting for Bobby Joe to do a job!"

"Shut the hell up Robbie! He doesn't need to know that shit!"

"Well, he was implying that we were doing something… you know…"

"Yeah, well we weren't, and he knows that. He just said that to get you to tell him what we are doing, dumbass!"

"Where is Bobby Joe?" Jack asked.

Silence.

"Look, I know more about what's going on than you think. Why else would I be here?"

"I don't know Jack… why are you here?" Conrad cracked.

"To save my brother."

"To save your brother? Which one?" Robbie inquired.

"Which one? Robbie, you dumbass! Do you honestly think Joseph would be out here on a night like tonight, involved in this kind of situation? Shit, Robbie… sometimes you are the dumbest asshole I've ever known, and I've known some stupid turd-cutters."

"Fuck you Conrad!" Robbie retorted.

"Look guys, I don't have a lot of time. Some crazy shit's going down in that barn fairly soon, and I need to know where Bobby Joe is."

The two childhood antagonists stared at Jack for a few seconds and then looked back at each other feeling a rare sense of empathy.

"He's up at the house, I guess. He's supposed to meet us here. He's really running late." Conrad offered.

"What was he planning to do? Why was he meeting you guys back here?"

"Well, he didn't tell us a whole lot, just that he needed a few sticks of dynamite, a huge coil of wiring and a blasting box." Conrad stated flatly.

"Dynamite? What the hell is he blowing up?"

"His barn."

"Why?"

Silence.

Jack turned on his heels and started walking toward Bobby Joe's truck. *He's blowing up his barn… he's blowing up his barn… why? It's a trap! That's it! He's trapping someone in the barn and then blowing it to hell.*

"Did he tell you who he was trapping in the barn and planning to kill?"

Silence.

"Why does he want to kill the Boss and his gang from the Zone?" Jack quizzed.

"Because they were planning to kill him tonight in the barn."

"Fuck Robbie! You talk too much! Why the hell do you talk?"

"Oh… Marcus X was planning to kill him here tonight…" Jack countered ignoring the ensuing argument coming from Conrad's truck. *Okay, it's all starting to make some sense. Marcus has probably arranged for Bobby Joe and Luke to come to the barn tonight to kill two birds with one swift stone. That would be consistent with the two, Bobby Joe and Luke, being in the barn in my dream. But why hasn't Bobby Joe come back here to set things up? Conrad said he's late… did something go wrong? Change of plans?*

"Hey guys, how about we walk through the woods and see what's holding him up?"

"Fuck that! I aint doing shit… in fact, I'm about tired of waiting here for him, and I'm sure as hell not comfortable with all this dynamite in the back of the truck. Shit, you know what? I'm outta here. I never felt good about taking that dynamite in the first place, and now Bobby Joe doesn't even show up. Fuck it and fuck him! I'm outta here. See ya Jack!" Conrad asserted shoving the truck's stick into drive and peeling out the wheels leaving a gravel dust in the wake.

Matthew returned from the hospital feeling mixed emotions: happy that Luke was no longer in legal peril with Alvin Wilkins, angry that his son was molested as a child years ago, and frustrated that Luke was not at home for him to console and offer his most profound apologies. *Dear Father in Heaven, place Your loving arms around my son, Luke, and give him the aid and comfort to endure and survive this awful tragedy inflicted on him. Give me the strength to forgive Alvin— to squelch the fire burning in my heart and mind toward that man. Help me to*

show Christ-like grace and mercy to those who have committed evil on us. I pray for the patience and understanding to counsel Luke's troubled soul. He has a restlessness that I fear was born that horrific Halloween night and will result in a fatal act. Please watch over my son! He's out of my hands and I fervently pray that Your will be done, not mine, Matthew prayed wiping tears from his eyes.

Matthew entered the house through the side kitchen door and found Melinda nervously pacing about like a cat on a hot tin roof.

"Melinda what are you doing? You've already washed those dishes and they've dried. Put them in the cabinet and leave them there… they're clean, honey."

"Oh, this whole sordid affair with Alvin assaulting and molesting our baby boy has me twisted in knots with needles pricking all over my body. I know its un-Christ-like to hate… but I hate that man with every ounce of blood in my body and if I had a gun… well let's just say, it's a good thing we don't own one cause…"

"I know. I know. But we can't be consumed by this anger and hatred brought about by Alvin's evil act. We can hate the sin but still love the sinner. I understand your raw, emotional feelings and desire to avenge the damage done to our son. But that's not God's way and He counsels us to love those who have sinned against us. It's hard… maybe the hardest thing for a Christian to endure but as I have been doing for the past hour or so, we should pray for God's guidance. It's tough and poor Luke has held onto this… this savage act for so long."

Matthew walked over to his wife of twenty-seven years and hugged her as they prayed together for God's strength, forgiveness and guidance.

"Hey dad! What's your theme for tomorrow's sermon? What scripture will it be based on?" Joseph called out from the den.

"The theme is aptly titled 'Jesus Has Your Back— scratch His back and He'll scratch yours!' I actually wrote this one years ago… when you guys were younger. How long ago was it, Melinda?"

"Oh, had to be ten, eleven years ago. Why didn't you do that sermon years ago?"

"To be honest, I lost track of it. I wrote it and it must have gotten shuffled in with other papers. Anyway, I found it recently in my office desk drawer— sitting on top. Plain for the eye to see and for some reason, I had never seen it there. I swear I use that top right-hand drawer a lot and had never seen that sermon sitting there until a few days ago. Really weird."

"Are you serious, dad? You don't think it's more than a little odd that a sermon you wrote years ago and had forgotten, suddenly appears?"

Matthew nodded and shrugged his shoulders.

"What's the scripture verse for the sermon?"

"First John 2:1."

"What's that verse about?"

"Don't you know?" Matthew teased his oldest attending seminary.

"I don't know every verse of every scripture in the Bible. Do you?"

"Well, we're supposed to as ministers of God… not unlike a doctor whose knowledge of medicine helps them treat their patients. While a doctor's knowledge of the medical field through exhaustive books and research papers, help them heal the body, a minister of God's knowledge of the Bible helps treat the soul. A good minister should be well-equipped in Biblical training and knowledge to deal with the multitude of human problems."

"Okay, I get it. Let's just say, I'm not there yet." Joseph laughed.

"Alright, Joseph… anyhow, the scripture in John addresses the younger generation as John is quite old by this time. He warns his spiritual children not to sin, but if you do, and you will, know that you have someone to defend you to God, the Father— Jesus Christ— the Righteous One. That's part of God's good news to all of us sinners— that our love and faith in God will be rewarded in heaven, for as we proclaim our love in Christ to men on Earth, so will Christ, the Righteous One, defend us of our sins to the heavenly Father. Amen."

"Wow… that's a powerful message… laced with hope for those sinners who may feel alone, abandoned, or betrayed by man. God never abandons, and though cloaked in sin, Christ defends us to the Father."

"Yes… God uses the terms father and children to help us mere mortals grasp a bit of God's love for us. Like a mortal father's love for his children, God's love is all-encompassing and forgiving as long as the child acknowledges the sin— asks for forgiveness— and our heavenly Father welcomes them back with open arms."

"That's a lot… a lot to think about… and so much of that message is relevant today. I mean to all mankind."

"Of course, the Bible's word never ages or grows old as other books do over time. It is the revealed word and guideline for how mankind could and should live their lives on earth. He sent His son, Christ, to show us the way."

"You say that's John chapter 2, verse 1?"

"No, First John chapter 2, verse 1."

"1-2-1… whoa…" Joseph scribbled on a pad.

"What's that?" Matthew asked.

"Hey mom, isn't Jack's real name, John? I mean his formal, legal name?"

"Why yes. Jack is the Irish nickname for John. We always called him called him Jack because his grandfather Fitzpatrick loved that name and called him that at his birth. So it stuck. I love the name Jack, but his Christian name is John."

"Jack… John… of course!" Joseph called out.

"What's all this mean, Joseph?" Matthew asked.

"It means I need to re-read that verse and pray over it. Thanks dad. Yet another illuminating discussion."

Luke turned down Calloway Drive in a slow cautious manner. His mind was racing with multiple scenarios of deception and double-crosses: What if Bobby Joe is part of the Zone's trap and was lying to draw him in?; What if Simon wasn't in on the Zone trap and was truly innocent and walking into a trap that he had set?— too many dangerous scenarios that had his adrenaline pumping. *Man, I'm putting my life in the hands of a guy that I really don't know very well and turning on a guy I've known my whole life. Bobby Joe or Simon? Both are preparing to eliminate the other and I'm the pawn being used to bring it about! Damn... how did I get here? What have I done in my life that brings me to this point? My parents, family, and friends have often warned me about Simon and I always defended him, but I guess somewhere in the back of my head, I knew there was truth to their warnings. Simon has gotten progressively worse through the years since... damn... since I met Janee. He always denied having real feelings about her but... seems like...Oh man... he was in love with her! He would never admit that but... wow... ever since that night of his party, he seemed to do little things to keep Janee and I apart. I always ignored it but...can this be Simon's revenge? Would he really set me up to get me killed? Bobby Joe, on the other hand, does seem more honest only because his ass is on the line as well. I'm sure the Boss didn't like him helping me escape and its entirely plausible that Bobby Joe is planning a power play to take out the Boss and take over his operations in the Zone... So much to think about... Oh shit there's Simon's car.*

Luke pulled over and parked his car about four houses away from Bobby Joe's farmhouse. He could see Simon's car parked further down in the distance as the street below seemed empty. *Can I really do this? I know for certain I'm walking into some kind of trap— Simon's, Bobby Joe's... maybe both! What to do? If I turn around and go home, its over for tonight but not finished. The Boss fully intends to kill me somewhere and sometime. Simon is definitely involved but whose side is he really on? Which scenario works best for him? There can be no doubt that he will turn me over to the Boss... he has to... too much debt owed to the Boss and apparently our friendship is over! Oh God, I feel so... so nervous... scared. What to do? Dear Lord... I know I haven't spoken to You in a long time... Hell, I'm not sure if I even believe in You... anyway, dad and Joseph always told me what a comfort it was to pray and unload my burdens on You. I never really believed them but... I never really believed much of anything after that Halloween night... my life was stolen from me! How could You allow that to happen! How could You allow a church member— a fucking deacon and Sunday school teacher— to assault a child? A child! I'm not blaming You... its Wilkins doing, and I know he'll have to pay the ultimate price for that...* Luke wiped away the tears as his body trembled. *Anyway, I'm not here to talk about that. That's over and done with. Apparently, I killed him and I'm truly sorry but, it really felt good to beat his ass, I'm not going to lie and for a long time sitting in the holding cell, I felt nothing but rage for the man. However, that all went away after I went to Waveland and started thinking about Janee… she was an angel that I blamed You for taking away from me. My rage for years was all encompassing because I missed her… then I met Candace and she seemed like Your replacement for Janee… and I had a new life… fresh perspective… she even has a daughter to take care of… Dear God, I know I'm rambling, but I pray that you give me the strength and courage to do what has to be done tonight! I know I can't do this alone and I feel terribly alone. Please Father show me the right way!* Luke prayed with eyes closed and head bowed. He saw several flashes of a light. He opened his eyes and watched Simon's headlights blink twice. *I guess that's Your sign that its show time! I commit myself to You, Lord!* Luke finished as he shoved his car into gear and drove down to face his fate.

"I thought that was you just sitting there. Having second thoughts?" Simon teased as he got out the car.

"Yeah, I guess. You sure this is the necessary? I mean, I know this is Bobby Joe's place. We're gonna repo his wrecker?"

"Yep! Big bastard is in too deep with the Boss and is also trying to take over his operation in the Zone. Just too much shit for the poor bastard to try to take on. But hell, that's on him. I'm trying to get you out of a mess both with the Boss and in Nicholasville. One man's folly is another man's gain." Simon reasoned slapping Luke on the back and leading him toward Bobby Joe's house.

"Yeah… I guess…" Luke mumbled as he followed Simon.

There was just one street light on several yards down the road but no lights anywhere coming from Bobby Joe's farmhouse. As they walked crouched and slowly up the front yard, Luke saw three rocking chairs and several hanging ferns gently swinging from the cold night breeze. It was an eerie desolation. *Man, Bobby Joe's doing a great job hiding out… but it almost looks too empty and barren… too easy a repo for Simon…*Luke assessed as he ambled down the side of the house toward the barn. Looking back at the street, he saw a car easing out of the shadows. It looked like the big muscle car from the Zone that he saw in the parking area at Shearer's Field. *Oh shit… its going down… it's definitely going down!*

Jack paced back and forth trying to think of the best approach to the barn. He knew the imminent danger but couldn't go to the barn unarmed. He hoped that Bobby Joe would help him as he had in the dream and was excited when he saw his truck in the embankment— again, just like in the dream. However, Bobby Joe and his powerful and explosive plan was a no-go. *Something went wrong! Bobby Joe's plan of attack has been altered or something happened to Bobby Joe! Damn… I really needed him. Okay, think. You've got to stop*

the murder of your brother in that barn but how? I'm not running to that barn armed with a tree branch or some pine cones… wait a second… in the dream, I had a gun… a gun from Bobby Joe's truck! Jack remembered as he ran over and opened the passenger side door of the huge truck parked in the embankment. *Holy crap, the door was unlocked! And yes!! There's a gun in the glovebox… and a flashlight!*

"Oh dear God, thank You! Thank You!" Jack called out as he kissed the revolver several times.

He shoved the gun in his back-waist band and started up the steep embankment. *Damn this is steeper than I remembered in the dream* Jack complained as he tumbled down several times before grabbing an exposed tree root and pulled himself up.

He jogged over to the entrance of the woods as a crosswind swept across his body. He pulled out the flashlight and peered into the dense woodland. The light beam gave little visibility as he struggled to get through the hanging vines and tightly packed pines. He was able to pick up his pace through a small clearing but coming out of it he hit his head on a branch and rolled down an unseen mound. Gathering himself at the bottom of the mound and rubbing his head, Jack checked his waistband for the gun. It wasn't there. He frantically scoured the pine needle covered floor for the one object he had to possess to move forward to the barn and his destiny.

❧ ❧ ❧ ❧ ❧ ❧ ❧

Luke trailed behind Simon in hopes of seeing some sign or signal from Bobby Joe that the trap was set, and he just had to make sure the mouse and its fellow conspirators got in as well. Simon adeptly yanked off the barn door lock, slid it open and disappeared into the unlit two-story structure.

Luke took several deep breaths casting his eyes toward the sky. He felt a cold wind blowing as storm clouds began racing to block the moonlit night. Once again offering a silent prayer, Luke cautiously pushed through the barn door and entered.

Squinting his eyes to adjust to the darkness, he heard the angry wind pounding on the side slats of the barn as a shutter from the hayloft banged on a loose hinge. He felt the draftiness of an old barn that saw better days and was in dire need of repair. He heard Simon moving about near a large vehicle before slamming the door shut on Bobby Joe's tow truck.

Taking several steps inside, Luke looked up toward the ceiling hoping to spy the red flag or bandana signaling Bobby Joe's trap. He strained his eyes scanning the ceiling's crossbeams but couldn't see anything remotely like a bandana or flag. Instead, he saw hovering twenty feet above his head a large mass suspended in mid-air. He could hear the twisted, gnarled rope holding a large object. Luke felt his heart beat faster, accelerating at a pace to burst through his chest. Staring at the swaying mass, he was hit with a wet droplet that landed on his forehead and raced down his face. Several more droplets hit as he wiped his brow without taking his eyes off the mysterious figure.

Suddenly headlights from the wrecker broke through the darkness revealing the horrific truth— Bobby Joe's lifeless body was dangling from a rope tied to a crossbeam. His dead eyes stared down at Luke as blood streamed out of a large gash about his neck and oozed off the rope in a slow steady descent. Luke felt dizzy as the barn started to spin and his vision blurred.

He could see figures moving from behind the tow truck as Simon climbed out. Frozen in fear, Luke could hear himself screaming though nothing came out. *Oh my God! Oh my God! Bobby Joe! Bobby Joe! What happened? What's happening? My heart's about to explode and I feel like I'm going to… No! No! Stay awake! Stay awake! Can't pass out! Not this time! Calm down… calm down… watch what's happening… movements… more people in barn with Simon… they're talking… laughing… Run! Run now!*

Luke turned to exit the barn but the large sliding door at the entrance abruptly slammed shut. Luke's hand instinctively ran across the door face searching for the handle. He found it, grabbed it, and yanked it several times but to no avail as he heard the outside clasp close shut. He turned back to the lighted figures standing in front of the wrecker. *Oh shit… it's that big fucker I hit in the Zone! My God, he's bigger… and the Boss… Marcus X… Oh God, what's happening?*

"Well, if it isn't the little white rabbit that attacked my compound, stole my packages, assaulted my people and had the fucking audacity to hit me at my God damn place of business!" Marcus barked as each word got louder for emphasis, "What's the matter white boy, can't talk? Got nothing to say? No words? I see you staring at your boy, Simon. Can't believe what's happening, huh? Thought you boys were tight… homeboys from the homeland… childhood friends, huh? Well, I got news for you red-neck, your boy hates you! Always has… has been playing you and using you to pay off his debts to me and to get rid of you!"

"Hey, Boss man… are we through here? I paid you what I owed and delivered your package. Are we straight? Can I get outta here? I have some packing to do." Simon pleaded.

The Boss stared at Simon for several uncomfortable seconds and then looked over at Luke awaiting a response.

"Aint you got anything to say to your boy— Simon? The Judas who turned you in for pounds of coke and a clean slate? You just gonna stare at him?" Marcus queried waiting for Luke to scream at or attack his rotund betrayer.

Again, after several agonizing seconds passed, Marcus continued, "Damn, you white folks are as soft as a fresh pile of dog shit! If my homey from back in the day turned on me like that… I'd beat the fuck out of him, rip his head off and shit down his neck… but that's just me."

Marcus allowed Luke a few more minutes to gather himself and his thoughts in hopes of watching a violent assault to avenge a grievous betrayal. Luke didn't move a muscle as he continued to stare at Simon. Simon nervously pivoted back and forth on his heels staring at the ground—unwilling and unable to look his trapped victim and childhood friend in the eye.

"Yeah, Simon… sure you can go." Marcus smiled as he nodded to Big Jr.

"Okay, open the door. You have one leaving… Sugar Booger is coming out." Big Jr. ordered speaking into his phone.

The door slid open. Luke could feel the cold wind rush through sending fresh chills over his body. He watched incredulously as Simon walked quickly towards him with his eyes down. As he approached, Luke stepped in front of him to block his exit.

"Luke… what are you doing? It's over, man. It's over." Simon sighed.

"Why Simon? Why did you do it? How could you do it? I always defended you… watched out for you… had your back! Hell, I'm only here because I tried to save you… save you from yourself!" Luke demanded.

"That's bullshit, Luke and you know it! You never had my back or my best interests at heart. You stole my girl! Broke my heart and altered my life!"

"What the hell are you talking about? Who stole your girl? Broke your heart? What girl, Simon?"

"What girl? What girl? Are you fucking kidding me, Luke? Janee! Janee! Janee! You stole her from me. She was supposed to be with me, not you and she would have been had you not sidetracked her, confused her…"

"Are you fucking serious? You're condemning me to death here in this shithouse because of a high school crush? Unrequited love? Simon, damn you to hell, she NEVER like you like that? You were never going to be her boyfriend. She didn't see you that way. She was too nice to tell you that to your stupid fat face." Luke added as his anger began to rise. "Did our friendship mean nothing? All those years together in school, going to parties, fishing, golfing… everything… you'd turn your back on me for a damn crush?"

"Get outta my way Luke. It's more than just Janee and goes way deeper."

"Bullshit! You aint leaving!" Luke declared with a shove and a quick pivot to the open barn door.

Reaching the entrance and through the threshold, Luke ran headlong into a tall dark figure with a pleasant face and a non-threatening demeanor. Luke pulled his fist back but felt it stop as a large beefy hand tightly gripped his wrist. He was spun around and, in a flash, saw a fist strike him across the left side of his face. He stumbled a few steps before another blow knocked him to his knees. Big Jr. grabbed a fist full of Luke's hair and dragged him away from the entrance.

"Make it quick, Boss. You promised no torture or beatings. Just a quick hit." Simon offered.

"Don't worry, Sugar Booger, he aint your problem anymore. Now get the hell outta here before I change my mind about you!" Marcus countered.

Simon looked down at Luke, shook his head and ducked out of the barn. Big Jr. grinned at C.J. and nodded for him to follow. C.J. lowered his eyes and shut the door but didn't clasp it. He stayed several yards behind Simon being careful not to be seen. Simon briskly darted to his car parked on the street.

As soon as he opened the driver side door, he saw a pair of headlights move rapidly towards him. The car screeched to a stop just in front of Simon's front fender. Two men quickly exited the vehicle toting baseball bats.

Oh shit! What now! Simon panicked as he jumped into his car. Just as he put the key in the ignition, he heard a terrible crashing sound as glass shattered all about him from the driver's side window. Leaning down in the seat he tried to start the car, but his door was opened, and he felt hands pawing at his body, gripping and grabbing and then pulling him out of the car. Lying flat on his back, he instinctively raised his arms to cover his face, but it did no good as the first swing came crashing down on his abundant abdomen. Simon screamed out but to no avail. He was pounded for several minutes and at different angles.

Jumpy and Wheels relished the opportunity to hone their batting skills on an unsuspecting victim. It was especially enjoyable if it was a person they knew. For some reason, the pair derived a devious pleasure from the beating of a contemporary or former employee. Killing rivals or unknown cheats was one thing, but a comrade in arms made it special. After taking one last shot on Simon's dead swollen head, Jumpy turned his attention to C.J.

"Damn C.J., aint you ever gonna hit someone? Are you always gonna be a big wussy?"

"What do you care? You two got plenty of shots in and seemed perfectly capable of completing the job. Why spoil your pleasure?"

"Why spoil my pleasure? Are you shitting me C.J.? Son, you better start participating, or you'll wind up on the wrong end of one of these beat-down parties. You understand, Dark Chocolate?" Jumpy added pointing his bloody bat at the taller man.

"Look, the job is done. Let's just load him into his trunk and get back to the barn, like Big Jr. ordered. Apparently, we will have a few more bodies to load before the night is through."

"Fuck that! I aint loading that fat ass into the car. Since you didn't do shit, you load his ass into the trunk!"

"Yeah, that sounds reasonable. Get going C.J., use those two wet noodles dangling off your shoulders to put that big boy in the car." Wheels laughed.

C.J. grunted and mumbled a few words under his breath as he leaned down to grab Simon's legs. Using his strong legs and knowledge of leverage, he dragged Simon's battered body to the back of the car, lifted the torso up against the trunk.

"Okay, can someone pop the trunk?" C.J. requested.

"Pop the trunk? With what? I aint got the keys? Do you got the keys, Wheels?"

"Hell no... and if I did I sure as hell wouldn't waste my energy popping the trunk. Why don't you pop open the trunk with that little bat of yours? Damn thing's never been used! Hell, it's like his damn wee-wee. Untried and unused!" Wheels screamed in laughter.

"Oh, that's cute... real funny, Wheels. Fine, I'll find the keys. They got to be around here somewhere." C.J. stated flatly as he walked around the car looking on the ground. He felt his phone vibrate and pulled it out of his pocket. "Yes, Big Jr.? What did you say? Are you sure? Uhh... okay."

"What's up C.J.? What did Big Jr. want?"

"He said to bring in the little girl."

"Aha! I knew it! Come on Wheels let's grab her and do the deed!"

"What? Do the deed? What the hell are you talking about?" C.J. demanded.

"Look Dark Chocolate, the Boss wants that little girl dead and delivered to the barn, now!"

"What? Big Jr. didn't say that! Where the hell did you get that insane idea about killing a little girl? No one ordered that!"

"Yeah they did!"

"Who? Not Big Jr.!"

"You're right! This goes higher up. Big Jr. would've never gone for that... that's why the Boss spoke to me and Jumpy separately. He definitely didn't tell you, for obvious reasons!" Wheels reasoned as he joined Jumpy walking back to the large dark muscle car. He yanked open the backseat door and scooped up the tiny figure wrapped in a blanket. She started to squirm.

"Now, now, sit still little one. This won't take but a second..."

C.J. slammed his bat against Wheels' head as he dropped to the ground. Julia landed on her feet and took off running back toward the barn. She never looked back but dropped her blanket as she sprinted past the barn to the open expanse. She didn't know where she was going. She was too scared to think. She just followed where her little legs were going.

"Run, Julia! Run! Run to the woods and hide!" C.J. screamed. "I'll come find you and take you home! Run! Run!"

"Oh, you done it now Dark Chocolate! You done fucked up and for the last time. Hitting Wheels was a huge mistake. Disobeying the Boss was a deadly mistake!" Jumpy warned.

"Bullshit! The Boss would never order the hit on a little girl. That's just you two twisted deviants looking to score another violent and outrageous act of violence."

"Good thing you hit like a little girl, C.J. or I might have been in real trouble. Should have known better than to turn my back on some soft-hearted little wuss. Now your day of reckoning has come! Time to beat your ass!" Wheels yelled out as he swung violently at C.J.'s knees. The bat crashed hard cracking both knee caps on one blow. C.J. cried out in pain and fell to the ground. He felt one more strike to his lower back and then his world went dark.

"Damn that didn't take long! I think the little girl would've put up a better fight!" Jumpy laughed cleaning the blood off his bat with C.J.'s shirt.

"Oh shit! Speaking of… we better find that little girl quick or it's our ass with the Boss!"

"Damn, you're right! She took off that way… past the barn!" Jumpy pointed.

❧ ❧ ❧ ❧ ❧ ❧ ❧

Remembering he had a flashlight tucked in his front pocket, Jack pulled it out and searched for Bobby Joe's revolver. Walking back and forth trying to retrace his landing sites during his fall; he grimaced in pain as he realized that he had twisted his ankle just before he fell and landed on it wrong during the tumble. Jack sat back down and gently rubbed his ankle. *Damn it! It's the same ankle I turned falling down the slope near the drug compound the other night! Does everything in my dream have to come true! Couldn't some parts, like being a stupid, clumsy ass, not happen? Man, this thing hurts and its already throbbing!*

Jack tightened his shoe laces and gingerly stood up as he resumed the search for the gun. *Without that gun, I can't possibly go to the barn and rescue Luke! I'm not strong enough or brave enough, to bluff my way in to getting him released. Calling the cops is a gamble but may be the best option if I can't find that gun! Damn there's a ton of shrubs and crap back here. That gun could've fallen anywhere. Oh shit, I heard a scream! Like someone getting their ass beat! Hurry! Please dear God help me find that gun! I'm nothing without it!* Jack prayed walking aimlessly about the bottom of the mound before stepping on a solid object that didn't snap. Reaching down he grabbed the revolver. *Oh thank God! Thank you, God!*

Jack shoved the gun securely in his back waistband and scrambled up and out of the mound. Flipping the flashlight on, he worked his way across the woodland towards the big barn he had only imagined in his dream. He was moving east solely on the knowledge gleaned from his dream.

He had no idea if he was making progress toward the clearing, and ultimately to the barn, or simply heading deeper into the woods and away from Bobby Joe's farm. Pushing through the pain and weaving in and out of bushes, low hanging branches and stepping in several decomposing tree logs, Jack had to stop and rest his ankle. It would do no good to arrive at the barn unable to walk— especially knowing a huge fight was supposed to take place. Jack had tried to put that idea out of his head ever since he raced out to Brannon Road to rescue his brother. Recollecting his nightmare, he shuttered at the thought of a brawl or physical confrontation with the Zone. Having it thrust upon you and reacting to a fight is one thing, but knowing a big fight was in the offing and willingly running to it was a completely different affair. Each time he thought of the imminent fight, he felt his cowardly instincts creep in, and scolded himself by repeating, "No! Not this time!"

Resting under an enormous hardwood tree, Jack heard the faint rustling of leaves, the crackling and snips of twigs snapping— it was a successive sound, like swift moving feet in short strides. Jack peaked out from behind the tree and peered into the direction of the sounds. He could just make out a small figure ducking and weaving through a gauntlet of tree limbs and vines. He could also hear soft sobs as the figure closed in on him. Jack pointed his flashlight at the moving object. *Oh my God, it's a little girl!*

☞ ☞ ☞ ☞ ☞ ☞ ☞

Luke rubbed the left side of his face and rotated his jawbone to make sure it was not knocked out of place. His cheek was swollen and throbbing, his vision blurred, and his hearing impaired. Though only two punches were thrown, it was the hardest Luke had ever been hit and the excruciating pain sent chills down his spine. He was in real trouble and that realization hit him like a Big Jr. roundhouse. Sitting on his knees, he heard mumbled voices before a swift kick to his ribs dropped him to the floor.

"Sit up and listen. The Boss is talking to you!" Big Jr. commanded grabbing Luke's hair and pulling him up.

"Ah... now that's better. Your eyes are a bit watery and your face is a mess. Not quite the same punk that visited me the other night, huh? Dumbest thing you ever did, son, was hitting me. Cheap shot at that! Caught me off guard and sucker-punched me. Oh well, let's just say I owe you." Marcus stated flatly before landing a right cross to Luke's face.

"Oh shit! That had to hurt!" Big Jr. screamed in admiration. "I mean, damn... I felt that over here!"

"Okay, okay. I owed you that. It's been a while since I've soiled my hands touching a piece of white shit but damn, sometimes its feels good!" Marcus announced rubbing his fist and savoring the moment. "Look, you throw a pretty good punch and my God, you can take a punch… I'll give you that. Most suburban white boys I run across scream like little bitches for a lot less than what you've just taken. I don't know if that's guts or you're just too hurt to make a sound. In any case, I admire the strong silent type that does most of their talking with their fists. Looking at you now, I don't get a sense that you're the type to beg or plead for mercy or cry about their doomed fate. Again, I admire that. Nobody likes a whiner or a crier."

"Hell no! Take it like a man! Stand up to it and face it head on!" Big Jr. added.

"That's right… at this point you haven't many choices but how you die is completely in your hands. Luke, you're going to die tonight. Do you understand that? I want that reality to sink in before it happens."

Luke lifted his head and looked directly at Marcus X. He didn't blink or lower his eyes. His heart rate had settled, and his nerves had calmed. Though he was in tremendous danger, and knew it, Luke seemed to accept his fate and was no longer afraid.

"Damn boy, you have a mean look. Like you could tear my head off right now, eh Big Jr.?"

"He still looks like a little punk to me, Boss."

"I don't know Big Jr., guys like him— suburban, white, middle-class college boy that takes his medicine without complaint are very rare. Trust me I know. Again, I admire that, Luke. I tell you what, boy, there's a job opening in this operation that I think you could easily fill." Marcus stated looking back towards the figure hanging from the crossbeam.

"Why did you kill Bobby Joe?" Luke garbled through a bruised jawbone as he sat up on his knees.

"Why did I kill Bobby Joe? Because he was planning to kill me." Marcus stated matter-of-factly.

"How do you know that?"

"Same way he knew I was coming here tonight… I have little birds all over the place singing information to me. You can't rise to my station in life, run the type of operation and organization I run, stay in power and alive as long as I have, without developing a deep and dependable network of informants that keep me several steps ahead of my rivals… and Bobby Joe was a rival. I saw it coming a few months back and watched it develop. I waited patiently for his opportunity to strike me. It just happened to coordinate with your crazy-ass attack on my compound."

"Did you have to kill him? Couldn't you just scare him like you did Simon?"

"Ha! Ha! Scare Simon!" Marcus roared with laughter looking at Big Jr. who smirked. "Is that what you think I did? Do you really think I just let him walk out of here knowing he stole money off the top of just about every drop and exchange he made as well as stole several pounds of product, principally coke, over the past year? That fat fuck was lucky he wasn't taken out sooner. But he came to me a few weeks ago with a plan to give back all the money he owed as well as deliver an old package that had gotten away from me a while back."

"Was that 'old package' Candace?" Luke asked.

"Damn boy, you are quick. Yeah, Candace… but we just call her Candy around here because that's what she is— candy! Get my meaning, boy? That red-head you chased after and put your ass on the line is nothing more than a cheap-ass whore. A two trick pony— she dances and fucks! That's all she's ever been… a fucking back-stabbing, lying-ass whore and now she's got your stupid ass in the sling!"

"It doesn't matter what you say or what you call her. She's a sweet, loving woman full of life and a devoted mother. I kept her outta your dirty hands! That's all that matters! She's alive and well and living safely with her daughter away from you!"

"Is that right?" Marcus smirked.

"Yeah, that's right. I made sure she had round the clock protection and was safely hidden from the Zone."

"Ha! Ha! Luke well played. Well, what about it Luke? You want to work for me?"

"Looks like I don't have a choice. Join or die. That's a helluva a recruitment tactic Boss man! How many recruits do you have on the team that joined under those circumstances? Huh? How has that worked out for ya? I know at least two that turned on you and later tried to kill you and another who simply escaped. Must be hell trying to sleep at night or operate in the daylight always having to keep your head on a swivel to guard against an attack. Never knowing who might turn on you next… when?... where?... how? Must be living hell being you, Boss man." Luke mocked.

"You have no idea. It's an amazing life I lead and the thrill of it all keeps my adrenaline flowing and sparking every cell in my body! The game is the ultimate way to live! You have no idea until you enter the arena. What about it Luke? You're a tough guy that doesn't scare easily and seems to be able to take care of himself. You want to join?"

"Do I have a choice?"

"Yes."

"Then, no."

"Wrong choice Luke! Big Jr…" Marcus nodded as Big Jr. lifted his 44 ounce bat above his head.

"Wait! Wait! Wait! I've changed my mind!" Luke screamed urgently.

"Hold up, Big Jr…. well?"

"Look, I'll join if you promise not to harm Simon. Let him pay off his debts and I'll work alongside him making sure he stays outta trouble, pays you everything and stays away from the product."

"Wow! Wow! Big Jr. did you hear that? Mother fucker still wants to protect the bastard that put his ass in here. You are unbelievable, Luke. Do you love that fat-ass that much that you would still go to bat for him?"

"He's still my friend."

"Bullshit! That fat fuck hated you, betrayed you and set you up to die. He doesn't deserve that kind of loyalty."

"Everyone should. I don't have a lot of close friends. One died, and I'm trying to keep the others alive."

"Well, I got bad news for you, boy! You lost another one! Simon's fat ass is dead and packed up in his trunk as we speak!"

"Bullshit! You did not kill him!" Luke reflexively screamed.

"Big Jr.?" Marcus nodded at his bodyguard who pulled out his cell phone and punched a number.

"Hey, C.J.?"

"Yes, Boss?"

"Jumpy, what the hell are you doing with C.J.'s phone?"

"He gave it to me while he took care of the Sugar Booger package."

"Oh… okay. What's the status of Sugar Booger?"

"Like Waffle House hash browns— smothered, chunked and covered. His fat ass is face down in his trunk as we speak."

"Okay… give C.J. his phone back and that's an order."

"Yes, Big Jr."

"Well, Luke what about it?"

Luke lunged at the Boss with a wild haymaker punch that Marcus easily side-stepped while Big Jr. smacked his backside with his baseball bat. Luke reached back writhing in pain, rolling about on the barn floor. The hatred in his eyes was intense and Marcus could feel it.

"Damn boy! You are loyal to a fault. Too bad you wasted all that on a piece of shit like Simon… damn. What am I going to do with you? It's a shame to waste your talent, strength and guts… I admire those qualities in a man. It's rare… you know what? I'm going to give you a legitimate choice. Do you hear me?" Marcus asked looking down at Luke.

"Yeah."

"Its real simple: join me and I'll put you in charge of the college campus operations making six figures. You won't have to get your hands dirty doing drops, running drugs, pimping girls… none of that shit. I'll set you up in a legitimate office downtown under a fake business. All you'll have to do is run my campus operations. Make sure things run smoothly and handle any mistakes that may pop up. Well what do you say?"

"You said I had a choice. What's the other option?"

"You walk… clean and clear."

"Bullshit."

"No bullshit, Luke."

"You're going to let me just walk outta here, right now?"

"That's right Luke. I admire you and you can ask Big Jr… how many times have you heard me say that?"

"Never." Big Jr. replied instantly.

"I don't believe you. You're going to send your dogs on me as soon as I leave like you did to Simon."

Marcus X nodded to Big Jr.

"C.J.?"

"Yes, Big Jr.?"

"Damn it, Jumpy. I told you to give C.J. his phone back. Where is he?"

"He drove Sugar Booger and his car back to the dump."

"I told him to wait until I instructed… damn it, he's getting as obstinate as you dumbasses. Anyway, The Boss ordered you guys to let the big white boy in here pass when he leaves the barn. Do you understand? You guys are NOT to harm Luke Miller."

"Right, Big Jr., don't harm the white dude when he leaves the barn."

"Good. Now, have C.J. call me as soon as he returns. And bring me that package like I called for a while ago!" Big Jr. ordered turning and looking back at the Boss.

"Well, Luke… what's your choice? Stay with me and make a fortune or walk away?"

Luke studied the "options" not trusting the outcome of the second choice. *There's no way I can trust Marcus to keep his word and the temptation to make that kind of money is great. It's not like I have a lot of business opportunities on the horizon and college seems like a huge waste of time— so much studying and for what? A shitty little nine to five job in a cramped little office or warehouse working for minimal pay. The work he's offering is exciting and dynamic but… its illegal and my parents would raise a shit storm. I can hear Joseph now, preaching against me… damn… I'm half tempted to do the job just to piss Joseph off! But I could never do that to my mom or dad. I love them too much to bring this world back into their lives and as soon as I enter the Zone's orbit it would expand down to Nicholasville and threaten my family… nah… could never do that to them!*

"Sorry, Boss! I appreciate the offer and the kind words of admiration, but I must decline." Luke replied as he stood up and walked toward the barn door.

"I'm sorry to hear that Luke. I really am. I thought we would make a great team. It's too bad you don't see as clear as I do… but then again, maybe you just need to have your eyes checked. Big Jr." Marcus stated as he nodded at his loyal lieutenant.

Big Jr. walked briskly around the Boss and headed toward the back of the barn. He grabbed a woman from the last stall and dragged her out. Her mouth was gagged with a red bandana and her hands were bound behind her.

"Candace! What the hell! How did you? ... where did you? ... Marcus let her go. Let her go now and I promise I'll work for you! Please, dear God! Don't hurt her and let her go. I'll work for you!"

"Why Luke... that's no longer on the table. You don't have choices anymore. You chose unwisely and now you're going to have to be punished." Marcus snarled with an evil lip curl staring deep into Luke's soul.

❦ ❦ ❦ ❦ ❦ ❦ ❦

"Shit! Shit! Big Jr.'s gonna kill us! What the hell did we just do?" Jumpy screamed pacing around.

"We did what we had to do! Dark Chocolate lost his damn mind hitting me in the head! You had my back and I got yours! Besides, the Boss told us to kill that little girl. So we got cover from the head man, himself!"

"I know! I know! But damn... Big Jr's gonna take this hard. C.J. was his boy. You should've heard how pissed he was that I was answering C.J.'s phone. We gotta go back and hide C.J.'s body in the trunk of Sugar Booger's car and then hit the woods looking for that little girl. We can't face the Boss without that little girl."

"You right! You right! But it doesn't take both us to put C.J. in the car. You start looking for the girl in the woods and I'll put C.J. in the trunk and join you." Wheels planned.

"Fuck that! You go to the woods first and I'll dispose of C.J."

"What the hell, Jumpy? You afraid of the woods?"

"Damn straight! Those woods in redneck country are scary as hell! You remember what C.J. said, the history of this area is bad for brothers of our color. So many of us lynched out here. Damn I can feel the ghosts of those fuckers haunting the woods now!"

"Come on, Jumpy. You're scaring yourself now! The only thing out in those woods is a scared little girl and we better hurry and find her. Alright let's both quickly put C.J. away and hurry together back to the woods!"

"Now you're talking!" Jumpy smiled.

❦ ❦ ❦ ❦ ❦ ❦ ❦

Okay, nice and easy. Don't rush up on her or you'll scare her, and she'll scream Jack told himself as he hobbled around shrubs, tree roots and low-hanging vines. Keeping his flashlight off so as to not alarm her, Jack would pause ever so often to listen to the small shuffling of feet through the leaves. It was a difficult task because the small figure would stop and listen as well— almost simultaneously. Jack got a glimpse of the small figure moving toward a grove of bushes and disappear. He stopped and heard nothing. Slowly he approached the backside of the bushes. He saw what appeared to be a head buried in her knees wrapped with her arms burrowed in a hole. Kneeling cautiously beside her, Jack covered her body with his and clapped his hand across her mouth.

"Julia… Julia. I'm a friend of your mother's, Candace, and I've come to rescue you and your mom from the bad guys. I'm not here to hurt you. I'm here to help you. I know you're running away from the bad guys and I'm a prince sent to save you, the princess, and your good mother. I'm gonna take my hand off your mouth now. Do you promise you won't scream?"

Jack could feel her little body trembling. He couldn't hear her assent but had to uncover her mouth as a sign of good faith that he wasn't there to hurt her. He uncovered her mouth and waited for a shrill scream, but it never happened.

She remained balled up and shaking. Jack sat up and scooped her beside him. He softly sang the "Itsy- Bitsy Spider" song next to her ear. She began to relax and, even sang the parts of the song Jack pretended to not remember. *She's absolutely beautiful and fearless! What a brave, tough little girl! I'm so glad Luke saved you! Now I have to make sure you stay saved. I'm sure it's only a matter of time before the goons come looking for you.*

"Hey, little girl! Little girl! Where are you? Come on now… hide and seek is over. Time for you to go see your mommy. You want to see your mommy, don't you?" Wheels called out.

"Come on little one! Come out, come out wherever you are… Uncle Jumpy's gonna give ya some ice cream!"

"What the hell are you saying? 'Uncle Jumpy'… damn you think that little white girl's gonna believe you're her uncle?"

"Yeah… why not? She's only two. Damn, son aint like she smart or nothing like us. You can talk stupid to them and they believe everything you say cause you bigger and smarter than them."

"I don't know about all that. I do know she's scared and hiding somewhere cause its quiet out here… I mean quieter than it should be with a scared two year old running around. They'd make a lot noise screaming and running and shit, you know what I mean?"

"Yeah, I feel ya. I feel ya. So she's probably not moving around… just sitting and hiding. Damn that's pretty smart. Okay let's split up, spread out, and move across the woods. If you come across the girl or see something just signal me with your hand like this." Jumpy showed him making a fist.

"How the hell am I gonna see your damn fist out here in the dark-ass woods?" Wheels reasoned.

"Oh… yeah… you right. You right. Shit, wasn't thinking." Jumpy laughed. "Okay, I kinda make the sound of a hoot owl. You know…

HOOT, HOOT!'"

"Why the hell you gonna make that sound. Aint like there's hunters out in the woods tonight shooting deers and shit. Damn, Jumpy! Just say 'I got the little girl!' and I'll come to you. I'll do the same… shit…"

"Yeah, okay that's a good idea"

Jack popped his head up from the bushes. He scanned the vicinity where he last heard the screamed pleadings from the Zone thugs. He could see one figure heading away deep into the far side of the woods. However, emerging from behind a tree was the second man from the Zone about a hundred yards away and moving in a direct line towards their position in the bushes. *He's moving right at us. Can't let him near us. No way he gets Julia. Think! What can I do to get him away from us?* Reaching down, Jack felt several pine cones. Loading them in his arms, he tossed a few like grenades in different directions trying to throw the scent of the game into another direction. He watched the darkened figure stop a couple of times, look about but slowly continue his trek towards them. *Shit! Shit! He's still coming towards us… now what? Wait a second… yes… gonna have to use it at some point… might as well be now* Jack reasoned as he pulled the gun out of his back waistband.

Bang! Bang! The unmistaken sound of gunfire erupted the serenity of the wooded enclave. He watched the predatory figure stop in his tracks and look about.

"Hey, Wheels… did you hear that?"

"What the fuck am I deaf or something? Of course I heard that shit?"

"Did you fire that off?"

"Did I fire that off? What the hell you talking about? 'Did I fire that off?' Hell no, Jumpy… I aint got no gun, you dumbass!"

"Great, you just announced to the whole world you aint armed, dumbass!"

"We're walking around with bats… that's as armed as we are and whoever fired those shots know, idiot! I think those shots came from near you. I'm coming now!"

Oh great! Instead of making those asses run away they're now coming towards us. Is it possible, they're too stupid to be afraid? Damn, got to move now and use flashlight like last time to confuse them and move them away from Julia.

"Okay, listen carefully Julia. The prince has to get the bad guys away from you. You stay still and very quiet while I take care those bad dudes, okay?" Jack counseled.

Julia lifted her head from her arms and wrapped them around Jack's neck. *Oh my God… she is so scared and doesn't want me to leave her… but there's no way I can take her with me on a bum ankle. I have to move swiftly, darting about. I won't be able to do that while toting her around and putting her in harm's way. Not a chance! Her life is too precious.*

"Listen to me, little one. I can't take you with me. Too dangerous. You're really, really, really safe right here. I'll be back real soon and take you home. Just so you know I'm coming back, I want you to hold on to my car keys. Here, hold them in your hands real tight." Jack added cupping her small hands in his. "See, I can't go anywhere without you, my little princess, okay?"

Julia nodded and played with the keys. The UK key chain was similar to her mother's and brought her a sense familiarity and relief.

"Remember Julia, stay very quiet and hidden under these bushes. I'll be back real soon, and we will go home." Jack reminded as he hugged her again and kissed her head.

Lifting his head slowly from behind the line of bushes, Jack saw the Zone predator resume his direct path towards them. Shoving the gun back into his waistband, Jack pulled out the flashlight. *Alright, time to play a little flashlight tag with these boys!* Jack darted out to the left, getting a better feel for the wooded terrain, he easily managed his escape to another series of bushes. He flashed his light at his closest pursuer. He could hear the man scream out and change his direction. Jack again ran away and deeper into the woods before flashing his light.

"Hey! You! Light boy! What are you doing? What do you want?" Jumpy shouted.

"Stop shouting dumbass! Chase his ass!" Wheels replied emphatically.

Jack could hear the rustling of leaves and shuffling of feet in hot pursuit of the latest flash of light. *That's right! Keep chasing the moving light... away from my little princess! Deeper and deeper into the woods. Maybe I can leave them out here chasing a phantom light and circle back to the barn, get Luke and grab Julia on the way out! Yes, that's a good plan!* Jack schemed just before tripping over a thick tree root and falling face first to the ground. The flashlight fell from his hand and down into a deep ravine that led to a creek bed. *Oh shit! My ankle is killing and my flashlight is at the bottom... too far away. Man... now what? Oh crap... I hear them getting real close.*

Jack crawled over behind a large oak tree spying his two pursuers who had somehow come together. He watched as they occasionally swung their bats at hanging vines and dead tree limbs. The swings were violent with a deadly intent. They stopped about twenty yards from Jack's tree peering down in the ravine at the light hiding under a shrub.

"Alright, we've got the little fucker trapped down there by the creek. Let's split up and come at him from different directions. I'll go this way... you go around that way and we'll pound the shit outta him at the creek."

"I don't know Jumpy. I'm not sure there's anyone down there."

"What do you mean? Don't you see that light? The fucker's hiding down there behind that bush."

"That bush looks awful small to be hiding someone. Maybe a trap... like we go down there and the fuckers attack us. We're not on very solid ground down there. Not a lot of room to move around, you know?"

"Damn, Wheels… for a second I thought I heard C.J. talking. But I know that aint true cause we just beat the shit outta Dark Chocolate and now you're taking his place." Jumpy challenged.

"Fuck you Jumpy! You know I aint scared. Just being cautious… trying to think, like Big Jr. told us to do. We don't know shit about this place. Its redneck country and only dumbass redneck white boys know how to run around here. Just looks too sketchy!"

"Alright little girl, you stay up here safe and sound and I'll go pound some ass!" Jumpy added in disgust and started scooting down the hill.

Jack watched in awe as the two pursuers descended into the ravine and toward the flashlight moving stealthily from different directions. He stood up and started moving back towards the barn when he heard them pounding the hell out of the bush. He stopped and hid behind and another tree. He could just make out an angry argument. *Now's the best time to get rid of these guys so I can get to the barn and save Luke!* Jack thought as he pulled out the handgun. Taking dead aim at the flashlight, Jack popped off two shots that hit a huge boulder between the two Zone thugs.

"Fuck! Fuck! Them damn white boys got us trapped down here and they're gonna shoot our ass!" Jumpy screamed.

"Not me! I'm outta here!" Wheels shouted back and darted down the ravine creek bed, closely followed by his associate.

Jack saw them running in the opposite direction of the barn which worked out perfectly. He spotted one of them turn his head around. Jack fired two more shots over their heads and heard squeals of obscenities fill the night air. Shoving the gun back into his waistband, he quickly turned on his heels and ran back through the woods to rescue his brother with a greater sense of accomplishment and determination. *I am not a coward and I will save my brother! I won't let him down again!*

❧ ❧ ❧ ❧ ❧ ❧ ❧

Luke stared at Candace's beautiful eyes that were streaming tears down her cheek. She looked disheveled and beaten to the core. Her mouth gagged and hands bound behind her back— she seemed defeated. Luke knew he would not leave that barn without her… alive.

"Seriously, Boss man! I will be your boy and run whatever operations you need me to do. Hell, you don't even have to pay me. Just let her go now and we have a deal. I'll sign whatever papers you need to make it legal and foolproof. Please I'm begging you… let her go!"

"Wow! Wow! Geoffrey was right. You've become quite attached to our little red-head, haven't you? Well, I can understand. She has many attractive qualities that draw you to her!" Marcus quipped as he ran his hand down the side of her body and cupped her breast.

Luke started toward him but the Boss quickly pulled out a large Bowie knife and shoved it under her throat.

"No, no, no, no, no, big boy. Just sit tight over there. One more move like that and I slit her throat wide open. You understand, boy!" Marcus barked.

Luke nodded

"Okay, then… listen carefully. Don't make another move like that! Big Jr. call your boy and tell him to bring in the package now. I have a little surprise for my love birds here and now's the time to deliver it!"

Big Jr. punched C.J.'s cell number and waited for an answer. Looking alarmed at how long it was taking for someone to pick up, Big Jr. turned back towards the Boss.

"Something's wrong, Boss. C.J. always picked up his calls without delay. First Jumpy answered a couple of times and now… no one…"

"Damn it, Big Jr! How fucking hard is it to do a simple task like bring me a dead two-year old!"

"What?" Big Jr. asked in disbelief.

"You heard me! Stop squirming, Candy or I'll fucking slit you right now!" Marcus ordered. He tightened his grip on her and stared directly at Luke. "Alright boy, since things aren't going as planned. Its time to improvise. One of the things that has sustained me and kept me in power for so long, is the ability to quickly improvise after a plan falls apart and this one seems to have been left in the hands of morons!" Marcus screamed glaring back at Big Jr. Gathering his thoughts and composure, Marcus continued, "Options are back on the table. You can leave right now! Go ahead and run. Big Jr. will never catch you and apparently my associates are missing in action."

"I'm not leaving without Candace." Luke replied firmly.

"Son, she aint on the table of options. You best forget her now or she'll get your ass killed!"

"I'm not leaving without her. Look, I'll still work for you, run your errands or operations or whatever you need but you have to let her go."

"You're playing a dead hand, Luke. You see… she's already dead…" Marcus smiled as he raised his knife from her throat.

Fuck! He's gonna kill her now! Luke sprinted into action toward the Boss. He saw the massive bear of a man move in front with his baseball bat cocked back. Luke remembered his baseball playing days and the pushup slide he was taught when stealing bases. Running toward Big Jr., Luke suddenly dropped to his butt with his left leg under him as his right leg kicked up. He felt the wind and whistle of the bat overhead as his right foot connected flush onto Big Jr's testicles. The behemoth doubled over wrenching in pain and rolling about on the barn floor as Luke scooped up the dropped bat and hammered the Boss's knife hand just after Candace stomped on his foot and fell to the ground. Marcus screamed in pain quickly rubbing his wounded hand. Luke pulled the bat back again and delivered a powerful swat across the Boss's knees.

"Run Candace! Run!"

Candace scrambled to her feet and ran into Luke's arms. He briefly hugged her and pulled the bandana from her mouth and easily loosened the rope binding her hands while watching the two Zone thugs rise up to full height. It was an imposing sight that Luke knew would be impossible to hold off for both to escape.

"Run now, Candace! Hurry and don't look back! I'll hold them off!"

"Come with me!"

"No... I can't. Not now but I'll catch up to you. Go get Julia! Now! Go! Run!" Luke demanded.

Candace sprinted past Big Jr. who lunged after her but she was too nimble and quick and his balls were too sore to chase after her. Luke watched with relief as she pulled the barn door open and disappeared into the darkness.

"Well done, Luke. Well done! You saved the damsel in distress but you and I both know you aint leaving this barn alive! My big bodyguard and I am gonna beat your white ass to a pulp. Oh sure, you have a bat and you swing it pretty good." Marcus stated as he rubbed his knees. "But, you really only have one swing on one of us and then the other will pounce!"

☙ ☙ ☙ ☙ ☙ ☙ ☙

Candace ran out of the barn and instinctively turned right heading back toward the street. She slowed down as she passed Bobby Joe's farmhouse and hid in the shadows of the old barn. She knew the Zone enforcers were watching her Julia in the backseat of Big Jr.'s muscle car. Scanning the road she immediately spotted the car parked askew in front of Simon's car.

Easing out of the shadows towards the cars, she cast her eyes about looking for any signs of her captors. As she approached Big Jr's car she noticed the back door open and blood splattered across the side of the car. *Oh no! Oh no! Please don't let that be Julia's!* Candace winced as she looked in the back seat for any signs of her daughter. Nothing.

She quickly ran over to Simon's car following a trail of blood that seemed as if a large body had been dragged across the road. The blood trail led to the back of Simon's car and into the trunk. Fearful of what she might discover, Candace hesitated, prayed and placed her hands on the trunk. Surprisingly the trunk lifted open. Candace let out a sharp scream as she covered her mouth while staring at two large adult bodies shoved tightly into the trunk. She could just make out a tall thin black male with a bludgeoned head lying atop a heavy white man. *Oh my God! That's gotta be Simon! Oh God, I'm sorry this happened to you Simon but you were a fool to put your trust in Marcus and turn on Luke. You never listened! I can never forgive you for taking my Julia and putting her into the hands of that monster, Marcus! You got what you had coming to you! Now where the hell is my Julia!*

Candace slammed the trunk shut and walked around the yard in search of some clue as to where her daughter had been taken. She felt like Julia was still alive since she hadn't been brought to the barn as ordered by Marcus. *Something went wrong! Big Jr. didn't get a response the last time he called and those other two idiots are missing. They probably have Julia with them.* Candace reasoned as she walked slowly around the other side of the barn. *Oh my God! Oh my God! Its Julia's blanket!* Candace reached down and pulled the soft quilt to her face inhaling the scent of her daughter. *She's alive! I just know she is and it looks like she ran out towards the woods.*

Candace sprinted across the open expanse and disappeared into the woods. She slowed her pace as she pushed through the vines dangling off the old oaks towering above her. Suddenly she heard two gun shots explode through the air about two o'clock in her sight range.

She had learned a few hunting rules from her father as a young girl. One of the first rules was to be very aware of where other hunters are in the woods. She ducked down behind a tree. *Those shots could not have come from the Zone thugs— they carry bats not guns. Big Jr. would never allow his crew guns— too stupid to take care of them and gunshots are too loud, drawing too much attention and witnesses. No, those shots had to come from someone else… but who and are they shooting at the Zone boys?* Candace rose and resumed her search through the woods.

Jack sprinted easily back through the woods with a better sense of direction. He was now much more familiar with the terrain and the lay of the land. *Before I go to the barn, I need to double back and check on Julia. Poor thing probably heard those shots and is scared to death hiding. I'll quickly comfort her and then go get Luke* Jack rationalized as he darted back and forth. Slowing his run to a fast walk, Jack found the row of bushes where he hid Julia.

"Julia! Julia!" Jack called out in a loud whisper. "Hey, its alright! It's the good prince Jack come to check on his princess!" Jack crawled down beneath the bushes and into a burrowed hole. Julia was balled up and sobbing. Jack scooped her up and hugged her. She wrapped her arms tightly around his neck. He could feel the tears running down her face as she sobbed more openly.

"Shhh! Shhh! Its okay little one. Its okay. Everything's gonna be fine. You're safe and prince Jack is here. But we still need to be very quiet… can you be brave some more for me princess Julia?"

"No! No! I want my mommy! I want my mommy! I want to go

home!" Julia cried out.

"Shhh! You can't scream like that in the woods right now. I've run off some of the bad guys but not all of them… in fact I still need to go to …. Shhh! Shhh! Quiet… I hear someone moving quickly towards us!" Jack warned as he covered her mouth and ducked down into the hole.

"Julia! Julia! Where are you honey? Julia! Julia! Mommy's here! Mommy's here!" Candace called scrambling through the brush and shrubs desperately tracking the voice she just heard.

Jack listened carefully to the voice and cautiously lifted his head out of the bushes. He saw a tall figure with long hair searching in a nearby clump of trees.

"Candace?" Jack called out.

He watched the figure spin around and head immediately toward him. As the figure got closer, Jack rose to his feet.

"Candace! Quickly over here!" Jack directed.

"Jack? Jack… Luke's brother… is that you?"

"Yes and I have someone eager to see you!" Jack smiled and lifted Julia out from the bushes and into Candace's arms.

"Julia! Julia! My precious baby! Oh mommy loves you! Loves you! Loves you!" Candace beamed as she hugged her daughter with tears flowing from her eyes. "Oh, mommy was so worried about you! Thank God! Thank God, you're okay!"

"Mommy! Mommy, I want to go home!" Julia replied in her mother's ear.

"Yes! Dear JuJu we're going home now… I'm not sure how but we're getting out of here."

"Take my car! Julia has the keys in her hands. Its parked on the outskirts of these woods on an old access road. You'll see it parked next to a huge pick-up truck. Hell it's the only car there. Will be easy to spot!"

"Are you sure?"

"Absolutely!"

"You're not coming with us? How will you get home?" Candace demanded.

"In Luke's car… with Luke!"

"Yes! Please, you must save him. He's in the barn now with only a bat against Marcus and Big Jr. I'm not sure how much longer he can hold them off. He saved me again, Jack!"

"I know… he did what I couldn't do."

"What do you mean?"

"There's no time now to explain… just know that Luke is the better man and he saved both of you and now, it's my turn to save him."

"How will you do it?"

"Well, let's just say I have a bit of an advantage… I've seen this once already and know what's gonna happen... I think. And I got this!" Jack exclaimed pulling the gun out of his waistband and walking to rendezvous with his destiny.

༖ ༖ ༖ ༖ ༖ ༖ ༖

Luke watched the two massive figures move in circles around him as he faked swings at each man's attempt to move on him. He knew he had one could swing to land on one of them and that the other would swiftly tackle him. He was calculating his odds of winning a head-to-head match-up with each of the thugs. *Obviously the massive six foot eight inch bear would be impossible to fight head to head— too large for me to take down... not sure he would feel anything above the waist. But he's slow-footed and heavy on his heels. I could move easier against him... maybe. The Boss on the other hand, I can knock out with several swift blows to the head— I've done that before. But he moves better than the bear— more nimble and much quicker... cat-like. Damn, neither option is ideal. The Boss has an evil look... a sneer... whereas the beast over there isn't quite as menacing... almost like he's going through the motions... can't trust that sentiment! That beast will kill me if he gets a hold of me... don't doubt it Luke!*

"Hey boy! Better make your decision soon while you still have that chance! Cause I aint waiting all night on ya!" Marcus taunted encircling Luke.

"Well why don't you develop a set of balls and come get you some! Don't stand out there talking the shit! Come in here and get it!" Luke countered.

"Don't tempt me boy! The last thing you want is Marcus X!"

"Marcus X aint shit without his posse and trained bear! You aint nothing but a punk in an expensive suit ordering others to do your dirty work while you keep your hands clean with manicures and lotions from the ill-gotten gains of better men!" Luke challenged.

"You don't know shit boy! How do you think I got on top? Nobody gave me anything that I didn't scratch and claw, beat and bruise, slice and dice, cut and kill with these hands! Look at them Luke! These 'clean hands' have killed more men, women and children— these hands Luke— look at them— they've choked, stroked and broken more lives than you'll ever do. You think you're clean Christian hands could ever do harm to either of us? Really?"

"I don't know... I've already killed once today! Didn't seem to bother me too much and trust me— you aint much different than that sick fuck!"

"Oh really? You killed someone... I don't believe it!"

"Then come in here and get some!" Luke screamed.

Marcus whistled at Big Jr. to move in immediately. The big bear followed orders and walked directly at Luke. Luke turned to swing at the big man but swiveled instantly wrapping his bat against the left side of Marcus's head. The bat popped like a club hitting a hollow coconut. Marcus fell to the ground. Luke pivoted just in time to watch a black fist explode into his left eye. He staggered forward several steps and looked up to see the next punch land on his nose causing blood to spurt like a fountain. His eyes watered, vision blurred as he covered his bleeding nose with his hand.

"Come on white boy! Take your best shot! You still got my bat in your hand! Let's see you use it! Swing for the fences!" Big Jr. taunted as he moved back and forth on his heels.

Luke gripped the bat firmly and shook his head trying to gauge the distance and images flashing before him. He could just make out the massive figure standing in front of him but his vision blurred in and out distorting his proximity. Suddenly the massive image rushed toward him. Luke pulled the bat back and swung directly into the midsection of the beast. He connected but the bat seemed to get swallowed up in the dense abdominal region of the dark land mass. He felt the bat trapped between the big man's ribs and arm. He tugged and tugged but there was no loosening.

"Damn boy! That was a weak Texas-leaguer! You know what that means? You play much baseball, boy? It means a little flair ball that landed softly outside the infield— a shit hit!" Big Jr. laughed. "For a boy who seems to think highly of himself and somehow hood-wink the Boss into thinking he was a badass— I got news for ya! You aint shit!" Big Jr. yelled seizing the bat away from Luke.

He took dead aim at Luke's legs and swung for the fences landing a terrific blow. Luke screamed in pain and dropped to the floor. He rolled over writhing and grabbing his knees. Looking up at the behemoth, Luke saw evil intention. He was in dire straits and had to act quickly. His body was wracked and he knew he was probably one blast away from that bat from being dead.

"You're seriously gonna hit me again with that pussy stick?" Luke wailed.

"Pussy stick? I guess it wasn't a pussy stick when you used it on the Boss and swung it all over the place trying to hold grown men back!"

"I used it only to fight a two-on-one. Not a solo, mano y mano fight. You got me back for hitting you a few nights ago in the Zone. I get it. We're even. Don't be a wussy and finish me off like that. Give me a fighter's chance!"

"Ha! You aint got no fight in you… look at your sorry ass! You're beaten and broken and bleeding all over the place. I landed some damn good shots on you and know you aint got much left! It would be merciful to bash your damn head in now! I can easily do it!" Big Jr. stated pulling the 44 ounce Louisville Slugger back.

"No! No! Don't do it. Yes, you could easily do it but there's no honor in it! You seem like a person who takes pride in their work and this would not be honorable."

Big Jr. stared at Luke without any sign of which way he would proceed.

"Let me stand up and face you… please gimme one shot. What do you have to lose? You're obviously gonna win but you'll do it honorably…"

Big Jr.'s expression didn't change as he contemplated the dilemma. He looked over at the Boss who was starting to stir rubbing his head and grumbling. *I aint never given a target or victim a chance to fight back or defend their honor… most punks never deserved a chance. Beating them was the only just thing to do. Rid the world of one less rat… but this white kid is different. He came back and fought for love. Saved the girl and her daughter… twice. Ran into an extremely dangerous realm and won! Seems a shame to finish true courage with a cowardly beating of the bat. Yeah… beating his ass with the bat would be dishonorable to both of us!*

"Alright… get up!" Big Jr. demanded as he slung his bat away.

Seeing Luke struggle to stand on his feet and not wanting to waste much time, Big Jr. walked over and grabbed Luke's hand and pulled him up. Luke swiftly threw a powerful punch to the large man's groin forcing him to double over again.

Once bent over, Luke drove his fist hard against the man's head knocking the hearing out of his left ear. The big man dropped to his knees screaming and holding his ear as Luke backed up a few feet and measured up an explosive kick to the face. His foot caught the big man's chin sharply snapping it back like a punted football. Big Jr. fell on his back as Luke, like a skilled MMA fighter, immediately jumped on the bodyguard's chest and began to pummel his face with left-right combos to the head. Big Jr's nose spewed blood as Luke continued to pound away at the misshapen face.

The adrenaline coursing through Luke's body began to ebb as fatigue set in. He stopped his assault to catch his breath. Sensing all the fight was out of the beast who was no longer moving, Luke let his guard down. *God… every part of my body aches and I can't see shit… eyes are blurry, nose won't stop bleeding and … damn… feel so tired… OH SHIT!*

Luke felt a sharp object enter his back. He screamed and twisted, reaching back trying to grab at the object but he felt another thrust push it in deeper. A large hand grabbed the hair from the top of his head and yanked him backwards as the knife was dislodged. Luke fell on his back and stared up at the barn's ceiling. He could see Bobby Joe's body swaying from the headlight's of his wrecker. He was having trouble catching his breath. The pain in his back was excruciating and his face was on fire. Through blurred eyes he saw the Boss standing over him.

"Man oh man. You are some piece of shit aren't you? That 'honorable' speech was a damn work of art! My God I thought there was no way in the world Big Jr. would fall for such sentimental bullshit! He's normally a ferocious animal who mercilessly pounds the hell out of people! Can't believe he fell for your bullshit! My, my Luke it is a damn shame to destroy your ass cause you and I would have worked well together. You're a pretty tough old boy, I'll give you that… but your time is up and well…" Marcus allowed as he pulled the knife high in the air preparing its descent on Luke's chest.

"NOOOOO!!!!" screamed a voice from the entrance of the barn.

Marcus squinted to try to identify the figure emerging from the front of the barn with his arm raised pointing an object at him. He reached down and grabbed Luke by the hair raising him to a stance with his knife tucked under his chin.

"Well, well what have we here? It's the chicken-shit coward who faints at the whiff of danger. Come on in Jack. I am surprised to see you here. Last time we talked, your boy up there," Marcus nodded toward the ceiling, "was carrying your weak-ass out of my office. Why are you here, boy?"

"You know why I'm here. Let Luke go and I don't bust a cap in your ass!" Jack asserted.

"Bust a cap in my ass? What movie is that from Jack? Huh? Look, you have a gun. No shock— the weapon of a weak white boy. That gun gives you courage and distance. You don't have to get up close to your victim… feel their fear, wrestle with their mortality, smell the sweat oozing from their pores. That gun is your defense against your own cowardice because you have no confidence in your ability to fight for your life! Your brother here, reeks of courage. That boy fought his ass off to save others while putting his life on the line… but not with no gun. He came in here with just his fists, cunning and guts! What do you bring to the fight… a God- damn gun! What a fucking coward!"

"Shut the fuck ass-wipe! You don't know shit! I'm here now and I have what you don't have— the advantage! Now take that knife away from Luke's throat!"

"Jack… run… you shouldn't have come." Luke offered meekly. "I'm finished. Look at me."

"No, damn it! You're not dying here tonight! It wasn't supposed to be you… it was me! In the dream, Luke, it was me! Marcus was about to kill me… not you! You will live!"

"Jack… it's okay, brother… you don't have to prove anything to me… you never did… you beat yourself up your whole life but you were right… to be cautious. I was headstrong and foolish. You and Joseph tried to warn me about my impulsiveness and look where its gotten me… Jack, I'm a dead man…"

"No… stop talking like that. I can't let you… end like this… its my fault! I let you down your whole life… going back to that shit Halloween years ago… I ran out on you… I always ran out! But not today! Not today damn it! Today, Jack's going take care of his little brother!"

"Wow… that's so fucking touching! I'm serious Jack! You boys are so sweet… good little suburban white brothers and their fucking Hallmark moment! Listen white pussy, neither of you boys is leaving this barn alive if you don't run right now… because we both know you aint got the God damn balls to pull that trigger!"

"If you don't let him go now, I swear to God, I send you to Hell!"

"Bullshit! Bullshit! You aint got the balls, boy! I'm tired of this fucking around! Pull the trigger or else!" Marcus demanded as his face twisted into an evil sneer. "Oh fuck it!" Marcus growled and slit Luke's throat from ear to ear. Sanguine fluid rushed from the arced line under Luke's chin as his eyes stared off into the distance.

"No! No!" Jack screamed as he pulled the trigger several times but there was no bang or explosion. Instead the air was filled with the clicking sound of an empty gun barrel and quickly followed by the laughter of his brother's assailant.

"Oh my God, Jack! I can't remember the last time I laughed so hard! You used a coward's weapon and even it let you down… looks like you let your brother down again by being a weak pussy that hesitates!" Marcus scoffed.

Jack felt a rage take hold of him like nothing he had ever felt before. It was as if another had taken over his body as he rushed forward and drove his body into Marcus. The tackle brought both to the ground but Jack was first to get up and drove his fist into Marcus's nose causing it to explode in a red fountain. He followed up with a series of right crosses to the eye. Marcus made no sound and even smiled after the last punch opened up a gash over his left cheek.

"Boy, you even hit like a pussy!" Marcus countered and then swiftly kneed Jack in the groin.

Jack instantly fell off Marcus twisting in pain. Marcus rolled over next to him and punched him squarely in the eye. He threw two more punches to Jack's head before standing upright.

"Alright little boy, time to show you what happens in a real fight for your life!" Marcus lectured grabbing Jack's hair and lifting his face for yet another devastating blow.

Jack took the punch but quickly grabbed the Boss by the legs and wrestled him to the ground. The two rolled around back and forth trying to seize the top. Marcus stabbed his fingers into Jack's eyes. Jack instinctively bit the hand tearing flesh from the bone. Marcus screamed pulling his hand back. In that moment, Jack scrambled to his feet and dropped a powerful punch to the man's throat rendering him defenseless and gagging for air.

Jack backed away to gather his energy which seemed to be draining from his body. Marcus rose slowly to his feet putting both hands on his knees and wheezing for air. *Shit that ass is back on his feet... he's so damn strong... can't let him gather himself! Gotta attack now and finish him!* Jack plotted and walked toward the bent over drug lord. Jack grabbed Marcus by the top of his hair and hit him in the face repeatedly as each blow pushed the criminal kingpin backwards until he landed up against the back wall of the barn. Marcus's face was severely swollen with blood pouring out of his nose and mouth. He lifted his head just in time to see another blast to his face.

"Is this what a real life fight looks like? Huh? I can't hear you through the blood bubbling out of your mouth? Is this what a fight for your life looks and feels like? Huh? This white boy just fought for his life and now he's going finish yours!" Jack exalted.

Just as he started to pull his fist back for what seemed like his final blow to the Boss, Jack was seized by a powerful, large body that bear-hugged the air out of his lungs. He was paralyzed. He couldn't feel his arms and was lifted off the ground and backed away from the Boss. He tried desperately to wriggle free but each attempt was met with more force from the giant.

"Boy, you aint going nowhere. The more you struggle, the tighter I squeeze!" Big Jr. warned.

Jack continued to squirm but to no avail and, to his horror, he watched Marcus open his eyes and wipe the blood from his face. Walking slowly and deliberately toward Jack, he said not a word, but drove his fist into Jack's stomach causing him to cry out. Marcus walked around like a cat eying and toying with its prey before finishing it off. He reached down and seized his Bowie knife from the barn floor.

"You had your chance, boy! You had old Marcus up against the ropes. Seemed like maybe I might be in trouble. But I'm a survivor boy! A survivor! Better men than you thought they had the better of Marcus but they always failed to follow through. They hesitated or celebrated too soon and then BAM! Marcus turned the tables! Cause that's what I do, son! I survive and thrive and stay alive!"

"Janee... Janee..." Luke offered softly from the ground as he reached in the air.

"What the fuck are you saying, boy? I thought you were dead! Damn that boy has a fierce force to live... gotta admire that!" Marcus stated flatly and then walked over and stabbed Luke several more times in the chest. Luke's arm fell as the life left his eyes staring at the ceiling.

"Why? Why did you have to do that?" Jack mumbled.

"What's that? Whatcha say boy? Your little brother is no longer your concern. He's gone!"

"He was never a concern... just a great brother... and friend... who was ruined, betrayed and let down... and I'm responsible for much of that..." Jack sobbed silently.

"Well, he should be your last concern. More immediately is what's about to happen to you now! Being that you're so easily scared, I wanted to give you a bit of time to come to grips with the idea that you're about to die! And it won't be a quick death like I gave your brother. No, a coward like you will die a slow, torturous death and the first blow starts now!" Marcus screamed pulling the knife and preparing to plunge it into Jack's chest.

"Stop! Stop, it now! Put that knife down or I'll blow your head off your neck!" barked a voice from the barn entrance pointing a rifle at Marcus X.

"Who the hell is that?" Marcus demanded.

"Joseph?" Jack inquired with his back turned being held by Big Jr.

"Joseph? Who the fuck is Joseph?"

"Oh shit! Joseph is the older brother." Big Jr. replied looking back at the barn door.

"Damn! How many Miller brothers are there?" Marcus remarked.

"There are three and this one is a man of God!" Big Jr. responded as he released Jack.

"What the hell's wrong with you Big Jr.? Grab that boy now! That's an order!"

"Sorry Boss... but no! I don't mess with no man of God!"

"Man of God?" Marcus asked.

"Joseph is studying to be a minister... a man of God." Big Jr. answered in awe staring at Joseph.

"Big Jr. you big idiot! There is no God. Don't you know that? God is a superstition... made up to dupe small-minded idiots like you into obedience and submission on earth. God is nothing but a myth"

"No Boss... you're wrong."

"Fucking idiot... well I aint laying down to some mythical supernatural being that don't exist! There aint no heaven or hell or some afterlife. This is it— life here on earth and you've got one shot at getting it right and I'm winning! Don't plan on losing and dying to some stupid myth!" Marcus demanded and grabbed Jack placing the knife up under his chin.

"Don't think about it! Drop that knife now or I'll blow you to hell to live with your master for eternity! What you call a myth is called Good News to us Christians who know that Christ died for our sins and will forgive us of our sins here on earth— but you have to believe... have faith! You can still turn it around and be saved! Even now as we speak. Drop that knife, turn yourself in and turn your life over to Christ! It's never too late!"

"Ha! Ha! You fucking idiots that cling to a false hope in a false god created by man. You guys are pathetic. I don't need forgiveness because I have committed no sins— not in the world I grew up in and survived. Now I suggest you put the rifle down now and walk outta here. I gave this brother here the same option I'm giving you and look how it worked out for your other brother!" Marcus called out.

Joseph looked down at his dead brother lying flat on his back with his eyes staring up at the ceiling. His blood began to boil as the rage coursed through his veins.

"Take your hands off Jack right now or I'll blow you to hell!" Joseph screamed.

"No, Joseph! Don't do it! Don't condemn your soul to hell for this! I'm not worth it. You were right! I let Luke down... again and now he's dead! I deserve to die and meet my fate! I'm already dead... please Joseph save yourself... like you said, you can't continue to protect us... you'll condemn your soul to hell!"

"Well... that's okay!" Joseph replied with tears welling up in his eyes. "Cause you'll have another friend who will always fight the damn devil protecting you and Luke! I always have and always will!"

"Well aint this shit sweet— brotherly fucking love!"

Marcus could not have known that this man of God standing before him with a .22LR rifle pointed at his head was a skilled avid hunter. He had spent years in the woods hunting small game with his paternal grandfather and honed his skills as a marksman. He was easily one of the best shots in the county having won many Turkey Shoots in Nicholasville. He learned in the woods how to move stealthily and when it came time to shoot— how to control your heart rate and breathing to steady the aim and squeeze the trigger. No, Marcus had no idea whose eyes were bearing down on him and whose skilled hands were holding the rifle.

"Look, we both know you aint got the balls to shoot that gun so you might else well put it down and run home. Also everyone knows that Christians are pussies that hide behind a make-believe faith to shield their own cowardice. Now, either shoot that rifle or get the hell outta here because I'm..." was the last words uttered out of Marcus X as the .22LR bullet entered his forehead spraying blood, bone and brain matter all over the back wall of the barn. His body slumped to the ground with his eyes wide open.

Jack peered down at the lifeless thug from the Zone who had terrorized him in the nightmare and in real life. The haunted image of an evil so frightening looked innocuous and benign lying prostrate on the hay strewn floor. In a state of shock, he looked back at his older brother who was talking to Big Jr. about something he couldn't hear. He watched the large man bow down as Joseph bound his hands behind his back. Everything seemed to move in slow motion as Jack tried to comprehend what had just occurred. He was alive and that, in and of itself, was shocking. His dream or premonition had stopped just short of his death— apparently that life lost was Luke's, not his.

Looking down at his younger brother, Jack began to weep. He saw not the man that had courageously fought for the lives of others, as well as his own survival, but that of a youth stolen and life robbed of its innocence by evil. A life he was too cowardly to protect and defend. *It should be me lying on the ground, not Luke. He was the good one, strong and courageous— constantly fighting the demons that haunted him from years ago on that fateful Halloween! I deserted him! I ran out on him and because of that he was irreparably harmed by an evil man! I was too cowardly to protect him then and too cowardly to save him tonight! God gave me the gift of a premonition and I blew it* Jack mourned as he scooped up Luke's body and closed his eyes.

"I was too late Joseph... too late to save our brother... he needed me and I let him down again! And this time it cost us his life." Jack sobbed as buried his head into Luke's shoulder.

Joseph leaned down and wrapped his arm around Jack.

"You did the best you could. You tried to warn him. You tried to stop him. You gave him every chance to survive this but he was too headstrong, Jack. You have to know that. He's been running on this course his entire life. No matter how much we counseled and advised him, he did his own thing. I'm not being critical of him or blaming him... just explaining him. He charted his own course and we have to accept his fate."

"If that was the case, why did you come back? If you believed Luke was destined to a fatal end, why did you come here tonight? I mean, you killed a man. Didn't you just condemn your soul?"

"I came here tonight... because that's what I do... I am responsible for you guys. I always have been... since day one when you all were born. Mom told me I had to look out for you... protect and defend you. Luke was... not a lost cause, but on a path of self-destruction that I couldn't stop. But I knew I couldn't lose both of you. I came here, realistically, to save you!"

"I wish I was worthy of your efforts. I don't deserve to be alive..."

"Don't say that Jack! Don't ever say that! You're being way too hard on yourself and ignoring the realities of what occurred. You couldn't stop this from happening even with the gift of a premonition. You tried and Luke simply did his own thing. This was ordained and we have to trust that this is in God's hands now." Joseph counseled.

"Aren't you worried about your own fate and the eternity of your soul, now that you've killed another? What changed your mind about killing? I mean, you came here tonight intent on killing a man, if necessary."

"You're right. I did. It's gonna sound crazy and maybe unbelievable, but I figured out those numbers from your dream."

"You mean 'one two one'?"

"Yeah."

"Well?"

"It's from First John 2:1. The scripture is and I quote 'Dear children, I write this to you so that you will not sin. But if anybody does sin, we have One who speaks to the Father in our defense— Jesus Christ, The Righteous

One'. That convinced me that we, as humans, will make mistakes and sin, but we also have a defender in Christ. Killing is always wrong and a sin, but Christ died for those sins. We repent, beg for forgiveness, and sin no more. The verse seemed to go perfectly with your cryptic dream. It gave me the confidence and assurance to come here tonight with bad intentions to save my brothers."

"I only regret that I could have saved Luke— acted sooner… before he died… he called out to Janee. It was like he saw her… he was reaching up to her. He had the most peaceful expression on his face, just before that murderous sack of shit finished him off."

"Oh wow… that's… that's amazing. I believe he did see her spirit and it brought him comfort at his most trying hour. That could only happen to… well, anyway that brings me great solace knowing that Luke is going to be alright."

"Yes, I was thinking that as well. He's gone from us now but in a much better place. His soul is no longer restless. I wish I could say or feel that same calm and peace. I feel lost, Joseph. What do we do now?"

"We live it, Jack. We live it… if that's even possible…" Joseph muttered looking back at the barn entrance silently whispering a prayer and then staring back down at Luke with tears in his eyes.

Tim F. Miller

Coming… "The Righteous"

22818220R00171

Made in the USA
Columbia, SC
03 August 2018